# frozen hearts

## HALSTON U PART ONE

R.A. SMYTH

**Frozen Hearts**


ISBN: 978-1-915456-13-7

Cover by Stephanie at Vicious Designs
Interior Design by Nikki Epperson.
Editing by Lunar Rose Editing Services.
Formatting by Rachel Smyth.

Halston University was supposed to be my fresh start, my chance to prove I can stand on my own, except it's not only passing classes I have to worry about.

Secrets...Desperation...Shattered dreams... my life is one big balancing act. But what happens if I fall?

And then there's *them* - three guys, each with their own darkness and allure. My demons.

There's Logan, the golden boy on the ice, who believes in soulmates and love at first sight. He sees me, *really* sees me, and I can't help but feel drawn to him.

Royce, the brooding one. He's like a storm, unpredictable and dangerous, pushing me to confront parts of myself I'd long buried and awakening something dark within me. Every interaction is charged with venom and desire, a twisted dance that's both enthralling and frightening.

Then there's Grayson, my estranged stepbrother, dead set on revenge. Plotting my demise in the shadows of his ire and resentment, even as it threatens to consume us both. But what do you do when you can't deny the lingering feelings of attraction, of something *more*?

No matter how far I run, there is no escaping my past.

And, if my trauma doesn't swallow me whole, Grayson Van Doren surely will.

# HALSTON U PLAYLIST

Fearless – UNSECRET & Ruby Amanfu
Let Go Now – Rayelle
River – Bishop Briggs
My Girl – The Temptations
Video Phone – Beyoncé & Lady Gaga
Unstoppable – The Score
Don't Forget To Breathe – Vanacore Music
All Roads Lead Home – Ohana Bam
I AM – CRMNL
Breathe In Bleed Out – Jared Lee
Sweat – HAYZ
... And many more!

# TRIGGER WARNINGS

- History of sexual abuse
- History of self harm and contemplation of suicide
- Sexual assault
- Kidnapping
- PTSD
- Dubcon
- Noncon
- Blood Play
- Primal Play
- Knife Play
- Degradation
- Violence

*****Spoiler Trigger*****

Sexual assault resulting in pregnancy (past event; does not occur on page)

***

This book is a dark, contemporary, new adult reverse harem romance, meaning the FMC will end up with 3+ males.

The book ends on a cliffhanger.

The series will ultimately have an HEA.

*To all those who have endured the darkest storms, faced their deepest fears, and found the strength within to rise above. May this book serve as a beacon of hope and a reminder that you are capable of overcoming even the most daunting of challenges. Your resilience and courage inspire us all.*

# RILEY

## PROLOGUE

The hinges on the bedroom door creak, and everything within me collapses. My lungs deflate. My heart tries to leap from my chest. My muscles go rigid with fear. I've come to associate that slow, agonizing screech with everything horrific that has happened in my life. It's the doorbell signaling the arrival of the Devil. A harbinger of imminent pain and suffering as his shadow slips into the room, growing in size on the wall in front of me as his malevolent presence chokes the air in my throat.

I cower in fear. Squeeze my eyes shut to the point of pain, hoping he might change his mind. Just this once. Only for tonight. My heart thrashes so loudly, I struggle to hear the soft pad of his socked feet against the carpet.

It feels like forever, yet not enough time passes before he's standing over me. Towering. Looming. Pricking. Prodding. Teasing. Tempting. *Savoring*. I know when he's there. Can feel his presence the same way the sick or elderly can sense the Grim Reaper when he comes to claim their souls for himself. And still, I do not move. Do not dare to even breathe.

*Pretend to be asleep.*

*Pretend to be asleep.*

*Pretend to be asleep.*

The plea plays on repeat in my head as though, if I can only wish hard enough for it, it'll actually come true.

I'm not certain it would make a difference, even if it did.

Regardless, I've learned by now there are no fairy godmothers or genies in bottles here to grant me wishes. Fairy-tales are nothing but pretty lies written in sharp black ink. Fantasies to fill the minds of young children until reality crashes brutally into their naive lives. Mesmerizing at the time; devastating when it's over.

"My sweet girl," he hushes, his fingers brushing over the top of my head. My muscles are locked so tight that my whole body trembles with the physical strain, giving away my pretense. Not that I had him fooled. He knew. He *always* knows.

His hand moves lower, and I choke on a cry too late, burying my teeth in my lower lip as a strangled whimper leaks out.

"Shhh," he soothes as his fingers curl around the covers and slowly peel them away. Cold air rushes in, prickling my skin like sharp needles, and still, I keep my eyes squeezed shut. If I don't see it, it's not real, right? Oh, how I wish that were true.

The dark brings out the worst kind of monsters. The kind that cannot be banished by wishing on stars or shining a flash-light under the bed. The kind that makes you feel dirty in your own skin. That steals pieces of you and refuses to take care of them, returning them shattered and tarnished. Unrecognizable.

The mattress dips, his familiar weight crushing me as his fingers find their possessive home on my hip. The warm puff of his breath against my neck smells like sulfur, burning against my skin.

I used to hope, pray, plead, *beg* for someone—anyone—to walk in, to see this, to stop it.

To help me.

information you'll need. If you're staying on campus, you'll need to make your way to the Landseer building to get your room assignment and key. The building is highlighted on the map."

"I'm staying off campus," I tell her, noticing the way her eyes widen in surprise.

"Oh. In that case, there will be a tour starting in"—she checks the delicate, rose-gold watch on her dainty wrist—"five minutes, right outside Mercer Hall." She points toward a large, grandeur building behind her on the opposite side of the quad, where I can already see a group of students gathering. With an hour to spare before I have to meet my studies advisor, I thank her and head in the direction she pointed.

I flick through the welcome packet as I walk, skipping past the emergency contact information and history of the university until I find the map. Unfolding it, it looks like the campus is quite widespread, which is surprising given the elite nature of the school. By university standards, Halston's student body is relatively small, with only one student in each year group offered an academic scholarship.

This year, that lucky student is me.

Glancing over the map, I take note of the English, Humanities, and Sciences buildings, as those are where most of my classes will be this year, before folding and tucking it back inside the packet when I reach the stone steps at the bottom of Mercer Hall.

I have to hide my grimace as I get my first real look at the other students waiting for the tour to begin. Every one of them is the epitome of a typical *Halston student*. AKA: students with money. Men dressed in chinos and ironed shirts with fancy loafers on their feet; women in designer outfits, high-heels, make-up on point, hair perfectly coiffed, and nails long, sharp, and manicured.

A moment of insecurity has me slowing my steps as I pull on the old band tee I'm wearing, the worn jacket I threw over the top that is too small to zip up, my stiff jeans and scuffed Converse.

I haven't even made an effort to fit in with these people, because why should I pretend to be someone I'm not? I know without a doubt that no matter how hard I try to fit in, I will never *be* one of these people. I would know it, and they would know it.

However, it's more than that. I don't *want* to fit in. I don't *want* to be someone I'm not. I've spent so much of my life being unhappy, putting on a fake smile, and pretending I'm not wasting away on the inside. I'm done with that shit. If you don't like me for who I am, then that's *your* fucking problem.

Confidence boosted, I lift my head and renew my pace up the steps. As I approach the awaiting group, my gaze catches on three girls huddled together, talking to one another with apparent familiarity. They look my way as I reach the top of the steps, their eyes raking over me with obvious disdain.

I can only imagine what they think when they look at me, face free of makeup, long, auburn hair pulled back into a loose ponytail, and nails bitten to the quick.

The funny thing is, once upon a time, I used to look exactly like these girls. I used to live in the big mansion with the chauffeur-driven car and servants at my beck and call. I had the wardrobe that was overstuffed with more outfits than I could wear in a year and the long painted nails.

I was also at my lowest, drowning in a pit of depression and unable to find a way out.

I tilt my chin higher, reminding myself that I don't care what these girls think. As a scholarship student, I knew I would stand out amongst my peers, and while I have no intention of changing anything about myself to fit in, I find myself wishing things were different. That entering campus didn't feel like striding onto a battlefield of *me versus them*. For a split second, I picture myself walking across campus with a group of friends, laughing over lunch together and late-night study sessions.

I blink and the image fades, the judgemental faces of the three girls filling my vision. With a sigh, I mentally shake my head, knowing the idea is nothing more than a whimsical dream. I refuse to change any part of myself to become anything close to what they deem *socially acceptable*, and at the end of the day, making friends here is so far down my list of priorities that I shouldn't be giving it a second thought.

"So you're this year's charity case," one of the threesome sneers, making my point for me. I note her perfectly straight blonde hair, unnaturally white teeth, and stick-thin frame.

Her remark isn't anything I wasn't expecting, so I don't let it upset me. "Looks like it. You must be this year's mean girl."

She gives me a withering glare before tossing her hair over her shoulder and turning her back on me as she returns to her conversation with her friends. *Whatever*.

Before any more snide comments can be made or I can garner everyone else's thoughts on the new scholarship student, a voice cuts across the group.

"Welcome, freshmen, to Halston," a girl greets with a bright grin, casting her eyes around the assembled students. "My name is Bella, and I'll be your tour guide today. Are we all ready to get started?"

A round of murmured agreements go up before she gets the tour underway, and we spend the next half hour being shown around the campus.

My jaw drops open when she shows us the large, glass building which houses the food court. Every available cuisine you could ask for is on offer, and there's even a cocktail bar on the mezzanine level.

"Of course, scholarship students eat in the *dining hall,*" the blonde bitch jeers in a low tone, solely for me.

I can't even argue back because she's right. The food court is incredible and my mouth waters at the delicious smells wafting in the air, but scholarships don't include a food allowance, and unless we can pay for it ourselves, our only option for on-campus eating is the school dining hall, which offers free meals three times a day, seven days a week, plus drinks and snacks in between mealtimes.

After the food court, Bella moves on to show us the newly renovated concert hall, a library containing some of the oldest texts in the world, and a state-of-the-art gym. She wraps up the tour by showing us Halston's ice hockey arena. Apparently, it's one of the largest in the country, with a capacity for nearly twenty thousand people.

"Ice hockey is our biggest sport here at Halston," Bella states. "The Huskies are D1 champions, having won the Frozen Four for three years running, all thanks to our star forward, Logan Astor." Bella says his name with literal hearts in her eyes, and I hear more than one girl in the group release a love-struck sigh.

Seriously?

I never did understand what the big deal was about sports players. Everywhere they go, they're greeted like royalty. Fawned over. Adored. Idolized. Why? Because they can catch a ball or knock a puck into a net? Big fucking whoop. Congratulations on being born with excellent hand-eye coordination. If you ask me, they're overrated. Overhyped. Overvalued.

I'm quite certain that this Logan Astor cannot be *that* amazing.

"I heard he's a Husky on the ice *and* between the sheets," I overhear one girl tittering to her friend.

Really? What does that even mean? That he's likely to growl at you like a rabid dog? How... kinky.

"I wouldn't mind letting him into my bed," her friend giggles, making me roll my eyes at their childish antics.

By the time we make it back to our starting point outside Mercer Hall, I have to rush straight to my meeting with my advisor, located in the main administration building. I follow the directions to his office, pausing outside his door to take a breath as I read the nameplate. *Dr. Edmund Whitaker.* Knocking on the door, I let myself in when I hear a gruff "come in" from beyond the door.

Dr. Whitaker is an older gentleman, I'd guess in his mid-to-late fifties, with a rotund body and gray, balding hair. He sits behind a large, mahogany desk that is bare except for a pen holder and a small stack of files. Sharply dressed in a hunter-green suit, complete with a mustard-colored shirt that speaks to the era he was born in, he stares at me from behind thin-wired spectacles, the deep wrinkles lining his eyes scored into his flesh as he closely scrutinizes me.

His shoulders drop as he heaves out a sigh, looking frustrated, although I'm not sure why.

"You must be Riley James?" His voice is sharp, authoritative-sounding in a way that can only come from years of teaching.

"Yes, that's me," I respond politely. Nervously.

"Mmhmm. And you are this year's scholarship student."

It's not a question, but I feel like I should answer him anyway. "I am."

"Right, well, have a seat. Let's get this over with."

I'm sure that's what every anxious freshman wants to hear from their advisor of studies; from the one person who is supposed to help them navigate the pitfalls and challenges of freshman year. *Yeah, I can already tell that we aren't going to get along.* With my hopes for this meeting diminishing by the second, I take a seat opposite his desk and wait patiently as he flicks through my student file.

"I see here that you have not yet declared a major." His lips are pursed in a severe frown, clearly unimpressed, although I don't understand why. From my understanding, most college freshmen have yet to decide what they want to major in.

"Y-yes, sir. I wanted to explore my options."

"Do you have any inkling of what you might be interested in pursuing?" he asks with blatant disapproval.

"Emm, well, I'm good with numbers, and I like science subjects, so maybe something scientific—Engineering or Pharmacology or something like that." Aware that I'm rambling, I snap my mouth shut.

Dr. Whitaker's bushy eyebrows furrow. "Those are... challenging career paths."

"Yes, sir," I state more resolutely.

Challenging may as well be my middle name. I welcome the gauntlet he doesn't realize he's throwing down. I'm not here for an easy ride. I might not have grand goals of winning a Pulitzer or the Nobel Prize, but I do intend to find the right career path for me. I'm not afraid of hard work. I won't be put off by a challenging workload.

When you claw your way out of the bowels of Hell, no challenge is too great. You can achieve absolutely anything with an inflexible resolve and a resolute mindset.

"Mmhmmm."

Although, I'm guessing Dr. Whitaker doesn't agree.

"And if you fail?" he asks casually, closing my file and leaning back in his chair as he stares at me.

"F-fail?" I question. I have no intention of failing. I've come too far. There is too much on the line for me to fail now. I might not know yet what I want to do with my life, but I will not *fail* at whatever I choose.

"Yes. What if you can't hack it?"

"I *will* hack it."

My conviction is met with a heavy silence, the weight of his gaze boring into me until I feel about an inch tall.

"Your file shows that you are older than our typical freshmen."

Jeez, he makes it sound as though I'm in my forties, not twenty. I'm two years older than the rest of the cohort. It's hardly a significant age gap. "That's right," I say politely.

"And yet, with those extra two years, you haven't figured out what you want out of life," he snidely remarks.

My teeth grate. I know *exactly* what I want out of life; I just haven't determined the best major to declare in order to achieve everything I want. There's a difference, *asshole.*

I don't respond, because I'm fairly certain if I open my mouth, he won't appreciate what I have to say.

Eventually, he sighs, placing his hands on top of my file and linking his fingers together before he meets my gaze. "Miss James, given your circumstances, I would be remiss if I did not advise you to choose less lofty goals."

"I'm sorry, my circumstances?" I can feel my palms sweating as nerves wrack my body.

"Your status as a scholarship student."

Oh, *that.* I let out a silent breath of relief.

"The careers you mentioned all involve extra years of studying beyond an undergraduate degree. Postgraduate degrees are competitive and only the best candidates are awarded scholarships. Given your situation, it would be wise to consider careers that only require an undergraduate degree."

He says it as if simply having an undergraduate degree is something to be sniffed at. Something only us poor commoners should settle for. The arrogant asshat probably has more letters after his name than there is space on a page.

"As you'll be able to see from my files, I have above a 4.0 GPA—"

"Yes, yes, I see that." He waves dismissively. "However, the academic rigor at Halston is of a much greater standard than what you are accustomed to. Frankly, I'm surprised the school even accepted you with your basic education. Competition must have been lacking for scholarship positions this year," he sneers. "A year of online courses, followed by two more years at Breakthrough Academy." He shakes his head. "*Delightful.*"

"My—" He holds up a hand, silencing any further argument.

"Let's see how you get on this semester, and if you are not failing out, then we can reassess."

Jeez, that's a positive pep talk. There's no point in arguing with him, so I nod my head in agreement, and once we set a date for the next meeting, I head out.

As I'm walking out of the admin building, I'm so busy looking at my map, trying to locate the dining hall so I can get my coffee fix after that tremendously horrendous meeting, that I manage to run right into someone.

"Oh my God, I'm so sorry," I blurt as something clatters to the ground and a strong arm wraps around my waist, pulling me against a hard chest. I'm forced to crane my neck back to stare up at the tall, broad, dark-haired man in front of me. Tattoos peek out from the collar of his black T-shirt, swirling designs of black ink that form indiscernible patterns before dipping back beneath the fabric, which is stretched across a solid chest.

Lifting my eyes higher, they clash with icy baby blues, two iridescent pools that instantly hold me captive and pull me in as I gape dumbly up at him. He's gorgeous. Incredibly so.

He takes a second to look me over, his eyes slowly cascading over my skin and turning my insides to mush, even as my body tenses, expecting the same reaction I've gotten from everyone else today—disdain. Instead, his eyes heat with a molten intensity that has me melting into his touch.

In the space between blinks, his heated gaze turns to stone, his hands moving to grip my upper arm to the point of pain. "You should be. Watch where you're going next time." His brutal words and harsh tone are a slap to the face, and I flinch away, gaping at him in shock as he levels me with a scowl.

I yank my arm out of his grip and step back, taking in the rest of his appearance—leather jacket and black skinny jeans that hug muscular thighs, tucked into matching black boots that give him a dark, biker vibe—before dropping my gaze to the ground. That's when I notice the notebook, which he must have dropped, lying open on the pavement.

To avoid looking at his angry face, I bend down to lift it, pausing when my eyes catch on the intricate drawing of the main Halston building. Despite being nothing more than a sketch, it's so life-like looking that I can't help but stare.

"It's rude to look through other people's things," the asshole snarls, ripping the notebook from my hand.

"Sorry," I mutter, not that he hears me as he levels me with a final glare before storming off.

*Jeez. What a fucking douchebag*!

"It was an accident," I snap under my breath, frowning in his direction before turning my back on him.

Why do the hot ones always have to be assholes? And right when I thought perhaps he was going to be different from everyone else.

---

Statistics 101 is my last class before the weekend. My first week at Halston has been relatively uneventful. The course load is intense, and the standards expected are high, but that's nothing I hadn't already foreseen. With the exception of unimpressed glances and whispering behind hands, I've been mostly ignored by the student population, which again is as predicted. And suits me perfectly fine. I'm used to being alone and didn't expect to make friends here.

Maybe if my life had worked out differently, I'd have fretted over fitting in and forming a solid group of friends, but that naive little girl is long dead and buried, and in her place is someone who doesn't give a damn what others think. Someone who recognizes that some things are far more important than having a friendship group and being accepted by superficial, rich brats.

Like security.

Safety.

Breathing.

I pull my laptop, notepad, and pens from my bag, prepared to take notes on today's lecture as the other students settle into their seats around me. Right before the professor is about to begin, the classroom door swings open, and the room erupts into hushed whispers as a tall, broad-shouldered, muscular man with messy blond hair and a cheeky grin steps confidently into the room.

He gives a slight nod to the lecturer, who ignores his tardiness as he waves him toward the tiered pews. Chestnut brown eyes scan the rows of seats, spotting the only empty one—right beside mine. He makes a beeline for it, deftly squeezing behind the other occupants in my row as he works his way down.

Eyes follow his journey with rapt fascination. Girls smile coyly and reach out to touch him as he passes, while guys nod or hold their fists up for him to bump. Whoever he is, he's clearly popular.

Dropping into the chair beside mine with a sigh, he leans over to grab his things from his bag. The move offers me the opportunity to check him out without him noticing. The thick cords of his biceps flex, and I can practically see the ropes of muscles around his shoulder, chest, and back through his top.

An athlete.

There's no way someone like him looks like that and isn't on some sort of sports team.

He doesn't spare me a glance as he sets his things on the desk, his dirty-blond locks falling forward and obstructing my view of his face, and I rip my gaze away from him as the professor calls the class to attention.

Professor Caldwell has barely introduced himself when the bitchy blonde from Monday's orientation tour leans into the hottie's other side and begins whispering in his ear. I roll my eyes but bite my tongue and keep my focus on the professor as he goes over the syllabus for the semester.

It's immediately apparent that this guy is a hard ass, and the class is going to be one of my tougher ones. Professor Caldwell makes it clear that he doesn't suffer fools and won't tolerate students who neglect their studies, and I make a mental note to ensure I don't fall behind.

"I would advise you all to get a head start on next week's reading," he calls out an hour later. "There will be regular class tests to ensure all of you are keeping up with the course load, and if your results are repeatedly subpar, you will find your place in my class in jeopardy."

Once I've jotted down a reminder to read the chapter on introductory statistical methods ahead of next week's class, I slam closed my textbook, glaring at the hottie beside me. He's oblivious, of course. As he has been all class while he flirted it up with blondie. The two of them whispered and giggled non-stop, their heads so close, I wouldn't be surprised if they were actually making out at one point. Her hands were all over him, stroking his arm and sliding across his thigh. There was a moment halfway through when I started to panic, thinking she might give him a hand job right then and there in the middle of class.

Not only were their antics annoying, but her high-pitched giggles made it impossible to hear and I kept missing what the professor was saying.

Those two might not have any concerns about flunking out of this class, but I sure as hell do. I can clearly picture the look on my advisor's face if I fail my first test of the year.

Gritting my teeth, I barge past the two of them—still oblivious to everyone around them as they flirt openly in the middle of the aisle—and stomp down the stairs toward the exit.

Unlike *some people*, I have places to be.

Leaving campus, I make the fifteen-minute walk to my apartment. Halston is an elite college town that is centered around the university, however, if you head toward the outskirts of town, that elite vibe gives way to a shabbier feel.

My apartment is situated amongst the living quarters for the working people of this small town. The ones responsible for the day-to-day running of the university and who work in the surrounding shops, bars, cafes, clubs, and restaurants.

I'm only a couple of blocks away when my phone rings in my pocket, and heaving out a sigh when I see the caller ID, I reluctantly answer.

"Mom." That one singular word is snapped off the end of my tongue as I fail to keep the bitterness out of my tone. I do not have time for her bullshit today.

"I haven't received this week's money," she hisses like a snake about to strike, and I grit my teeth in an effort to keep my temper in check. No *hello, how are you doing?* No inquiries about my classes or how I'm getting on at university. Not that I expected any such concern. My mother has never been maternal or caring; she has become downright spiteful over the last four years.

But she knows how to play people. Anyone who meets her thinks she's such a sweetheart—a mother with a heart of gold who can do no wrong.

Bull-fucking-shit.

It's an act she puts on to ensure she gets what she wants—men, money, status. Doesn't matter what the end goal is.

The worst part is, it works every time.

I'm the only one who sees her for the snake she is. The only one privileged enough to be subjected to this side of her.

I don't get the sweet smiles and pouty lips.

Nope, all I get is the bitter bitch that resides underneath.

Pressing my fingernails into the palm of my hand, I mentally count to three before responding. "I don't get paid until tonight. You know this. I'll transfer it to your account tomorrow."

"Why can't you do it tonight?" she whines, and I'm forced to close my eyes and take a calming breath before I bite out a response that will only make the situation worse.

"Are the bills paid and the fridge stocked?" I ask in response, careful to keep my biting tone to a minimum despite the anger bubbling inside at her callous demands.

"Of course, Riley. Honestly, what do you take me for?" She huffs haughtily and I roll my eyes at her dramatics.

Fighting back a wave of frustration, I calmly retort, "Then it can wait until tomorrow. I'm already late for work, and I don't get off until two."

"Fine," she sighs as though her generosity knows no bounds.

"How is—"

The line goes dead, and I pull the phone away from my ear, blinking at the screen in disbelief as I realize she hung up on me.

"Nice talking to you, too," I sneer, shaking my head and stuffing the phone into my pocket. My mother knows exactly how to piss me off.

Rolling my shoulders, I shake off the fiery pit of hurt and anger that takes up residence in my stomach every time I have to deal with her and push open the door to my apartment building. Hurrying up the stairs, I let myself into my tiny one-bed apartment to change for work.

# LOGAN

## CHAPTER TWO

"Good practice, boys," Coach bellows over the echoing shouts and clang of metal doors as the various conversations that were taking place cease. A previous NHL hockey player himself, Coach's once jet-black hair has faded to salt-and-pepper, his face etched with lines that tell stories of dedication and determination. He knows what it takes to perform at this level, and more importantly, he knows the grit required to make it in the NHL.

Coach's astute gaze scans over each of us in the locker room. Even though he's well into his fifties, there's still a robust strength about him. It's in the broad set of his shoulders, muscles still refined from years spent on the ice. His presence alone commands respect, and when Coach speaks, we all shut up, sit up, and pay attention.

"If you play like that against Denver next week, the season will be off to a fantastic start!"

The room erupts into chaos as everyone hoots and hollers. I cup my mouth with my hands and throw my head back, howling to the ceiling. My howl is quickly joined by that of my teammates, all of us united in our goal for this hockey season.

"Don't worry, Coach," Gavin, a fellow senior and one of our defensemen yells. "We're going all the way to the championships again this year!"

The locker room gets even louder as my teammates bang their sticks against the floor and yell their agreement.

"Lovin' the confidence, Anderson," Coach says with a smile before he grows serious, "but let's not count our chickens before they hatch, yeah?"

Gavin scoffs, flinging his arm around my neck and dragging me into his bare, sweaty chest. The dude reeks.

"What the fuck, man," I growl, attempting to wriggle out of his iron hold.

"With Astor on the team, there's no way we aren't making it to the Frozen Four," he preens, ignoring my fist as I drive it into his side in a bid to get him to let go.

"Damn right," one of the other guys yells as I finally manage to break free from Gavin's hold and shove him away from me with a grin.

I forget all about Coach still standing in the room as I banter with Gavin and the others, giving them shit and talking about the pussy we're all going to get when we win our game against Denver next week.

"Astor," Coach barks, startling me as the smile drops from my face and I turn to face him. "I want to see you in my office once you've showered and prettied yourself all up."

"Aww, Coach, finally taking me up on that date?" I tease with a wink as the guys howl with laughter.

Coach returns my ribbing with a deadpan stare before stomping out of the locker room, and knowing nothing pisses Coach off more than being left waiting, I hurry my ass into the shower.

"What's up, Coach?" I ask as I saunter into his office five minutes later. Coach is a hard ass but a great coach and mentor.

Everyone on campus thinks I'm responsible for winning us three championship titles in a row, but he's the man behind the glass helping me perform at my best. Without him, we never would have made it past regionals.

"Astor," he grunts, sounding positively irritated as he lifts his head to pin me in place with his glare. Leaning back in his chair, he folds his arms across his chest, and instantly my back straightens, knowing I'm in deep shit. "Tell me how we're only one month into the school year, and you're already flunking?"

*Fuck.* I should have known Coach would find out about that.

I grimace. "It was one test. Doesn't mean anything."

"Don't peddle that shit my way. You were nearly benched freshman year because of this class, right?" He waits until I give a brisk nod before barking, "Is that how you want to play out your senior year—on the bench?"

"No, Coach. Absolutely not."

Lips pursed, he stares at me, seeming to contemplate something before he shakes his head and sighs. "The Pacific Penguins were on the phone asking about you the other day."

I immediately perk up, eyebrows hitting my hairline as I gape at him. I wasn't fortunate enough to get drafted right out of high school, and I've spent the last three years working my ass off to prove myself to the scouts. This is my final year to show them what I'm made of and ideally land an NHL contract.

This year, I have to make every game count. Every minute of ice time. This is my opportunity to prove to the scouts that I'm not just another player but an unstoppable force.

I can't afford to be benched for one game, never mind an entire season!

My team is depending on me. My future is relying on me. If I can't get my grades up and play the best damn season I've ever played, I might as well throw in the stick right now. Tell Coach I'm quitting and walk away.

Except I could never do that. Could never willingly walk away from hockey. It's who I am. All I've ever wanted. Since I was three years old and someone put a stick in my hand, I knew this was what I wanted to do.

I refuse to let one measly grade, one stupid class be the reason that dream slips through my fingers!

“They wanna come watch you play,” Coach states with an engrained frown, unaware of the rapid pitter-patter of my heart. "But they won't get that chance if you’re sitting on your ass all season. Not to mention that, as team captain, it doesn’t set a good example if you can’t keep your grades up, and not having you on the ice will affect team morale.”

*Damn it!*

This is it. This is my shot. And I might have already fucked it all up.

“Coach!" I plead, grinding my teeth against my frustration. "You can’t bench me just because my brain takes offense to numbers! I’m this team's best shot at getting that championship title, and you know it!”

“Maybe so, son, but rules are rules,” Coach returns, unfazed by my outburst. “If you don’t wanna be warming your ass on the bench all year, then I suggest you find a way to pass that class.” He's unwavering in his stance. It doesn't matter how much I protest, he's not going to change his mind. I get it. Respect it, even. But that doesn't mean it doesn't piss me the hell off.

The principle of it all is what infuriates me. It's fucking unfair. What the hell does one stupid test have to do with my ability to perform on the ice? My grades don't define me as a player or a captain. Sure, I need to pass the class in order to get my degree, but that should be a wholly separate issue. One I can deal with after the scouts have seen me play, and I ideally have the championship trophy in one hand and an NHL contract in the other.

Seemingly done with me, he drops his gaze to the pile of paperwork on his desk—my sign that I'm dismissed.

"This is fucking bullshit," I grumble to myself as I march away from his office with my duffle bag slung over my shoulder. How the hell am I meant to pass a class that's next to impossible?!

It's not like I'm not trying. Despite the bad rep athletes get for not studying, I actually do put the work into my classes, and I fucking studied for that test! Regardless, it might as well have been in Chinese, for all I could understand of the questions. It didn't seem to matter that I'd poured hours of my time into understanding the concepts Professor Caldwell discussed in class. I couldn't figure out how to apply them to the issues presented.

Like I said, it's fucking bullshit.

Maybe I can ask someone in the class to help me. Although, who? Neither my teammates nor Grayson or Royce have had to take Stats, and most of the class either wants to fuck me or party with me—neither of which is conducive to getting good grades.

Guess it would do no harm to find out who is acing the class and suss them out. If that doesn't pan out, I can always try putting the moves on Professor Caldwell. Maybe I'll get lucky, and he will fall for my charms and give me an A anyway.

---

The puck bounces off the post a second before the game ends, and close to exploding, I toss the controller aside. Before I do something stupid like punch Grayson, who is grinning cockily at me, I slump back against the couch cushions and stare up at the ceiling.

"Dude, I'm kicking your ass," Grayson taunts. Asshole is just looking to get a black eye.

"Video game hockey is nothing like the real thing," I retort half-heartedly, frowning at the TV screen as fireworks explode and the game players celebrate Gray's win.

Leaning back beside me, Grayson nudges my shoulder to get my attention. "What's eating you? I rarely kick your ass, even on the screen."

I huff out a small laugh. "Coach found out I failed my stupid Stats test. Said he'll bench me if I don't pull my grade up."

"Shit, man, I'm sorry. That sucks."

We might give each other shit, but he knows how much hockey means to me.

As much as football meant to Royce—though we are still cleaning up the aftermath of *that* disaster. We can't afford for me to get benched and lose my shit as well. Fuck knows Grayson has enough on his plate to deal with, never mind babysitting both of our pathetic, sorry asses. Royce is trouble enough, getting into all sorts of mischief when he is feeling particularly melancholy and violent. It's taken the two of us to keep him from killing himself—or *them*. And we'll keep doing it, but if I lose my dream and join him in Miserableville, Gray will lose his ever-loving shit trying to wrangle us both under control.

I wouldn't be surprised if he washed his hands of us.

So nope, no wallowing. No giving up. I *will* figure out how to pass this stupid class. Somehow. For Grayson's sake as much as my own. Because the man looks stressed out on the best of days, so he doesn't need me adding to his problems.

The three of us have been best friends since freshman year, when Royce got into a fight at one of the campus bars. Some chick hit on him in front of her boyfriend, and when the boyfriend got in Royce's face, Royce, naturally, incited a fucking riot. It took both Gray and me to peel him off the boyfriend and drag his drunk ass out of there and to Leon's, an all-night diner out of town where the three of us bonded over stale coffee and the fluffiest pancakes known to man.

We talked about everything that night.

Hockey. Football. Halston. Our pasts. Our families.

We were like kindred spirits; always meant to find one another. We formed an unlikely threesome, but we work.

Gray and Royce connected over their hatred for womankind. At the same time, I enjoyed the challenge of dragging those two antisocial nitwits out of their comfort zone and having people to chill with when I wasn't feeling a raging party on a Friday night.

They both have a lot in common, so their friendship makes sense. Me, not so much. I freakin' *love* women. And unlike Gray and Royce, my family isn't a total mess. My parents are good people and they love and support me.

My father built his company, Bolt Media, a marketing agency, from the ground up, turning it into a tremendously successful business. One he expects me to take over one day, and I will, but hockey has always been my dream. My passion. Thankfully, my parents support my dreams, and Dad is happy for me to pursue a career in the NHL for as far as I can go, and when I retire, then I'll take over for him in the business. Eventually. Running the company isn't necessarily the future I'd have picked for myself, but I appreciate all the hard work he has put into building it into the company it is today, and the time they are giving me to pursue my own dreams, so the least I can give back is the promise to protect his life's work after he's gone.

Although, if I don't get my grades up, I could be taking over for him a lot sooner than I anticipated.

"I thought you studied for that test?" Gray queries, pulling me out of my morbid thoughts.

"I did," I whine. "But I may as well not have wasted my time for all the good it did me."

"And you can't drop the class?"

I shake my head. "Not if I want to graduate with a degree in Marketing." Which I do. Seems pertinent, what with one day running a marketing company. I know I can probably learn everything I'll need to know on the job, but I want to prove to my dad and those working at his company that I deserve my place among them, and when I one day take over as CEO, I want them to know I earned it. That the job is going to the right man. That I deserve the responsibility. And not that I was handed it out of nepotism.

"Shit." Gray sighs, his forehead creased as he frowns. "What are you going to do?"

"I'm going to have to find someone to tutor me," I state, defeated. "I've already emailed the professor and asked him if there's anyone suitable in the class who I could study with."

Grayson actually laughs out loud at that. "Good luck with that one, man. There isn't a single student here who doesn't fawn all over you. They'll all be too busy drooling at your feet to actually teach you anything."

Smirking, I shove his shoulder playfully. "Are you including yourself in that, Gray? Do you go moon-eyed in my presence?"

"Fuck off, asshole." He shoves me right back, but his lips are hooked up in a grin.

"What's he done now?" Royce asks as he stalks into the room and drops into an empty chair beside us. He sprawls out, the chair creaking precariously beneath his weight as his hands clench around the arms. My gaze instinctively drops to his knuckles, noticing the split skin, but I bite back my retort. It will only piss him off.

It used to be a fun thing we did to blow off steam—head to The Depot. It was a rush. A high we chased in the off-season. Royce is a fucking champion, a natural in the ring, but now that he doesn't have football to expend all his energy on, he practically lives there. Bruises permanently litter his body and his knuckles are constantly swollen, the white scars now tattooed on his skin.

Still, he agreed he wouldn't go to The Depot without one of us with him. He has a penchant for getting into trouble when he goes alone. Okay, he also manages to find trouble when we're with him, but at least we're there to drag his sorry ass out.

"Just being his typical dumb self," Gray retorts with a roll of his eyes. However, I do notice the tightness around his mouth. He's spotted the same tell-tale signs I have. The ones that tell us, no matter how *okay* Royce seems, he's still stuck in self-destructive mode.

Smirking, Gray adds, "Guess who has to find themselves a tutor."

Royce's eyes snap to mine, filling with mirth. "No shit, really?" A bark of laughter rips from his throat. "That should be interesting for the poor bastard who ends up stuck with you for the semester."

"Who says my tutor won't be a girl?" I argue.

Royce arches a dark eyebrow. "Ehh, because you'll fuck her and never call her again? Not exactly conducive to a constructive tutor-tutee relationship."

Grabbing a cushion, I toss it at his smug face. "Shut up, dickhead. I won't fuck her. I have puck bunnies for that. I'm capable of keeping it in my pants."

It's Gray's turn to look at me skeptically. "Are you? Cause I've yet to see that."

"You're both the absolute worst," I grouse as my phone

buzzes in my pocket. "Worst friends ever. I don't even know why I put up with you idiots."

Royce scoffs as I open the email from my Statistics professor. "Probably because we're the only ones on campus who don't think the sun shines out of your asshole."

Ignoring him, I smirk down at my phone.

"What are you grinning at?" Gray asks, leaning in to peer at the screen.

I quickly lock it so he can't see, and looking up, I grin at both him and Royce.

"I found myself a tutor."

"And let me guess," Royce says with an exaggerated eye roll. "She's a girl."

"Dude, you're totally failing that class," Gray says, all the while laughing his head off.

Nah. I may love pussy, but I love hockey more. Whoever this girl is, I'm not going to let her interfere with my dream. I'm going to convince her to help me, and I'm going to play my best game on the ice this year. I'm going to be in the middle of my teammates when we win that championship title, and I'm going to be a forward for the Pacific Penguins next year.

Because when you visualize, you materialize, and all that *go-getter* nonsense.

Maybe, at the end of the semester, when I've aced my Statistics class and I've dominated every game, I can reward us both with a fun night between the sheets.

Later that night, I'm lying in bed, searching social media as I try to find a picture of this girl—Riley James—so I know who she is. Annoyingly, all of her accounts are set to private. Who does that? The entire point of social media is so you can post pictures of the food you're eating or the random dog you walked past on the street for complete strangers to roll their eyes at as they scroll past it on their feeds.

# RILEY

## CHAPTER THREE

My skin is clammy with sweat and I can feel a trickle run down my spine. My breaths are heavy in my ear as the classroom door comes into sight. *Thank God.* Some idiot ran into me while chasing a football, spilling my coffee, and I had to duck into a bathroom to mop it up. However, the brown stain stands out like a beacon against my white top, *and* I'm now late for Statistics. *Just great!*

Attempting to calm my breathing and swipe down my hair so I don't look like a complete mess, I push open the door. Professor Caldwell stops mid-speech, sparing me a scathing look that promises trouble if I dare interrupt him like this again. Muttering an apology, I ignore the giggles of the other students as I clench the front of my coat in my hands, holding it closed to hide the coffee stain blooming on my chest while I scan the room for a vacant seat.

I nearly groan aloud when I spot one beside Logan Astor—yup, I uncovered the identity of the blond-haired hottie and wasn't entirely surprised to discover he was the one the girls were moon-eyed over during my orientation tour.

*Why?* I moan to myself. The man is *never* alone. Boys and

girls alike flock to his side the second he steps into the classroom, and no one has ever left an empty seat beside him—not that I've been specifically looking. Other than ensuring he doesn't sit beside *me* again, I don't care where he sits. Or who he sits with.

Skipping over the empty chair, I scan the rest of the lecture hall, hoping to find another one, but when Professor Caldwell clears his throat in an obvious *sit down this instant,* I admit defeat and hurry toward the ice hockey god.

He continues with his lecture the second my ass hits the seat, and I hurriedly pull out my things, hoping I haven't missed anything important.

"I'm open to creative forms of payment," Logan murmurs in my ear, his voice low and heady.

I stiffen, side-eyeing him in confusion.

He winks, and dear Lord does it do inappropriate things to my ovaries. No wonder girls fall all over him. He's sex incarnate —and he knows it.

"For keeping the seat beside me free for you."

*Oh, hell no!*

If sitting here comes with a price, then I'd rather skip the entire class.

My expression turns thunderous as I begin shoving everything I just lifted out back into my bag, willing to risk Professor Caldwell's wrath if it means I don't owe this arrogant asshole a damn thing.

"Relax." He sighs as though frustrated, resting his hand on my arm to halt my movements. "I was only joking."

I give him a withering glare that could turn glass to ice. "Well, it wasn't funny."

He nods, his features fixed into a serious expression, but I can't tell if he's being genuine or mocking me. "Noted."

I glare at him a moment longer, but when I can't figure out

his intentions, I dismiss him altogether and turn my attention to the front of the class.

He leaves me alone for all of thirty seconds before he leans over, invading my personal space. "I *did* keep this space free for you, though."

My gaze shifts to the side, narrowing before I promptly dismiss him. He's only trying to get a rise out of me. He's the type who needs everyone's attention constantly on him.

"It was quite a feat," he continues, undeterred. "I thought one girl was going to burst into tears when I told her she couldn't sit there."

I roll my eyes, although I wouldn't be surprised if he was telling the truth.

When I remain mute, he sighs. Frustratingly, it makes me want to laugh, and I have to bite down on my lower lip to stifle it. I bet he's never had to work so hard to get a girl to talk to him.

He drops his face to stare at his tabletop, and I silently hope he's given up and decided to focus on his studies instead of bothering me.

Unfortunately, I am shit out of luck, and while I'm jotting down notes, he takes the opportunity to drag his chair impossibly closer. His muscular arm presses against mine and it's my turn to huff out a frustrated breath as I do my best to ignore him.

However, apparently, Logan is persistent. His knee bumps against mine beneath the table as he leans into my personal space and glancing at him out of the corner of my eye, I find him intently watching me while I write. His nearness leaves me feeling off-kilter, and I don't like it. The way my heart rate spikes and my palms grow clammy. *He's just a boy*, I remind myself, even as pressure wells in my chest, a sensation I can neither shake nor deny. It's like a magnetism between us that I'm trying desperately to pretend doesn't exist.

"Has anyone ever told you you smell like strawberries?" he murmurs in a low voice that elicits goosebumps along my skin. As if to prove his point, he inhales deeply, humming with pleasure. "Because you totally do. Sweet and juicy." His nose is practically buried in my hair, and it takes everything in me not to react to his words or the brush of his lips against my skin.

Teeth gritted, I glare at the notepad on my desk, willing myself not to respond. I'm no longer paying attention to the lecture. Every atom in my body is attuned to the gorgeous man currently *sniffing* me like he's a damn dog and I'm a juicy steak being dangled in front of him.

"You could at least acknowledge my existence," he grumbles in exasperation when he gets no further reaction from me. Stifling my laugh, I tug my lower lip into my mouth, pleased to have irritated him as much as he is currently irritating me.

Because irritation is definitely the only emotion I am feeling toward him.

Yup. Only irritation.

Quietly clearing my throat so he can't tell how much his close proximity affects me, I keep my eyes carefully focused on the front of the lecture hall as I mutter barely loud enough for him to hear, "I didn't ask you to save me a seat, and contrary to what you seem to think, I don't owe you anything."

Unfazed by my harsh tone, he mock gasps and claps his hand against his chest. "She speaks!"

*Dammit, lips, don't twitch! He is not amusing!*

"Okay, fine," he admits in defeat. "You caught me. I had ulterior motives for wanting you to sit beside me."

My body stiffens as I once again flick my shuttered gaze his way.

"I need your help," he mutters, face scrunched as though the confession cost him.

How the hell could *I* help someone like him?

He stares at me expectantly before cocking a brow. What? Does he think I have telepathy? I can't read his damn mind!

Appearing frustrated, he sighs. "Haven't you wondered why a senior is taking a freshman class?"

I had, actually. When I first learned who he was—and more specifically, that he was a senior—I questioned why he was in a freshman Stats class. However, I am not intrigued enough to go out of my way to find the answer... or to encourage whatever this is.

Masking my curiosity, I lean in as though I'm about to share a scandalizing secret and whisper, "This may come as a surprise to you, but I don't actually think about you all that often."

Instead of the frown I was expecting at my admission, his face breaks out in a smile. The most breathtaking one I've ever seen. It's blinding. Dazzling. Literally wipes all rational thought from my mind.

"So what you're saying is you think about me *sometimes.*" My eyes widen, and he chuckles at my horrified expression. "What I want to know is *when* do you think about me, Shortcake? 'Cause if it's when I'm hoping, then perhaps the two of us should hang out and think about each other *together.*"

His cocky smirk is positively devious, and I hate how my body heats at the idea of his offer. My fingers quiver slightly with anticipation and I have to curl them into my hand to hide my reaction. Is this how other girls feel beneath Logan's attention?

So... blindsided. Intoxicated. Swept away.

I have to physically snap myself out of my daze as I tear my gaze from his. This isn't some romantic comedy, and Logan isn't a sweet kid searching for some great love. He's a sweet-talker—a player. Allowing myself to be taken in by him would be foolish. Irresponsible. Especially when there is so much riding on my success at Halston.

Wrangling myself under control, I scowl at him. My voice comes out low but harsh. "If *that's* what you need my help with, then you may look elsewhere. I'm sure someone from your fan club would gladly help you out."

He barks out a laugh, loud enough to draw the eyes of half the class, and I snap my head toward the front of the classroom, ignoring the heat in my cheeks as Professor Caldwell glares in our direction. *Great, as if being late to class wasn't bad enough, now I'm definitely going to be in Professor Caldwell's bad books.*

"No doubt, I could easily find someone to *help me out*, but that's not the sort of help I need." He leans in, and I catch a whiff of his cologne. The scent reminds me of a sharp winter breeze, and I involuntarily breathe in deeper until it fills my lungs. His scent wraps around me like a gentle caress, revitalizing my senses. I feel as though I just stepped outside into a whipping gale. Alert. Awake. Adrenalized. It's pure. Invigorating. And it completely catches me by surprise. "The help I need, only you can provide."

I blink at him. His words slowly process through the fog that has taken residence in my brain at his mere proximity.

His words finally resonate, and my entire body melts.

*Fuck, why does that sound so sexual?* Heat gathers low in my belly and I have to resist the urge to clench my thighs.

*He's not talking about sex,* I mentally chastise myself. *And even if he was, you would not be taking him up on that offer.* I'm not here to get distracted by hot hockey gods that look like Logan Astor, and I just have to look at him to know one night with him would ruin me.

Hell to the motherfucking no.

No distractions. There's too much on the line.

I glare daggers at him, sharp enough to penetrate skin, and his teasing expression melts away as he drops his gaze from mine, rubbing sheepishly at the back of his neck. It's an interesting look on him... seeing this confident sex symbol appear bashful, nervous even.

"I failed this class the first time around," he mumbles, refusing to meet my gaze. "Me and math... we don't gel. Anyway, I put off retaking it for too long—if I don't pass it this time, I won't be allowed to graduate, and well... I'm already flunking."

I swallow hard before asking skeptically, "Why do you think I can help you?"

"Because you're top of the class."

"How do you—"

He interjects smugly, "I sweet-talked the professor into telling me."

Of course, he did. And because he's a real-life god come to grace us mere mortals with his presence, the professor just handed over that confidential piece of information.

He must see the refusal on my lips because before I can put it into words, he cuts across, "Please don't make me beg. 'Cause I will. I'll get down on my knees right here in the middle of class and beg you to help me."

He shifts in his chair as though he's going to do precisely that. Honestly, I wouldn't put it past him, and horrified that he's going to cause more of a scene than he already has, I hastily snap out a hand, ignoring the searing heat of his skin against my palm and the exhilaration that shoots along my nerves as I squeeze his forearm.

"Don't do that," I blurt, not altogether hating the grin slowly gaining traction as it spreads across his face.

"Does that mean you'll help me?"

I worry my lips as I mull it over, conflicted feelings threatening to drag me under. On the one hand, I respect his ability to reach out and ask for help. That takes guts and determination, something that I realize Logan has in spades, even if I don't entirely appreciate how he's gone about asking for my help.

However, there's also this underlying tension between us. This is our first conversation and I already feel the sheer intensity of it. The rawness. The potency. It's both inviting and menacing. Enticing and dangerous—primarily for me—and I no longer know what to do as I try to steel myself against his gaze.

Flicking my eyes to meet his, I run them over his rarely serious face. He's patient, waiting, but I can see the apprehension, the desperation he's trying so hard to hide. Emboldened, I turn to face him. "What's in it for me?" I ask, cocking a brow at him.

His eyebrows lift before his typical cocky smirk curls his lips. "You mean other than getting to bask in the presence of my company?" I can tell he's teasing, but I still roll my eyes, making sure to pierce him with an unimpressed glare. "You'll get a nice bump in your social status, being seen with me. If I get an A on next week's test, I'll even tell people you're cool."

Seriously? Is that why other people do shit for him?

"Social status means nothing to me," I deadpan. "I have no interest in being 'cool' or fitting in with anyone here."

He merely blinks, surprise flashing across his chestnut hues. "Then what do you want?"

I tilt my head, thinking it over. It's a good question. *What do I want?*

I want a secure job with a stable income.

I want to be able to pay my bills each month without stressing.

I want to provide for myself and my family.

I want to offload my good-for-nothing mother.

None of which he can give me.

"I guess I don't want anything from you."

He rears back, face contorted in shock. A strange moment passes between us where his eyes rake over my face as though he is seeing me for the first time. His scrutiny is unwavering, his brow flattened as though he's trying to solve for *k* before he wipes away all trace of confusion, replacing it with a frown so severe it looks foreign on his usually peppy face.

"Everyone wants something from me, Shortcake." His tone is so blunted that it physically stings. "You can let me know when you figure out what it is *you* want."

I open my mouth to argue, to tell him that he genuinely has nothing I want. I'm not interested in his fame or popularity. I don't want *his* money. Do I want money? Of course. Anyone who would say otherwise is kidding themselves, but I know exactly what happens when you accept money with strings.

The cost: one already tarnished soul.

And it's a price I'm not willing to pay.

Honestly, even if there was something I wanted from Logan, I'm not certain I'd ask for it. Not now, when I suspect most of his interactions revolve around what he can do for others. It's sad and hurts my heart for him.

Has anyone ever gotten to know Logan for Logan? Has anyone ever looked behind the veneer to acquaint themselves with who lies beneath?

Why do I find myself wanting to do exactly that? My fingers itch to reach up and pry off his mask, to catch a glimpse of the real Logan. The one that I suspect no one on this campus truly knows.

Logan's gaze takes on an icy quality, his tone equally cold. "So, do we have a deal?"

I search his face, all traces of humor gone. I'm reminded of his notorious reputation. One that runs rampant on campus.

His ruthlessness. His ability to take down any opponent who stands in his way without hesitation. Logan might come across as a harmless golden retriever, but according to the student body, he's vicious on the ice. Which is why the Huskies are undefeated champions for three years running—soon, I imagine, to be four. I see now that he's also capable of that same ardency off the ice. If hockey ever doesn't work out for him, I'm certain he would be a force to be reckoned with in the boardroom.

Perhaps it's because I feel bad for him, or maybe it's simple resignation that leads me to utter, "We have a deal." The words slip from my tongue, sealing our contract and binding us together, and despite not having asked for anything in return, I feel as though I've unwittingly signed my soul over to Logan Astor.

---

I'm still thinking about the deal I made with Logan as I stretch out my hamstrings on the floor of the stage that night.

"Give me all the juicy gossip," Tara demands as she sits down beside me and begins stretching out her long, toned legs. Her black hair is piled on top of her head, emphasizing her unusual gray-violet eyes that remind me of thunderstorms.

I laugh as I lean forward, reaching out to touch my toes with my fingers. She demands the same thing at every rehearsal.

"There is no gossip."

"Seriously?" She arches a disbelieving eyebrow at me. "A bunch of rich hotties all crammed onto that campus and there isn't a single bit of gossip?"

"Not so much as a whisper."

"Uh-huh. At least tell me you went to one party this week."

Tara is five years older than me. She never attended college, and on my first night here, when she discovered I was a Halston student, she declared that she was going to live her college years vicariously through me.

I did warn her that I was not the party type. That I was barely social, and I would be the most boring college student she's ever met, but she didn't seem deterred. If anything, I'm a tad worried that she saw my declaration as a challenge—which is why, I believe, she keeps giving me asinine goals like attending one college party, each week.

At this point, I'm clinging desperately to the hope that she will give up on reforming me before I cave and do what she wants of me.

"Ry!" she exclaims when she sees the guilty look on my face.

"I'm not interested in hanging out with a bunch of people in skimpy dresses and doused in too much cologne."

"How do you know? Have you ever done it?"

I give her a deadpan look. "I don't need to be bitten by a snake to know it will hurt."

"Before you know it, you'll be gray-haired and wrinkly and wish you could go partying without having to pop your arthritis pills first."

"You mean, I'll be like you."

She gasps, eyes brimming with mirth. "You bitch!"

We both crack up laughing as we continue stretching.

"Give me something before I grow concerned that you're a robot. Is there even a guy who has caught your eye?"

She wags her eyebrows, and I look away, pretending to stretch out the muscles in my lower back as I twist my spine.

"Oh my God, there is, isn't there?"

"No!" I answer a little too quickly. Too aggressively.

She laughs at my outburst. "He's hot, right? Ugh, please tell me he's like the school's quarterback or someone out of one of those dark romance novels with the damaged male characters that only soften for the one woman they truly love."

Dear Lord, there's going to be no dealing with her. If I don't tell her anything, she's going to make up a fake guy and probably concoct an entire drama-filled relationship for me. Yet, the second I tell her Logan is captain of the hockey team, she might actually have a heart attack.

Thankfully, Chrissy saves my ass, clapping her hands and gaining everyone's attention as she bounces into the center of the stage with a beaming smile. "Alright, girls. Positions. Let's go through the routine a final time before we need to get ready."

Dressed in my lycra leggings and a slouchy, off-the-shoulder crop top, I get to my feet. "Don't think this is over," Tara warns, pointing her finger at me before we separate to move into our positions. It's usually the same handful of girls working on the weekend. We work well together and we're a close-knit team.

The opening notes of Cannon's *Fire For You* play through the club's sound system, and we get through the routine without a hitch.

"That was perfect, girls! Do exactly that tonight, and you will be amazing!"

Dismissed, I head to the dressing room to change and prepare for tonight.

Lux is a high-end burlesque club that opened only a few weeks before the term started. It's a ten-minute walk from my apartment, and while I was out exploring during my first week in town, I came across an advertisement for performers. Despite the premise being outside my comfort zone, I jumped at the chance to be able to dance regularly. Plus, it pays better than anywhere else in town, and the tips on the weekends are an added bonus.

Dancing on stage, feeling the heavy stare of men's eyes on

you while wearing provocative clothing designed to entice, was incredibly challenging for me. Before I started working here, I shied away from exposing my body in such a way, preferring to hide behind oversized hoodies and loose clothing.

That first night, after my performance, I threw up backstage. I came so close to quitting and walking away. It was Tara who talked me out of it. She saw the state I was in, and while she didn't ask questions, she seemed to instinctively understand exactly how I was feeling.

Every performance gets a little easier to step onto that stage. It's still not something that comes easily to me, but I'm discovering my inner sexy tigress and learning to love my body —flaws and all.

"Alright, ladies, show time!" Chrissy calls out a short while later, and with one final look in the mirror, I add a final swipe of lipstick and tell myself I've got this before heading onto the club floor.

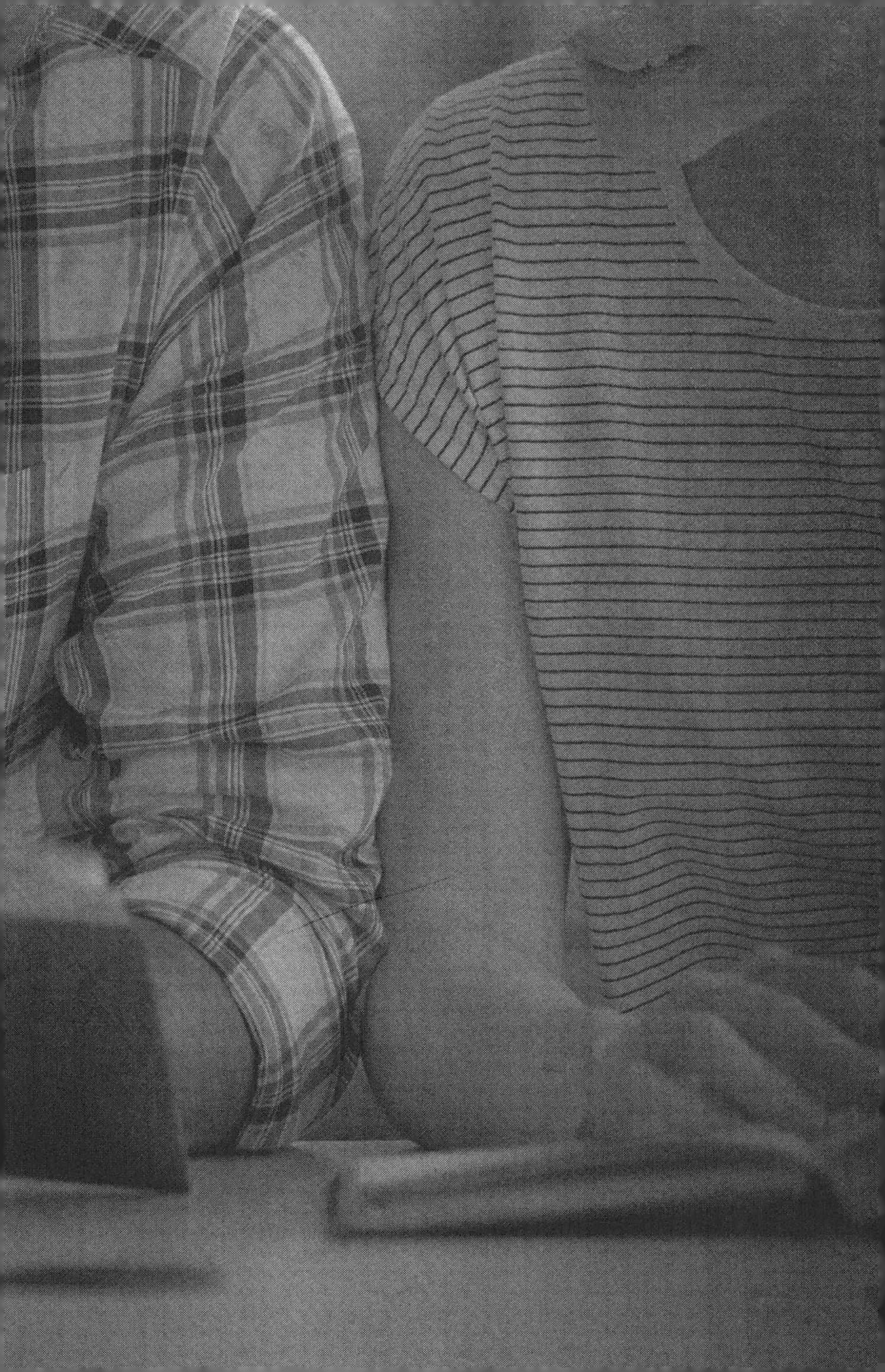

# RILEY

## CHAPTER FOUR

An invisible weight presses on my chest, making it impossible to breathe. My lungs spasm, my entire body seizing until clawing panic scrapes at my insides, begging me to move, to fight.

I'm trapped in a twisted realm somewhere between reality and illusion. A state where malevolence douses the air in toxic waste, making every inhale feel like glass shards shredding my lungs. Dread turns to ice in my veins, gripping my heart and clenching until it shudders and threatens to stop beating altogether.

My body teeters on the precipice, desperate for oxygen as it screams at me to inhale. Right when I think I'm going to pass out, my airway expands and my eyes snap open.

Fear is a palpable thing, beating a hasty retreat against my flesh as my eyes bounce around the room. In the darkness, my surroundings are warped and twisted, shadows dancing in the corners, morphing into grotesque shapes and distorted forms that have me inching closer to utter terror.

He's back. He's here.

I should have known he wouldn't let me go.

The air grows heavy with my labored breaths, sweat dripping from my trembling body and soaking into the sheets. With numb fingers, I reach out blindly until I find the switch. I flick it.

The room is immersed in a bright, white light that sends the monsters scurrying and hissing into the shadows, and I take my first real breath as I scour the room. The seconds tick by, each one cementing me more firmly in reality as I leave the nightmare behind. However, it does nothing to ease the terror flooding my limbs as I grapple for control of my own mind.

Blowing out a long, shaky breath, I fall back on the methods I've learned to quell the panic and ground myself when attacks like this leave me reeling.

*You're safe. You're in your apartment at Halston. You're alone.*

When I've gathered enough moisture to form actual words, I repeat them aloud, needing to hear my own voice. To know this is real. That I am real.

"I am safe. I'm in my apartment. I'm in Halston." I do one final search of the room before confirming, "I am alone."

*He's not here. He can't hurt you. He* won't *hurt you ever again.*

My hands are still shaking as I slide one beneath my bed sheet and run my fingers along the lining of my pajama shorts until I find the bumps. The sharp, straight edges are my only source of comfort on nights like tonight.

Breathe in; bleed out.

It's something I used to take quite literally, but now I use it to find a sense of calm.

More than anything, that helps push away the curling tendrils of black mist still clinging to the recesses of my consciousness.

Relief is a visceral thing, flooding through me as I finger the scars, recalling the solace inflicting each one brought. At the time, it was my only outlet for all the hurt and anger. The only thing that stopped my world from completely spinning out. And when memories of that time resurface, the reminder brings me a sense of calm.

Remembering that I got out. That I am alive.

I scrape a hand down my face, frustration welling as I scour my mind, trying to identify what might have triggered tonight's nightmare. Nothing obvious stands out, but sometimes it's not always clear cut. Logan's warm brown eyes come to mind, and I pause. Is my interaction with him earlier what triggered me tonight? Sometimes it's as simple as that. As unassuming. I didn't feel fear in his presence, but I did feel... alive. Drawn to him.

Pushing all thoughts of Logan aside, I blow out a shaky exhale, continuing with my usual routine. My hand trembles as I rest it over my heart, the rhythmic *thump, thump* steadying me further.

"I survived," I say aloud, voice hoarse and scratchy. Still, there's a strength in it that bolsters me. "I can feel my heartbeat. The air in my lungs."

There was once a time when that knowledge would have shattered me. When all I wanted was to die. If it hadn't been for divine intervention, life's twisted idea of a joke, or whatever you want to call it, I would be. I'd be worm food in a pine box six feet under, and not a single soul would miss me.

But I'm not.

I'm alive. And I'm fucking fighting to stay that way.

Even when I'm drowning, and I don't know which way up is the surface, I have to remind myself that at least I'm still alive. Still here to fight for the life that I want. The one I deserve.

My inner candle, once unlit, now burns brightly. Some days the flame may be low, the wick close to extinguishing, but I refuse to ever allow that candle to be snuffed out again.

Coming to Halston has been a humongous step forward.

Putting some distance between me and my mother has helped enormously, but it's more than that. It's knowing I'm one step closer to financial freedom, job security, and proving that I can stand on my own two feet.

It's claiming back a sliver of control and carving out a life that is purely mine. Based on *my* decisions, on *my* actions. I'm sick and tired of living an existence beneath the heel of someone else's boot, to be used, abused, manipulated, and subjugated.

Sleep is all but forgotten as I gather the textbooks I dumped on the floor last night and flick them open, ready to dive back into the English assignment I was working on yesterday. Despite the flicker of paranoia still wreaking havoc somewhere in the back of my head, a fire has been ignited in my veins. A thirst for life. For freedom. And glaring at the open page before me, in a low voice, I vow, "I'm taking back control, starting now."

---

By the time that afternoon comes around, I'm flagging, whispering words of love and awe to my coffee as I make my way toward the library for my first tutoring session with Logan.

To say I'm anxious would be an understatement. I'm not sure what to expect. Logan is flirty and full of himself, and I don't for one minute think he will simply sit there and listen to me explain statistical theories to him.

I'm also aware that, despite my best efforts, he has an uncanny way of wriggling beneath my defenses. The fact he managed to sucker me into taking precious time out of my already packed schedule to do this is emphasis enough of my inability to say no to him.

My phone buzzes in my pocket as I make my way up the library steps, and I swiftly pull it out, glancing at the screen.

LOGAN

Got us a table at the back.

Logan and I swapped numbers that day in class. I needed to check my work schedule before confirming a date and time for us to meet. I'd been hesitant to give him my number, imagining him abusing it by texting me at all hours. Although he has been surprisingly honorable, only messaging to arrange today's tutoring session.

Of course, he tried relentlessly to get me to come to his place to study, spouting some bullshit about getting more peace there than he will in the library, but I wasn't having it. Alone with him in a bedroom when he has no concept of personal boundaries and flirts as effortlessly as Logan does? Yeah, that's a recipe for disaster!

Thankfully, he relented and agreed to meet at the library instead.

As I'm weaving my way through the tables, I spot him in a corner at the back of the room, away from prying eyes. Again, this is a surprising move for someone who loves being the center of attention.

*Perhaps he's embarrassed to be seen with me.*

The school heartthrob and the scholarship student... now, that would get tongues wagging, no doubt.

"Hi," I greet awkwardly as I approach the table, setting my bag down as I pull out the chair beside him. "Sorry I'm late. I needed a caffeine fix."

I hold up my steaming coffee cup as if that proves I was genuinely getting coffee.

He gives me a lopsided grin. "And there I was, beginning to think I'd been stood up."

I snort. "You've never been stood up a day in your life."

"No, but there's a first time for everything. And how typical would it be that it'd be with the one girl I actually want to spend time with?"

My cheeks blush, something I'm learning is a commonality around Logan, even though I know he doesn't mean it like that. It's his naturally flirty demeanor.

*And because he needs your help,* I remind myself. *Not because he's actually interested in you.*

Not that it would matter if he was. *No distractions, remember?*

With that reminder, I throw up my mental walls against his charm. "Shall we get to work?"

Just like that, the teasing glint in his eye slips away, and an uncannily serious Logan appears before me. "Sounds good, where do we start?"

The next couple of hours fly by. Logan continues to surprise me. Not once does he try to flirt or goof off. He's wholly focused and pays attention to everything I say and, as I discover, is actually quite smart. *I know, shocker, right?*

He doesn't take offense when I point out that he's doing something wrong or that his answer to a problem is incorrect.

As a hockey player, I guess he's used to criticism, though it's still surprising to see him so intent and pensive. Especially on school work.

"Ugh, my head is fried," he groans, leaning back in his chair and rubbing his hand through his hair. He's done that a lot while we've been here, and it's now sticking up everywhere. Sadly, it does nothing to detract from his handsomeness. If anything, it makes him look as though he's spent the last few hours fooling around with someone who has been dragging their fingers through his hair... presumably while he rocks their world.

Clearing my throat, I say, "We've covered a lot today." I busy myself with packing my things. "You did good, though."

"Yeah?" I can hear the flirty tone back in his voice. Just like that, the switch is flipped, and teasing, flirty Logan is back. I don't know how he does it, going from focused and intent to jokey and chill.

Before I glance at him, I already know one side of his very kissable lips will be hooked up in a teasing smirk. He waits until my green eyes clash with his brown ones. "Do I get a reward?"

I don't know what comes over me—I blame his charisma—but instead of telling him to get over himself, I lean in and lower my voice. "Yeah..." I watch, amused, as his eyes widen with surprise, focus intent on me, and when his gaze drops to my mouth, I run my tongue along my lower lip. "You get the satisfaction of a job well done and, if you're really lucky, an A on next week's test."

It takes a second for my words to penetrate, but when they do, he throws his head back and laughs, this deep, masculine bark that should not be sexy but totally is.

All I can do is stare at him, my gaze dipping to his throat as it vibrates with his laughter. An Adam's apple shouldn't be so sexy. Feeling that now familiar burn in my cheeks, I tear my eyes away, tapping on my phone to check the time.

I smile at the photo on my lock screen until a gasp has me snapping my attention to Logan.

"She smiles," he says with mock seriousness, gaping at me.

I frown at him, not understanding what he's getting at. "Of course I smile."

He shakes his head. "Nope. That's literally the first time I've seen you smile."

"So?" I question with furrowed brows. "We've only talked like twice."

"Yeah, but I've seen you on campus several times this week, and you never smile."

I blink at him, momentarily stunned. He's seen me on campus? Has he been looking out for me? We haven't crossed direct paths since our Stats class last week. I know I've seen him, but he's impossible to miss. You'd have to walk around with blinders on to miss him, and the way everyone flocks to his side when he's around. But me? I melt into the background. I don't stand out, not like him. How would he even notice me if he wasn't actively looking?

"That doesn't mean anything," I mutter, feeling strangely exposed and off balance by his perceptive observation.

He holds up his hands. "I don't mean anything by it. I'm just saying smiling looks good on you. You should do it more often."

I shift in my chair, uncomfortable and unsure how to respond.

"So, who's the kid who has the power to make you smile like that?"

My eyes bug out. *Damn, he really is a perceptive fucker. I'll have to remember that.* I hadn't even realized he'd been looking at my phone screen.

"My niece," I blurt.

He gives me a soft, genuine smile. "She's cute. I love babies. They're like baby animals, ya know? You can't help but lose your mind over them."

I blame the fact that he has caught me completely off guard for the words that tumble from my lips. "It's an old photo. She's three now."

"Oh, does she like Paw Patrol?"

I can't help tugging my lips at the thought of this two-hundred-pound ice hockey player watching kids' cartoons. "She loves it. It's her favorite show."

He nods knowingly. "I come from a large family. I have like ten nieces and nephews, and every single one of them was the same at that age. Who is her favorite character?"

"Skye, obviously," I say, properly grinning now.

Logan laughs, this rich, deep timbre. It's genuine and hearty, unlike his typical laugh that I've come to recognize as the one he uses when talking to the other students on campus.

"Of course it is."

"I'm pretty sure it's because she's the only female, but who am I to argue when she promotes all the qualities you want to instill in a kid? She's dependable, fearless, and smart as hell."

"Is Skye your niece's favorite or yours?" Logan teases.

Wholeheartedly failing at suppressing my smile, I confess, "Okay, so she might be mine." I nudge his shoulder playfully. "You can't tell anyone my role model is a dog."

He mimes zipping his lips. "Your secret is safe with me." Leaning in, he lowers his voice. "This will probably shock you, but Chase was always my favorite."

Recalling the brown-haired police dog who is known as the gang's leader because he's the mature one, always willing to make the hard decisions and step up when needed, I tilt my head, viewing Logan in a new light. Yeah, he comes across as playful and carefree, but he's also the captain of the hockey team, which I imagine comes with a lot of responsibility, and it's a role I doubt he would have accepted unless he'd earned it.

At first, Logan struck me as someone who takes the easy route but here he is, putting in the work. I'm sure he could simply pay someone for the answers or flirt his way into cheating off someone, yet, he's here. Because he wants to earn it. Because behind that goofy front is someone who values integrity and hard work.

No, Logan is not at all who I believed him to be.

And I get the impression I'm only touching the surface of what might possibly be the real Logan.

An unfathomable depth lies behind his veneer, and against all reasoning, I find myself wanting to delve deeper; to know more. Because, despite myself, I think I might actually like the Logan I'm beginning to uncover.

In a soft voice, ringing with too much emotion, I say, "That doesn't surprise me as much as you might think it does."

He stills. It's subtle. His chest still rises and falls, but there's an unnatural stasis to his posture that I wouldn't have noticed if I wasn't already watching him closely.

Astonishment flashes across his face, and something softens his features for a moment. I quickly glimpse a raw, more vulnerable side to him before he erects his cocky grin, his version of a brick wall keeping everyone at bay.

Turning away, he haphazardly tosses his belongings in his bag. I get to my feet and wait until he slings his bag over his shoulder before falling into place beside him.

"You should come to my game on Friday. It's our first of the season," he says casually as we walk through the library toward the exit.

"I'm working," I answer on autopilot, although it's not a lie.

He shrugs off my refusal. "Come to the party after, then."

"I work late, and I'm usually dead on my feet by the end of the week anyway."

He stops on the steps of the library, the late afternoon sunlight glinting off his blond hair.

"Why do I get the impression that all you do is work and study?" he asks, watching me with a knowing look.

I shrug, unable to meet his eyes.

"I know the workload here is intense, but it's still college, and you're only young once, right? You should get out and have some fun every now and again."

Yeah, that's easy for him to say. He's one of those who *'work hard, play harder'*. Only I don't have that luxury.

"Yeah, maybe," I mutter noncommittally. "Anyway, I'll see you in class."

I turn on my heel, but when I'm two steps away from him, he calls out, "Aren't you going to wish me luck?"

I glance back at him over my shoulder. "Do you need it?"

He smirks cockily. "No, but that doesn't mean I don't wanna hear it."

Rolling my eyes, I snark, "I'm sure your fan base will wish you all sorts of luck."

"Maybe I want to hear it from you."

Shaking my head, I turn my back on him and walk away.

---

I'm wiping the sweat from my face when Ava walks into the studio.

"Hey," she greets, giving me a wave. "Sorry to interrupt, but I have a class in half an hour."

"It's your studio. I was just finishing up, anyway."

"Cool. Come join me in my office. We can chat for a few minutes before I need to get set up."

Grabbing my water bottle, I follow her into her small office at the back of the dance studio.

"How have you been?"

"Good," I respond. "Busy. How's Isabella?"

Ava is my next-door neighbor. We met the first day I moved in when her five-year-old daughter tried to swipe my feet out from beneath me while she raced down the stairs dressed in a bright pink tutu and lime green tights. Once Ava wrangled her child, we got to talking and became easy friends.

Ava chuckles to herself. "As energetic as always. She keeps asking when you'll babysit again."

"You know I'm happy to help you out any time."

Shortly after I moved in, Ava's mom slipped and fell in the shower, and Ava had to rush to the hospital. Out of desperation, she knocked on my door and asked if I could look after Isabella and, of course, I agreed. I was more than happy to help her out, and I adore kids, so it was no hardship.

Afterward, Ava kept asking me what she could do to repay me, and when I discovered she had a studio and told her how much I loved to dance, she gave me a spare key and told me to stop by anytime there wasn't a class on.

I rarely take advantage of the opportunity, but some days I need the time to myself, to escape the world around me. I'm heading home tomorrow, a trip that will inevitably involve seeing my mother, so I needed the release dancing brings tonight more than ever.

"I was thinking you could come over for dinner, even. Perhaps tomorrow?"

"I would love to," I say sincerely, "but I can't tomorrow. I'm heading home for the day."

"Oh, that's lovely. Don't worry. We can do it another time. Are you excited to be going home? I'm sure it's been a major adjustment, moving away and starting college."

"Yeah, it has. Home is... complicated, though."

Ava nods. "I get it. No need to explain, but if you ever need to talk or drink wine and bitch, I'm your girl."

Laughing, I thank her.

"How are you getting home?"

"I still need to sort it out. There's a train from Springview early tomorrow morning that should get me in about midday. Then I can get the last one home tomorrow night."

"And travel on public transport alone in the dark? Definitely not. Here." She rummages in her purse before pulling out a set of keys and holding them out for me. "Take my car. I barely use it. It's a heap of junk. The heating barely functions, and sometimes the windows have a mind of their own, but it runs."

"I can't do that," I protest, refusing to take her keys.

"Yes, you can. I only keep it because it wouldn't be worth anything if I sold it, and having a car in case of emergencies is handy. You helped me out when I needed it," she tacks on when I don't waver. "Let me repay the favor."

Groaning, I reach out and take the keys from her outstretched hand. "Fine, but I'm leaving the tank filled, and I insist that when we do dinner, I cook."

Ava grins. "Deal."

The next morning, butterflies swoop in my stomach as I climb into Ava's beat-up blue Honda with a coffee cup in hand and sunglasses perched on my head to combat the low sun. It's October, and the days are rapidly growing shorter.

Setting my coffee in the center console, I start the engine and tune the radio to a station I like before setting out on my journey. It's only a two-hour drive to where my mom lives. I deliberately chose a college that was far enough away from her but wasn't so far that I couldn't make the journey home when I needed to.

I'm only half an hour out of Halston when the ringing of my cell phone interrupts the song on the radio, and grabbing it from the passenger seat, I frown as my mom's name flashes on the screen.

Pulling over to the side of the road, I answer it.

"Mom? What's going on? Is everything okay?"

"I can't do today," she states, skipping over my questions.

My stomach plummets. "What? Why?"

"I just can't, Riley." Her tone is sharp as a blade. No wavering. No negotiating. However, it doesn't stop me from arguing.

"Mom!" I plead, tears of desperation lining my lower lids. "I'm already on my way. You can't do this!" When my protests are met with resolute silence, I continue, growing angry, "You agreed to this. This is the arrangement *we* came to. This is our first meeting since I started college and you're already canceling?"

"Don't take that tone with me, Riley. There's always next month."

"Next month? No, Mom. That's not fair!"

"Fair?!" My mother shrieks. "Don't you dare talk to me about *fair*, Riley James! Do you think any of this is *fair to me*? I am stuck living with the consequences of *your* childish, attention-seeking actions."

"Attention seeking?" The accusation stings like a slap to the face, leaving me wide-eyed and dazed as tears stream down my cheeks and my heart cinches in my chest. Gone are the anxious butterflies from this morning, replaced with dying moths, disintegrating with each passing second on the floor of my stomach.

My mother won't listen to me. She never does.

Desperately grasping for a solution, I plead, "Can we FaceTime instead?"

A deep sigh reverberates down the line before she responds, "Not right now."

My voice quivers. "Later, then. Tonight."

"Maybe."

"Please, Mom. I'm only asking for five minutes. *Please*. Mom! Mom?!"

Pulling the phone away from my ear, a sob wretches from my throat when I see she hung up on me.

Hurt, angry, and sad, I toss the phone onto the passenger seat and bury my head in my hands.

Unfair. She thinks the life she's living is unfair. She hasn't a fucking clue. With my pain stabbing me in the chest like icicles, I rage, screaming out my torment as I bang my fists against the steering wheel until I'm breathing heavily, exhausted, and completely empty inside.

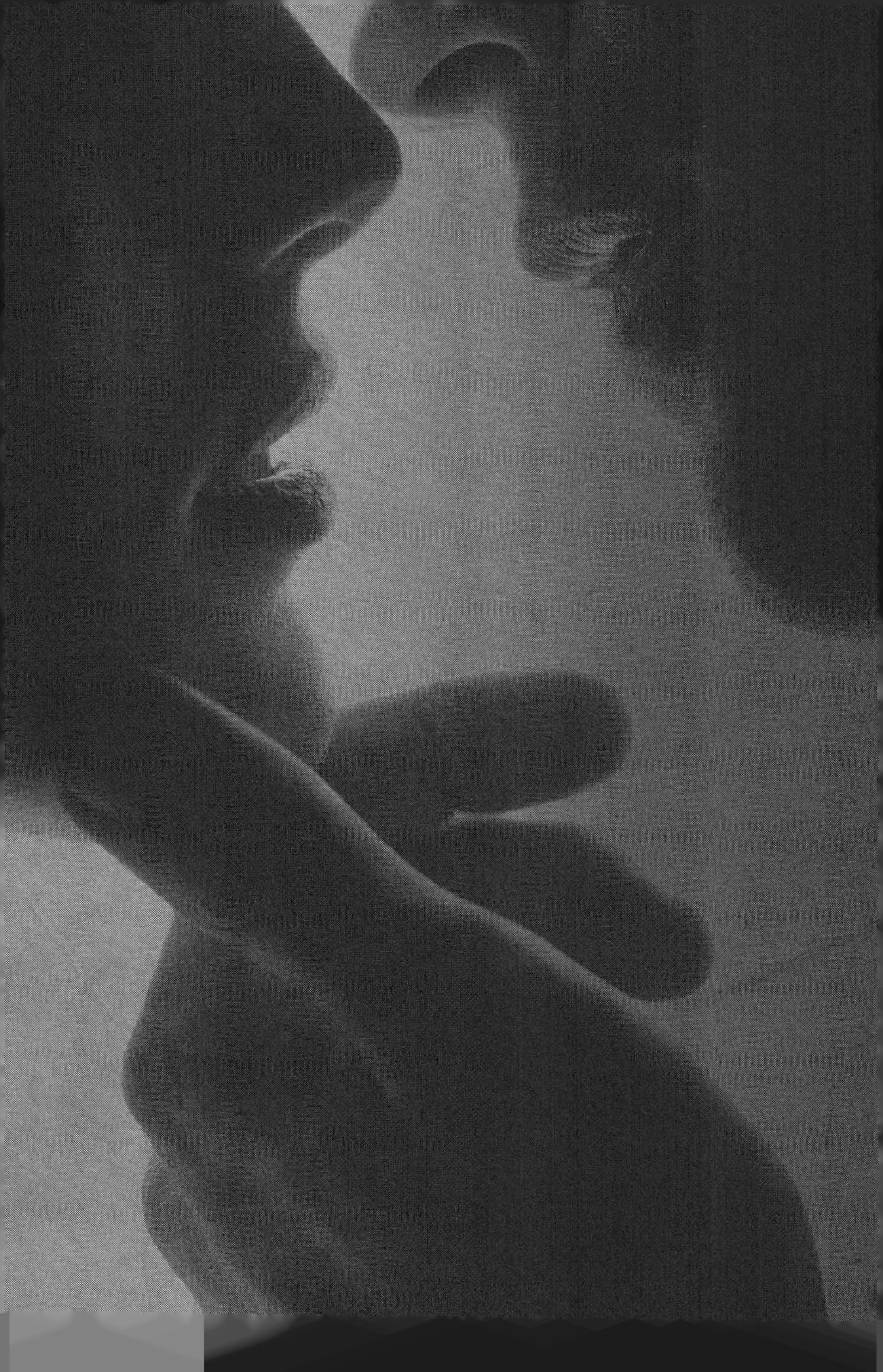

# RILEY

## CHAPTER FIVE

"We won our game," Logan says smugly as he drops into the chair beside me at our table in the library on Tuesday and unwittingly shatters through the glass box I'd locked myself in. Dark clouds have been hanging over me since my mom canceled my visit. She still hasn't agreed to FaceTime, and with each passing day, the clouds grow darker, more threatening. I'm expecting a downpour of misery at any moment.

Or rather, I was...

In a surprising move, the clouds have parted, allowing a rare moment of sun to break through in the form of Logan Astor. Simply staring at his beaming smile is enough to brighten my day. To pull me out of the funk I've been stewing in for days now.

Forcing my lips into an upward slant, I look up at him. I haven't seen him since our Statistics class last Friday, right before his big game. He was surrounded by students, everyone wishing him good luck—exactly as I'd predicted—and more than one girl promising to help him burn off the remaining adrenaline afterward.

He even winked at me, and I had deliberately looked away, picking a seat on the far side of the room to avoid getting dragged into that circus. However, thirty minutes before his game was due to start, I caved and texted him *good luck*. Despite the hoards of people surrounding him on game day, it was my good luck he'd asked for. *Mine* that he wanted. And, well, apparently I'm incapable of saying no to anything Logan Astor asks of me.

Like looking at a solar eclipse, I can't stare for too long for fear his smile will blind me. Tearing my gaze away, I shuffle the pages in front of me. "I heard," I state in a bland, uninterested tone, purely because I know it will irk him. I'm not sure I could handle what it would do to his ego if Logan knew I watched his game with rapt fascination before I had to leave for work. "But I'd rather know how you did on your Statistics test."

If I wasn't subtly watching him from the corner of my eye, I'd never have believed it, but Logan Astor, the almighty hockey god, blushes. *Blushes.*

"I, uh, haven't looked," he confesses bashfully.

"You what?!" I turn to outright gape at him, studying his expression. It takes a second before I connect the dots, a teasing smirk forming when I do. "Don't tell me you have no issue going skate-to-skate with some guy broader than you, but you're afraid of a measly test result?"

He gives me a lopsided, knowing smirk and my ribbing chuckle drops as I realize my error. "Well, well, did Riley James just admit to watching my game?"

"What—" I stutter. "No. Not, all of it." *Dammit, I hadn't meant to admit that.*

I'd gasped aloud when I watched that asshole shove him into the boards before skating off, but it was the look of pure thunder on Logan's face that kept me riveted as he took off after him, stealing the puck before skating down the ice toward the net.

They nearly came to physical blows later in the game. Logan's teammates had to literally drag him away as he started to peel off his gloves. I have no idea what was happening or the rivalry between them, but I was *hooked.*

Leaning in, Logan drapes one arm across the back of my chair, batting those long, thick eyelashes of his that probably get girls and guys alike to do whatever he asks. "So? What did you think?"

My teeth sink into my bottom lip, and I relish the way his gaze dips, pupils dilating as he tracks the movement. It's good to know he's as affected by me as I am by him. I can't explain this attraction between us, and I don't plan on acting on it, but it's definitely satisfying to know he feels it, too, this magnetism between us.

"I think..." I begin in a low, seductive voice that I'm confident all the girls use when they're trying to lure him into their beds. "You should check your grade on last week's test."

His gaze remains riveted to my mouth while I talk, before he finally wrenches it away, meeting my stare as he blows out a breath. "What do I have to do to get a compliment out of you?" he asks in a teasing tone.

Rolling my eyes, I jest, "Your ego doesn't need me to feed it."

"No, but you'd make its day if you did."

The way he's looking at me is too much. Too intense. Too beyond superficial flirting. It robs me of air, making me feel things I have no right feeling.

Glancing away, I clear my throat. "You should check your test score."

As though we didn't just share a moment—or perhaps it's all in my head and *we* didn't share anything—he relaxes back in his chair and pulls up the email on his phone containing the result of last week's test.

While he's distracted, I take the opportunity to scan his profile. Saying Logan is fit would be an understatement. His T-shirt clings to his muscles, tightening around his biceps in a way that makes it appear as though the fabric would tear if he flexed.

His pale skin is dotted with the occasional tattoo, small ones here and there along his arms. *I wonder if they mean anything to him or if they're just for show.* It's more than just his obvious good looks and the fact his body has been sculpted into a piece of art. It's in the way he holds himself, with a quiet confidence. Every step he takes is done with effortless ease. He owns his body. It responds perfectly to his commands. He's confident in his looks and ability, and he wields it at every opportunity.

At first glance, Logan comes across as obnoxious, arrogant, and completely full of himself. And he is all of those things, don't get me wrong. But he's also down-to-earth and easygoing. He doesn't act as though the world owes him anything or use his popularity and fame on the ice to get ahead. He acknowledges when he doesn't understand something and has taken my advice and listened to my explanations without interruption.

Having gotten to know him better, I can honestly admit, Logan Astor is not the brash, cocky man he presents to most of the world. Which begs the question: who is the real Logan Astor, and why does he keep himself hidden?

He turns his phone so I can see the screen, a bashful, pride-filled smile lifting the corners of his lips.

"Oh my God," I squeal, throwing my arms carelessly around him. "You got a B! That's amazing!" His body tenses for a moment before his muscular arms squeeze me tightly in his embrace. His warmth radiates through me and I'm suddenly keenly aware that I am hugging Logan Astor—the ice hockey god that half of campus shamelessly throws themselves at.

I quickly pull back, ignoring the pang in my chest at the loss of his touch as I grin at him. "Next time, you'll get an A!"

His lips curl into a mischievous smirk and he shakes his head at me, but I can see the pride shining in his eyes. "Don't get ahead of yourself. I'll humbly accept my B."

"Nonsense," I insist boldly. "This clearly shows how capable you are. You'll be acing Stats before the end of the semester." A teasing smirk pulls at the corners of my mouth as I waggle my finger in his face. "Just you wait and see, Logan Astor. I don't doubt you for a second."

One minute I'm praising Logan, and the next his warm lips are pressed to mine, and all rational thought has fled the building. His lips are soft and supple, and I'm helpless to do anything other than kiss him back when his tongue runs along the seam of my lips.

My lips part, our tongues tangling in a gentle exploration as fireworks go off in my head. Time stands still. The world ceases to exist. His teeth nibble playfully on my bottom lip, his masculine groan flooding my mouth, zapping through my veins, and heading straight between my thighs.

When we finally break apart, I'm left panting for air, staring at him wide-eyed as I bring my fingers to my swollen lips. They tremble as they rest there beneath Logan's desire-laden gaze.

His pupils are blown wide and peering out is a burning lust that ignites something within me.

"Sorry," he mutters, his voice like gravel as his gaze darts between my eyes and lips. He doesn't look at all apologetic. In fact, if I had to guess, I'd say he looks very much like he wants to kiss me again. I'm not even sure I'd push him away if he did. That kiss was... *wow.*

I can count on one hand the number of people I've slept with. There's only been a handful more that I've kissed, and none of them were terribly memorable. Sweet, nice even, but never *wow*. Never indescribable.

"You looked so... proud," he says sheepishly. "I couldn't help myself. I needed to know how it tasted on your lips." He shrugs, and I can't tell if it's because he views what he did as no big deal or because he's playing it off as that.

Because, for me, that was a *very big deal.*

Any kiss that has the ability to leave you breathless is a big deal, right?

Except, I shouldn't be letting it mean anything.

I can't afford for *Logan* to mean anything.

"It's fine," I respond awkwardly, voice catching. I'm unable to meet his eyes as I fiddle needlessly with the pages sitting on the table in front of me. The air surrounding us grows uncomfortable, and unable to stand the silence, I say, "We, uh, should start on the material from last week."

"Right," he agrees with a nod, thankfully willing to move past that kiss. The one still causing my lips to buzz as I suck them between my teeth and try to focus on my notes on Bayesian statistics.

---

Walking across campus, the trees are a beautiful burnt orange and yellow, leaves falling into piles on the ground as they fight against the upcoming winter. The air is crisp, and I burrow deeper into my coat as I stuff my hands in my pockets and pick up my pace, keen to get a warm drink into me.

As I pass by, I glance longingly at the coffee cart, noting the long line of people waiting for their drinks. I've heard the other students rant and rave about their coffee. I've never tried it myself, but *damn* does it always smell good when I walk by. Like freshly baked croissants and coffee that hasn't been stewed in a pot all day. *Oh, what I'd give for even a taste.*

Knowing that I can't afford it, I reluctantly tear my gaze away and, instead, stride through the double doors into Halston's dining hall. As much as I'd *love* a pumpkin spice latte, it would be stupid to waste my hard-earned money on it when the coffee here is free.

The dining hall is mostly empty at this time of day. It's late afternoon on a Friday, and most students are either done for the week or close enough that they're powering through the last of their work so they can begin their weekends.

Grabbing the pot of black coffee, I pour it into a large to-go cup and add a decent amount of creamer before popping on a plastic lid. I only have one class left this week, but I'm working tonight, and knowing I'll be on my feet until the early hours of the morning, I am in desperate need of as much caffeine as I can get my hands on.

Bringing the steaming cup to my lips, I inhale, pretending I smell the fragrant notes of cinnamon, cloves, and nutmeg. Despite the bitter taste, which is nothing like a pumpkin spice latte, I smile against the rim of the cup, simply happy to be getting my caffeine fix.

Sometimes, it's the simple pleasures in life, ya know?

Croissants and gourmet coffee sound great, but as long as I have caffeine, I'll be a happy girl.

Besides, perhaps I could treat myself to one of the fancy coffees from the cart outside at the end of the month if I don't fall behind on any of my schoolwork. That seems like a reasonable reward for keeping up with my studies and doing well in my classes.

I'm still dreaming about that coffee as I push open the dining hall door and step outside into the cold October afternoon. With my coffee securely held in one hand, I use my other to hitch my bag higher onto my shoulder as I turn the corner…

…and collide with a solid mass.

"Oomph."

The wind is knocked out of me as I ricochet off a granite chest. Even beneath the leather jacket, I can feel the hard planes of the guy's pecs. *Seriously, he should come with a warning sign—or a blaring alarm.*

Blinking, I pull my eyes up over his chest, along the thick cords of the muscles in his neck, to a dusting of dark stubble. His jaw tics, and as I lift my gaze to meet ice-blue eyes, my grip loosens on my coffee cup.

*Just my fucking luck!*

Of course, it's the same guy I crashed into my first day on campus.

And he looks just as pissed as he did last time.

The hot liquid of my coffee splashes over my feet, but nothing can melt the ice I feel slithering into my veins from his hostile glare.

"You," he sneers. "*Again.* Are you that clumsy, or is this some sort of ploy?"

"Ploy?" I mimic, confused and struggling to wrap my head around what he's saying. The guy might be an asshole, but *damn,* he is a *hot* one.

His top lip curls back on a snarl, making him appear more animal than human. Really? Does he think he's going to growl and send me running away?

"Whatever your game is, it won't fucking work." His eyes drop, slowly running over me. I hate that they harden in disgust, and I self-consciously glance down at myself. I get that I'm not dressed to impress in jeans and a hoodie. Despite what this ass seems to think, I didn't get dressed this morning with the intention of crashing into him—or anyone else, for that matter.

It's Friday. I'm exhausted, and I have a weekend of work ahead of me. The only person I dressed for this morning is me.

"You think I ran into you on purpose?" I bite back rather aggressively.

I'm all for simply apologizing and moving on purely to avoid confrontation, even if it's not necessarily my fault, but this has happened twice now. Honestly, though, I'm tired and pissed at his shitty attitude.

I bark out a caustic laugh. "Why the hell would I deliberately run into you when you have *that* on your forehead?" I point with my index finger between his brows.

His eyes crinkle, and he lifts a hand to rub at his forehead before looking down at his clean fingers.

"Oh. It must be permanent. Did you tattoo it?"

"What the hell are you talking about, woman?" he growls angrily.

"The *fuck off* stamped on your forehead."

His chest rises and falls in a silent, aggravated huff, and he shakes his head. Still, I swear I catch the corners of his lips twitching, almost as though he were about to smile, before he quashes the action.

He wouldn't want to ruin his bad-boy image, after all.

"Other women may ignore your very obvious warning and fling themselves at you, but I do not have such self-destructive tendencies." I fix my bag on my shoulder and glare at his sharp, handsome face. "I suggest you look up the word *accident* in the English dictionary." Moving to step around him, I toss over my shoulder, "And while you're at it, you might want to look up the word *sorry*, too," before storming off, absolutely furious that I only got a sip of my coffee before I foolishly dropped it.

# ROYCE

## CHAPTER SIX

The soles of my shoes stick to the beer-stained floor, and if it weren't for the thudding bass and screaming crowd pressing in around me, I'd be able to hear the *rip* every time I lift my feet.

Not that I care. I barely even notice the stench of sweat and BO hanging heavy in the air, or the waving of dollar bills as bets are placed. The only thing I'm aware of is the sense of belonging that settles deep into my bones every time I step in here.

It's a far cry from the screaming stadium of fans calling my name as I ran onto the field. Hard to believe it was less than a year ago when the football field was my home.

I thought football was my entire future. I was standing on top of the world with endless possibilities lying before me.

Before it was cruelly ripped away.

Now, I've replaced a grass field and shiny locker room with steel-sheeted walls and a blood-stained boxing ring. I can't bear to even look at the football stadium. I haven't set foot in it since everything went to shit. The game that was once the love of my life, I now avoid with a sickening passion. Along with my old teammates. I rarely show my face on campus. I go to my classes and go home, and that's it.

The only pleasure I allow myself is this.

Although, I dunno if you'd call beating the shit out of someone pleasurable. It's cathartic—a necessity in order to function. To expel the pent-up energy I no longer have a release for.

It's not something I do for pleasure.

However, I have found a surprising comfort in this old warehouse on the outskirts of Halston. It speaks to the lost soul I've become. Perhaps because it has become the only place where I feel fully in control. Where the outcome is solely based on me—my performance.

"What we bettin' tonight?" Logan asks, bouncing on the balls of his feet as he takes in the crowd with excited eyes.

"Like you need the money," I drawl, rolling my eyes. His dad runs a multi-million dollar marketing company, and if he can keep his grades up, he'll be a shoo-in for an NHL contract this year. He's practically swimming in money. But that's not why he's doing it. He's an adrenaline junkie, just like I am. Except, his vices are girls, booze, and betting. Whereas mine is solely in making people hurt. In bashing their heads in. In watching the fear bleed into their eyes and leach them of color.

He shrugs, not giving a shit. "If you're going to drag me out here the night before a game, then I may as well make it interesting."

"Didn't hear you complaining when we were leaving the house."

The asshole is full of it. There's nowhere he'd rather be. He gets off on the crowd's energy as much as I do. He, more than anyone, understands what a high it is to have people screaming your name.

He also understands how that isn't enough. It's like the

opening note in a song. It sets the scene. Gets the blood pumping. But more has to come after.

The piano solo is poetic, and the drum base is invigorating, but combine them, and you get fucking nirvana. The taste of blood in the air is my piano. The screams for violence are my drums. The vibrating of the floor beneath pounding feet is my bass. The feel of skin bruising beneath my fists is my chorus. The *oomph* of air as it's punched from his lungs is my verse. The *thump* of my opponent hitting the mat is my bridge.

All individual elements. All build the hype. But together? Together, they make the most addictive of songs. One I could play on repeat for the rest of my life and never grow tired of hearing it.

"Here," Grayson grunts, shoving a beer into Logan's hand. He knows better than to get me one pre-fight. I'll save the alcohol for after I've taken down tonight's poor bastard.

The three of us turn our attention to the current fighters. Sweat-slicked skin, tinged with blood. One guy is barely on his feet and I know all it will take is one well-placed hit to take him out.

"You up next?" Grayson yells in my ear.

I nod before pushing my way through the crowd. No one has recognized me yet, but it won't be long until someone does, so I use the anonymity to my advantage as I shove forward until I'm standing ringside.

Grayson and Logan follow, and catching the referee's eye, I jut my chin so he knows I'm here. As the fight before mine comes to a predictable end, and the loser is helped out of the ring by his buddies, the air around me becomes charged, whispers building in momentum as the gathered crowd catches sight of me.

*Ruthless.*

*Ruthless!*

*RUTHLESS!*

*Ruth-less! Ruth-less! Ruth-less!*

The chanting threatens to blow the roof off the large warehouse that holds these illegal fights. One of the guys claps me on the back, and rolling my shoulders, I step through the rope and into the ring.

Standing beneath the spotlight, I lift my arms in the air. The screaming becomes deafening as the crowd catches my fighter name printed in large, bold letters across the back of my hoodie.

*Ruthless.*

Royce "Ruthless" King.

Ruthless in the ring and ruthless out of it, because the only way to survive in this life is to be fucking ruthless. To take or be taken. To win or be won. To fight or to die.

Spinning, I turn to face the crowd still screaming my name, giving them my usual cold, empathetic stare before I dismiss the room entirely and turn toward Gray and Logan. Unzipping the hoodie, I toss it to Logan before I kick off my boots and socks and begin to bounce on the balls of my feet. Blood pumps through my veins. The Depot fades until all that exists is me, the ring, and my opponent.

Wearing only a pair of dark jeans, I step up to the ref and look at my opponent for the first time.

He's tall, wiry, with crew-cut hair, and when he grins at me, I notice one of his front teeth is gold. Dropping my gaze to his bare hands, I see the white scars, telltale signs that he's a regular on the circuit. His knuckles are already swollen, most likely from a fight earlier in the evening, and I shake my head. *Idiot.*

Doesn't matter how skilled a fighter he might be. He'll drain of energy before I do.

We bash our knuckles together, stepping toward our respective corners. For a split second, the crowd swells. Their chant a pressure wave that rushes toward me, crashing against my body and energizing me until I feel as though I'm going to explode if I don't expend the excess energy.

As quickly as the noise rushes in, the ref blows the whistle and the world goes deathly silent. Like a lion latched on his next kill, my gaze zeroes in on my opponent as we size one another up. Who will be the predator, and who will be the prey? Who will be the victor, and who will be the poor chump left bleeding on the floor?

I can tell you one thing for certain: I'm never the chump.

One corner of my lips quirks in a cocky manner, and I turn my fist. Flexing two fingers, I tell him to bring it.

He rushes me.

I duck beneath his flyaway fist, smirking as I deliver a rapid one-two punch to his gut before stepping out of his reach. Snarling, he chases me. I allow him to land a solid hit to my jaw. The move brings us close enough that I can easily swipe out his legs, and he crashes to the mat. I pounce. Pinning him to the mat with my tree-trunk thighs, I lay blow after blow on him until he's a bleeding, whimpering mess beneath me.

My opponent's face blurs. I no longer feel the impact of his skin beneath mine nor the strain of my muscles every time I pull back my arm. The constant burning resentment rages like a forest fire, screaming for release with every punch.

One punch for the unfairness of it all.

One punch for the life torn away from me.

One punch because it's all I know anymore.

Round and round I go, the anger bubbling until my punches slow. The rage ebbs. I can feel it slowly draining, trickling from me like water until it's sitting at a low simmer, when someone pulls me off the lump of bloody meat.

My tunnel vision widens from a pinpoint at the high-pitched blare of the ref's whistle as he barks for someone to remove my unconscious opponent. I blink, his face coming back into focus. It's swollen and bloody, eyes glazed. Tilting my head to the side, I spit blood-tinged spit onto the mat as I shake off the person's—Gray or Logan since no one else would dare to touch me—hold and get to my feet before striding away.

Blood rushes in my ears, deafening me to the screaming happening around me as I stuff my feet into my boots and throw on my hoodie.

The guys clap me on the shoulder as I step out of the ring, and knowing me as well as they do, they direct me to the bar. Seeing me approach, Xander—barman and owner of The Depot—sets a bottle of beer in front of me, along with a bag of ice for my hands.

"Ruthless as always," he says with a smirk, before moving down the bar.

Ignoring the ice, I grab the bottle and turn, leaning my back against the bartop as I suck down the bitter liquid, half-watching the next fight as it commences.

Only once it's over do I take my eyes off the ring and look around the warehouse, noticing how everyone gives the three of us a wide berth. I'm sure it's partly to do with how I nearly killed some guy, but I can't help remembering how the feisty girl who crashed into me last week pointed out the obvious *fuck off* I keep stamped on my forehead.

It brings a reluctant tug to my lips, which I quickly squash with another pull from the beer bottle. Women only ever fuck shit up. A lesson I learned the hard way five years ago. One that is still biting me in the fucking ass today.

I allow one psychotic chick into my bed, and I nearly get disinherited and lose all hope of a future in football.

Sure, sounds like a fair trade.

Now, I don't allow any woman into my bed. A singular moment of pleasure is not worth a lifetime of consequences. I haven't had sex in five fucking years, and I don't see that changing any time soon.

Most girls at Halston thought I was just playing hard to get, constantly turning them down and ignoring their advances, but I didn't give a single fuck about them. I was protecting myself.

I fight, drink, and draw; those are the only three pleasures I need.

So the fact the feisty hazel-eyed girl is infiltrating my thoughts is disturbing.

When she crashed into me outside the admin building, I pegged her as just another desperate chick. I chewed her out before storming away, and when we collided again outside the dining hall, I thought for sure she was going for attempt number two... until she showed me the fierce temper that matched the color of her hair.

She shouldn't have been alluring, dressed in a hoodie that practically drowned her and left me to imagine the curves that hid beneath. But she was. I wanted to bend her over my knee right there in the middle of campus and tint her ass red with my handprint until my jeans were soaked with her arousal.

And that thought alone is fucking terrifying.

"Yo, man, what are you thinking about?" Logan asks, interrupting my thoughts as he nudges me with his shoulder. "You look pissy, but in a weird, turned-on kinda way. It's freaky."

I shake my head, snorting a laugh. "Nothing."

He simply shrugs, used to vague non-answers from me by now.

Bringing his beer bottle to his lips, he takes a swig before confessing, "I kissed my Stats tutor."

"Of course, you did," I mutter as Grayson snorts, the two of us sharing a look. Typical Logan behavior. I'm only surprised he stopped at kissing her. I have no doubt it will only be a matter of time before he gets her into his bed.

Glancing his way, I notice Logan's lips are tugged tight in a frown as he picks at the label on his beer bottle. "Was it not good?" I question, realizing he didn't just mention it to brag. "You realize you don't *have* to kiss her. I'm sure she will still tutor you even if you don't stick your tongue down her throat in every session."

"That's the thing," he mutters, looking thoroughly put out as he terrorizes the label, ripping it into shreds and dropping it onto the floor at his feet. "It was good. Really fucking good."

"Then what's the problem?" Grayson asks, arching a brow.

Logan shakes his head. "I don't think she wants me to do it again. She completely shut down afterward. Refused to discuss anything that wasn't Statistics."

I scoff. "You're Logan Astor. There isn't a person on campus who doesn't want to suck your face. She's probably just playing hard to get. Making you work for it."

*Fucking women.* Always playing some sort of head game. Always with some ulterior motive.

"Nah, man. I don't think so. Not her." Lifting his eyes, his conflicted gaze meets mine. "She's not like the usual puck bunnies or girls on campus. She's shy. Reserved. Innocent."

Yeah, right. It's probably all an act. In my experience, all girls are the same. They're all out for one thing—themselves. They don't care what they have to do or who they have to exploit so long as they get whatever they want.

And they say men are dickheads. Women are ten times more manipulative.

Yet, green-brown eyes and auburn hair swim to the forefront of my mind.

I scoff internally. *Yeah, right.* She might seem different, but I bet she's just like all the others.

ITEM 1 OF 2
**LOGAN
PUMPKIN

# RILEY

## CHAPTER SEVEN

"Don't forget, lab reports are due next week," my Chemistry Professor shouts over the cacophony of noise as everyone gathers their things and begins to file out of the classroom.

I groan internally, stressed over the quickly mounting workload sitting heavy on my shoulders. I swear I have like eight assignments due within the next week. How do the other students have time to party and socialize and still stay on top of the workload? I'm barely managing to balance working and studying, never mind any of the rest of college life.

I'm mentally configuring my study plan for the rest of the week as I walk down the corridor when my phone vibrates in my pocket. Pulling it out, I pause, staring at the screen in confusion as Logan's name flashes across it.

"Hello?" I ask, half convinced he's butt-dialed me.

"Where are you?"

I glance around, confused. "Outside Jefferson Hall, why?"

"Oh, cool." The background noise becomes more prominent, and my face scrunches as I strain to listen. It almost sounds as though he's running. "I'm nearby. I'll be out front in a sec. Meet me there."

Pushing my way through the double doors leading outside, I keep the phone pressed to my ear as I search my surroundings. "Okay..."

"So, how's your day going?" Logan asks casually. What the actual hell is happening right now?

"Ehh. Good, thanks. Yours?"

"Pretty decent so far. Coach definitely didn't get laid last night, though. He was a total dick this morning. Pushed us in training until I thought I was going to puke."

"Is that why you sound like a forty-a-day smoker?" I tease, hearing his heavy breathing over the line.

He huffs a breathy laugh. "Are you sassing me right now? You realize I'm doing cardio *for you*."

"I don't remember asking you to run for me."

"That's because you've crammed your brain with too much book knowledge. There's no room to remember all the things you say to me, but don't worry, Shortcake, I'll remember for you. You're still coming to mine for a sleepover tonight, right?"

I can't help laughing. I don't know how Logan does it, but even when I'm having the worst day, he always seems to pull a smile from me.

"I definitely did not agree to that."

"You totally did."

"When?" I counter.

"It was late last night. You were all alone in your bed, missing me like you do every night"—cue another laugh—"and when you finally worked up the courage to call and tell me, I said *'Shortcake, you know you're always welcome to share my bed'*, and you said *'Oh Logan, I was hoping you would say that, but my pajamas all shrunk in the wash so I'd have to sleep naked...*"

Okay, I full belly laugh at his ridiculous attempt at mimicking my voice, and the absolute horse shit coming out of his mouth. "I feel like you're confusing me with whatever porn site you were perusing last night."

"Nope, I don't think so," he says, tone serious. "She looked and sounded just like you."

"How could you see me, I thought I called you?"

"Huh. Guess it must have been a FaceTime."

"Yeah, or your imagination is playing tricks on you. Maybe you've taken one too many pucks to the head. You should probably see a doctor about that. It's a real thing now—traumatic brain injury."

"I do not have a traumatic brain injury," Logan scoffs. "I'll have you know my brain is in perfect working order, just like a certain other head—"

"Oh. My. God! Logan!"

He chuckles, thoroughly amused by his own childish joke. "Oh, I see you."

Looking up, I spot him as he jogs toward the building, ignoring the other students as they wave or try to catch his attention. He's still got his phone pressed to his ear, sights set on me, until he's standing right in front of me, his cheeky grin aimed solely at me.

"Hey, Shortcake."

He pulls the phone away, and I do the same, tucking it back in my pocket as I scan his face, wondering what was so urgent that he wanted to meet. We rarely talk outside of class or our tutoring sessions.

"So, is that a yes to tonight?"

Snorting, I shove his shoulder playfully.

"Only in your dreams, Astor."

He smirks, the expression sinful and making me momentarily wonder what it would be like to spend the night in Logan Astor's bed. I bet it would be mind-blowing.

Coughing to clear my throat, I glance away as I tuck a strand of hair behind my ear. "So, what's up?"

I swear I hear him laugh, but when I snap my attention back to him, he's scrolling through his phone before holding it up.

"Just wanted to show you this," he says, his grin wide and proud.

"No freaking way! Logan, you got an A!"

The results must have been emailed while I was in class.

"Yup." His smile is bright enough to outshine the sun. "I knew I had to find you the second I found out."

"That's amazing, Logan. You should be really proud of yourself."

I swear his cheeks turn the slightest shade of red. It's adorable.

"Thank you."

We stare at one another for a moment. I can't stop grinning at him, genuinely proud of the effort he has put in—and look how all his hard work has paid off! "So, I was thinking we could grab a coffee or something to celebrate?"

"Oh. I, uh..."

"Or will being seen with me in public tarnish your rep?" he teases.

"Are you sure *you* want to be seen with *me*?" I counter, not entirely joking.

He scoffs, moving to throw an arm over my shoulder and escort me away from Jefferson Hall. "I don't give a shit what any of these people think, but for the record, I'd be proud to be seen hanging out with you, Riley."

I duck my head, hiding my smile as we meander through campus.

"What do you want?" he asks as we approach the coffee cart.

"Oh, I'll just grab a coffee from the dining hall," I say, attempting to slide out from beneath his arm as I gesture toward the dining hall behind us.

His nose scrunches in disgust. "You'd rather drink the piss they give away in there?"

I grit my teeth, embarrassed that I have to spell it out. "It's free," I say, unable to look him in the eye.

My confession is followed by a moment of silence, and I can feel his eyes scanning my face. Still, I refuse to meet his gaze. "This is my treat, Shortcake. A thank you for taking a chance on this dumb athlete and turning him into a full-fledged nerd."

With the awkward moment instantly brushed aside, my lips reluctantly curl upward.

"So, what do you want?"

"A pumpkin spice latte," I answer immediately.

He orders our drinks before we move to sit on a bench nearby, away from the hustle that always seems to surround the coffee cart. Logan sits beside me, leaving only a sliver of space between our bodies. To distract myself from how close we are, I lower my nose to the cup and inhale deeply, ingraining the scent of cinnamon and nutmeg into my brain. *God, I could live off that smell alone.*

Taking a sip, my eyes drift closed as I relish that first taste. "God, that's so good."

I feel eyes on me, and I glance in Logan's direction, finding him watching me with an expression I've never seen before. His lips are slightly lifted in a soft smile, a twinkle in his eye that I can't place.

"So..." I look around as I grasp for something to talk about. "What are you majoring in that you need Statistics? I would have thought most degrees athletes usually obtain require very little mathematics."

"My degree's in Marketing." He must see my surprise and confusion as he explains, "My dad owns Bolt Media."

"The marketing company?" I question in awe. Everyone knows Bolt Media. It's world-renowned for its year-on-year growth, even when we've been going through a recession.

"That's the one."

*Well, damn.* Now I feel even more inadequate to be in his presence. I mean it's one thing to have the attention of the campus hockey god, especially knowing how popular and beloved he is by students and teachers alike. And obviously I knew Logan came from a wealthy family since, unless you're a scholarship student, it's basically a requirement for Halston. However, I had no idea he was *that* well off. Success is practically woven into his DNA.

Logan's dad is a true inspiration. I remember reading an article regarding his climb to success. Unlike a lot of the students attending Halston, Logan's family doesn't come from money. His dad has earned every penny they have. He worked his way up from nothing and founded the number-one marketing company in the world. I mean, talk about inspiring!

What I remember most about that article is how his dad said his family was his motivation, the driving force behind his success. It was something I really resonated with. It helped me connect with him as a person and gained him role model points in my book.

My goals aren't as grand as to earn my own billions, but who doesn't dream of being successful in their career and providing for their family?

"Is that your plan, then, after college? To go into marketing? I thought hockey was your passion."

"It is. Playing for the NHL is my dream. I actually have

scouts from the Pacific Penguins coming to one of my games this weekend."

"That's amazing, Logan."

His excitable grin is adorable.

"And your parents support your decision to play hockey for a living?"

"Yeah, my parents are pretty great. Dad is all for pursuing your passions. Although, I think he was hoping I'd discover a love for marketing while studying it."

"I'm guessing you didn't. Or at least, not as much as hockey?"

His chest vibrates with a short laugh. "Nothing compares to hockey. I don't hate marketing..." He trails off, his face pinched as he stares at a spot in the distance.

"But it's not hockey," I finish.

He turns to face me, nodding. "It's not hockey."

It feels right when I touch his arm, giving him that little bit of comfort. "It sounds as though your parents love you. I'm sure they just want you to be happy."

He gives me a small half-smile, but it lacks its usual shine. His chestnut hues sear into mine, searching for I don't know what before he breaks the moment and shakes his head. "I don't know why I told you all that. It's probably not what you wanted to hear."

"I was the one who asked what your plans were after graduation, why wouldn't I want an honest answer?"

Unable to look me in the eye, he shrugs, clearly embarrassed. "Most people don't want the truth. They just want to talk about hockey. I'm not even sure of the last time someone asked me what my major is."

My hand, which I'd left resting on his arm, tightens, garnering his attention as he stares at the point where we're touching before slowly lifting to my face.

"Logan, you're worth more than purely the goals you make on the ice and the wins you bring home. Anyone who only sees you for those things is missing out. At the risk of inflating your ego any further, you're a good guy, and anyone who can't see that... that's their loss."

The air crackles between us, alive with anticipation, as Logan's gaze drops to my lips. Memories of the kiss we shared engulf me, and I can't resist any longer; I lean into him, instinctively seeking his touch and craving another kiss even though I know it will destroy me entirely.

He closes the distance, gaze heavy on my face, and I hold my breath. His fingers skate up my arm, eliciting little bolts of lightning that send sparks straight through my veins to jump-start my pulse. Fingers sinking into my hair, he tilts my head back and holds me in place as his lips linger over mine. Our breaths mingle. Teasing. Tantalizing. Torturing. Until I'm ready to beg for more.

"What are you doing to me, Shortcake?"

His voice is a low rumble that has my nipples pressing painfully against the restraining fabric of my bra while desire pools within me like molten lava.

My eyes dart between his. "Only what you're doing to me."

And then his lips crash down on mine, and I'm lost. Utterly robbed of oxygen. My hand fists the front of his sweater and I pull him closer as our tongues tangle in a titillating dance.

No one kisses better than Logan Astor. His kisses have the power to transport me to an alternate dimension. One where my problems don't exist. Where the world isn't a dark, ugly place riddled with injustices. They ignite a fire in my belly and flood me with light until I feel as though I'm on top of the world, high on endorphins without a single fuck to give.

"Come to my game this weekend," he rasps, his firm grip still holding me in place as he stares into my eyes. "I know you work weekends, but there are two games—Friday and Saturday. Come to one of them. I'll leave tickets for both at will-call."

My lips part, my denial tasting sour on my tongue. However, no words come out, and before I can gather the fortitude to let him down, he kisses me, quickly. "Don't answer now. Think about it."

One more hurried peck, and he lets me go, grabbing his bag and getting to his feet. My eyes are glued to his lips, swollen from our kiss, before I manage to drag them upward to meet his. I swallow at the sheer intensity I see shining in his chestnut depths. Fuck, if this is what it is to have Logan's full attention, I'm not sure I'm going to survive.

With his cocky smirk back in place, he says, "I'll see you there," before leaving me dumbfounded on the bench, watching his delectable ass as he walks away.

---

My foot taps impatiently as I glare at my phone screen. She's five minutes late, which really shouldn't be surprising, but I have to be in class in fifteen, so I need her to call me, like, right now.

Annoyed that I always have to make the effort, I stab my thumb angrily against the screen, hitting the button to call her instead.

The phone rings and rings until I get the standard *"Unfortunately the person you are trying to reach is unavailable."*

Since she's supposed to be calling me right now, she shouldn't be *unavailable*!

I jam my thumb down on her name again, growing increasingly furious with every unanswered ring.

"Mom," I snap when I once again get her voicemail. "Call me."

As I pull the phone away from my ear, it rings.

"Finally," I grumble, answering immediately. "Mom," I sigh in frustration. "I have to be in class—"

"Uhh, sorry to disappoint..."

"Logan?" Pulling the phone away from my ear, I realize the caller ID says Logan. Not Mom.

"Erm, hi," I say somewhat awkwardly, internally grateful that he cut me off before I said something I'd rather he did not hear.

"Hi."

Despite the fact he's not the person I'd been hoping to hear from, it's impossible not to smile at his teasing tone.

"Where are you right now?"

"Umm, I'm about to head into English."

"Hennessy building?"

"Yeah."

"Cool. I have something for you."

"You do?" I ask, surprised. "What is it?"

"Now, what sort of surprise would it be if I told you?" he teases.

"The kind where I know what I'm getting."

He chuckles. "That doesn't sound very fun."

"How would you know? Have you ever tried it?"

"Sound reasoning, smarty-pants, but it's not going to work. You'll just have to wait. I'll be there in one minute."

He hangs up. Then a few seconds later, he strides toward me with a coffee in hand.

"Hey," he greets with a broad grin that hits me right in the chest and instantaneously makes my day.

"Hey."

Uncaring of the students walking past, most of whom are watching and taking note of our exchange, he leans in and presses a chaste kiss to my cheek.

"I'm supposed to be in my Marketing Ethics class, like, right now, so I can't hang about. I just wanted to give you this."

He shoves the coffee cup into my hand.

"Your coffee?" I question, confused.

He shakes his head. "Not mine." Leaning in, his warm breath tickles my skin as he murmurs, "Sniff it."

My entire body responds to those two words, and flashes of his face buried between my thighs as he sniffs *me* flood my mind, turning my cheeks beetroot as I duck my head and inhale the sweet aroma of cinnamon and nutmeg.

He remains so close, that when I smile, my cheek brushes his. "Pumpkin spice latte," I murmur before glancing up at Logan through my lashes.

"*Your* pumpkin spice latte." His voice is just as soft as mine, adding an intimacy to the moment.

My teeth sink into the plump flesh of my lower lip as I stare at him with what are probably literal hearts in my eyes. *Damn, this man has figured out the direct line to my heart.*

He tracks the movement like a man starved, giving me the impression he wants to devour me the same way I want to devour my latte—and him, for that matter.

Lifting his hand, he brushes his thumb along my lower lip before applying pressure and gently freeing it from the confines of my teeth.

"Thank you," I say softly.

"You're welcome, Shortcake." Running his nose from my cheek to my ear, he whispers, "Enjoy the rest of your day," before stepping away and hurrying down the hall toward his class.

As I turn toward my own classroom door, I notice various eyes on me—everyone having witnessed our exchange—including Whitney, the bitchy blonde from orientation. Her face is pinched, eyes narrowed as she glares at me with disdain.

*Whatever.* The scent of nutmeg and cinnamon has me damn near groaning, and I refuse to let her or any of the rest of them ruin my sweet sweet caffeine fix. Instead, I turn my backs on them all and smile to myself as I take my first sip of heavenly bliss.

# RILEY

## CHAPTER EIGHT

"Ehh, where are we?" I ask as I peer out the windshield at the fields surrounding us. I lost phone reception when we turned off the main highway before we drove up a mile-long, pot-holed road that had me fearing the car would conk out and we'd be stuck out here in the middle of nowhere all night.

Alas, we made it here. Although I still haven't figured out where *here* is, other than the obvious... a field.

A dark, creepy-as-hell field.

I watch horror movies. I see what happens to young girls when they do stupid shit like this. I knew letting Tara talk me into going out with her tonight was a bad idea, but I'm only now appreciating how truly idiotic it was of me.

And to top off my dummy sundae, I let her dress me up like a hooker in a maroon-colored dress that leaves absolutely nothing to the imagination. I blame the time I've been spending at Lux. Before I started working there, I would never have been caught dead in such a revealing outfit. Now, it seems modest in comparison to what we wear on stage. Or at least, it did seem modest until I pictured myself running away from an ax-wielding murderer wearing a bodycon dress that would happily ride up to reveal my ass crack if I didn't keep tugging it down.

The only plus side is that my makeup is on point tonight, thanks to Tara. Winged eyeliner and dark red lips give me a sultry look, and she put mousse in my hair to give it extra volume, making me appear a little wild. Begrudgingly, I have to admit that I look pretty hot. A statement Tara readily agreed with when I hesitantly appeared from my bedroom earlier. It's just so far from my normal that it has a twinge of anxiety piercing my chest. However, Tara dragged me out of the house and into her car before I had a chance to back out of whatever it is we're doing tonight.

"You'll see," Tara sing-songs, not appearing to have the same serial killer fears as me as she pushes open her car door and steps out onto the soft, wet grass in her sky-high hooker heels like she was born with them on her feet. Unlike me, Tara isn't the slightest bit fazed at the amount of skin she has on display. She looks hot in a sleek, black, backless romper that dips low between her ample breasts and shows off her long, tanned, legs toned from years of dancing.

Me, on the other hand... I totter through the long grass like a baby deer learning to walk for the first time as I repeatedly wrench my heels out of the ground each time they sink down.

Laughing with amusement, Tara takes pity on me and links her arm through mine, helping me navigate the uneven terrain as we head toward a large, abandoned warehouse that looks as though it's one winter storm away from collapsing in on itself.

*It would be a perfect setting for a murder house,* I can't help but think as we approach the side door where a bouncer is standing guard in the dimly lit entrance, a hulking presence with a rugged appearance that mirrors the murky wilderness surrounding us.

What the hell is a bouncer needed for all the way out here?

Is whoever owns the place afraid a herd of drunken sheep will try to bash their way inside?

I titter at my own joke, earning a questioning look from Tara. "What are you giggling about?"

I wave off her question. "It's nothing. Just some drunken sheep."

"What?"

"Tara," the bouncer grunts when we're within earshot. "I didn't know you were coming tonight."

"Me and my girl here needed to let off some steam before the weekend shift begins," Tara says with a wider-than-normal grin plastered on her face.

My eyes dart from her to the bouncer. He is even more imposing up close, standing well over six feet tall, with a heavily muscled frame that suggests countless hours spent working out. His shaved head, adorned with intricate ink added to his intimidating aura, and as he folds his arms over his broad chest, I notice little white scars criss crossing his knuckles.

"You're supposed to let Xander know if you plan on comin'," the man practically growls, features pinched in anger as he narrows his gaze on Tara.

"And would my brother also like to know when I'm on the rag? Maybe he'd like to be kept informed of what brand of tampons I use? Should I text him next time I cry because I'm hormonal and realize I forgot to wash my comfort thong?"

I bite down on my tongue to restrain my laughter at the look of utter horror on the bouncer's face. "No man needs to know that shit," he hisses, making Tara beam.

Clapping her hands together, she bounces on the balls of her feet. "Perfect. Glad we got that cleared up. Catch you later, Ro-Ro." With that, she drags me past... Ro-Ro? and to the door.

"Who was that?" I whisper as she pulls open the door.

She waves a dismissive hand. "That overbearing pain in the

ass is Rome. He's all mean and scary looking, but he's a teddy bear at heart."

I'll have to take her word for it because he *was* mean and scary looking.

"What is a comfort thong?" I question aloud.

She snorts. "How the hell do I know? As far as I'm concerned, *no* thong is comfortable."

*So true.*

The near bursting of my eardrums drowns out any further conversation as I'm blasted with ear-splitting screaming and loud heavy rock music. In between beats, I can hear the thud of fists against flesh and pained grunts, drawing my attention across the crammed-in crowd to the large ring situated in the center of the warehouse, where two men are currently fighting like animals. Blood and sweat slick their skin, momentarily captivating me.

Someone jostles into me, and pulling my gaze from the men fighting, I stare upward toward the steel roof perched high above us. It's then that I notice one major problem.

When Tara called and said we were going out tonight and that she wasn't taking no for an answer, I inevitably assumed we were going to a club. An assumption I believed to be correct when she handed me the skin-tight bodycon dress that's currently sneaking closer to my ass every time I shift my hips. However, wherever we are is definitely not a club. Instead of the dim lighting providing a sense of anonymity, shrouding you like a cloak and allowing you to get away with things you never could in the light—such as wearing a short-ass dress—the lights are turned up bright, putting everything inside the building on display.

"Come on," Tara yells. She yanks on my hand, but I hold firm, remaining rooted in place.

"I can't."

Panic pushes against my skin. It was one thing for me to dress up like this to go to a club. I convinced myself it wouldn't be all that different from going to work, but this... no. I can't do *this*.

"Hey," Tara says, planting herself directly in front of me so all I can see is her face. Slim features framed by long black hair complete with bright pink tips. Her hands cup my cheeks, forcing my eyes to hers. "You're safe here. No one will hurt you so long as you stick with me."

My eyes scan her face for any hint of a lie, but I don't catch one. I give a jerky nod of my head, but I still don't feel ready to face the packed crowd and bright lights.

Sensing I need more time, Tara remains in front of me as she runs her hands up and down my arm in a soothing gesture that helps to ground me and slowly helps to push the panic down.

"You all good now?" she eventually asks.

When I nod, she smiles warmly, utterly unfazed by my freak out, before linking her hand with mine and leading me through the crowd. She ensures I'm always right behind her as we cross the sticky, booze-coated floor, not seeming to have any issue with jamming her elbow into people's sides when they stumble into us or refuse to get out of our way.

I occupy my mind by scanning the steel walls of the warehouse, noting the exposed pipes and industrial fixtures. The space is vast, the loud noises echoing off the sheeted walls and vibrating through my skull.

Eventually, we pop up at the other side of the room in front of a makeshift bartop, a rough slab of reclaimed wood and rugged steel just as sticky as the floor beneath my feet. Behind it, shelves are lined with various bottles of alcohol, with a neon sign stating *The Depot* hanging above.

As I look around, a lone barman works his way down the line of patrons toward us, wearing a white vest top that showcases well-defined arms and chest, a canvas of tattoos adorning his skin. Tousled jet-black hair frames a rugged face, a hint of stubble covering his jaw and chin, and when he lifts his head, his eyes are the color of steel as they survey the warehouse with a quiet intensity

"Tara," he growls in a rich, commanding baritone, spotting us at the far end of the bar and making a beeline, ignoring everyone else. "You're not supposed to be here."

"Hello to you too, big brother."

*Big brother?* My eyes dart between her and the barman, noticing the small nuances—like how they both have sharp, straight noses and prominent cheekbones. The same jet-black hair and similar eyes. Does that mean this is *Xander*?

For whatever reason, her big brother's scowl only deepens, and he casts a sharp glance around the room, seeming to search for something—*or someone*. "You're supposed to tell me when you're coming. I don't have any spare men to babysit you tonight."

"And that's why I didn't tell you I was coming," Tara retorts. "I don't need a babysitter." Before her brother can argue with her further, she wraps her arm around my shoulders. "This is my friend, Riley."

Her brother's gaze shifts to mine, his scowl still firmly stuck in place as his eyes rake over me before he snaps his attention back to his sister. "Since when do you have friends?"

"Since now," Tara snaps. "So be nice to her, or I'll peel your skin from your body and turn it into my own personal puppet."

Her brother rolls his eyes, not appearing fazed by the extent of her violence. "When you say shit like that, it makes me regret allowing Dax to teach you how to wield a knife."

Only because I've been watching their exchange closely do I catch Tara's flash of hurt at the mention of this Dax character, and I make a note to talk to her when her brother isn't around.

He mustn't pick up on it as he returns his attention to me, wiping his large, calloused hand on a threadbare cloth before holding it out for me. "I'm Xander, this one's big brother and keeper," he teases with a slight smirk.

"You are not my keeper," Tara protests, flicking her curled black locks out of her face. "I'm twenty-five, for Christ's sake. I'm not a child."

Ignoring her, Xander rests his muscular, tattooed forearms on the bartop and continues talking to me. "It's nice to meet you. You're always welcome here, just not alone. Things can get out of control quickly when a fight doesn't go someone's way—or even if it does. Mob mentality and all that. It's easy for people to get carried away when their adrenaline is pumping and alcohol is flowing." He tilts his head toward his sister. "Stay with this one tonight, and if you ever want to come back, let me know in advance and I'll arrange for someone to keep an eye on you."

That's the second warning I've been given, so you can bet your ass I'm going to heed it. I nod, and seeming appeased, Xander turns to pierce his sister with a stern glare. "Both of you are to remain at this bar and within my line of sight all night. Got that?"

Tara rolls her eyes. Crossing her arms over her chest, she stares her brother down for a long, tense moment. The tension between them grows hot and humid as I wait on tenterhooks to see who will fold first.

I'm not altogether surprised when Tara blows out a frustrated breath and her body sort of deflates. "Fine. We'll stay here, but I want drinks in our hands all night."

Shaking his head, Xander reaches beneath the bar before setting two beers on top of it. He pops off the caps then hands one to me before giving the other to his sister.

"Thank you, Xander. You're the best," she says in a sweet

voice. Still shaking his head, he hides the twitch of his lips behind his hand before he moves down the counter to serve the other men waiting.

I wait until he's out of earshot before leaning over and asking, "Brother, huh?"

"Yup." Tara fake glares over my shoulder toward her brother, but I can see the affection hidden in her eyes. "Perpetual thorn in my side since my druggie mom chose meth over her daughter and dumped me on the front door of my dad's trailer."

"Shit, I'm sorry. That's... messed up."

She laughs, but it lacks any humor. "You can say that again."

"What age were you?"

She shrugs. "Three, I think. Xander was five. He and Dax—his neighbor and best friend—took me under their wings."

I scan her face before hedging, "And you and Dax?"

"There is no *me and Dax*," she states in a bitter tone. "I had a crush on him for as long as I can remember. Probably since that first day when he and Xander walked up to the trailer and saw me sitting there, shivering and crying. I was a total mess, and yet, Dax didn't give a shit. He just pulled me in for a hug and told me everything would be okay." Her eyes have glazed over, and I can tell she's stuck in the past as she goes silent, so I remain quiet.

"Anyway," she says, shaking herself out of her memories. "I thought for a moment there when I was a foolish, naive teenager that we could be something more, but then he took off."

"And you haven't seen him since?"

"Nope. Apparently, he's a big name in the underground fighting circle now. He comes back every now and again to see

Xander and fight here, but I make a point of staying away. I'm not ready, you know?"

Reaching over, I squeeze her hand. While I might not understand exactly how she's feeling, I do understand how it feels to not be ready to face your past.

Instead of prying further, I glance around the loud, bright, testosterone-pumped bar. "I never would have guessed a place like this existed in Halston."

All traces of sorrow are gone as Tara throws her head back and laughs. "Oh, sweetie, we're not in Halston anymore." At my quizzical look, she explains. "We're about five miles outside of Halston right now. Technically, this is Boxum County, where the rednecks and trailer trash live. We're a dirty little secret that no one likes to talk about. The rich folk prefer to pretend we don't exist. God forbid even mentioning the word Boxum might tarnish Halston's good name.

"Wow. I had no idea."

She shrugs, unbothered. "Why would you? Halston is the one on the map. The town people flock to to get themselves an education or follow in mommy and daddy's footsteps."

I nod, unsure what else to say. "And your brother works here?" I ask, once again changing the subject.

This time, Tara grins proudly. "Riley James, my pain-in-the-ass-but-equally-amazing brother owns this fine establishment."

"Shit, seriously?" I look around the drabby interior with new eyes. It's rough and ready, masculine and basic, but it's filled to the brim with men and the occasional woman, all jeering, laughing, and screaming as another fight takes place in the ring.

"Yeah, he and Dax were really into fighting when they were teenagers. They set this place up together before Dax got noticed and took off to take part in the circuit."

"Your brother didn't get noticed?"

"Nah, he did. He was just as good as Dax, but I was only sixteen and he refused to leave me behind." Her eyes are lowered in a wistful expression. "Anyway," she says, shaking it off. "Enough chit-chat. Let's go watch the fights. There's this one guy who has been making a name for himself recently, and I am seriously hoping he is here tonight."

With her beer bottle in one hand, she wraps her other around mine and yanks me away from the bar.

"Don't you dare leave my sights, Tara," Xander bellows after us.

Tara simply giggles, ignoring her brother as she pulls me closer to the large ring.

"Alright folks," the referee shouts into a microphone. "We have a special fight for y'all up next!"

"Fuck yes," Tara squeals, jumping up and down while tugging on my arm. "It's him!"

"Who?" I shout into her ear.

"Ruthless."

I don't get the chance to ask any more questions. The crowd goes into an uproar as a large, muscular man easily five times my size steps into the ring dressed solely in a pair of loose black shorts. The pale skin of his back and arms is decorated in black ink, which moves as he flexes his muscles. He glances briefly out over the crowd, and I swallow a gasp as my eyes clash with bright blue ones.

Not seeing me, his gaze moves on, roaming over the crowd, but I see him... the man I crashed into on campus. The asshole who thought I was deliberately trying to get close to him.

I shouldn't be surprised to see him here. While I imagine no other Halston student would be caught dead in a shithole like this, the dark, carnal energy that exudes from this asshole fits in perfectly with this place's tense, animalistic vibe. Truthfully, he looks more like he belongs here than on a college campus, with his swirling ink, tormented features, and shadowed eyes.

As he steps into the center of the ring to stand opposite his opponent, I know without a shadow of a doubt that he's *Ruthless;* the fighter Tara was referring to. He dominates the ring. Even though his opponent is no starved chicken, he lacks the feral nature that drips from the asshole like oil from a rusty car.

The next few minutes pass in a brutal, violent dance that steals my breath and tantalizes my senses. I feel each one of their punches as though it were my own fists doing the beating. I resonate with the hedonistic mood that hovers like a cloud over our heads. It's erotic. Charged. Savage. It should spark fear in me, should send me running for the exit, but I can't look away as blood-tinged spittle flies from the opponent's mouth, sending the crowd into a frenzy.

All too soon, Ruthless sends his opponent tumbling to the mat with a final punch to his face, and the crowd goes wild, screaming, "Ruthless reign, no pain, no gain!"

Grinning, Tara turns to face me, laughing at the expression on my face.

"Yeah, I recognize that dazed, star-struck look. Come on, let's get you another beer."

She tucks her arm through mine and we push our way back toward the bar. "He's incredible, isn't he?" Tara says, sounding just as star-struck as I am.

I nod, needing another moment to find my voice. "I, uh... He's a student at Halston."

Gaping open-mouthed, Tara pulls me to a stop. "Are you shitting me right now?"

I shake my head. "No. I've accidentally run into him a couple of times."

She laughs. "Girl, you're lucky you don't have a broken nose. His chest looks like it's been carved from granite."

"It feels like it, too," I grumble, recalling how hard it felt beneath my face.

"I'm unbelievably jealous." Tara pouts. "He's got all the damaged, bad-boy vibes that just suck me in. Please tell me he's as sexy up close as he is from over here."

"Sexier," I tell her with a twist of my lips. "But he's a total asshole."

"Ugh, you're only making me want him more," she teases.

I shake my head at her as we reach the bar and she stretches over the countertop to grab us two fresh beers. "Nah, like a *total dick*," I tell her. "I accidentally crashed into him, and he accused me of following him and deliberately trying to get him to notice me. Sure, he's hot, but get over yourself, dude."

"Ugh, what a dick," Tara groans in agreement. "Doesn't mean he isn't hot, though. Or that we can't come back and drool over him the next time he's fighting."

Chuckling, I shake my head and turn to look out over the rest of the room as another fight commences.

"Where are the bathrooms?" I ask as I finish off my second beer.

Tara points toward a door to my left. "Just through there. I'll be right here," she tacks on when I set down my empty beer bottle before heading toward the door she pointed out.

I step through it into a narrow hallway that looks as though it runs the length of the building. Spotting two doors up ahead, I amble toward them. The first one has a sign indicating it's the men's room, but as I pass by, the door flies open, making me jump back and flatten my body against the wall as Ruthless storms out, looking as enraged as he did in the ring.

His black hoodie is unzipped, hanging open so I can see the white muscle shirt underneath that clings to every one of his large, sharply defined muscles.

"You," he snarls. "What the fuck are you doing here?" He

doesn't give me a chance to answer before snapping, "I fucking knew you were following me." His lip curls up in a sneer as his gaze lowers over my skimpy outfit, and I swear I'm going to punch Tara in the tits for forcing me into this damn dress.

*You'll totally fit in. No one from Halston will even be there*, she said.

Lies. All of it was lies.

"Well, what are you waiting for?" he growls in that deep, rough rasp that must have women everywhere suddenly searching for new underwear. "Get on your knees."

His harshly barked words snap me out of my fantasy. "Excuse me?"

"You're desperate enough to follow me all the way out here, so you might as well get what you came for."

All I can do is blink up at him, my mouth slightly parted.

The fucking audacity of this guy.

He steps closer, eliminating the space between us. His piercing blue eyes scour my face before slowly trailing down my neck and lingering on my sharp nipples poking against the fabric of my black dress.

"You're pretty, I'll give you that," he says in a husky tone.

Dragging his eyes back to mine, he quirks a brow. "I don't have all night. If you want to know what my cum tastes like, you better hurry up and get on those knees."

It's the arrogant way that he lifts his eyebrow that snaps me into action, and I don't register what I've done until I feel the sharp sting against my palm.

*Fuck, that hurt.*

"You entitled fucking asshole," I snarl at him, absolutely furious, as I shake my hand out to abate the sting.

His blue eyes darken with anger as he glares right back, but despite his feral glint and the fact that he could crush me like a bug beneath his shoe, I jab my finger into his rock-hard chest. "I could accuse you of stalking *me*, only I'm not that fucking conceited. As for tasting your cum, I'd rather bathe in horse shit. Dunk my face in a vat of acid. Rub my body in gasoline and set myself on fire. Lick—"

"Think I've got it," he hisses, a new hostility in his tone.

"Do you?" I bark, still plenty riled up. "Do you actually? 'Cause if you pull this shit the next time we meet like this, I'm going to slap your balls instead of your face."

For some asinine reason, one side of his lips quirks in the faintest of smiles. One I'd have missed if we weren't standing so close.

I'm so glad the asshole is finding this amusing.

"You're planning on making this a thing? And there I was, beginning to believe you weren't stalking me."

Lips pursed, my nostrils flare as I blow out a frustrated breath. "Fuck me," I mutter to myself.

He chuckles. "You're only making my point for me, Babydoll."

"I mean it," I bite.

"So do I." Leaning in so his breath whispers along my skin. "If it's my dick you want, you'll have to try far harder than following me around like a lost puppy."

I'm still reeling from the audacity of the asshole as he stands to his full height before striding past me down the hall.

"I'm not fucking following you!" I yell after him, eyes raking over the word *Ruthless* written across the back of his hoodie.

The asshole only ignores me as he shoves open the door and heads back into the warehouse.

"God, I hate him," I grumble before turning my back on where he disappeared and heading in the opposite direction to the women's bathroom.

Once finished, I push through the throng of people back toward the bar. As I sidle up beside Tara, I spot the dickhead himself standing further down the bar with a glass of amber liquid. Xander stands behind the bar, their heads bent close together as they talk. He nods at something Xander says, his lips moving around syllables I can't make out. There's a casualness in the dickhead's relaxed posture that I haven't seen before, yet his expression is still sharp and guarded.

As if sensing my eyes on him, Ruthless' head turns in my direction, those piercing eyes boring into mine. I tear my gaze away, striding toward Tara at the opposite end of the bar, and astutely ignore the weight of his stare drilling into me with every step.

"Hey, you were gone for ages," Tara says when I reach her side. "Everything okay?"

"Yeah." I give her a tight smile. "I definitely need another drink, though."

"Girl," she says with a laugh, "It's like you read my mind."

# RILEY

## CHAPTER NINE

I'm nursing my third beer of the night as the current fight comes to a brutal end. A warm buzz penetrates my veins, relaxing my muscles, my paralyzing anxiety from earlier long forgotten amid masculine sweat and the metallic tang of blood.

Tara hasn't left my side all night, the two of us remaining within viewing range of the bar, where I suspect her brother has had one eye on us the entire time he serves customers.

Despite the predominantly male crowd, pushing and shoving at one another to get a better view as fists drive into flesh and grunts of pain rise from the ring, cursing like sailors when bets don't go their way, beer sloshing over the lips of bottles at bellowed outbursts, I don't feel out of place, or as uncomfortable as I had expected when I first walked in. Unlike at a club, where everyone is there to dance and grind and fuck a stranger, most of the focus has been on the fighting ring. That is not to say that debauchery isn't happening in dark corners of the warehouse or in bathroom stalls. Just that, so far, I haven't felt as though I'm being leered at.

"I'm going to grab another water," Tara says, voice raised to be heard over the heavy bass of the music and chattering of the crowd. She switched to water after her first beer since she's driving us home later. "Do you want anything?"

I hold up my still, mostly full beer as I shake my head. "I'm good."

Lips pursed, she makes no move to step away. "Don't move from here. I'll be back in a sec."

She waits for my nod, still appearing reluctant as she peels away, leaving me alone in the jostling crowd. I watch her go until she slips between the bodies gathered around the long bar, only the top of her head visible.

I scan the rest of the bar, searching for a familiar scowling feature and blue eyes, but I don't spot him among the throng of people. I guess he left after he finished his drink. Relief and a twinge of something that feels far too close to disappointment settles in my stomach, so I quickly push it aside and turn back to the ring, where two fresh-faced fighters circle one another. The one with a shaved head and tattoos crawling over his scalp and down his neck is the epitome of vicious as he gives his opponent a feral grin before snapping forward with all the ease of a trained fighter—someone used to scraping and clawing for survival.

Flesh meets flesh, and I wince, the sting of it sharp enough to reach my ears, yet I don't look away from the savagery of that blow. The brutality it instigates. *This* is survival in its rawest form. It might be in a ring, put on for the amusement of others, but it's no less of a battle for survival. Hell, based on bets placed and winnings tonight, perhaps for some of these fighters, it *is* a battle for survival. That money might be all they have to live off for the week. These fights... this show of dominance, of power and control, might be the only thing getting them through the week. The thread of light that keeps them from succumbing to the darkness.

I don't know what it's like to fight with fists. For your palms to be coated in the blood of another. But I do know what it's like to split yourself open and bleed for survival. For breath. For life. For the hope of a better tomorrow. A more promising future. An end to the ceaseless abyss.

Perhaps that is why I watch the violence unfold with a perturbed fascination. An understanding that I can't wholly explain and yet comprehend in its entirety.

So wrapped up in the savage violence unfolding before me, I fail to notice that I have gained unwanted attention until he sidles up behind me.

A large, unwelcome hand wraps firmly around my hip, squeezing with a sense of possession he has no right to as I am held in place. Warm, putrid breath, ripe with bitter beer scrapes against my cheek as I'm pulled against a rigid body, some asshole's crotch pressed firmly against my ass. "You like watching the fights, sweetheart? Enjoy seeing them bleed?" He leans in even closer, and my already stiff spine turns to ice. "Do you get off on it? Can you feel your adrenaline pumping? I bet your cunt is begging to be brutalized in a similar way. To be fucked hard and fast."

Bile.

Bile burns my throat. Ravages through cartilage and muscle until I'm incapable of speaking, even as that one syllable forms a chant in my head.

*No. No, no, no, no, no.*

With every blink, the warehouse goes in and out of focus. Steel-clad walls are replaced with cream ones. The cement floor beneath my feet switched out for a bed with pink sheets and frilly pillows.

*Always such a good girl.*

My stomach cramps, my next moves occurring on autopilot as I drive my elbow into the asshole's side. He grunts, air whooshing from his lungs as he doubles over. One foot planted in the present, the other in the past. I spin to face him, seeing his tear-stung, mud-brown eyes and scruffy beard, his worn cotton T-shirt with pit stains and scuffed-up jeans without actually taking any of it in.

Red colors his cheeks as he recovers, teeth gritted as those eyes snap to mine, hardening in anger. "Bitch," he snarls, the vulgar word my only warning before he lunges.

A strong hand grabs my arm in a bruising grip, nails caked with dirt digging into the skin as he tugs me toward him. Wide-eyed and frantic, I gaze at the crowd of towering men around us. A crowd that is either unaware or uncaring of what is happening. Is this what Xander meant by being careful, by not going off alone?

I flick my eyes to the bar, frantically searching for Tara or Xander. I find the two of them at the far end, in the middle of what looks like a heated argument. Neither of them looks my way and fear rattles my bones as I realize I'm alone. They haven't seen what is happening. I can't rely on them to come to my rescue.

A scream builds at the base of my throat, lips parting as I suck air into my lungs. However, before it can burst free, a heavy hand clamps down on my shoulder before swiftly sliding to the back of my neck, giving a gentle squeeze.

Frozen in place, my very bones quake as I watch the man in front of me tear his eyes away from me to glare daggers at whoever stands behind me. Except, that murderous rage bleeds out of him, pupils dilating in awe and... fear.

Fuck, who the hell is behind me to cause such a reaction?

The man before me visibly swallows. "R-Ruthless."

Fuck. If possible, my spine straightens further, and I become irrevocably aware of his hand like a brand on the back of my neck as long, slender fingers rub slow, gentle circles over my pulse point.

"I-I'm sorry. I d-din't know s-she was y-yours." The man stumbles over his words, stripped down to a stuttering fool in Ruthless' presence.

"Now you do," comes Ruthless' flat yet deadly response. "And if you don't want me to break every bone in your hand, you'll walk away and never so much as glance in her direction ever again."

"Y-Yes. O-Of course." He's barely got the words out before he backs away, scurrying like a city rat into the nearest drain in his haste to blend in with the mob around us.

Too stunned to move, I stare at the spot where the man disappeared for several blinks before I catch ahold of myself. Spinning, I dislodge Ruthless' hand as I stare into those cold eyes, like chips of ice, as they glare down at me.

Endless seconds tick by. Me staring. Him glaring.

"Looks like you bit off more than you could chew with that one," he drawls. One side of his lips is hitched in a sneer, although the rest of his expression remains perfectly blank. Unaffected. Except for those eyes that blaze with a thousand fires. Fires of ice. Of cold, brutal rage that I can't even begin to comprehend.

Through the shock, it takes a moment for his words to penetrate, but when they do, I snap back into myself as though I'd somehow become disconnected from my body. As if the terror and shock of the situation had separated my body from my mind.

"Oh, go fuck yourself," I snarl, any and all gratitude I may have felt dying a quick death.

He sighs, tucking his hands into the pockets of his jeans as though he hasn't a care in the world. "This again? I thought we'd been over this already, Babydoll. Or have you already forgotten about your desperate attempt to follow me into the bathroom earlier?"

Teeth gritted, I'm surprised steam doesn't stream from my nose. "I was not. Following. You," I hiss with deadly venom.

He smirks, pure, masculine cockiness in every twitch of those muscles, and before he can spout some other bullshit that will only enrage me further, I spin on my heel, giving him my back as I storm through the crowd toward the bar.

I feel his eyes on me the entire time. Even after I've found Tara and asked her if we could leave. Even after she agrees and leads me through the crowd toward the door.

Even after we've gotten into her car and driven away from the warehouse, I still feel those ice-cold eyes digging into my back like arrows of icicles embedded in my skin.

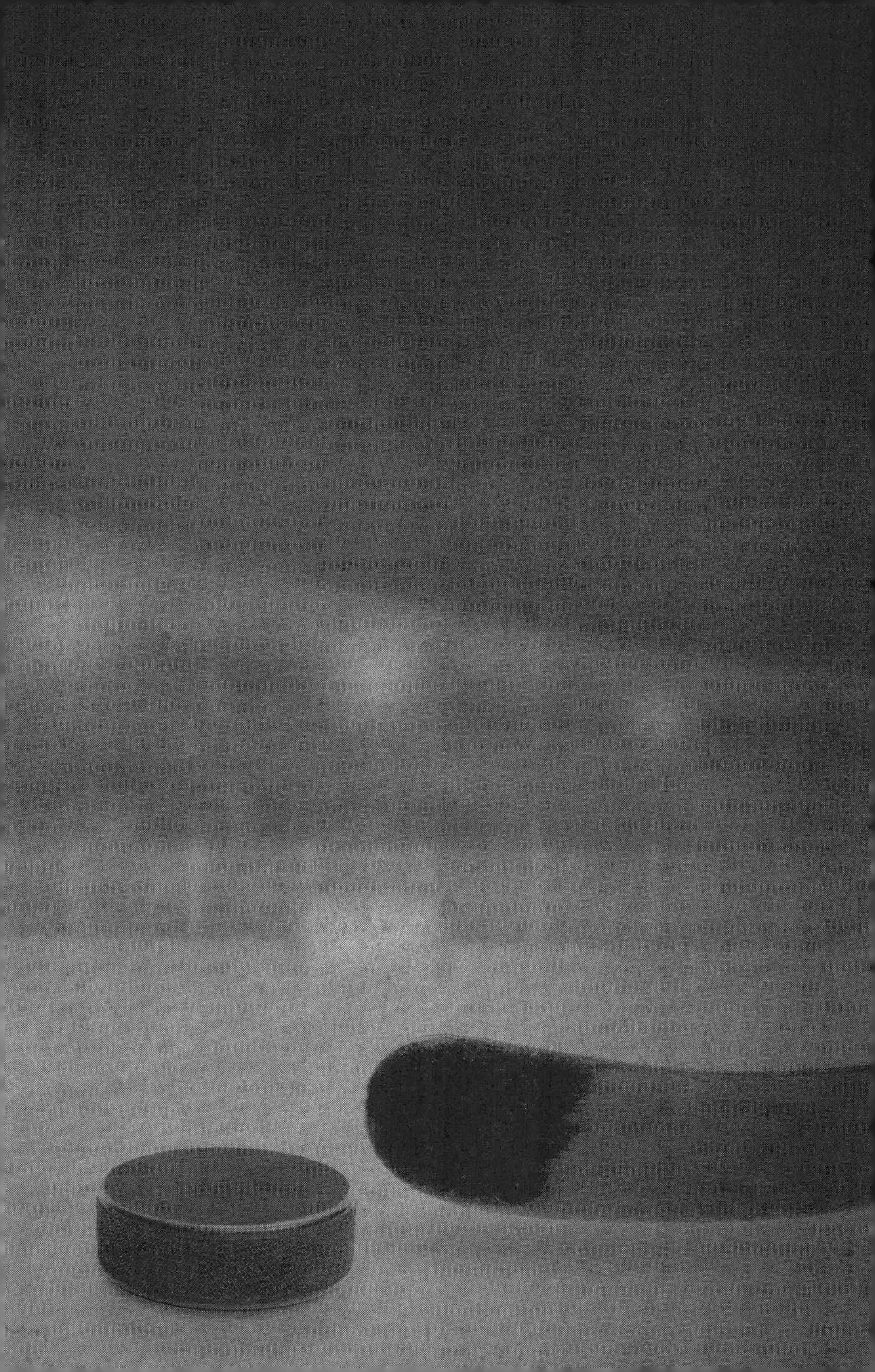

# LOGAN

## CHAPTER TEN

My knee bounces as Coach goes over his typical pre-game spiel. However, instead of hanging off his every word like I usually do, my mind is stuck on her. Is she here? *God, I hope so.* I left tickets for her at will call, and because I'm a glutton for punishment, I got her a seat rink-side, so I'll fucking know if she doesn't show.

*Fuck, please show.*

It's insane how much this girl is in my head. The fact I'm thinking about her and not the imminent game or the fact scouts could be in the stands at this very moment—so it's imperative that I remain in the zone—says everything about how deeply under my skin Riley is embedded.

The way I feel when I'm around her, I've never had that before. Other than some of the guys on the team, Grayson, and Royce, I've never been able to talk so openly to another person. Definitely not a girl. And I've never had them genuinely care.

What she said on Monday... It felt so fucking good to hear. I hadn't meant to open up to her. No one other than Grayson and Royce knows of my struggle to follow my own dreams and to ensure the continuation of everything my father has worked so hard to build. No one has ever cared to ask. I appreciate that most people assume my future is hockey, and they probably wouldn't even consider that there could be any other option. Still, I hadn't realized until Riley asked, how much people just assume or don't care.

People come up to me all day long, wanting to be seen with me, to become my friend, or hoping for a date. Yet they don't want to actually get to know *me.* They want Logan Astor: star forward and soon-to-be drafted NHL player.

For the first time in I don't know how long, Riley sees the real me. The me outside of the jersey. The me beyond hockey. Beyond the popularity and the flirty, outward persona I present to the rest of the world.

"Astor. Astor!"

Gavin shoves my shoulder and I whip my head up, finding Coach glaring at me.

"Does our captain have any words of wisdom before we hit the ice?"

I glance around the locker room, shocked to realize Coach is finished with his speech and everyone is looking at me expectantly, game faces on.

Clearing my throat, I meet the gaze of each of my teammates. "This is our year. The team has never been stronger, and it shows. The rest of the league should be afraid because we're fucking coming for them. So let's get out there and kick some ass!"

The locker room erupts into cheers, sticks banging against the floor as the guys all fist bump.

"What are we?" I yell over the din.

"Huskies!"

"What do we do?"

"Win."

"How do we do it?"

"Together."

Grinning like a fucking savage, I roar, "Let it rip, boys!" before throwing my head back and howling alongside the rest of the team before we skate out onto the ice to a battlefield of screams and cheers.

I keep my focus on the center of the ice, refusing to look into the stands, just like I did all during warm-up, knowing my eyes will betray me and zero in on her seat. The need to know if she's here itches beneath my skin, but the fear that she isn't keeps my eyes on the ice.

However, right before the puck drops, I can't help myself. My control wavers.

I turn my head.

I look.

And a stone drops into my stomach.

Her seat is empty.

She didn't come.

It shouldn't bother me, but *fuck*, I've never been so disappointed. It's only at this moment, as the puck hits the ice and everyone bursts into action, that I realize I've never wanted anyone in the crowd more than I wanted to see her cheering me on.

Of course, Gray and Royce come occasionally, and my parents do too, but I've never asked a girl to come before. Never wanted one here until her.

And I hadn't realized how much it meant to me until this moment.

For the next two hours, I spend more time looking at her empty seat than on the game happening around me.

I play like shit, not scoring a single goal, and when the final buzzer goes, I glance up at the scoreboard. 0-1. *Fuck.* Our first loss of the season.

Pulling off my gloves, I ignore everyone around me as I skate off the ice, so fucking done with this day.

"What the hell was that?!" Coach barks when we're all back in the locker room, heads hanging, and the weight of our first loss of the season putting a damper on the mood. "What I saw out there tonight was not the team I have spent the last several months cultivating. Where was the communication? The coordination? Astor." He barks my name, and I know he's about to tear me a new asshole. "Where the hell was your head because it sure as fuck wasn't in that game. A statue would have been more useful than you were out there tonight. You're goddamn lucky there were no scouts here, but if you play like that tomorrow, you can say goodbye to your future in the NHL."

The reality of what he's saying hits directly in the chest, only darkening the ominous cloud hanging over my head. He isn't saying anything that isn't true. It just fucking sucks to hear. To know I could have thrown away my entire future, and for what, a girl? I need to sort my head out and get it back in the game before tomorrow. Since the Penguins scouts didn't show tonight, you can bet your ass they'll be there tomorrow—and there's no way in hell I'm going to play like I did tonight.

---

I'm in a foul mood as I hit the ice on Saturday night for our game against the Boston Eagles, but I don't dare so much as glance in the direction of *her* seat. I keep my focus entirely on the game, and the second the puck drops, I take off down the ice, ready to purge my emotions.

Tonight is about the scouts. About making my dream a reality. The disappointment and hurt eating away at me for the last twenty-four hours need to be channeled into a productive outlet. I can practically feel it pouring out of me and into the stick in my hand as I tackle a player on the opposing team, driving my elbow into his side before I gain possession of the puck.

Coach yells something—probably telling me off—and I know I'm lucky the ref didn't call a penalty as I pass the puck to Jonas and shoot down the ice, getting into position.

Jonas knocks the puck to Barnes, who manages to dodge an Eagles` defenseman before sending the puck in my direction. Smirking cockily at the goalie as the puck slides across the ice, I deftly whack it into the corner of the net, officially scoring the first goal of the game.

Now that's what I'm fucking talking about!

"Hell, yes!" Jonas yells, skating over, and we bump fists as the rest of the team joins the celebration.

"Don't think I didn't see that elbowing," Coach warns when I skate past, before calling Jonas and a couple of other players off the ice.

Whatever. I scored the goal, didn't I?

Unfortunately, things go downhill for us over the next twenty minutes and my ire rises with every missed opportunity and goal the Eagles score.

"Astor! Penalty!" the ref yells when I cross-check an Eagles defenseman. "Two minutes."

*Fuck.* We're down by two, and who the fuck knows how much worse it will be by the time my two minutes is up.

For the next two minutes, I either check the clock or watch as my team fumbles the passes and fails to block. By the time I'm allowed out of the box, I'm full-on pissed off and ready to rip off some Eagles' wings.

"Astor!" Coach bellows before I can join the fray. He indicates for me to get my ass on the bench, and I skate over, scowling.

"Coach. This is my game!"

"And you're fucking it up. Sit your ass on that bench and when you've got that temper under control, you can go back out there."

Cursing under my breath, I dutifully oblige, teeth grinding as I watch the game unfold.

At the start of the next period, Coach reluctantly agrees to let me rejoin, and determined to make up for lost time, I jump the half-board and dive right in.

In the first thirty seconds, I have an Eagle pressed against the boards as I steal the puck. I glance up, my eyes connecting with startling green ones, and the entire stadium disappears.

I'm faintly aware of a whistle blowing behind me, but it's nothing more than white noise as I rake my eyes over her face, unsure if what I'm seeing is a mirage or reality.

Her smile is timid but encouraging, and time stops as I lose myself in her.

*She's here. She came.*

Seeing her in the stands, knowing she's been cheering for me hits like a bolt of lightning, and a feral grin splits my face as I take in her pink cheeks and the black and gold Huskies scarf protruding from her puffer jacket.

Her responding smile lights me up from within, and I'm shoving away from the boards with renewed energy when the ref bellows, "Astor! Two minutes in the box. One more penalty and you'll be out for the rest of the game."

*Fuck.*

No. She came to see me play, and she can't do that if I'm stuck in the fucking box or riding the bench.

Reluctantly tearing my gaze from hers, I skate over to the box and sit my ass down. For the next two minutes, all I do is stare at her. I watch as her wide eyes dart around the rink, flicking every thirty seconds to where I'm sitting here twiddling my thumbs.

*She fucking came!*

I still can't believe it. I was certain she wasn't going to come. Had convinced myself this chemistry between us was one-sided and that she didn't feel the same way.

Except, she's here.

By the time I'm allowed back on the ice, I've made a promise to play the best fucking game of my life, and I take off with renewed energy, ignoring Coach's calls to behave.

I'm untouchable as I join the game, racing toward the attack zone where Barnes and Rickman, the other two forwards, are currently battling with the Eagles' defensemen to score a goal. The ice is smooth as clouds beneath my skates, the other players a blur.

Seeing me coming, Barnes manages to get a clear shot, whacking the puck my way. I fly toward it, focusing solely on the puck and the goalie. He's a beast in all of his gear, easily managing to block all but the first goal we've tried to score all game, but I've watched tapes of the Eagles' recent games and I know he's slow.

I feign right before I whack the puck into the top left corner of the net.

The crowd explodes.

Grinning like a fool, I hold my stick in the air as I do a celebratory loop of the rink. My eyes go immediately to her, and that light, happy feeling in my chest expands, a wide grin tugging at my lips as I skate toward her.

Throwing up ice, I come to a stop in front of Riley's seat and take a second to appreciate the fact she's fucking here. That she saw that. That she's clapping her hands and screaming *my* name. It's the best fucking sight I've seen all night.

I smack my gloved hand against the glass, her eyes narrowing in confusion as she glances at it before returning her gaze to mine. I repeat the action, and the older gentleman sitting in the next seat takes pity on her. He must explain what I'm after as she nods knowingly before leaning forward and pressing her hand to mine, still smiling that dazzling smile that makes me feel like I'm the only person in this entire stadium who she sees.

I grin at her from behind the cage of my helmet, the bright blue of my mouthguard visible, but it makes her laugh as she shakes her head before waving me away. It's right then that I know this is going to be my best game ever.

---

"A fucking hat trick, man!" one of the guys screams in my ear as the rest of the team crowds around me. Lapping up the high from our phenomenal win tonight.

"You were on fucking fire!" Gavin yells as he cuffs me around the neck.

I can't stop grinning, but untangling myself, I scan the slowly emptying stands for my girl. Because, after that game, that's exactly what she is—my girl. My good luck charm. I have never played the way I did tonight. It was on a whole other level. And the only difference... her.

The fact she was here.

For me.

Her seat is vacant, and not seeing her amongst the crowd, I skate toward the edge of the rink, eager to get changed and find her.

"Fantastic job tonight, Logan," Coach praises as I step off the ice. "Good to see you managed to pull it together when it counted." He lifts his chin toward the stand, and for the first time since I saw Riley, I remember that Pacific Penguin scouts were in the crowd. I can't believe I forgot all about them.

When Riley is around, my brain short circuits. I forget about everything and everyone except her.

"They were here?"

"They were," Coach confirms. "After tonight's performance, I don't think you have anything to worry about." Coach pierces me with a scowl. "However, you could have done without the penalties."

Too happy to give a shit, I clap him on the shoulder. A couple of penalties won't be held against me. For the most part, I've been a solid player. My record is clean and I've never been banned from a game for fighting.

Floating on fucking clouds, I hurry through a shower before throwing on my clothes and texting Riley as I'm leaving the locker room.

Where are you?

RILEY

I had to get to work, sorry!

Disappointment has my shoulders dropping, my steps slowing as some of my excitement fades. My fingers hover over the screen as I debate asking her where she works. If her shift is only starting, it's probably one of the campus bars. I could stop by and see her. Except, she might not like that. Most girls would love it if I stopped by their job, but Riley isn't like everyone else. She'd probably be embarrassed and flustered, and that's the last thing I want to do to her.

Before I can think of a response, another message comes through from her.

Sorry I didn't make it last night. I had to go into work early.

You played amazing tonight, even if I struggled to follow what was happening half the time.

I hadn't realized hockey was so interesting to watch.

ME:

Hopefully there was one hockey player more interesting to watch than the others.

RILEY

Mm number seventeen had a pretty decent ass.

I grin stupidly down at my phone, fingers flying over the screen as I push my way out of the stadium and into the chilly night air.

ME

Just pretty decent?

Usually, after a celebration, I'd head to a bar with the team, or hit up a party if there's one, but I'm not feeling it tonight. So instead I begin the walk across campus toward the townhouse I share with Grayson and Royce.

RILEY

I figure you have enough supporters there to inflate your ego. I wouldn't want your head to explode.

I actually burst out laughing, causing a couple walking my way to look at me strangely.

ME

Incredibly thoughtful of you.

But on a scale of 1-10 how decent was this ass?

RILEY

17

OMG that was corny. Forget I said that.

ME

Not a fucking chance, Shortcake. No takesies backsies.

I chuckle under my breath, picturing the red blush spreading over her cheeks at this very moment and wishing I was with her to see it for myself. However, I'm enjoying this more playful Riley. The distance offered by texting has made her bolder. There's not a chance in hell she'd have said that if we were face-to-face.

RILEY

Go celebrate your win, superstar.

Fuck, why am I picturing her calling me that as she strangles my cock?

ME

Nah, the only person I wanted to celebrate with had to work, so I'm just heading home.

I watch as the ticks turn blue, indicating she read my message. There's a pause before dots appear. They seem to sit there for ages, and I make the walk through campus on autopilot, not once removing my focus from the phone screen as I await her reply.

When I'm beginning to think she's writing an entire essay, the dots disappear. I watch the screen intently for the remainder of my walk home, but by the time I insert my key into the front door, she still hasn't responded, and I reluctantly tuck my phone into my pocket as I step into the house.

Grayson and Royce are sitting in the living room, and both give me expectant looks when I walk in, probably surprised to see me since I usually head out with the team after a game—win or lose.

"Well?" Gray questions with anticipation.

Smirking, I'm all swagger as I stalk across the room and drop onto the opposite end of the couch. "We won."

He grins, smacking my chest. "Nice one, man."

"Got a fucking hat trick," I tell them.

"Seriously?" Gray gapes at me. "Fuck, that's... wow. Congrats. You deserve it."

Grinning, my gaze shifts to Royce. The morose bastard has been in a particularly delightful mood since we were called to pick his ass up after he beat the shit out of some dude at The Depot the other night. And *not* in the ring, where he's *supposed* to be delivering the punches. Asshole wouldn't explain shit, except to say that he touched something he shouldn't have—which we all know is a trigger for him, and Gray and I both have the good sense not to poke or prod at *those* wounds.

Still, despite his sulking, his voice is genuine when he says, "I'm happy for you, man. Gray's right. You deserve all the recognition. You'll have scouts banging down your door after tonight's performance."

Fuck, I hope so.

Exhilaration pumps through me, and for a brief moment, all feels right in the world. I'm with my best friends. Riley came to watch me play. And I kicked ass tonight. Hope flutters in my stomach as I picture a future in the NHL. A future with Royce and Gray at my side. Hell, there's even a part of me that can imagine Riley slotting easily into that future, as crazy as that sounds.

A light smack to the chest jolts me out of my thoughts. "The big winner gets to pick the movie tonight," Royce states, tossing me the remote.

A teasing smirk slides across my face, and spotting it, Gray groans. "Why?" he whines, shifting to glare at Royce. "Why would you give him that power? You realize he's going to make us watch reruns of *The Office* for the rest of the night now. I spend half my week in an office."

Already having navigated to the tv series page, I scoff. "Your office is *nothing* like this. You'd probably be far less grouchy if it was."

"Ass," Gray grumbles, kicking me half-heartedly in the shin. Giving him the middle finger, I press play on a random episode and smile at the TV as I sink into the couch cushions.

Except, as episode bleeds into episode, I find my attention wavering, and I spend as much time staring at my phone as I do the TV, waiting, hoping for a response from Riley and wondering if I'd be coming on too strong if I messaged her.

"Dude, are you even watching?" Gray grumbles as the theme song for our third episode of the night plays out.

"Of course I am," I retort, snapping my head up to the TV.

He makes a noise of disagreement. "Then how come you're looking at your phone every thirty seconds."

"Shit, did tutor girl go to your game? Is that why you're in such a good mood?" Royce teases.

"Logan Astor is actually falling for a girl. Who'd have thought we'd see the day?" Gray joins in, the two of them ganging up on me.

"Shut up," I snark, but there's zero heat behind it, and based on their matching shit-eating grins, the assholes know it.

"We're going to have to suss her out," Royce continues. He's still teasing, but there's an edge to his tone that has me narrowing my eyes on him.

"No." I point a finger directly at him. "I haven't even been on a date with her yet. I basically had to beg her to come to my game tonight. She's skittish and I don't need your moody ass scaring her off so don't go poking your nose where it doesn't belong."

With a sigh and a roll of his eyes, Royce grunts out a "fine," but I know I've only put him off for now. It won't be long before he—or both of them—seek Riley out for themselves and I want to be certain neither of them scares her away. Not when she's only just started letting me in. Not when I want so much more.

I make it through another couple of episodes of *The Office* before mumbling a goodnight and heading to bed. There's still no response from Riley as I slide between the sheets and reluctantly I admit that I'm not going to get one. Not tonight, at least. And that's okay. I'll leave her in peace tonight, but tomorrow... tomorrow, I'm making her mine.

# RILEY

## CHAPTER ELEVEN

My eyes drift shut as my hips trace a sinuous arc through the air, the sultry rhythm of the music thrumming through my body. My thoughts drift to the frigid ice rink bathed in the harsh lights of the arena. To the precise and determined way Logan moved across the ice, performing a dance of his own kind.

Remembering how effortlessly Logan's powerful legs propelled him around the rink, I find my own movements shifting. My body mirroring his. Each twist and turn evokes the sensation of gliding across the ice, my fingertips tracing invisible lines as I echo Logan's prowess.

For a moment I'm there with him. Not watching from the stands but skating alongside him, my graceful spins mimicking his agile turns, hips swaying with the same rhythm and power that he displayed as he maneuvered the puck.

Then my thoughts drift to how it would feel if the roles were reversed—him sitting in the audience watching *me.* My skin heats, muscles tightening at the notion. Shivers skate down my spine as I picture his chestnut orbs locked on me with that same intensity he had on the ice. Desire floods my veins at knowing

I'm the only one who has his attention. It's heady. Intoxicating. And has me momentarily wishing he was here. That I had the courage to tell him what I do for a living.

He hasn't asked, although I know if we continue to hang out, it won't be long until he does. Until I have to tell him. It makes me nervous. Nervous to see how he will react. To know what he might think. Will he care? I hope not but you can never really know.

My steps falter, and I focus my thoughts back on Logan and tonight's game. From the second he hit the ice, I couldn't take my eyes off him. And every time he scored a goal, I got swept up in the excitement of the crowd, screaming his name and clapping my hands like a lunatic.

I struggled at times to follow what was happening. I looked up the rules of the game before I went tonight, but factoring in the speed at which everyone moved around the ice, it made it challenging to follow at times. However, even when I wasn't sure what was going on, it didn't detract from the game. From the atmosphere. The energy in the crowd and the effortless way in which Logan moved captivated me. He owned the rink with every slice of his blades and whack of his stick. The hard, determined look in his eyes when he was on the ice. How focused and in the zone he was. I didn't need to know anything about hockey to know he's a natural at it. He was born to be on the ice, adored by screaming fans and taking down men the size of mountains.

I'm not entirely sure if the way he was playing was normal for him or not. The man beside me kept cursing every time he elbowed another player and the couple of times he pulled stunts worthy of a penalty and time in the glass box. Yet, after he saw me, he stopped playing so aggressively. It was as if whatever anger he was harboring disappeared and his head was fully in the game. Even the spectators around me noticed the change in his behavior, and I received some sideways looks after that.

*I* couldn't have been the change in Logan's mood... could I?

The only time he took his focus off the game was when he looked at me. I'd be lying if I said that didn't make me feel all sorts of special, especially when he came right over and basically declared for the entire stadium to see that I meant something to him.

Meant what, I'm not sure, but whatever it is, I can't deny it feels pretty damn good.

Or that I feel the same way, too.

My thoughts revolve around Logan for the entirety of my shift, which catches me by surprise. Normally when I'm on stage, I lose myself in the performance, falling into the practiced routine alongside the other dancers. Dancing has always been my outlet. The thing I turned to when I needed to get out of my head and forget the world for a while.

It's the only reason why I even felt comfortable accepting this job. Putting my body on display for everyone to gawk at is not something that comes naturally to me. It's not that I have body image or self-esteem issues, but knowing I'm deliberately encouraging men to look at me, enticing them, is triggering for me.

I can't even be at a swimming pool without wearing a one-piece that covers as much skin as possible, and the second I'm out of the pool, I'm pulling on a top and shorts to cover up.

So, applying for a job where I dance half-naked in front of a room full of strangers was a *huge* deal for me. I probably wouldn't have applied for the job, except reality came calling in the form of my mother, reminding me I have responsibilities and I can't afford not to. So I learned how to block it all out. To focus only on the movements, the way I do when I dance solely for me.

"I need you to stay behind and help me lock up," Ben, the club's manager, says when I'm nearing the end of my shift.

Rocks settle in my stomach. I hate it when he asks me to stay late. From the minute I met him, I was wary. He always gives me ick vibes, with his greasy, slicked-back hair and the overwhelming stench of aftershave that threatens to drown me. However, it's more than that. It's the way he leers at me and the other girls, always watching us a little too closely, a little too often.

"Sure," I say, resigned, as I go to change out of my skimpy outfit and into my normal clothes.

"I can wait for you," Tara offers in a quiet voice when we're backstage.

"No, it's okay. Nothing's going to happen. He'll try his luck, I'll turn him down, and that will be that."

Tara stares at me for a moment longer, searching to see if I'm telling her the truth before she relents. "Okay. Well, let me know when you're done, yeah?"

I give her a quick smile. "Will do."

Once I've changed, I begin wiping down tables and stacking chairs on top of them before moving over to the bar and tidying it up. I'm leaning over the prep area to wipe down the bartop when Ben emerges from his office.

"You danced well in tonight's performances," he says in a leering tone that raises the hairs along the back of my arms. I appreciate that, as a manager, he would be watching the shows to ensure everything goes smoothly. However the way he says it, like he was watching *me* specifically... it creeps me out. "Is that what you're going to college for? To become a dancer?"

Yeah, I'm sure he'd like that. Bet he's picturing it right now, all that bending and stretching. I guarantee he's thinking about how flexible I'd be in bed. The other girls talk, and word is that Ben is a creep. He has hit on a couple of the other girls, offering them rides home and inviting them to his place so they can 'get to know each other better'.

Dude, professionalism! It's a thing, look it up!

"No. I haven't decided what I want to do yet."

The last thing I want to do is give this guy any information about me. Equally, I don't want to come across as rude. It's a challenging balance.

He steps closer, within touching distance and effectively corners me behind the bar. "You're young," he says, voice lower than a moment ago. "You've got plenty of time to figure it out. In the meantime, you should let loose, have some fun, enjoy yourself."

The insinuation is clear. My body is coiled tight as I stare pointedly at the bartop I'm now furiously wiping in an effort to distract myself. Perhaps it will serve to remind him that we're actually meant to be *working*.

He shifts so his chest brushes against my back, deliberately leaning in and eliminating any possibility of it being an accidental graze. My blood turns to ice in my veins, my heart rapidly thumping against my ribs. Reality blends with the past in a cruel clash as memories rise like a tidal wave, threatening to crash over my head.

Another heavy body.

Different warm breath.

Someone else's raspy voice.

*Not real. Not real. Not real.*

My eyes slam shut as the acidic burn of vomit floods my mouth. It takes everything in me to regulate my breathing and not lose my shit.

*Breathe in; bleed out.*

*I survived.*

*I survived.*

*I survived!*

I manage to pull myself back from the edge of a full-on panic attack, but I'm still nowhere near calm. My thoughts are clear enough to remind myself that, despite Ben being the one at fault here, I can't afford to freak out and lose this job. The sad fact is, I need the money, and doing something impulsive like pulverizing his balls is a surefire way to get myself fired.

"I could help you." His voice slicks like oil against my skin, leaving a sticky residue behind that will need a scalding-hot shower to remove.

Panic seizes me. It renders me immobile. Mute. Frozen as I fight to quash it.

My throat is so dry, my brain feels scrambled. Words are impossible. *Breathing* is impossible.

I have no response. No reaction.

Misinterpreting my silence, he chuckles, his warm breath nauseating against my skin. His hand grazes my hip before he moves away.

I still don't breathe. Don't dare to look until I hear his office door snick shut. Then it's like the bow holding me upright snaps, and my body sags forward, air gushing out of me as tears track silently down my face. My hands are shaking so badly, and the absolute last thing on my mind is my job as I drop the cloth and race from the club.

Despite the late hour, I walk home in a fog, stripping out of my clothes and crawling beneath the covers, where I cry myself to sleep.

I cry for the girl I used to be. For the shell of her that I have become. For all the broken parts of me that were once whole yet savagely stolen. Taken against my will. The fractured pieces that are irreparably damaged.

I do a good job of convincing the world—of convincing myself—that I'm okay. But it's in moments like this; at times like tonight, when I remember just how fragile I am. How close I am, at any given moment, to shattering.

I tell myself I survived, but some days it feels as if I'm still living in hell. Regardless of the time that has passed or the work I have put in, my heart is still one giant wound laced with scars that have not fully healed.

I try so hard to be strong. I have no other choice. But on days like today, on nights like tonight, I allow myself to be weak. To break. To cry. To scream at the injustice in the world.

So, I hide beneath my covers where no one can see my tears, unleashing all my carefully compartmentalized pain for only me to hear.

---

I sleep restlessly, every moment plagued with nightmares until I give up trying shortly before dawn breaks. I have a ton of assignments that I need to work on, but my head isn't in the right place to achieve anything productive. Instead, I pull my hair into a high pony, throw on an oversized hoodie and leggings, then grab my keys and walk out the door.

The street is quiet this early in the morning, the yellow-orange of the street lights shining like fireflies in the soft blues and dark purples of pre-dawn as I walk down the street to the small, rundown dance studio.

As I reach the entrance, a sense of peace washes over me and I unlock the door, pushing it open. The studio is empty and silent as I flick on the lights, and I smell the faint scent of lemon cleaner as I move through the room, tracing the lines of the wooden floor.

I don't get to come here often, but on days when I feel as exposed and vulnerable as I do today, I'm eternally grateful for the private space that feels more like home to me than my own apartment.

Taking off my shoes, I wiggle my bare toes against the cool floor and take a few minutes to warm up my muscles.

Once I feel loose enough, I connect my phone to the Bluetooth speaker and scroll through my playlist until I find the perfect song for how I'm feeling. *Fearless* by UNSECRET and Ruby Amanfu begins to play as I move into the center of the room.

As I take a deep breath, I close my eyes and willingly surrender myself to the melody of the track. With every passing chord, the world slips away. The song is about strength. About recognizing your scars and still having the courage to face your fears. Each chorus cuts deeper as my body leads me in a dance across the room, arms stretched and legs extending.

With every arabesque, I shed myself of fear. I banish the shadows with each twist of my core and toss aside the nightmares with every pirouette. I hemorrhage over the floor with each passing beat, the music ripping me apart until nothing remains. Until I'm an empty vessel, drained of emotion. Only then, when I've been hollowed out and carved anew, do I begin building myself back up. I piece myself together, one fragment at a time, until the lyrics *you won't break* are stitched into the fabric of my being.

Until I no longer feel alone.

Until my inner strength shines from within.

Until I truly do feel fearless.

As the final notes play out, I reach for the sky with tightly clenched fists and scream out, filling every corner of the studio with courage before crumpling onto the floor, exhausted yet empowered.

Tears track down my cheeks, and I know I've left an essential part of myself in this dance studio. However, I also feel stronger. Tougher than I did before.

The waves of power taper off slowly, leaving me breathing heavily as I remain on the floor, surrounded by the fragments of my past self. Taking one last deep breath filled with renewed confidence, I rise up and face this stronger me in the mirror.

Sharp, glittering green-brown eyes stare back at me, features fixed into one of fortitude. An indomitable spirit that refuses to be broken again.

I've made it this far. I will continue to persevere. To fight. To live. Despite the challenges I am facing, I will endure, and I will rise.

Because in the end, it will all be worth it.

The end goal is worth whatever I have to sacrifice to get there.

Song bleeds into song as I lose all track of time until the music is interrupted by the ping of an incoming text. It jars me out of the dance, and wiping the sweat from my forehead, I move to grab my phone.

For the first time today, a genuine smile lights up my face as I read the message from Logan.

Good morning, beautiful.

I never responded to his text from last night, but I'm happy to hear from him today. Checking the time, I'm shocked to realize I've been here for hours and it's nearly midday.

ME

Are you only waking up now?

Sundays are the only day I get to sleep in. What are you up to today?

I have errands to run and assignments to finish.

We could study together.

I chew on my bottom lip as I grab my keys and exit the studio, locking up behind me. My stomach flips at the thought of seeing him, and choosing not to analyze it too closely, I fire off a response.

Meet me at the library in an hour.

---

"Riley!"

At the sound of Logan's voice, I turn with my hand pressed against the dining hall door to find him stalking toward me.

His gaze drops, grazing over me in an appreciative way that causes my skin to buzz. When our eyes connect, there's a heat that wasn't there before, and he stares at me with an undeniable hunger as he eats up the space between us within seconds.

His hand wraps around my wrist as he shoves open the dining hall doors, pulling me off my feet. As soon as we've crossed the threshold, my back hits the door. Logan's lips descend to devour mine as his hard, muscular body presses firmly against my softer curves.

Logan's kiss is an exorcism for my soul. Every swipe of his tongue expels the dark thoughts, the moments of self-doubt, the plaguing fears, and replaces them with pieces of him. His radiance fills the residual cracks, lighting me from within until my skin glows, pulsing with a warmth and energy it doesn't normally contain.

Our lips are swollen when he pulls back, his eyes shining as he stares into mine. “I’ve been wanting to do that since the moment I saw you in the stands last night.”

All I can do is blink at him. The man has warped my brain, leaving me incapable of a response. Sensing his effect on me, one side of his lips lifts in a slightly cocky yet secretly pleased smile, and he threads his fingers through mine.

“Come on, let’s grab coffee and get to the library. I booked us a private study room.”

He pulls me back out the door and over to the coffee cart. Thankfully, there is no line today, and Logan places our coffee orders while my brain is still playing catch up.

“Why did you book a private room?” I eventually manage to ask while we wait for our drinks.

His eyes bounce between mine, and there’s no edge of suggestion when he says, “I wanted to be alone with you.”

It’s not like how it was with Ben last night. Logan doesn’t want to get me alone to take advantage of my body—although, with how his eyes eat me up, I have no doubt he’d like to do exactly that. Nevertheless that’s not what this is about. He genuinely just wants to be alone with me. It doesn’t matter to him if it’s only so we can study.

I’m fairly certain it’s at this moment that I fall hopelessly in love with Logan Astor. It’s certainly the moment that I come to realize the fall is going to hurt like a bitch when I hit the bottom. But I’ve already tumbled over the edge without a parachute. There’s no slowing down, no stopping. I can only hope that the crash doesn’t entirely shatter me.

He grabs the recyclable tray with our drinks when they’re ready, carrying them in one hand as he drapes his arm over my shoulder, steering me along the path toward the library.

Being a Sunday, campus is relatively quiet. However, there are still people milling around. Most of them cast second glances our way and whisper as they pass us. Logan appears completely oblivious to the attention as he talks about everything from the TV show he binged last night to the weird dream he once had about a talking hamburger that tried to eat him.

I, on the other hand, feel each one of their searing gazes. They burrow beneath my skin, picking at my insecurities and preventing me from paying attention to what Logan is saying.

It isn't until the door closes behind us in the small, private study room at the back of the library, effectively blocking out the rest of the world, that I no longer feel the weight of everyone's questioning gaze on me.

Setting our coffees on the table, Logan spins to face me. Expression pinched as he searches my face. "I actually wanted to talk to you."

"Oh?"

"Last night, I was on top of my game. I played the best I ever have, and when I was thinking about why that might have been, I realized there was only one difference last night."

He pauses, eyes darting back and forth between mine, and I feel like he's hinting at something I should understand, but I don't. "What?"

"You. *You're* what was different. The fact you were there, cheering me on."

"Okay..." I can't for the life of me figure out where he's going with this.

Stepping closer, he slides his large hands around my upper arms. "I played my best game ever because you were there screaming my name." When I still don't latch on to what he's implying, he says. "I need you at all my games. I'll get you tickets, pay for your transport, accommodation, whatever you need."

He's still rambling, even though I've zoned out. "Wait." I

hold up a hand to shut him up. "Hold on. You want me at all of your games? For the rest of the season?"

"Yes."

"Even your away games?"

"Yes."

Eyebrows scrunched, confused as all hell, I stare at him. "Why?"

It's his turn to appear confused. "Weren't you listening? You're my lucky charm."

I scoff. "The last thing I am is lucky. Cursed, would probably be more accurate."

Not believing me—and why would he—he shakes his head. "To me, you're a blessing in disguise. One I hadn't realized I needed, yet I'm so damn thankful to have." Closing the distance, he brushes the back of his knuckles along my cheek. "I know it probably sounds crazy, unreasonable even, but the fact you were there last night and I played so well... it's no coincidence."

"And, what? You think if I don't attend the rest of your games you won't play as well?"

He glances away but nods in confirmation.

"Logan, that's insane. You played amazing last night because you're talented and dedicated. Didn't you say there were scouts coming this weekend? You probably played your best game because of them."

He scowls. "Then how come I played like shit on Friday, huh? I had no idea which night the scouts were going to show. I took one look at your empty seat on Friday, and I played like shit. Yet, I saw you on Saturday and it was like I wanted to play my best... for you."

Smiling sweetly, I reach up to cup his coarse cheek. "That's really sweet, except I can't come to every single one of your games for the rest of the season. It's just not feasible. I have to work. I can't afford to lose my job."

"But..."

"There is no *but*, Logan," I interrupt, remaining firm. "I'll come to your home games... so long as they don't interfere with my work schedule. But there is no way I can take the time off to go to your away ones. Not to mention the expense and the time it would take away from my studies."

His lips purse into a thin, tight line, and I can see the cogs working behind his eyes.

"Okay," he eventually agrees. "You'll come to all of my home games."

"So long as they don't interfere with work."

"So long as they don't interfere with your work," he repeats in agreement.

"And for away games, and any other games you can't attend, you agree to FaceTime me instead."

"Logan," I groan.

"Or send a photo at the very least. I need to see your face before each game, Shortcake. Ideally, I need to hear your voice and see you standing in the crowd, preferably wearing my jersey. *But,* if I have to, I'll settle for a photo."

I release a long exhale, staring up at him for a long moment.

His desperate plea is impossible to say no to. And the fact he believes I'm his lucky charm? What more could a girl ask for? He's literally perfection personified.

"Fine," I relent. "I'll attend your home games, and the ones I can't make, I agree to FaceTime or send you a photo."

His boyish grin is the best reward as he wraps his big, muscular arms around me and lifts me off my feet. I laugh as he spins me around in the small room.

"You know, feel free to get creative with the photos. Something in lingerie, or nude." He wags his eyebrows, making me chuckle as I shove his shoulder to put me down.

"Don't push your luck, mister."

Grinning, he keeps his arms loosely wrapped around my waist. His chest brushes mine as the teasing moment disappears and he grows serious. "I had one more thing I wanted to ask."

"Don't you think you've asked for enough favors today?" I tease.

"Just one more."

I arch a brow, waiting.

"Go on a date with me."

He doesn't phrase it as a question, but his usual cockiness is nonexistent. There's a vulnerability I haven't witnessed before hidden in the depths of his eyes as he waits for my answer.

"I don't want to only see you at hockey games or in the library. I want to be able to text you, to hear your voice before I go to sleep at night. I want to take you on dates and show you off on campus. I *want* to get to know you—all of you—because what I've seen so far... well, it has me pretty damn obsessed."

"Okay."

His eyes widen almost imperceptibly. Did he really think I'd say no? How could I after that little speech? His surprise vanishes as quickly as it came, his impish grin spreading across his face as he leans in to kiss me.

My lips part, my tongue swirling around his. His arms tighten around me as he tilts his head, deepening the kiss. In the privacy of the study room, it quickly turns heated. Hands on my hips, Logan backs me up against the wall before sliding his thick thigh between mine. The friction against the thin fabric of my leggings causes me to gasp into his mouth.

He groans, his hard body towering over me as his hips press against mine. Feeling the long length of his arousal against my abdomen, my core clenches with a hunger I hadn't known was possible.

I whimper as he works his thigh against my clit.

"Fuck, Shortcake. You're so hot. The sounds you make are so sexy."

His hands slide around to grasp my ass, moving me up and down his jean-clad thigh.

"That's it, baby. Use me. Take what you need."

"Logan."

He groans, sounding pained. "My name sounds so good falling from your lips. You're going to come for me. Nod your head if you understand, Shortcake."

I nod, unable to form words as he coaxes me to move faster. His lips move to devour my neck, and I lean my head back against the wall, allowing him better access as he leads my body toward total bliss.

Our breathing grows labored as we each chase that high. Sensations build in my core as everything grows taut.

"Logan."

"Eyes on me, Shortcake."

I hadn't even realized I'd closed them, but I snap them open, staring into Logan's deep chestnut hues as my fingers curl around his shoulders, nails digging into his skin.

Our breaths mingle, breathing synced as our hips grind, that delicious friction encouraging us on.

"Fuck," he curses at the same time energy races along my skin and my panties flood. "So good. So fucking perfect."

Moan after moan passes my lips as my body goes up in flames, and I fall into the pits of his eyes, held captive as he holds me through my release.

His hips continue to rock slowly against mine, dragging out the pleasure until I can't bear it anymore, and we sag against one another, catching our breaths. His head drops and he nuzzles my neck as I stroke his hair, relaxed in my post-orgasmic glow.

"For the record, that was not at all what I intended when I booked this room."

Feeling so light that I fear I'm at risk of floating away, I chuckle. If it were anyone else, I might not have believed them, but this is Logan, and I know he doesn't lie. He tells it how it is. If all he wanted was sex, he'd have been upfront about it, but I get the impression he feels what I do. He recognizes that this is somehow... *more.*

"Sure you didn't," I tease. "I bet you had it all planned. Beg me to be your own personal cheerleader, somehow convince me to go on a date with you, then decimate my brain cells with an orgasm so I can't back out or change my mind."

He hooks his lips up in a grin as we disentangle. "There are so many things in that sentence, Shortcake, that I don't even know where to start. Firstly, I *decimated your brain cells*, huh?" He arches his eyebrow, causing me to roll my eyes.

"Secondly, there was no begging. I did not beg. If that's how you remember it, then I think you need your memory checked. Thirdly, my own personal cheerleader? You have no idea how hot that sounds. I'm totally picturing you in a short little skirt, a tight crop top, and your hair tied up in one of those high ponytails. Do you own pom poms? 'Cause you might make me come in my pants for a second time today if you do."

"Oh my God, Logan!" I shove at his chest, cackling. "No, I do not own pom poms, and no, I am not buying any. And if you buy them for me, I'm throwing them in the trash."

"What about a cheerleading outfit?" His eyes dance with mirth.

"Not. Happening." I pin him with a stern expression until he relents.

"Fine. Not into role-playing. Duly noted."

"I never said I wasn't into role-playing. I just don't want to be a cheerleader."

His mouth drops open and he gapes at me before groaning. "Fucking hell, Shortcake, you *are* trying to make me come in my pants again."

I shake my head at his antics. "Go clean yourself up so we can get some *actual* work done."

He winks, leaning in to press a quick kiss to my cheek. "Yes, ma'am."

I swat his ass and he booms out a laugh as he steps out of the study room.

# RILEY

## CHAPTER TWELVE

I'm standing at the campus gates, my stomach churning with nerves as an all-black Range Rover rolls to a stop and Logan jumps out from behind the wheel.

"I wish you'd let me pick you up at the dorms," he says as he strolls around the front of the car.

Yeah, if I lived in the dorms, I would have.

I didn't tell him I wasn't staying in student accommodation because I don't want him to see where I actually live. Not because I'm ashamed, just that it's very different from the campus dorms or wherever I imagine he lives. I don't need his pity when he realizes the university didn't provide me with accommodations. Nor do I need the questions if he asks how I'm affording it. I already dread him asking where I work—an inevitable question at some point if we continue to see one another.

He stutters to a stop in front of me, lips curling upward as his gaze drops to take in my outfit. "Fucking hell, Shortcake. You look incredible."

I stare down at myself, self-conscious as I take in the cute hunter-green dress that shows off the curve of my hips before falling to my mid-thigh. The top half is hidden beneath my thick coat but looks just as good, showing a hint of cleavage.

Usually, I rock up to class dressed casually in age-old jeans and an oversized hoodie or plain top, not giving a shit what the other students might think or say, but tonight I wanted to look good for Logan. Something I haven't wanted to do in a really long time.

For far too long, I have been trapped in a cycle of self-hate, shrouding my body under oversized garments that hide any hint of femininity, afraid to show the world that I was all woman because of the attention it might draw. It has taken years for me to feel comfortable in my own skin, to not panic if I wear something flattering and sexy.

Even then, I still have moments where the fear renders me immobile—like at The Depot. The second I walked in there and saw all those people and the bright lights, I was rooted to the spot. Thank God Tara managed to talk me down, or I would have had to leave.

Moments like that show me that, despite the work I've done, I'm not entirely there yet. My past, my fears and insecurities, still linger, ready to leap forward and remind me that no matter how far I come, I'll always be a little bit broken inside.

Thankfully, those moments are few and far between. Mostly because I rarely dress up and go out. And when I'm on campus or in Halston, I generally wear comfortable, loose clothing—clothing that enables me to fade into the background and move around unseen.

I can put on a tight dress and go out when I need to, and if I know in advance, I can usually keep the panic to a minimum, but I don't feel truly comfortable until I'm back in my sweats and burrowed into a sweater.

The only time when it is different is when I'm at Lux. Whenever I step through the doors of the club, I set Riley aside and become someone else, and ultimately, pushing myself to get up and dance in revealing clothing has helped me to claw back some semblance of control. It has gone a long way toward helping me feel confident in my body and acknowledging that it's okay to like the way I look. To show it off. It doesn't mean I'm inviting unwanted attention. I'm not giving men a free pass to take advantage. If they deem it acceptable to cross that line, that's on them. Not me.

Tonight, I wanted to look good for Logan, but I also wanted to feel sexy for me. Although it might not look like it, tonight is important to me. It's my first real date, and I know I'm on it with the right man. I want it to be perfect.

Lifting my gaze, my throat goes dry as I take in Logan standing there in his dark denim jeans and white fitted Henley with a pale-blue open shirt thrown over the top. He looks hot in a casual sort of way. Perfectly Logan. He's put some gel through his hair, giving it that mussed *just fucked* appearance that does sinful things to my insides. "So do you."

He grins, leaning in to press a chaste kiss to my cheek before moving to open the passenger door and helping me in.

The interior of the car is sleek and modern, with a black leather dashboard and seats that feel like butter against my skin.

"Where are we going?" I ask when he climbs in beside me and pulls onto the road.

"I remembered you saying you wanted to see that new psychological thriller that came out several months ago, and I found it still showing in a theater in Springview, so I thought we'd do that."

All I can do is stare at him in surprise, shocked he remembered. It had been an offhand comment I made several weeks ago while we were discussing something else.

"But if you don't like that idea, we can do something else."

His face scrunches, his focus on the road as he rubs at the back of his neck. "Umm... we can go grab something to eat, or, uhh, do you like miniature golf? We could go do that."

I reach across the center console and rest my hand on his thigh, giving it a light squeeze to stop his rambling. "The movie sounds perfect."

He glances down at where I'm touching him before turning his head to meet my gaze. "You sure?"

"Absolutely. I've been dying to see it. I should probably warn you that I'm a jumper, though. So be prepared for flying popcorn."

My jesting does the trick, and the tension bleeds out of him as he relaxes into his seat, laughing. "Maybe I'll be responsible for holding the popcorn."

"Probably wise." Now that he seems more relaxed, I start to pull my hand away, but as I do, he encases it with his, keeping it in place.

Fighting a smile, I turn my head to look out the passenger window as we travel down the street heading out of town.

"How are you feeling about tomorrow's game?" I ask, breaking the comfortable silence we'd been sitting in. The dark country road is starting to give way to street lights and more and more buildings as we drive into Springview.

"Good. Great, even. Penn State is a tough team, but with the way we've been playing, I'm confident we'll beat them." He glances my way. "I'll FaceTime you beforehand?"

Tomorrow and Saturday's games are both away games, and true to my word, I've agreed that we can FaceTime before they begin and before I have to leave for work. I have rehearsals on Friday before my shift, but I can watch his game on the TV on Saturday before I have to head to Lux.

"Yup."

We park in a parking lot across the road from the movie

theater, and Logan takes my hand in his before we cross the street. He buys us our tickets and enough food to feed a small army before we grab our seats.

"Fucking hell," he groans when I remove my coat and place it over the empty seat beside me. "You're going to have to give me a play-by-play of the movie later because I'm telling you now, I'm going to be too busy looking at you to pay it any attention."

My cheeks heat and I duck my head as I settle in beside him. He drapes an arm over the back of my chair, his fingers grazing my upper arm as his other hand comes up to pinch my chin. He lifts my head until I'm staring into his eyes. "I'm serious, Riley. You're so beautiful, and I'm not just talking about your bangin' body. You're beautiful inside and out."

"Kiss me," I demand in a quiet rasp, because how could I not want to kiss his perfect lips when he says the most incredible things?

Seemingly as desperate as I am, he presses his lips to mine, and for a moment we forget where we are. It isn't until the lights dim and the opening credits roll that we pull apart, and he tucks me into his side, offering me some popcorn as we settle in to watch the movie.

---

"Holy crap, I was not expecting that plot twist," Logan exclaims as we exit the movie theater.

"Mmmhmm."

It's the only response I can form. The last two hours have been literal torture, and I can't figure out if it was deliberate on his part or if he was completely unaware of what he was doing to me. There wasn't a single moment where he wasn't touching me. Whether it was his fingers grazing my upper arm or his hand resting on my leg, tracing patterns on my inner thigh. All any of it did was drive me crazy, to the point where I barely paid attention to the movie.

Meanwhile, Logan was hooked from the opening scene. Every time I subtly glanced his way, his gaze was riveted to the screen. Yet, his fingers continued to torture me with their light, seemingly innocent teasing.

I shiver when we hit the cold air outside, my skin clammy, and my body wound too tight after the movie for me to put my coat on, making me welcome the cool breeze as it dances over my tormented skin.

Logan pulls me deeper against him, and I inhale the sharp, wintery scent of his aftershave as I burrow into his side. We hurry across the street, and Logan opens my door for me, helping me into his car before he rounds it and climbs in beside me.

As soon as he's maneuvered the car onto the road, he reaches over and rests his hand on my thigh. Immediately, he begins tracing circles on my skin. Already primed, my body instantly reacts, thighs clenching as need builds in my core.

I do my best to hide it, to block out my reaction to his touch, but when I squirm in my seat for the third time, and his fingers slip beneath the hem of my dress, steadily climbing up my legs, I know he's completely aware of my response to him.

"You alright over there?" he asks with a knowing smirk.

"Yup." The word is a high-pitched squeak that causes him to laugh while I bite down on my lower lip to stop a needy moan from escaping.

He glances my way. "You sure? 'Cause you seem a little worked up. Perhaps there's something I can do to help."

His fingers continue their tantalizing teasing. They are now so high that if I parted my legs, he'd easily be able to touch where I need him most. The knowledge has me close to combustion, and with another sweep of his fingers, I'm unable to hold it back. A small whimper escapes.

"Fuck, Shortcake," he rumbles, his hand clenching the steering wheel. "I love the noises you make. They make me so fuckin' hard."

My gaze drops to his crotch, noticing the outline of his dick pressing against the stiff confines of his jeans.

"Are you wet for me, baby?"

There's an edge of desperation to his voice, and I lift my gaze to his face. Instead of answering him with words, I swallow back my nerves and tentatively part my thighs, granting him entrance as his fingers stroke along the drenched fabric of my panties.

He groans, low and deep. "Jesus Christ." Pressing his thumb against my overly-sensitive clit, my hips jerk and my head falls back as I moan.

Ripping his hand away, he growls, "Touch yourself."

"W-what?" I ask, blinking stupidly through the fog of endorphins.

"I wanna touch you so badly," he states in a strained tone. "But if I sink my fingers into that sweet pussy, I won't be able to stop at fingering you, and I don't want our first time to be a quick fuck in the front seat of my car. When I finally get you naked, I want to have you spread out on my bed, with the entire night dedicated to memorizing every inch of your body.

"However I may crash this fucking car, knowing you're sitting right there, soaking wet, and begging me with your eyes to make you feel good. So I need you to touch yourself for me, Shortcake. Make yourself come so I can hear those delectable moans of yours."

Jesus, when he talks like that, Logan could get me to do just about anything.

"I—I can't."

For most of my late teens, I was as good as dead inside. Sex and orgasms were the farthest thing from my mind. It took me several years before I was healed enough to acknowledge those feelings of sexual attraction. Longer still before I was brave enough to act on them. However, with that came terrifying nightmares and panic attacks, and it didn't take long for me to decide the experience wasn't worth the mental fortitude required.

I was so focused on not panicking while I was intimate with someone that I didn't have a mission of reaching an orgasm, and after failing to get myself off even alone in my room, I came to the conclusion that I was broken. That *he* had broken me.

From that point on, I focused on my studies and building the life *I* wanted. Boys didn't matter. Sex wasn't important. I was alive. I had my freedom, had everything I needed to be happy.

Yet here is Logan, making me feel more than I've ever felt for anyone else and giving me the courage to *try*. He already achieved the impossible in the library when he made me come without even touching me. Something about Logan puts me at ease. He pulls me out of my head and I'm entirely in the moment with him, attuned to the way our bodies react to one another, the static charge of electricity in the air.

"Yes, you can, Shortcake." Logan's words drip with certainty. "Close your eyes and pretend it's me touching you, and know that I want to be the one making you feel good so fucking bad that it's killing me not to stop this car and climb over there."

Before allowing time for self-doubts to build, I slip my hand beneath the lining of my panties. My middle finger swirls around my clit, before I slide it lower and into my wet heat.

"Fuck, that's so hot," Logan rasps, his eyes darting back and forth between me and the road. "Does that feel good, Shortcake?"

Leaning my head against the headrest, I close my eyes. "Mmm, yes."

Unbelievably, it does feel good. More than good. Then again, I shouldn't be surprised at the things Logan can get me to do. My body reacts to him in a visceral way no one else has ever elicited. One look and my blood heats; one touch and I melt.

"Tell me what you're imagining."

"I'm pretending it's your fingers inside me," I say breathlessly, as I insert a second finger. My insecurities have fallen by the wayside as I fall headfirst into the fantasy, pretending it's Logan's hand instead of mine coaxing pleasure from my body. "They're so much thicker than mine. Longer too. They feel so good."

The car swerves, and I snap my eyes open, gaping as Logan veers to the side of the road, slamming his foot on the brake.

Turning, he faces me with black, dilated pupils. Our eyes clash before he drops his gaze to where my hand is buried in my panties.

"I haven't heard you screaming yet, Shortcake." His voice teeters on dangerous, as though he's grasping for control, on the verge of saying fuck it and launching himself across the car.

I have no idea where my newfound boldness comes from. I blame the way Logan is currently looking at me, nearly unhinged by his need to watch me come. It makes me feel emboldened. Empowered. Seductive and Sensual. Enough that I remove my hand from my panties, and instead loop my fingers around the edge and peel them down my legs.

Shifting in my seat so my back rests against the door, I part my legs. Logan watches intently as I trail my slickened fingers up my thigh until they disappear beneath the hem of my dress, and I reinsert them.

My back bows at the intrusion.

"That's it, baby."

At his low rasp, I lift my gaze, finding him rubbing his hand over the bulge in the front of his jeans. Hooked to the sight, I lick my lips and move my fingers faster.

Realizing he has my attention, Logan lifts his hips, and popping the button on his jeans, he pushes them and his boxers down until he can palm his erect cock.

"See what you do to me, Shortcake? I've spent weeks sitting in that library trying to calm my need for you, but I'm done holding back. I want you to see exactly how hard that big brain and smart mouth of yours gets me."

He glides his hand up and down his impressive length, emphasizing his point. "I've been jerking off in the shower for weeks now, picturing that blush spreading across your chest, conjuring the sweet moans when I make you come. I don't want to imagine any more, Shortcake."

He stares spellbound at where my arm disappears beneath my dress as I work myself over, while he tugs on his weeping cock until our heavy breaths steam up the windows and tension crackles in the air.

"Do you have any idea how hot you look, fingering yourself?" he asks, voice strained. "The way you're looking at me..." He's jerking furiously on his dick now. "I'm about to fucking explode."

I can see how close to unraveling he is, and it's my undoing as an orgasm swells, and I cry out as I come apart. I hear him grunt his release, my name scraped out in a guttural tone.

As the post-glow begins to fade, an uneasy shame seeps in. I've never done anything like that. Never even been tempted to. My own actions bewilder me. It was as though Logan took possession of my body and made it his. Embarrassed and unable to meet Logan's eye, I fuss with my dress, all too aware of the dampness clinging to my inner thighs.

Leaning across the console, Logan plants one hand on the window beside my head while his other gently turns my face so I'm staring right at him. "Don't shy away from me. That was so incredibly hot, and I fully intend to watch while you get yourself off again in the very near future."

Swallowing nervously, I shyly lift my eyes to meet his. Nothing but authentic compassion and heat stare back at me. He's not embarrassed, not any less interested. If anything, I'd say the opposite. The depth with which his eyes are boring into mine, I almost swear he's trying to burrow into the very core of my being.

"I've never done that before," I confess.

His eyes dart between mine, narrowed slightly. "You've never gotten yourself off?"

I give a small shake of my head, feeling the heat in my cheeks. "I've tried, I just could never..."

"Fucking hell, Shortcake. How is it that every time I find out something new about you, you only get more perfect for me?"

My eyes round in surprise as I stare up at him.

"That doesn't... put you off?" I ask, confused.

"What?" He seems genuinely taken aback. "Hell no. Why would it?"

"Because it makes me difficult?"

"Baby, don't you know hockey players love a challenge? Nothing good in this life comes easily."

Fearing he doesn't grasp the severity of the situation, I blurt, "Logan, I've *never*..."

His brows dip until they're sitting low over his russet eyes. "Wait... You've *never* never."

I give another shake of my head.

"But what about in the library the other day?"

My cheeks flame. "Well, yes, I did then—"

"Hold up, Shortcake." Moving back so he can see my entire face, Logan asks, "Was that your first ever orgasm?"

*Okay, world, now would be a great time for a crater to open and swallow me whole.*

When no such fortune comes to save me from this embarrassment, I duck my head and squeak out, "Yes."

The world falls silent at my admission, the only noise the rapid thump of my heart against my chest as I wait on tenterhooks for Logan's response. For him to push away. To tell me this has been fun, but he doesn't see it going any further.

Except none of that happens. Logan remains exactly where he is, perched directly in front of me, waiting until I muster the courage to lift my face to his.

As soon as I do, his lips tenderly brush mine and he whispers, "So. Fucking. Perfect."

Pulling back only enough to meet my questioning gaze, he cups my cheek in his hand, brushing his thumb along my heated skin. "I've never been so fucking glad to fail a class in my life," he states, voice husky and ringing with sincerity that makes my eyes water. "But don't hide from me again, Shortcake. I don't care if you're embarrassed. Your innermost thoughts; your insecurities and vulnerabilities are the aspects of who you are that I most want to know. The pieces that no one else gets to see."

I'm left speechless as I stare at him, thinking of the Jenga tower of vulnerability that has been precariously stacked over many years of self-hate, trauma, and pain. Tonight's admission is barely a drop in the ocean of fragility residing inside me. Despite his heartfelt sentiment, I don't believe Logan is ready for me to offload anything more profound onto him, however, it gives me hope that maybe one day Logan could be someone I can confide in about the darker aspects of my life.

Voice laden with emotion, I softly respond, "Okay."

He holds my gaze for a moment longer until he is satisfied with my agreeableness. I see when he is because his eyes soften, the lines in his forehead smoothing out, before he reaches into the back of the car. He grabs a t-shirt from an open gym bag and, in an unexpected move, begins to clean me up. He wipes the residue from between my legs before falling back into his seat while I slide my panties back on.

Tossing the t-shirt into the back seat, he pulls the car back onto the road, his hand settling on my thigh as though it belongs there. And perhaps it does. Is it too much to hope that Logan Astor may have been put on this earth to insert color into my monochrome life?

"I'm back on Saturday night, but it's Jonas' nineteenth, and the team is taking him out. I'm free Sunday, though, if you wanna grab dinner or something," Logan converses, as though the ground didn't monumentally shift beneath our feet.

"Sunday is good with me, but don't feel like you have to if you're tired or hungover or whatever. I'll still see you on Tuesday."

"I told you I want more than library dates and seeing you at my games," he argues, giving my thigh a squeeze. "I don't think you quite realize what you've gotten yourself into yet. I'm going to be that pesky little bug you can't get rid of. The tick that latches on and refuses to let go. The puppy that endlessly follows you around." I chuckle at his dramatics, but when he turns to pierce me with his intense stare, I realize he's not entirely joking. "I don't plan on going a single day without seeing your pretty face or hearing your sweet voice."

*Yup, I am officially done for when it comes to Logan.* He knows precisely what to say to have me cracking open my chest, ripping out my heart, and handing it over to him on a silver platter.

"Okay. Sunday, then." I fail miserably at hiding my smile as he pulls up outside the Halston dorms. It would have raised questions if I'd asked him to drop me off at the gate.

I go to open my door, but he calls out, "Wait. Stay there. Don't move."

Quirking a brow, I watch curiously as he hurries out of the car and jogs around the hood to open my door. He holds out his hand, helping me out with a stupid-ass grin on his face.

"You're such a goof," I tease, as he reels me into his arms and I press my hands against his firm chest.

"Your goof." His large hand slides up and down my back, our teasing falling aside as the moment grows heavy.

"Thank you for tonight. I really enjoyed myself."

Tucking a wayward strand of hair behind my ear, he murmurs, "I'm pretty sure I should be thanking you, and for a lot more than being my date tonight. Hockey has always been my one true passion. While pursuing that dream, I always believed I would have no time or energy to spare on anything else. Then you came along, and with each passing day, you're proving me wrong."

Leaning in, he presses the sweetest of kisses to my lips. Our tongues dance, but we keep it light. "Go on inside before you get cold," he murmurs, kissing my temple before handing me my coat and encouraging me toward the dorm with his hand at the base of my spine.

Wishing him goodnight, I step into the building, waving at him until he drives out of sight. The red rear lights of his car have only just faded into the distance when my phone pings, and curious as to who it could be, I pull my phone out of my handbag.

LOGAN

Us both getting off in the front seat of my car: 10/10

Hottest thing I've ever seen.

Chuckling, I text back.

What is this? What are you doing?

His response is instant.

Letting you know I'm still thinking about it.

I walk home with a goofy grin on my face. Not once do I feel the chill from the November air. I have the remnants of Logan's touch keeping me warm.

An hour later, I'm curled up in bed when my phone goes off again.

LOGAN

Jerked off to the thought of you: 6/10

It wasn't you.

That night, I fall asleep with a smile on my face.

# GRAYSON

## CHAPTER THIRTEEN

As I step into the club alongside my two best friends, the vibrant stage lights illuminating the dimly lit space and casting a kaleidoscope of colors along the walls, a rush of anticipation washes over me, and I am more than ready to let off some steam.

While I'd rather have hung out at home with my boys, I'm just glad to finally have a night off—even if Logan had to practically drag me away from the computer. Senior year has been grueling so far. The irony is, it's not the workload that's getting to me. The tests and assignments are manageable. It's all the fucking shit I'm dealing with outside of college that eats up every spare second of my day and results in me working until the early hours of the morning more often than not.

No other student has to deal with the crap I do. They aren't awake at 3 a.m. poring over contracts and agonizing over the hiring and firing of employees. They don't spend their weekends holed up in an office doing paperwork, or their spare time between classes fielding business calls. All they have to worry about is getting good grades, wearing a rubber when they fuck some chick at a party, and ensuring they don't piss off Mommy and Daddy.

What I'd give for such superficial problems.

To not feel as though I'm carrying the weight of the world on my shoulders.

To not be responsible for the livelihood of hundreds of others.

However, that's not the hand life dealt me.

If I fuck up, it's not only my life that will suffer, but those of my employees; of my investors. Of those who believe in me to sustain the family business after everything went to shit.

Admittedly, there are *some* things I wouldn't change about my life—my friends, the control I have, the influence. And the aspects I wish were different... well, I can't change them, but I sure as hell can drink my problems away on a Saturday night.

The thumping beat of the music fills my ears, enveloping me in its rhythmic embrace as I cast my eyes around the decadently styled interior. The low lighting creates an intimate ambiance, the soft glow of old-fashioned chandeliers casting a warm, golden hue across the room.

The walls are adorned with rich, velvet drapes in deep crimson, adding an erotic, heady aura. Taking up a significant portion of the floor space is a large, center stage, lavishly decorated with ornate carvings and elaborate gilding, with a spotlight overhead bathing the stage in bright light as performers move rhythmically across the stage in sensual, glamorous costumes complete with feathers, sequins, and tassels.

Heavy velvet curtains frame either side of the stage, ready to be pulled at the end of the performance, providing an opulence that likely appeals to the wealthy Halston clientele.

Peeling my focus away from the stage, I take in the rest of the room. The space is divided into various seating areas—small, plush booths along the walls are draped in gossamer curtains, providing the illusion of privacy. At the same time, round tables are decorated in satin tablecloths, and vintage-inspired velvet chairs are interspersed around the remainder of the room.

A dark mahogany bar with a long, golden-framed mirror lines one wall, and I make a beeline toward it. Following me, Logan claps a hand on my shoulder. "Try not to look like a raccoon pissed in your cereal, yeah?" My nose scrunches in disgust and he barks out a laugh. The energy emanating from him is exhausting. He's still high from the adrenaline of his wins this weekend and the incredible season his team is having, and I'm hoping one of the performers will catch his attention or he'll get distracted texting his little tutor friend so I can have some peace. "This is supposed to be a celebration," he reminds me.

"Yeah, for some rookie on your team that we don't know," Royce gripes, as pumped to be at a club as I am. I don't want to be here because I'm an antisocial bastard, but it's probably taking everything within Royce to remain inside the building. He hates these things, with good reason. "What nineteen-year-old comes to a burlesque club?" he continues to gripe. "Shouldn't he be at a strip club in Springview or something?"

Logan simply shrugs, too busy casting his eyes around the room. The club only opened during the summer. However, it has become immensely popular, especially with the rich Halston U students. It's classier than a typical bar or club, and less sleazy than your standard strip club—although I've heard, if you talk to the manager, you can avail of the same services here. While most people probably come for the performances and the atmosphere, others will be seeking the more private, intimate services the club provides on a *hush-hush* basis.

"Have a drink, bro," Logan says, nudging Royce's shoulder. "Let some girl wiggle her tits in your face and go blow your load in the bathroom. Might help loosen that rod you've got lodged in your ass."

"Fuck off, asshole," Royce growls, grabbing Logan in a chokehold before the two of them proceed to act like idiots in the middle of a crowded club.

Shaking my head, I increase my strides as I close in on the bar. Once I reach it, I hold my hand up to gain the bartender's attention and order myself a whiskey. As soon as he slides the glass my way, I knock it back, instantly feeling the tightness in my chest loosen.

Even getting blind drunk won't be enough to obliterate the weight on my shoulders, but a few drinks will help, for a while at least. It's not as though my problems are going anywhere. They'll be there waiting for me tomorrow, alongside my hangover. And most likely a barked phone call of orders from my father.

*So much to look forward to.*

The other two order their drinks before the three of us wind our way through the room, searching for Logan's teammates.

It's impossible to miss a crowd of hockey players. They stick out like sore thumbs with their height and broad shoulders, so it's surprising when we don't immediately spot them.

"Yo, bro! Over here!" Gavin, one of Logan's teammates, calls, waving us over to a portion of the club sectioned off behind thick, red velvet ropes.

"VIP. Nice one," Logan mutters as we step into the exclusive area currently occupied by the entire Halston U ice hockey team, all of whom are sprawled across various booths and chairs.

There is a second, smaller stage, where a performer is putting on a solo show, garnering the attention of most of the team.

"Hey," Logan greets, giving some of the guys a chin lift in

greeting as we walk past. "Happy birthday!" He reaches over to fist-bump the birthday boy while I move to the side of the cordoned-off area and lower myself onto one of the plush booths.

From here, I can look out over the entire club, my gaze landing on the main stage as I watch the performers sway their hips, teasing the audience with the silver sequin pasties covering their nipples.

I'm distracted by red-painted nails as they stroke along my shoulder, and a woman wearing a red and black stripe corset with frilly black lace around the edges and a short, black, tulle skirt that most likely shows her panties when she bends over as she moves to stand in front of me.

"Can I get you a drink?" she asks in a low, seductive voice that implies she's offering a lot more than a drink. I rake my eyes appreciatively over her body before lifting my gaze to her face as I mull over my answer.

*Fuck, when was the last time I got laid?*

A no-strings-attached blow job would probably be a better stress reliever than alcohol. Despite that, I settle for a scotch —for now.

Nodding, she saunters off and I go back to watching the main stage as the next performance gets underway. This time, it's a sole performer. She strides confidently into the center of the stage where she stands with her head lowered, legs hip-width apart, dressed in a shimmering, ruby-red corset adorned with black lace and sequins that glitter beneath the bright stage lights. Long, elegant gloves reach up her arms which are held out at her sides as the first sultry note drifts into the air.

She begins to move, and I stare, captivated. With a flick of her wrist, she expertly removes her gloves, letting them slide down her arms and fall gracefully on the floor. The move gains the attention of every red-blooded male in the room, and my dick twitches in my pants as the music intensifies and she sways her hips in time to the rhythm, teasing the audience with each subtle movement.

From this angle, I can't see her face, and I find myself mentally demanding that she look this way. I'm so caught up in her performance that I don't notice the red-nailed woman has returned until she pushes my drink into my hand.

"Who's that?" I ask, indicating the dancer on the stage.

The waitress follows my line of sight before answering, "Aurora Noir."

"Aurora Noir," I repeat, liking the way her name rolls off my tongue. It's a stage name, obviously—one that has my blood heating with a desire I haven't felt in a long time.

"She's a *performer*," the waitress states, emphasizing the word *performer*. The subtle implication isn't lost on me—she *only* performs on stage. I can't say I'm disappointed. Though as my attention drifts back to the stage, I decide that for now I'm happy to sit and watch my enchantress lure every man in the room into her web.

Huffing under her breath, the waitress moves to step away, but I snap out a hand and ensnare her wrist. Wrenching my eyes from the stage, I trail them over her body. It's not the one I want, but should the need arise, it would do. "Stay close. I might have use for you later."

She gives me a coy smirk, nodding before I let go of her wrist and turn back to the stage as the performance reaches its climax. Aurora unhooks her garter, sliding it down her leg before hooking it over her heel and tossing it into the audience. The hypnotic display results in a moment of silence as the music ends, before the room erupts into thunderous applause.

"Fucking hell, that was way hotter than it should be," Royce mutters, momentarily startling me. I hadn't even realized he'd joined me.

Ignoring him, I lean forward in my seat as the woman on the stage bows, before lifting her head to bid the crowd farewell.

*Look this way. Look this way.*

My fingers dig into the arms of the chair as I silently plead for a glimpse of her face.

And then, as if granted this one singular wish, she turns and my vision is eclipsed by soft, pink lips, upturned in a shy smile, long dark lashes, and seductive rosy cheeks.

I suck in a shocked gasp, momentarily taken aback by her beauty.

However, it's more than that...

Not only is she beautiful, but I fucking *know* her.

"Hey, man, you alright?" Royce asks, nudging my shoulder.

I absently nod, gaze still riveted on the girl across the room.

My eyes bounce over her body as my pulsing desire gives way to something darker, dangerous. My teeth grind, the muscles in my jaw pulling tight.

Not one to give up easily, Royce pushes, "You know her?"

Fuck yeah, I do.

"What are we staring at?" Logan asks, apparently done socializing with his teammates as he drops into a seat on my other side, taking a sip from his beer bottle before also peering in the direction I'm staring.

"Whoa, who's the hottie?" She turns in our direction once again, giving a final wave before she flounces off the stage, and as she does, Logan's body stiffens. His eyes flash with confusion as he leans forward in his chair. "What the fuck?!" he mutters to himself. "Riley?"

At the sound of her name on his tongue, I tear my gaze away from the now-empty stage to focus on my best friend. Eyes narrowed on him, I bark, "You know her?"

He doesn't seem to hear me as he continues to gape in the

direction she disappeared, so I take the time to observe him. Each one of his emotions is plain to read on his face—confusion, hurt, surprise, uncertainty. And buried underneath each of them is lust.

Finally feeling the pressure of my stare, he turns to face me, eyes wide and brows furrowed. His focus shifts to Royce before returning to mine. "She's the one who's been tutoring me this semester."

Tutoring him? But he's taking a freshman class. Does that mean Riley is a freshman? It would be unusual, given that she's only two years younger than us, but not impossible.

"No way, that's her?" Royce gapes. "And here I've been picturing a shy, quiet, nerdy girl who spends all her free time in the library."

Still laughing, he focuses back on the stage as a group of dancers appears. The three of us fall silent, and I scour the stage until I find her. Her auburn hair is a beacon drawing my eyes as she moves into position for the next performance.

Royce shifts beside me, shuffling closer as he curses under his breath, and I turn to look at him, arching a brow in a silent question, which he ignores as he glares at the stage.

Not sure what to make of his change in behavior, I focus back on Logan, determined to get some answers from him. "She attends Halston?"

"Yeah," Logan confirms. "She's this year's scholarship student."

*Guess that explains how she's affording the astronomical Halston U fees.*

But why the fuck is she here? At *my* college. In *my* town. In *this* club.

"Why wouldn't she tell me this is where she works?" Logan mutters, clearly talking to himself.

That's when it *really* clicks. She's not *just* his tutor. She's the girl he's been chasing. The one who went to his game and who he took on a date last week.

She's the girl Logan has fucking fallen for.

"Seriously?" I snarl more furiously than I intend. "*She's* the one you've been chasing after?"

His eyes narrow on me in warning. For the most part, Logan is a golden retriever. It makes it easy to forget he's an absolute pitbull on the ice—or when someone threatens the people he cares for.

"No. Abso-fucking-lutely not. You are not to go anywhere near her."

I'm practically yelling at him, and realizing I sound completely unreasonable I clamp my mouth shut. I have no idea what game she's playing at, getting close to Logan and toying with his emotions, but I downright refuse to let her sink her claws into him, too.

By now, he's staring at me like I've grown a third head.

"Dude, chill out," Royce says in a low voice. "You're drawing attention."

Forcing myself to take a deep breath, I stare Logan straight in the eyes, and in my most serious tone, I hiss, "She's off limits. Trust me, man, you do not want to put your dick in that."

"Holy shit," Royce gasps. I'm guessing he's put two and two together while Logan still looks mystified. "She's the girl?"

They both know about my tumultuous past that has led me to this point, and Logan cops on immediately, eyes widening in shock and a silent plea for me to be wrong.

Holding his gaze, I nod. "She's the girl."

"No way." He shakes his head, refusing to believe what his ears are hearing. "That can't be. There's no way she's the same girl."

"Believe me, man. She is. I wouldn't lie to you."

"But, she's so sweet. And innocent." Tearing his gaze away,

he turns to watch her as she dances on the stage, oblivious to our piercing gazes. His eyebrows flatten in uncertainty. "We had a connection."

When the performance comes to an end and the spotlight dims, the lights in the rest of the room brighten and I catch sight of the pain etched into his features.

*Fuck. He truly fell for her.*

A fresh wave of anger crashes through my veins, igniting the oil drum of hatred that has been simmering for Riley James for the last four years. How dare she cause Logan, of all people, pain.

This is all her fault. I understand that and yet, knowing my confession has gutted him makes me feel like total shit. Guilt gnaws at me despite knowing, in the long run, I'm doing him a favor.

The blame lies with her. She's the one who lied to him. Used him. Who is pretending to be someone they aren't... and for what purpose? What does she want with Logan? Hasn't she done enough damage? She has to sink her claws into him, too? Logan who is a genuinely real and decent guy. Who would sooner give someone the shirt off his back than see them go without. Who struggles daily to appease his friends and his family and do right by everyone while also fighting for what he wants.

Fuck no.

I refuse to let her destroy another life.

To steal the happiness that emanates from Logan and provides the only source of hope Royce and I cling to on our darkest of days.

My vision blurs with the intensity of my rage, and I struggle to maintain control over my thoughts. Everything is screaming at me to get up. To hunt her down and demand my pound of flesh. The anger is relentless, fueled by memories as it pushes me to the brink of losing myself to the darkness within.

It's only a hand on my shoulder that pulls me back from the edge. My vision clears, a sliver of awareness breaking through the maelstrom of emotions as a small voice whispers *she deserves worse than what you can do now.*

That one thought pushes back the darkness and enables me to tune back into the conversation as Royce asks, "What is she doing at Halston?"

"Same as every other student?" Logan says with too-casual of a shrug. "Getting a degree."

Ignoring him, Royce shifts his attention to me. "Do you think she followed you here?"

I shrug, only half paying attention as I mull over the words *she deserves worse.* "No clue."

I never had any intention of letting Riley get away with what she did. Between school and everything else, I haven't had an opportunity to give her any real consideration.

However, now that she's been hand-delivered to my doorstep, I think I'll move dealing with her to the top of my to-do list.

Deciding the voice in the back of my head is right, and Riley deserves far worse than anything I could do if I confronted her here and now, an evil smirk tugs at my lips.

Spotting it, Royce nudges my shoulder, a conniving twinkle in his eye. "Why do I get the feeling you're scheming?"

"Maybe because I am."

The three of us lapse into silence, and I lose myself in my thoughts as Riley reappears in a new outfit for another group performance. She remains oblivious to our eyes on her, and while I watch the lying enchantress, my dick twitches like a traitorous bastard, paying no heed to the warning I just gave Logan.

Despite the hostility simply seeing her elicits, there's no denying how beautiful Riley has become. The last time I laid eyes on her, she was fifteen and painstakingly beautiful. Seventeen and ruled by hormones, she held me captivated. No other girl at school held a candle to her. It made it next to impossible for me to be around her, and instead I resorted to lurking in the shadows and watching from a distance...

*The sound of water splashing in our pool has me gravitating outside, wondering who would be up this early. The sun is barely cresting the horizon, my hangover hitting me hard from last night's party. I should still be passed out in bed, but when I woke up in Charlie's guest bedroom with some naked chick beside me, I knew it was my opportunity to sneak out before she woke and the waterworks began.*

*I pause in the doorway, my gaze landing on a now familiar lithe form as it cuts a path through the pool, reaching the far end before doing a flip and coming back. I should leave. It's not appropriate for me to be standing here watching her, yet my feet remain rooted to the floor, the shadows of the doorway hiding me from view as I watch her like a creeper.*

*Slick creamy skin. Auburn hair, the copper strands shining in the early morning rays.*

*Riley James has become an inconvenient obsession. One that space and distraction have not succeeded in purging from my mind.*

*At the end of her next stroke, she hauls herself out of the pool, water sluicing from her slim form as every inch of her dancer's body is put on display for me to memorize. It doesn't matter that she's two years younger than me and one hundred percent off-limits. I can't drag my eyes away as she turns to sit on the edge of the pool, her legs and feet dangling in the water.*

*Even in a basic one-piece, she's more captivating than the girls strutting around wearing basically nothing at last night's party. I'm held entranced as she tips her head back, face lifted to the early morning light. She's beautiful. Sadness clings to her features, carved into each of the tiny freckles dotting her cheeks. I overheard Dad saying she's been having a hard time adjusting. I wish I could help. I want to help. I've done everything I can to put her at ease from afar —friendly smiles, saying hi when we cross paths at school—but I'm afraid to get any closer. I'm sure she just needs time. She'll make some friends, settle into her classes, start dating someone in her year.*

*I try not to think about that last one. By fall, I'll be off to college, and with that distance, I'll be able to get over this little... obsession.*

*But for now, I stand and drink in every inch of her beauty.*

Yes, Riley James was pretty when she was fifteen, but watching her on the stage now, she's... magnetic. Her body has filled out in all the right places, changing from that of a teenage girl to a curvaceous woman. However, her face is the same.

So familiar, even after all this time.

Not that I could ever forget the face of the girl who destroyed my family.

Who tarnished our generations-old name.

Who ruined my entire life.

My fucking stepsister.

## CHAPTER FOURTEEN

Tapping my pen against mine and Logan's usual table in the library, I check the time on my phone for what must be the hundredth time. He's late. Beyond late. Is an hour late, late? Or does it officially count as a no-show at this point?

A sinking pit opens in my stomach.

I've been worried for days now. After his speech on Thursday night about wanting to see and talk to me every day, things were great on Friday and Saturday. He texted me good morning, and we chatted on and off during the day. We had Statistics together, and I FaceTimed him before Friday and Saturday's games.

But since then, it's been radio silence. No good morning text. No mention of meeting up on Sunday. I'm not *that girl*, so after he didn't respond to my text on Sunday morning, hoping he had fun with his teammates on Saturday night, I didn't harass him any further.

Initially, I'd figured he was simply hungover, but I began to worry when I still hadn't heard anything yesterday. Yet, I stil

However, now he's a no-show for our tutoring session—the first time all semester that he has missed one—and that festering concern has become a bubbling pit of worry.

Feeling queasy, I open my chat with him while gnawing on my bottom lip.

ME

Hey, are you running late?

Did you forget about our session today?

Just wanted to check that everything is okay...

Every single one of my messages has gone unread, and I refuse to send any more and come across as desperate or needy, or give away the fact I'm just a little bit worried. What if something happened? I know he wasn't injured in Saturday's game, although what if something happened when he was out that night? Or he could have been hurt in training since then.

*Or perhaps it was all pretty words and he's done with you now.*

I hate how that negative voice pipes up, trampling over my self-esteem.

Is it possible that I misjudged Logan?

*God, I hope not.*

However, his continued silence is leading to more and more self-doubt.

Turning my phone upside down on the table so I'll stop glancing at the screen every five seconds, I focus on the Chemistry textbook open in front of me. Or at least, I *try* to focus on it. Chemistry barely holds my interest on the best of days, and today is definitely not one of those days.

I struggle through another hour, barely retaining anything before I give up. Slamming the textbook closed, I pout at my phone before reaching out a hand, already knowing what I will find when I look.

*Oh, look at that. No response from him.*

Sighing, I drop it on the table and lower my head.

"Look who it is! The charity case," a snide voice interrupts my pity party. Snapping my head up, my eyes narrow on the bitchy blonde from orientation—Whitney White. Her father is a big name in green energy. His innovations actually show the most promise with regard to reducing global warming... doesn't mean his daughter isn't a complete bitch, though.

Unsurprisingly, we run in very different social circles, so other than a few classes we share together where she's constantly giving me the stink eye, I haven't had to endure her sunny personality.

However, I do feel the full weight of her glower on the back of my head in every Statistics class, which I'm pretty sure I'm earning because Logan keeps sitting beside me instead of her. She wins points for persistence, though. Every week, she tries to coax him to sit with her. And every week, he refuses.

Despite that, she hasn't caused me any issues... until now.

"Should have known I'd find you in the library."

"Here I am," I state, in no mood for whatever this is. "If you want help with Stats, you're barking up the wrong tree."

Her nose scrunches. "Eww. No. Why would I need your help with anything?"

I could point out the fact that she's failing Stats—something which I heard her complaining to one of her friends about after our last class test—but I don't give a shit, so I don't bother.

Instead, I do my best to ignore her as I shove my belongings into my bag, making a point of not looking at my phone screen as I stuff it into my jeans pocket.

Blondie stands there, watching me the entire time, until, huffing, I spin to face her.

"Well, this has been a great chat, Tiffany. Let's not do this again."

Her nostrils flare as her eyes flood with petty righteousness. "It's Whitney."

Whatever.

I step around her but she slides into my path, planting her hands on her hips. "Why is Logan hanging around with you?"

Giving her a deadpan look, I state, "I'm his Stats tutor."

Rolling her eyes as though I'm dense, she huffs out a breath. "I know that, stupid. I mean, why did he acknowledge you at his game last week? Everyone is talking about it." They are? "And people say he's been hanging out with you outside of your little... study sessions." Brows furrowed as though she's been presented with a complicated math equation, she flips her long blonde hair over her shoulder. "I thought he was just using you to pass Professor Caldwell's class." Her eyes rake over me, face scrunching in disdain. "Maybe pity fucking you on the side." *Truly delightful girl... I'm thoroughly enjoying this exchange.* "But to acknowledge you at the game... that's like WAG behavior. It just doesn't make sense."

"WAG?"

"Even if he was fucking you. You'd be like a desperate, less attractive puck bunny; he would never pull that stunt with one of them. I mean, Logan has never acknowledged any girl at one of his games before. So why you?"

I merely blink at her, and when I take too long to answer her supposed question, she tilts her head and raises her eyebrows. Does she seriously expect me to answer that? Even if I had an answer for her, I wouldn't share it.

"Sounds like this is a question you should be asking Logan."

She rolls her petulant eyes. "Like anyone can find him. He's been AWOL all week." An evil smirk tugs at her lips. "Maybe he's come to his senses and realized how damaging it would be to his reputation to be seen with you. Poor guy is probably holed up under his bed in a ball of shame." She taps the center of her botoxed lips with her long, manicured nail. "I should take him a bowl of chicken soup—make sure he's okay."

Yeah *chicken soup.*

"You do that," I snap, irritated. "At least if you're with him, you aren't here bothering me."

Unwilling to listen to her tear me down anymore or discuss exactly how good her *chicken soup* is, I move past her, shoving my shoulder into hers and smiling as she stumbles into the table.

"Hey!"

I ignore the entitled brat as I walk away, doing my best to pick out the thorns left behind by her sharp barbs.

I know there's no truth behind what she said, but that doesn't stop her words from seeping into my brain, unlocking my insecurities and sending them surging to the forefront.

Is that why Logan has been hiding all week? Because he's regretting spending time with me? What if someone said something to him and made him realize he shouldn't be hanging out with me? Has his attention been out of pity?

The questions cycle round and round in a vicious circle, slicing deeper with each rotation until my heart is bleeding freely and the walk to my apartment is a blur.

*Honestly, this is a good thing,* I try to tell myself. It's a necessary reminder not to lower my guard around Logan. He's excellent at making me feel as though I matter. I thought we were friends. Hell, after last week, I thought we were more than friends. However, even if everything Whitney says is bullshit, his silence only proves that this relationship is nothing more than a simple transaction to him. One that leans heavily in his favor.

Shoving my disappointment in the hockey player aside, I stomp into my apartment. Thankfully, Ava and Isabella are due any minute for dinner tonight, which will distract me from thinking about Logan for a few hours.

I've barely had time to quickly tidy the apartment when there is a knock at the door.

"Riley!" Isabella cries, rushing into my apartment. "Sleepover!"

I sweep her into my arms, giving her a hug.

"No, baby. Not a sleepover," Ava clarifies, rolling her eyes at me as she follows Isabella inside. "Only dinner."

Isabella grins mischievously, and it instantly brightens my mood. *God, I really needed this.*

I wink conspiratorially at her before setting her back down on her feet. "I have Frozen set up on my laptop if you wanna watch it?"

Her eyes widen and she nods her head vigorously. I point to where I left my laptop sitting on the coffee table, and she grabs her blankie from her mom before getting cozy on my small sofa.

"Sorry about that," Ava says, setting a casserole dish on the counter. "She got it into her head that it was a sleepover, and no matter how many times I tried to tell her otherwise, she wouldn't listen."

"It's okay," I insist, secretly loving the fact Isabella wants to have a sleepover in my apartment. "She can absolutely spend the night."

"I don't want to put you out," Ava begins instantly.

"You wouldn't be," I admit, glancing over to where Isabella is curled up on her side on the sofa, head resting on a cushion and her hand wrapped around her blanket, thumb in her mouth as she stares unblinkingly at the laptop screen. "Honestly, I'd love to have her and could do with the distraction."

"Uh-oh, bad week?" Ava asks while I lift the casserole and put it in the oven to heat before grabbing a bottle of wine and two glasses. The two of us get comfy at my small, rickety kitchen table before I answer.

With my full glass in hand, I groan. "C-R-A-P-P-Y," I spell out, since young ears are always listening, even if you think they aren't.

"What does that spell?" Isabella asks, making us both laugh. *See!* Always listening, even though her focus didn't once shift from the screen.

"Watch your movie, and let the grown-ups talk. Otherwise, there will be no sleepover," Ava warns her daughter.

Isabella gasps before slamming her lips shut and covering them with her hands.

It takes everything in me not to laugh.

Ava points at the laptop and Isabella goes back to watching the movie before Ava asks me. "Why? What happened?"

I shake my head. "Nothing, really. I, uh, went on this date with a guy last week. We've been hanging out a lot recently. I was tutoring him, but we both seemed to develop feelings and anyway, we went on a date last week. And I thought everything went great, but I haven't heard from him all week."

Ava looks at me with sympathy. "I'm sorry. That sucks. I know it doesn't make you feel better, but it's his loss if he's decided to ghost you."

"Yeah, I know," I sigh. "I just thought he was different."

"Yup," Ava says with an attitude, sounding as though she knows all too well. "Those are the guys that'll get you."

I don't know the specifics of her circumstances, who Isabella's dad is, or if he's in the picture at all, and because I know I don't want people prying into my life, I don't ask. If she wants to tell me, she will.

"I'll get over it," I say, more nonchalant than I feel. "It just sucks."

Reaching across the table, she squeezes my hand. "Well, if you ever need to talk, I'm here."

"Me too!" Isabella shouts from the sofa.

Laughing, I grab my glass of wine and move to join her, pulling her into my lap as all the stress of the day washes away.

I don't set eyes on Logan for the rest of the week, but it doesn't stop me from constantly thinking about him. In class. During rehearsals. At the dance studio. I search for him when I walk across campus and check my phone religiously in the hopes of there being a text from him.

Yet I'm always disappointed. So by the end of the week I'm wondering if I imagined everything I thought was between us. Or did I just completely misjudge him?

---

As soon as I step through the doors of Lux on Friday night, Ben glances up from his phone. His leering gaze trails over me, leaving an oiliness on my skin despite the layers I'm wearing, before he drawls, "You have been specifically requested for a private performance."

I stiffen. "I'm only supposed to be on stage," I remind him as an elastic band tightens around my chest, making breathing difficult. At my interview, I made a point of ensuring this job didn't require me to be on the floor. As uncomfortable as I was when I first started dancing on the stage, I would have been ten times more discomfited if I'd had to work the floor as a member of the waitstaff.

Then, I discovered that Lux offered more than just dancing

and delivering drinks. Tara had assured me that the girls partake willingly and that if I didn't want to, I didn't have to, but now Ben is looking at me like I don't have a choice in this, and I feel as though my lungs have forgotten how to function.

I have nothing against the girls who choose to do *extras.* I understand better than anyone that you will do whatever is necessary to make ends meet, but anything other than being on the stage is a hard limit for me. I doubt patrons want to see me curled up in a ball, mumbling to myself and rocking back and forth because they touched me, and I freaked out.

I'm sure Ben doesn't want that either. It wouldn't be good for the club after all. However, I can't make my lips form the words to express my deepest vulnerability, especially when he looks down his nose at me in that superior way.

"Nothing I can do about it."

*Of course, there isn't. It's not like he's the manager or anything.*

Lux doesn't even provide private shows other than what is offered in the VIP area. This arrangement has been made off the books between Ben and whoever requested me—a thought that makes my stomach sour and nerves take flight as I fight to quell my internal panic. Who is this person? What do they want from me? How can Ben so easily pimp me out like that without even asking me?

I blink dumbly at him. "I can't do it," I blurt, voice pitched in panic. "It's not part of my job description. I don't have to do it."

He arches an arrogant eyebrow, lips pressing into a tight line.

The seconds tick endlessly before he straightens, sighing as he lowers his hand holding the phone. "If you don't want to do it, that's fine..." There's a split second of hope before he crushes it beneath his malicious smirk. "You're welcome to quit, and I'll find another girl to take your spot."

Such a fucking asshole. He knows I won't quit. That I can't.

Like most of the girls here, I *need* this job. I make more money a night than I would a week in any other job. In such a small town, there are slim pickings for jobs, and most are minimum wage or based primarily on tips—shitty tips that would barely cover my rent.

Normally, the Halston scholarship covers educational fees and accommodation, but the university is renovating one of the student dorms this year, reducing the amount of student housing available.

Accommodation had to be provided to the school's full-paying students first, along with those scholarship students in later years with whom they'd already signed contracts. Which left little old me without any student dorm to stay in. Not even a converted supply closet—trust me, I practically begged for them to offer me that as an alternative.

Instead, I was left to find my own accommodation and means of paying for it. I'd already planned on getting a part-time job while here, but I could have done without the extra expenses eating into my paycheck. The only small mercy is the free food in the school's dining hall—so you know damn well I eat breakfast, lunch, and dinner there.

I hold his unwavering gaze as defeat beats a noxious drum against my chest. He already knows what my answer will be. I do, too, but it takes a moment for the reality to fully register. For me to accept the situation I've found myself in.

"No, I'll do it," I state in a weak voice, worrying my bottom lip as I try to gather the mental fortitude to do what is required of me. *I'm only giving a little,* I remind myself. *It's really not all that different from being on stage.*

I walk into the dressing rooms as though I'm heading to the gallows, thankful that Tara isn't there. I'm barely holding it together, and if I had to see her sympathetic face, I'd crumble. Going straight to the rail with our costumes hanging on it, I pause with my hand outstretched, realizing I shouldn't wear my costume for tonight's first performance if I'm not in it.

My brain is foggy, and I'm unable to think straight as I stare absently at the other racks of clothing, only managing to snap out of it when the door bangs open and two of the waitstaff stride in, giggling as they gossip with one another.

Unfortunately, I can't hide out here all night, and the longer I keep Ben and whoever this man is waiting, the worse it will be for me. With unsteady hands, I grab the closest outfit and fumble through getting changed, careful to not thoroughly look at myself as I apply my makeup and slide on my heels before walking out the door on shaking legs.

"He's in booth number four," Ben states when I emerge onto the floor, unaware that his words have my adrenaline spiking to dangerous levels. The booths Ben is referring to are large semi-circular areas draped in gauze curtains, which can be pulled to provide an element of privacy or tucked back and left exposed to the rest of the club.

Glancing toward booth number four, I notice the curtains are already drawn. My feet are cemented to the floor, and I can't seem to make myself move toward it.

"Well, go on," Ben barks. "Don't want to keep him waiting."

My head whips to face him, and he smirks at the unmistakable dread drenching my features. I won't find any sympathy from him. "W-who is he?" I ask, voice wavering.

He shrugs. "No idea. Just waltzed in and asked for you."

"Y-you're sure it's me he wants?"

"Do you know of another Aurora Noir I'm not aware of?"

Fuck, if he knew my stage name then it's definitely not a mistake. I watch my last thread of hope disappear like a balloon into the sky, and when Ben gives me a warning glare, I force my feet forward.

It's only when I'm standing, shaking like a leaf, outside the gauzy curtains that I realize I never asked what the man wanted. A dance is one thing. Dancing I can do... I think, but anything more...

Blackness rushes in and I fight to push it away.

*No!*

Would Ben do that? It's one thing to make a bit of money on the side facilitating private dances and extras with willing girls. That could be perceived as a gray area, but forcing me to do anything sexual—that's a far greater crime.

*It's just a dance,* I tell myself.

*God, what if he's some fat, old man who saw me on stage?*

*What if he* has *paid for more than just a dance?*

*I can't...*

The loud music fades, *his* deep, demanding baritone replacing it.

*Such a good girl.*

Cold sweat breaks out along my skin, bile burning a rancid path up the back of my throat.

"I won't bite... unless you want me to."

A rich voice, smooth like dark chocolate, brushes against my skin, chasing *his* away, and I blink back into the dark, sultry atmosphere of the club.

Swallowing, I slowly count to three before pulling the gossamer curtain aside. Ignoring my still trembling hands, I tuck Riley away before stepping into the secluded booth, replacing her with Aurora Noir. Simply the reminder of my daughter's name reminds me why I'm here. Why I'm doing this. Whatever is required of me, I will persevere—for her. To win her back. To provide for her. To be the mom I never had.

Lifting my chin, I portray a confidence I don't feel as I slip into Aurora Noir—a mysterious, unattainable sexual symbol.

One which men can look at yet cannot touch.

The persona only lasts until my eyes fall on the man's wild, dark hair, sharp cheekbones, and ice-blue eyes before my walls crumble.

"You." The word falls from my lips before I can stop it.

What is *he* doing here?

Ruthless.

The last time I saw him, he saved me from some handsy asshole and I told him to go fuck himself. And all that after I told him I'd rather eat horse shit than taste his cum. Admittedly, neither were my finest moments, but I felt it was sufficient to get the point across that I wasn't interested.

Clearly, I was wrong. Not only did he not believe me then, but the fact he's here surely means he's decided to move the ball to his court.

Except, the ball was never in *my* court. There is no fucking court. We're not even playing the same sport.

On the plus side, my crushing anxiety has given way to anger—an emotion I'm far more comfortable managing.

"Me," he retorts, smirking like the cat who got the cream.

There's a raw cunning behind his eyes. An astute awareness that hints at the deliberate nature of this move.

How the hell did he even find me?

This can't possibly be a coincidence. The fact he specifically *asked* for me tells me it isn't. It tells me, since the last time we crossed paths, he's been looking into me—a fact that sits uncomfortably in my stomach as I scowl down at him.

Tilting my head, I run my gaze over his relaxed posture, taking note of the *I could destroy you with the flick of my wrist* vibes he's practically pumping into the air.

"Why are you really here?"

He glances lazily past me, out onto the main club floor. "For a dance, of course. Why else would someone come here?"

"I'm not sucking your dick," I blurt before closing my eyes as I internally cringe.

*Subtle, Riley.*

His chuckle is the most pompous sound I've ever heard.

"I believe you've given me this spiel already. If I remember correctly, it went something like you'd rather bathe in horse shit, dunk your face in acid, and rub your body in gasoline before you suck my dick."

I'd feel bad if he didn't look so fucking cocky.

"Then why are you here?" I repeat. "I thought I made my point last time, but if you need me to spell it out more clearly..."

That unwavering smirk continues. Is the asshole enjoying this?

"Maybe I plan on making you eat your words, Babydoll."

Ignoring his stupid nickname meant to rile me up, and how rough and rasping his voice is—it's totally unfair that such an ugly personality can be wrapped in such a sinful body—I scoff, momentarily forgetting that pissing him off could result in me incurring Ben's wrath and ultimately losing my job.

"How did you know who I was? That I worked here?" I ask instead, moving the topic of conversation to safer territory.

At my sharp tone, his gaze narrows, eyes scouring my face before slowly lowering to trace over the swell of my breasts and curves of my hips, enhanced by the restraining fabric of my corset.

His facial features may as well be carved from stone. I couldn't read him if I had a magnifying glass and a map.

"I paid for a dance, not an interrogation," he drawls in a detached tone, following it up with a haughty arch of his eyebrow when I fail to move.

After a drawn-out moment, his gaze shifts to something behind me. "*Or,* I could go tell your manager that I'm not getting my money's worth."

My fingers twitch with the desire to curl into a fist as I grind my molars. One side of the asshole's lips lifts in what can only be his version of a smile. He knows damn well he's cornered me.

Reluctantly, with stiff, awkward movements, I step between his parted legs and begin to sway my hips. There's no enthusiasm behind it. No desire.

Only pure, mechanical movement.

After several tense moments, where the air thickens with tension until it's suffocating, he huffs out a breath. "You can do better than that, Babydoll. I've seen you on that stage." Lowering his voice to a whisper, he says, "I know how bewitchingly you can dance."

# ROYCE

## CHAPTER FIFTEEN

Riley forces her body to relax, but it's obvious she isn't as confident as she was when I watched her on stage last weekend. The fluidity; the ease at which she moved, none of that is present. Her body was like a piece of art, the way it gracefully transitioned around the stage that night, but now... the movements are stiff. Forced. There's no desire. No compulsion to bend to the music's will.

Regardless, she looks just as beautiful as she did last time, in her deep navy corset with black lace, short black skirt, garter, and stockings. She's every man's wet dream, her auburn hair and smattering of freckles along the bridge of her nose only adding to her appeal.

What truly holds my attention, though, is the anxiety pouring off her like a perfume. Her pupils are dilated with it, her breathing out of sync, even as she tries to hide it behind her blazing eyes and defiant attitude.

Knowing she's highly uncomfortable brings a smirk to my lips. It was incredibly easy to get the manager to agree to letting me spend some time alone with her. In any other circumstance, I'd be revolted, but then I recalled the fucked up shit Riley pulled that destroyed Grayson's family and any sympathy I have for her quickly gives way to hatred.

Women like her... they reel you in. Make you feel sorry for them. Have you wanting to help them, then they stomp all over you in their effort to accomplish their fucked up agenda.

It's fucking disgusting.

I'll admit, after her attitude when we crashed into one another outside the dining hall, and again when I cornered her at the warehouse, I was intrigued. Not enough to seek her out, but enough that those hypnotizing green eyes have occasionally weaseled their way into my dreams. The defiant glare the first time I snapped at her was so unlike the haughty arrogance of other Halston girls. The fact she called me on my shit—no one has ever had the balls to do that. Even Gray and Logan have been tip-toeing around me these last few months.

When I realized the girl on stage was the same one who throws nothing but attitude at me, even when I tell her to get on her knees in a dirty, dingy bar, I was taken for a loop. I can't make sense of any of it. I've been struggling to separate the lies from the truth all week. Which is ultimately why I ended up here tonight.

After what she did to Grayson, was she planning on making me her next target? Did she hear of my history and think I'd be an easy target for her next conquest? And what of Logan? What were her plans with him?

There are too many unknowns. Too many questions I don't have answers for. Past experience has taught me there is no such thing as coincidence, and if this girl is targeting me or Logan, then it's up to me to do my due diligence. This time, I won't ignore the signs and look the other way.

I almost fucking believed the words that came out of those poisonous lips of hers, but knowing what I do now, I can only come to one logical conclusion... She was playing me.

Of course she was.

That's all girls like her do.

Play people like they are their own fucking puppets to manipulate and control.

I can feel my anger reaching a boiling point, and I close my eyes, forcing myself to take a deep breath. My hand clenches into a fist on my knee. I can't lose my shit here, in front of her. Can't allow her to pick up on any weaknesses.

Opening my eyes, I banish those thoughts as I focus on her smooth skin, toned thighs, and tight ass as she twirls in front of me. Trailing my gaze skyward, I smirk when I spot her jaw ticking.

That anger gives way to a sense of accomplishment. I had no specific plan in mind when I waltzed in here and demanded a private performance from Aurora Noir, but now that I know how uneasy it makes her to be off the stage and this close to me, I can sense a plan forming.

Knowing that my proximity gets a rise out of her. That my actions are forcing her to do something she doesn't want. That I'm pressing her buttons and getting on her nerves.

I like knowing that I'm pissing her off. Even better, I like the thought of being a thorn in her side every single time she steps through those doors. She doesn't deserve peace after what she did to Grayson and whatever game she was playing with me and Logan. She doesn't deserve that moment of tranquility that washed over her when she was dancing on the stage.

Her eyes flare with a defiant spark, promising all sorts of retribution that I know she won't deliver on. She can't. Not if she wants to continue working here, and based on her scholarship status, I'd hazard that she can't afford to lose her job.

Grayson hasn't figured out his plan for her yet, so until he does, I intend to keep a close eye on her. I'm going to become the shadow that stalks her every move. The leech stuck to her skin. As annoying as the incessant buzzing of an overhead fly.

I'll be the bane of her existence. The constant reminder that her actions have not gone unpunished.

And I'll take great fucking pleasure in watching her face crease with annoyance every time she sees me. Watching the way her spine straightens when she's forced to dance for me. Seeing the fear in her eyes when she feels my presence looming nearby but doesn't spot me hidden in the shadows.

Riley James thinks she has the world wrapped around her dainty little fingers, and I'm about to prove how one harsh tug will have everything she thought she knew ripped out from beneath her feet.

---

Half an hour later, I stroll through the front door of the townhouse I share with Logan and Grayson. We've lived here since our sophomore year at Halston. Most students choose to stay in the Halston dorms all throughout college, but for us, one year of that was enough.

"Where have you been?" Grayson grouses.

His mood has been shittier than a blocked toilet ever since he set eyes on Riley at the club. Not that I can blame him, per se. Between the three of us, we're a sorry bunch these days. Before this, *I* was the one with issues—not that I didn't have a good reason to be. Grayson has always been a moody asshole, but Logan has always been the one who lifts us all up. I genuinely believed nothing could ever get him down for long—until this whole shit with Riley. Depressed and Logan don't belong in the same sentence, but that's the best way to describe his mood since he discovered the girl he was crushing on was the same one who destroyed Grayson's life and blew up his family.

My attention shifts to where he's slumped in his seat, looking exhausted and defeated. It only serves to light my anger anew. The fact this girl has the power to bring Logan down... she doesn't deserve to have that control over him. Not when every little thing she has said and done to wiggle her way into his life has been a lie. It has to be.

She can't be the sweet, innocent girl Logan claims she is *and* the lying, selfish, manipulative bitch Grayson knew. Even I know she's not as sweet and innocent as she portrayed to Logan. Every time she looks at me, defiance pours from her eyes. Her attitude is always front and center. It's only a matter of time until I push her too far and she shows me the rest of that hideous personality she's kept hidden from him. She's put on an act for Logan—for what reasons, I'm determined to find out.

"Out," is the only answer I give Grayson. I don't know why I didn't tell him I was at Lux. He's the one who said we need to learn everything about her life here before we can act out whatever revenge plans he has cooking. "What's been going on here?"

I glance between Gray and Logan.

"Logan was just saying how he pussied out of going to his Statistics class today."

"I'm not ready to face her," Logan grouses, face scrunched. "Do you know what a mind fuck this is for me? I had fucking feelings for this girl. We... she..." He blows out an exasperated breath, managing to look both pissed and contemplative at the same time. "I wasn't fucking ready."

"You're the only in we have," Grayson pushes. I can tell his desire for vengeance is overriding his compassion. He's had a one-track mind since Saturday. Dude may as well have fucking blinders on cause all he can see is her—and his desire to fuck with her.

"You can find out everything you need online these days," I

toss out, throwing Logan a bone. "And anything about her we can't find online, we can probably get by asking around campus or flirting with the admin staff."

"It would still be better if we had an inside man," Gray pushes relentlessly.

Incensed, Logan jumps to his feet, his face like thunder as he glares at Gray. "Well, I'm not fucking ready. I get that you have a fucking vendetta against her, and I wanna help. I do. But, *fuck.* You've no fucking clue how into her I was. I thought she was my fucking soulmate or some shit." He blows out a ragged breath, looking tortured. "I've never felt like that before. I've never felt so... *seen* by anyone." Shaking his head, he drops his face into his hands. "Thinking she was one thing, then finding out she's the opposite is fucking with my head. Which is fucking with my game. I just... I need to get my head on straight before I fuck up the rest of this season."

Basically, he's just fucked all around.

Looking chagrinned, Grayson nods. "You're right, man. I'm sorry. Your future is more important. Your focus needs to be on tomorrow's game. I shouldn't have said otherwise." Collapsing back in his seat, he rests his head against the back of it and swipes his hands down his face as he groans. "It's just, knowing she's here—right fucking here—is stirring up all sorts of shit. I can't stop seeing her wide, innocent eyes the day the cops showed up."

The day the world was ripped out from beneath his feet, he was sent into a tailspin, left to gather the remaining pieces and attempt to fit them back together.

"There's this dark, hungry pit inside me demanding to be filled with her tears and suffering. It won't let me fucking sleep or eat or think about anything else other than having her at my feet, tear-streaked and begging for my forgiveness."

"And we'll help you achieve that," I insist, understanding

that dark desire. At least Grayson has the opportunity to sate that beast. To get some form of closure for the wrong that was committed against him. I will never have that, and it eats at me —that feeling of helplessness.

Logan nods in agreement. "Absolutely. I dunno if I can do what you need, but I do wanna help," Logan insists, and I know he means it, even if his face is pinched and he hates himself a little for even saying it.

Gray lifts his head and gives Logan a grateful smile, knowing how hard this is on him, even if his own head is a mess. Grayson has stepped up and taken on the fallout of everything from that day. He's dealt with all the shit with his dad, the publicity and public scrutiny on his family, and he's taken over the responsibilities of running the family company. All while starting college and maintaining a 4.9 GPA.

It's fucking commendable.

But he's given every fucking part of himself to his family and the company, and the few pieces he's kept back for himself are tarnished and stained, corroded with Riley's betrayal.

He *needs* this. For his own fucking sanity.

So he can gain some closure and move the fuck on from what she did.

We spend the next couple of hours determining what we need to know about Riley—who she interacts with, what she does with her time, and who is important in her life. Grayson comes up with an ambitious but admittedly sinister plan, and we agree that Operation Payback's a Bitch should take place over winter break.

This gives us four weeks to do reconnaissance and figure out a way to ensure Riley won't be missed over the winter break —if, you know, she just so happens to disappear off the face of the earth for a couple of weeks.

# RILEY

## CHAPTER SIXTEEN

It's been a solitary two weeks without Logan's presence in my life. I hadn't realized how much of an impact he had made in such a short time. Of course, Logan's energy consumes everything in its immediate vicinity, so naturally, his absence would have left a gaping hole.

I just hadn't expected my life to feel this empty without him in it.

Without the good morning texts, which made me smile.

Without his laidback, cock-sure smile to brighten my day.

Without his easy presence to offset the gloom.

Without Logan to talk to on campus, I don't speak to anyone. The quiet, loner life I'd been happily living before he came along now feels empty and muted. There are no smiles to break up my day. No laughter. No light moments.

One day bleeds into the next in a dull, monotonous gray. My heart feels heavy, my spirit dampened, and my nights are plagued with questions and insecurities. I can't understand his complete one-eighty behavior. Logan was the one who pursued me. Who instigated intimate contact. Who sought *me* out.

So why the radio silence? Did I do something wrong? Was it

all just some game to him? A dare to fuck with the scholarship student?

I'll be furious if that's what this was—some sick form of entertainment.

However, if that was the case, then I don't understand the end result. Shouldn't he be rubbing it in my face or telling the entire student body rather than pretending I don't exist?

After his being absent all week, I've spotted Logan a few times on campus. Always from a distance, and always surrounded by his usual horde of adoring fans—mostly girls.

What hurt the most though, was when I saw him staring down at some girl with that same dazzling smile he used to give me. After that, I hid in the bathroom for half an hour, trying to convince myself I was pissed rather than hurt. It was a lie, of course. It felt like he reached into my chest and ripped my heart out.

I knew it would hurt when Logan was done with me, but I hadn't expected it to be quite so unbearable. The only way to mask the pain is with my anger—something I have plenty of. It's become a permanent state of mind, and I pull that rage to the forefront as I step into my Statistics class on Friday afternoon, preparing to see him up close for the first time since our date.

Even with my armor wrapped tightly around me, my feet stick to the floor the second I spot him. *Goddamn.* In my head, I'd tried to diminish his attractiveness, but even from here, I'm rendered mute as I openly stare. *So much hotter than my imagination allowed me to recall.*

He's sitting near the back of the hall, surrounded by his usual groupies. Of course, Whitney is cozied up beside him, and spotting me, she smirks before placing her hand on his arm and nuzzling closer. Murderous rage pumps through my veins, vibrating along my nerves as I picture myself stomping over there and ripping her goddamn arm off.

Tearing my eyes away from her, I scan Logan's face, searching for any signs that he's been as tormented these past few weeks as I have.

Does he sleep at night? Can he swallow down more than a mouthful of food at a time? Can he focus on his schoolwork? Because I sure as fuck can't do any of that. I'm a robot, simply going through the motions.

One of the groupies says something that has the rest of them laughing, and Logan graces them with his winning plastic smile before his eyes clash with mine.

Gaze guarded, I can't get a read on him. It's the most shuttered I've seen his expression since I started tutoring him. His fake smile cracks momentarily, his stare searing into mine and rooting me in place for what feels like an eternity. Caught in a riptide, I'm unable to pull away. All I can do is stare back, searching for answers to the unasked questions I know he can read in my eyes.

When he finally wrenches his gaze away, I swear he's somehow managed to lasso my soul and tug it from my chest. My entire body jerks forward with the momentum, and I gasp, blinking as I stare around the lecture hall, seeing it for the first time since I walked in.

Conversations continue around me, life going on as usual. Everyone wholly oblivious to the gravitational pull that was holding Logan and me hostage while a chaotic storm of emotions battered my defenses.

If I thought his absence was bad, it's nothing to the devastation I feel at seeing him. At having him dismiss me as though I meant nothing. And still somehow managing to steal pieces of me.

Professor Caldwell clears his throat, and I hurry into an

empty seat on the opposite side of the room. Thankfully, Logan isn't in my line of sight, so I can just pretend he doesn't exist.

Except, for the next hour, I can feel the raw energy he naturally emits pulsing around the room. It brushes against my skin like expensive silk and pokes against the back of my neck with the prickling of sharp needles.

The professor's voice is nothing more than background noise to my discomfort, and I don't take in a single word. It's unfair how easily Logan takes up space in my world. How effortlessly he has stomped his way into my life and irrevocably messed it all up.

During the whole lecture, my anger slowly boils until it's a scalding pot on the verge of bubbling over. Then, when the professor dismisses us, I'm the first out of my seat.

Stuffing the notepad I didn't even bother to open back into my bag, I push past dawdling students, twisting my head back and forth as I press onto my toes in an attempt to spot Logan in the crowded room.

I need to confront him. To find out what happened; what changed. Whether he had a change of feelings or this was some game, I just need to know. So I can throw my hands up and say *okay,* or *he's a dick*, and move the fuck on.

'Cause to me, what we had felt pretty significant. It was in the early days, yeah, but the potential was there, hanging so heavy in the air between us that I could practically taste it on my tongue.

Spotting him barreling toward the door ahead of me, I shoulder past students, ignoring their scowls as I chase after him.

"Hey!" I yell as I reach the door. "Logan!"

He ignores me, whether because he knows it's me or because he's so used to randomers calling his name.

Once I've made it through the bottleneck at the door, I move to the edge of the hallway, slipping along the wall as I chase after his tall frame.

"Logan!" I try again, closing the distance between us.

I again receive no response, but his shoulders stiffen, so I'm pretty sure he knows I'm shouting after him.

"Logan." This time I growl out his name as my outstretched fingers wrap around his bicep. Tugging on his arm, I suck in a gasp when he turns to face me with an expression carved from stone. His ordinarily light and mischievous eyes are darkened in anger. Two rich mahogany pools.

"What?" That one word is a harsh snap that hits me with the force of a sharp whip. It's all I can do to gape at him open-mouthed before I regain my composure.

"Don't *what* me!" I seethe. Glaring right back at him, I tug more forcefully on his arm as I drag him through the nearest doorway into an empty classroom. Of course, it would be effortless for him to remove himself from my grip and storm off, but for some reason he allows me to drag him into the room.

As soon as the door closes behind us, he pulls away, crossing his arms over his chest in a defensive posture that has me scrunching my eyebrows. "What do you want?"

*Again, with the attitude.*

"Why are you angry with me? I'm the one who should be pissed at *you*."

A derisive snort escapes as he shakes his head, unable to meet my eye as his focus bounces around the room.

I wait for his response until it becomes apparent he's not going to elaborate.

*Oookay then.*

"Why have you been ghosting me?" I snap.

Silence.

"And you've missed two tutoring sessions."

Again, no response. Although, in fairness, that didn't technically warrant one.

Perplexed and affronted by the fact that he can't even look at me, I reach out to touch his arm. "Logan," I say more softly.

The second my skin touches his, he flinches away as though burned. However, it's the look of disdain that wrinkles his nose and pulls at his lips that sucker-punches me.

"Did I do something?" I question, considering that's the only thing that makes any sense.

Still no response, and I wrack my brain to understand.

"Talk to me," I plead, desperate to understand what happened. How we went from *I'm going to be that pesky little bug you can't get rid of* to... this.

His teeth grind, the muscle in his jaw popping so profoundly that I'm momentarily worried he will burst a blood vessel or something.

When I think he's going to ignore me yet again, his eyes finally snap to mine. The sharp edges slice through my skin. "I think it's more about what you *didn't* do."

His fingers fly over the screen of his phone before he turns it to face me, and my eyes go wide as I stare at a photo of me, dressed in a gold one-piece and stockings, standing on the stage at Lux alongside the other performers.

Unable to form words, I stare at the photo.

"Lux is the club we were at on Saturday."

*Fuck.*

"Imagine my surprise when the performer my teammates were drooling over turned around, and it was *your* face I saw."

There's a careful neutrality to his tone, making it impossible for me to decipher his feelings.

Running my tongue along my dry lips, I rip my gaze away from the phone screen to glance up at him. His expression is just as guarded.

"Logan," I hedge. "I'm sorry I didn't tell you. If I'd known that's where you were going, I would have."

He scoffs, clearly not believing me.

"I would have," I persist. "Besides, it's not like you ever asked where I worked. You knew I had a job and that I worked late, yet not once did you ask *where*."

His eyebrows climb his forehead. "So you're saying this is *my* fault."

Blowing out a frustrated breath, I say exasperated, "No. That's not what I'm saying. It's just, this isn't all on me."

That muscle is once again popping in his jaw. My eyes scan his face, searching as I tilt my head. "Unless this isn't about the fact I didn't tell you..."

Fucking silence.

I bark out a caustic laugh. "Right. I get it now." I can't even look at him, I'm so fucking angry. "I thought you were better than that, Logan. I really did." I shake my head in disappointment.

"I dance on a goddamn stage," I snap, reaching boiling point. "It's exactly the same as if you went to see the ballet or a concert."

He doesn't even bother to argue with me, which somehow only cuts deeper. However, his lack of eye contact and derisive snort fire my easily triggered temper.

"I don't do any of the extras," I snap, confident that he's more than aware of the seedier aspect of Lux. "But even if I did, there would be nothing at all to be ashamed of or disgusted by. It's alright for you to stand there with your holier-than-thou morals and judge me, but you've never had to rummage in the couch cushions for spare change in order to afford something to eat that day. You aren't the one reliant on the free food in the dining hall for sustenance."

My temper escalates with every sentence out of my mouth,

reaching a crescendo. "You haven't lived my life. You don't know the path that has led me here. You don't know the courage it takes for me to get up there every night just so I can have money in my purse each week."

Jamming my finger in his chest, I hiss, "And until you have any fucking idea about my life, you have no right to judge how I choose to live it. The decisions I make."

Throughout my entire incensed speech, he has glared at a point in the wall behind my head, but as my chest rises and falls with haggard breaths, he glances down at the finger still jabbing him in the chest, before finally looking into my eyes.

"Doesn't your scholarship cover food and accommodation? What can you possibly need money for that you couldn't earn in a restaurant or cafe?"

"Scholarships don't cover everything," I seethe. "I still have expenses."

His narrowed gaze bores into me, prodding, searching, seeking.

I've already broken down walls I hadn't intended to. I refuse to give him any more than I already have.

Dropping his head, he cuts off our staring contest and releases a breath.

I wait on tenterhooks, unsure where we go from here. If he can get over himself, then this isn't an insurmountable problem. I am disappointed in him. I honestly thought he was a better person than that, but I can equally appreciate he would have been taken by surprise when he saw me on Saturday night, so his freak-out is somewhat warranted.

Forcing the indignation out of my system, I soften my tone. "I'm sorry I lied to you, Logan. That was never my intention. I wish I'd known you would be there on Saturday so I could have told you, but this doesn't change anything. It doesn't change who I am. I'm still the same girl you know."

The shaking of his head silences anything else I might have said as my airway closes over.

"I... can't," he sighs, still staring at the floor.

Can't? What does that mean?

Taking a step toward the door, he repeats, "I can't right now." He *still* won't look at me, and the butterflies that usually take flight in my stomach in his presence drop like stones, an ache forming in my chest. "This. Us. It shouldn't have happened. It was a mistake. I appreciate the tutoring, but the rest of it... forget it ever happened."

Forget it ever happened? Is he for real?

"Logan." His name is a broken plea as he takes another step backward, away from me. With each step, a bottomless cavern opens between us, and the string that connects me to him, the one that has me immediately locating him in a room, knowing he's nearby before I ever set eyes on him, is pulled taut.

A sharp tug pulls at my chest, the strain becoming unbearable as he opens the door. Without a backward glance or so much as a goodbye, he exits the room, and as the door snaps shut behind him, that cord connecting us is severed.

I'm left staring at the door long after he's gone, my brain rifling through the murky mess of confusion as it tries to make sense of how everything went so wrong so quickly.

Somehow, I'm left even more bereft than before I dragged him in here. Before, I still had hope. Hope that this was a misunderstanding. Hope that whatever might be wrong had nothing to do with *us* and that we could work past it.

And in the absence of that hope, I had anger to cling to.

But now, I have nothing.

Nothing tethering me to him.

Nothing to ground myself.

He walked out the door as though *we* meant nothing. As though *I* meant nothing.

And perhaps it shouldn't have slayed me.

But it did.

It fucking did.

Because despite all the warnings I issued to myself, I went and fucking fell for Logan Astor.

Emotion lies thick in my throat, and my eyes burn with tears I refuse to shed.

My phone chooses that moment to go off in my pocket, and I groan aloud at the sight of my mom's caller ID. I swear she knows when I'm having a crappy day and chooses then to heap more dung on the steaming pile of shit that is my life.

"Mom," I grind, in no mood for her bullshit today.

"I need an extra $100 this week."

"Why?"

"What does it matter why?" she snaps. "I just need it."

Pursing my lips to hold back my retort, I instead demand, "I wanna speak to Rora."

She sighs in exasperation. "You can't right now."

"Then I can't get you your money right now."

I'm so goddamn sick of her shit. I've been walking around on eggshells, terrified to do anything to upset her and lose the few privileges she's allowed, but I'm too raw from my confrontation with Logan to care right now.

"You haven't upheld a single one of your agreements since I started college," I point out. "Why should I uphold mine?"

"Fine," she hisses. "You have five minutes."

"FaceTime," I bark, pulling the phone from my ear and switching it to video mode before she can argue.

A moment later, a little girl with freckles across the bridge of her nose and brown hair with a slight red hue through it pops onto the screen, and tears threaten as I grin at her. I inject as much enthusiasm into my voice as possible, saying, "Hello, baby girl."

“Mommy!”

My eyes are glassy, and I have to blink the tears away to get a proper look at her. Scanning my sweet little angel from head to toe, I imprint every inch of her to memory while simultaneously cataloging the differences from when I last saw her.

“You’ve gotten so big!” I exclaim. “How old are you now? Seven?”

She giggles. The kind that only children can produce that burrows seeds of warmth deep inside you. Seeds that fill every dark crevice left behind by the withdrawal of Logan’s light. “No, silly. I’m *three*.” She holds up three fingers to emphasize her point, and I laugh, even though all I want to do is curl up and cry my heart out.

Cry for all the time I’ve spent away from her. All the important life events I’ve missed.

All the shitty decisions that have led us here.

“How have you been, baby?” I ask instead. “Are you doing okay?”

She nods her head, her hand wrapped possessively around a stuffed teddy bear sporting a Halston U T-shirt that I bought for her right before I left.

“When are you coming home, Mommy?”

It takes everything in me to hold back the tears. “Soon, baby. I’m going to see you real soon.”

“Time’s up,” my mother cuts in.

My heart clenches, needing more time with my little girl more than I need my next breath. “Mommy’s gotta go,” I say to Aurora. “But I’ll see you soon, okay, sweetpea?”

She nods again, tears shimmering in her eyes that threaten to shatter the flimsy dam I have erected.

“Mommy loves—”

The screen goes black before I hear my mother’s grating tone.

"Send me that money, Riley."

"I will," I respond, utterly defeated and stripped raw. "You're still coming up here next weekend, right?"

"We can't."

"What? Why?" I begin to protest. "You canceled the last two meetings, Mom. You can't keep doing this for the next three years!"

"It's not my fault, Riley. That piece of crap car you bought me won't start."

"Well, have you taken it to the mechanic?"

"And how do you think I'm going to pay for that? Not all of us are so willing to offer up our bodies as payment."

I close my eyes and count to three.

Fucking hypocrite. She might have never danced on a stage for tips, but offering up her body in exchange for a lifestyle upgrade is exactly what my mother has always done.

More than that, I have to get up on the stage at Lux every weekend because *she* point-blank refuses to get a job, meaning I'm left to provide for myself, my daughter, and my good-for-nothing mother, all while attending college full-time.

"I'll send you the money to get it fixed," I grind through clenched teeth, even as I mentally tally up the amount in my bank account. I might be able to scrape by if it isn't too expensive. Worst case scenario, winter break is only a couple of weeks away and I have no plans other than to work every available shift I can get, so that should help tide us over for a while. Assuming my mother can stop demanding extra money each month. "It better be fixed by the next visitation," I tell her, unable to keep the irritation out of my voice. "I want to see my daughter on Christmas Day. And get her hair cut! It's getting straggly."

"Yes, yes," she retorts off-hand. "We'll see what we can do. Don't forget to send me that money."

On that parting note, she hangs up, and it takes every ounce of my self-control not to launch my phone across the room.

Agitated and emotionally wrung out, I know exactly where I'll be spending the rest of my afternoon before I have to go to work—the dance studio, attempting to work out the impact of this particularly grueling day from my system.

# ROYCE

## CHAPTER SEVENTEEN

"Yo, man, hold up!"

*Fuck.*

Ignoring him, I continue walking, even though I should have known it wouldn't do me any good.

A moment later, I hear the thundering of footfalls as what sounds like the entire football team approaches.

*Just fucking great.*

"King!"

A thick, heavy forearm is thrown over my shoulder a moment later.

"It is you." Todd pulls me to a stop as the rest of the team surrounds us. "How you been, man?"

"Fine." Todd and I are both seniors. We were on the football team together, both competitive as hell and gunning for the captain position. Glancing down at his Halston U hoodie, I notice the word *Captain* stitched beneath the husky mascot, with the academic year written beneath. *I guess he got the position.* Unsurprisingly.

"Yeah? What you been up to? We never see you anymore."

"I've been busy," I grit out, uncomfortable as fuck with the questioning eyes of every player from the team on me. There was once a time when I would have lapped up having everyone's attention. When these guys felt like brothers to me, regardless, those days are long gone now.

Todd's eyes bounce between mine. "You coming to the party after the game?"

"Nah, not my scene anymore."

"Yeah, thought that. Haven't seen you there all year."

*There* being the football frat house where most of the team lives and where we—they—throw an epic party after every home game.

"Look, man. None of us know what went down at the end of last year, but you're still one of us." No, I'm not. Despite the bobbing of heads in agreement from the other guys. "I get it if coming to a game is too much, but seeing you at the house would be great."

Giving nothing away, I blandly state, "I'll think about it."

I won't.

"Good. I hope you do," he says genuinely. "It was meant to be you and me this year, living it up and making the rookies' lives hell."

Yeah, it was. Until *they* caught wind of the win we pulled at last year's championship game. When *they* heard I was on the team. Found out I was making a name for myself; that I had the potential to go somewhere. To be someone.

Now, it's *his* year, and I'm simply trying to navigate the fallout of yet another ass fucking.

"Todd, man, we gotta get to training," one of the younger players says.

"Yeah, alright." Todd sighs, clapping me on the shoulder.

"I'll see you around, man."

With that, he takes off, the team giving me chin tilts and head nods before they follow after their leader.

I watch them go with a resignation.

That should have been me.

I should have been the one leading the team to victory this year. The one being looked upon by the rookies with reverenced awe.

And the fact I'm not, is still a devastating blow. Especially when I have to fucking *see* the consequences.

This is why I barely set foot on campus unless it's to go to class. Why I haven't attended a single game this year, never mind an after-party. It's one thing to know in my head that that part of my life is officially over, but it's another to witness what could have been with my own two eyes. To see everyone else moving on with their lives while I'm fucking stuck.

*"What do you mean, suspended?" I argue, my mouth dry as I gape first at my coach, then the Dean of Halston. Both of them stare at me with stern expressions, but there's disappointment in my coach's eyes that makes it impossible for me to look at him for more than a second.*

*It's been a long time since I've had that look directed at me. I'd almost forgotten how fucking awful it felt. And now that I'm reminded, I never want to see it again.*

*"Just until we can sort this issue out with the Mountbattons," the Dean attempts to explain, but I'm barely listening. The future I've been working my ass off for is being flushed down the toilet. It's slipping through my fingers and there's not a damn thing I can do to stop it.*

*I should have known my past would come back to haunt me. That as soon as life started going well for me,* they *would spring out of the woodwork to ruin it. God fucking forbid I move on and be happy.*

*"I didn't do anything," I argue, but just like the first three times I said it, my words fall on deaf ears.*

*"Nothing will be decided until a thorough investigation of the allegations has been completed," the Dean appeases fruitlessly.*

*I scoff, shaking my head.*

*Not if my father has anything to do about it. I already know there isn't going to be an investigation. That's not how my father works. He wouldn't dare let me drag the King name through the mud—not again.*

*The doors to the meeting room bang open, and I turn in my chair as my father strides in, his long coat billowing out behind him.*

*"What is the meaning of this?"*

*"Mr. King," the Dean simpers. "As we were just explaining to your son. Mr. Mountbatten contacted me with some disturbing information—"*

*My father waves away the Dean's words. "Yes, yes. That was already settled with Mr. Mountbatton years ago. We came to an understanding. He shouldn't be bringing it up now."*

*"Regardless, now that it has been brought to my attention, I cannot simply overlook it," the Dean continues, her lips pursed as she stares down my father.*

*"And what are you suggesting?"*

*"Two-week suspension from school, including football, for the time being while this is sorted. At which point, we will reconvene to discuss Royce's continued education at Halston."*

*"You'd expel my son?"*

*A muscle in the Dean's jaw ticks. "I will not have a student at my school who has... who is a risk to other students."*

*Frustration and anger coil around my father like a cape, and I know I'll have to face his wrath after this little meeting is over. I'd laugh at the irony of this being the first time we've been in the same room together since I was in high school, except there isn't a damn thing about any of this that is funny.*

*"And* what *exactly, Dean Reynolds, would I have to do to change your mind?"*

*"Mr. King, you cannot—"*

*"How much?" he barks, causing the Dean and my coach to jolt in their seats.*

*"Money is not sufficient to sweep this under the rug," the Dean persists. "Mr. Mountbatten has explicitly stated that he wants to see action taken."*

*"He has insisted that Royce be removed from the football team," my coach interjects.*

*His admission is met with a tense silence. My palms sweat against my jeans, my mouth so dry it's a struggle to swallow. That can't happen. Football is my future. It's who I am. I don't know what I'd do if I couldn't play any longer.*

*"Fine," my father snaps, unaware of the devastation he is wrecking. "The boy is off the team, and I'll donate ten million to the university. Will that be sufficient?"*

*"Mr. King."*

*"Twenty million," my father counters, cutting across the Dean, who is now blinking at him in stupified silence.*

*I will her not to agree, but I know it's useless. No one says no to my father.*

*"Your generous donation is appreciated," the Dean responds slowly, eyes darting to me before returning to my father. "And Royce is removed from the Football team and won't be allowed to rejoin."*

*With a curt nod, my father spares me no more than a passing glance as he stalks out of the room, leaving my world in shambles at my feet.*

Shaking off the memory, I stomp across campus with a newfound tension hunching my shoulders. As I'm passing the quad, I dare to look up. My hasty retreat slows when I spot a familiar head of reddish-brown hair up ahead.

I can only see part of her face. Her expression is pulled tight, and she looks like her day is going as well as mine is. She bisects the path in front of me, and instantly, my plans to head directly home alter.

Rather, I turn to follow her, remaining a healthy distance behind as I track her across campus and out onto the street.

"Where are you going, James?" I mutter as she crosses the road, moving further away from campus.

She should have no need to leave other than for work, and I know it's too early for Lux to be open.

Trailing her across town to the outskirts, I step into a doorway when she stops outside a shabby apartment building. *Who does she know that lives in there?* No one from Halston U would be caught dead living in this part of town.

When she slips inside, I look both ways before jogging across the street. Approaching a door that looks like it's one bad winter from rotting away, I peer through the small, smudged pane of glass etched into the center of the door into an equally shabby lobby. I try the handle, but the door is locked. Spotting a buzzer system, I scan the list of names until I come across one that says *James*. Huh, unexpected.

I hang around for another few minutes, too curious to leave but unsure what else I can do. As I step away from the entryway, she pops into view. Her head is lowered as she hits the bottom of the stairs and moves toward me, now wearing a pair of skin-tight lycra leggings and a workout crop top.

"Shit," I mutter to myself as I scurry across the street and back into my hiding place just in time for her to emerge from the building.

Looking up and down the street, she turns and walks in the opposite direction, and unable to resist, I follow.

She doesn't go far, only a couple of blocks until she reaches what appears to be a dance studio. Letting herself in, I count to five before approaching. By the time I'm at the door, I hear the fast-paced tune of *Let's Go Now* by Rayelle, and shifting so I can peer through the large window that looks into a studio without being seen, I watch mesmerized as she moves around the dance floor like a woman possessed.

Even from out here, I can feel the energy radiating from her. She's a storm, unleashing on the room as her body twists and contorts in an alluring, entrancing way that makes it impossible to do anything other than stare.

I swear I hear the crack of thunder. The flash of lightning.

Rain pounds ferociously with every step she takes.

Clouds gather along the ceiling of the studio, heavy with the weight of the emotions she's exuding. Her movements are sharp and quick, her spins and twirls fast-paced and impeccably executed.

Watching her on the stage in Lux had been alluring. Having her dance for me, her moves had been slow and sultry. Intended to entice and seduce.

But this... this is a catharsis of the soul.

I feel as though I'm intruding on a truly intimate moment, and yet I'm helpless to look away as I watch her purge herself.

She doesn't belong on a stage in some club. She should be dancing in opera houses for all the world to see.

As the song comes to an end, she maneuvers back into the center of the room. She seems lighter, somehow, yet I can tell by the set of her shoulders and slight pinching around her eyes that she's still carrying the weight of the world on her shoulders.

The final notes play out so softly I hardly hear them as she folds her long, slim arms around herself and drops her head to the floor. Even after the song has finished playing and another has started up, she remains like that. A frozen statue except for the steady rise and fall of her shoulders with each inhale.

I should leave now, before she glances this way and spots

me lurking outside. Yet, I can't bring myself to do that. Something I can't explain and refuse to look too deeply at has me rooted in place as she finally lifts her head, and I catch a true glimpse of her.

She's completely unguarded, every one of her emotions exposed. She's an open book for only me to read, and I absorb every word. I wade through the monumental pain she carries, navigate the heartache, and traverse the sharp peaks of her determination.

And all the while, I ask myself, why?

Her chest expands with a deep inhale, and I watch as she tucks each one of her feelings back into their respective boxes. Only when she's fully back in control do I step away, turning my back on her and the studio as I head down the street.

The entire walk back to my house, I can't stop picturing the look on her face when she lifted her head—the sheer intensity of her emotions.

Whatever she has been through doesn't excuse her actions.

But I find myself curious to know more.

And not only to help out Grayson.

"Hey, man," Logan greets, glancing up from his video game when I walk through the door. "How was class?"

I don't answer as I sit down in an empty chair, still lost in my thoughts.

"Thought you said Riley lived in the student dorms?" I eventually ask.

"Fuck sake, that was a cheap shot!" he snaps at the television before tossing his controller aside and giving me his attention. "Ehh, yeah. She does. Isn't that where all freshmen stay?"

I shrug. "Usually, but not necessarily."

"It's where I dropped her off after our..." He trails off, face scrunched, before he wipes his expression clean. "She didn't correct me or ask me to drop her somewhere else."

"Well, I just followed her to an apartment building on the far side of town."

Logan gives an unsure shrug. "Maybe she was visiting someone."

I arch a skeptical eyebrow. "She changed her clothes, re-emerged and went down the street to a local dance studio. Plus, her name was on the buzzer."

Logan's eyebrows hit his hairline. "You think she lives there?"

I lift a shoulder. "It looks that way. I'll keep an eye on the place. See if she goes back. Shouldn't be difficult to find out."

The sound of the front door opening is followed by Grayson walking into the house, dressed in a smart suit.

"Where were you?" I question as he drops into a seat and tugs at his tie like it's a noose around his neck.

"Fucking board meeting."

"Fun," Logan quips.

Gray grunts, closing his eyes as he rests his head against the back of the chair.

"What's been going on here?" he asks after a moment, still not opening his eyes.

"We think Riley is living off campus," I tell him, filling him in on my sleuthing session.

That gets his attention. His head snaps up, focus intent on me. "As a scholarship student, she's entitled to free accommodation on campus. Why would she rent somewhere off campus that she'll have to pay for?"

I shrug, not having an answer for him. "No clue. I'll stop by the administration building tomorrow and see what I can find out. Martha loves me there. Shouldn't be too difficult to get answers from her."

Snorting, he shakes his head.

Hey, it's not my fault the woman is a huge football fan. She might be sixty and hard of hearing, but she showed up at every single one of our games and screamed like a banshee. I've never heard an old lady curse so colorfully before.

Thankfully, she doesn't know what happened to get me kicked off the team. She also isn't the slightest bit put off by my *fuck off* vibes—just like someone else I know—and always stops to chat with me when we run into one another on campus.

"Why wouldn't she tell me?" Logan whines, clearly still hung up on Riley. The idiot sounds totally put out, although I don't know why. She didn't tell him where she worked, or how she earns a living by essentially getting men hard, so why would she tell him where she lives? The girl evidently likes her secrets.

"She, uh, tracked me down after class," he states hesitantly. Gray and I share a look, waiting him out as he appears to get lost in his thoughts. "Demanded to know why I ghosted her."

"What did you say?" Grayson asks.

Logan gives a nonchalant shrug of his shoulder. "Gave her some bullshit about how I found out she worked at Lux. Pretended that's why I'd been ignoring her."

"You didn't—"

"No, of course not," Logan growls, glaring at Gray. "I'm not an idiot. She knew I was heading out with the team on Saturday night, so I told her the truth, that we went to Lux, but I didn't say anything about you two fuckers."

"How did you leave things?" I ask.

He glances at Gray, before admitting, "Told her we were done. And I didn't want anything to do with her. I'm sorry, man. I just fucking can't. Not yet. I need to get her out of my system for what we have planned. If I think about her the way I have been fucking thinking of her, then I won't be able to do it."

"Don't sweat it, I understand," Gray reassures, casting

Logan a concerned glance. "Like Royce said, we can watch her from a distance."

Logan's forehead wrinkles as his brows tug down. "She did say some stuff, though. Made it sound as if she's been through some shit."

Gray scoffs, looking disgusted.

"Do you know what her situation was before her mom married your dad? Or what happened to them afterward?" I ask.

"I remember Dad saying when Riley was a kid, they had no money. Think they lived in a trailer park and everything, but when Dad met them, they were living in a house in an alright part of town. Nothing special, but not a shithole either."

"And after?" I prompt.

"No idea. Didn't exactly make it a point to keep in contact with them, but with no access to my Dad's money, they were probably broke. Would explain how Riley got offered a scholarship and why she's working at Lux—if she needs the cash."

I nod. Casting Logan a sideways glance, I find him frowning at the floor. "You alright, man?"

"Yeah," he grunts. "I'll be fine. I gotta run, though. Got a team meeting before tonight's game."

"Gray and I are coming."

We hadn't actually discussed it, but the way Logan's face lights up lets me know it's the right call. He's been in a crappy head space since discovering who Riley truly is. I know she went to one of his games... before everything blew up between them, and he hasn't been playing as well since. Not that he's been playing badly; there just isn't the same fire that there was during that handful of games when they were... whatever they were.

"You are? Sweet! I'll leave tickets at will call for you."

With a pep in his step, he heads upstairs to change, and I look to Grayson.

"She really did a number on him," he states with a frown.

"Yeah."

"You did the right thing. He needs to know we're there for him. Will you manage okay, though?"

Tensing, I grunt, "I'll be fine," before shoving out of my chair and heading to my room.

Football games aren't the only ones I've been avoiding. I haven't been to a sporting event, period, since my football goals were stolen from me. But Logan is my best friend. He's been there for me while I've spiraled out of control these last few months, picking me off the floor when I've been black-out drunk and cleaning my wounds when I get into a particularly nasty fight.

The least I can do is have his back while he mends his bruised heart.

# RILEY

## CHAPTER EIGHTEEN

"Your admirer is back," Ben comments after I step off the stage after our third performance of the night on Friday. He gestures toward the booths, and I follow his gaze past the open curtains of booth four to where Ruthless is currently lounging, eyes on his phone and looking awfully at home.

My lips dip in a frown. *Dammit. I'd been hoping one weekend of bothering me would have been enough to satisfy him.*

"He requested *me*?" I ask, futilely hoping he might be here for tonight's performances.

Ben nods, and reluctantly, I go to change and entertain my *admirer.*

Although I still feel nervous as I approach him, there's none of the clawing anxiety I felt last week. Ruthless is terrifying to look at. He's built, his tall stature and bulky muscles meaning he dwarfs most men, covered in tattoos that scream unapproachable, and that sign on his forehead would have any sane person running away from him. Yet, I feel an odd allure in his presence. I know he's bad for me. He has *damaged* written all over him, but there's also something that piques my interest.

That has me feeling at ease even when I'm confident that's the last thing I should feel in his proximity.

I had a lot of time to study him while acting as his performing monkey last weekend. Had the opportunity to run my fingers along his chipped edges, to feel how worn they were, the sharp prick against my flesh from where they've been sharpened into weapons.

However, occasionally, I came across a soft spot. An unknown area of exposure. In those crevices, I uncovered a deeper understanding of this perplexing man where I sensed an unspoken similarity—an instant familiarity. Perhaps I was reflecting my own scars onto him, but I could have sworn I saw it...

His pain.

It felt so like my own.

So real.

Like veins of crystallized minerals carved into stone, pulsing with vibrancy.

A live wire ready to wreak havoc.

A land mine waiting to be triggered.

It was so raw, so exposed, I was tempted to reach out and touch it.

But I held back, recognizing that I could not weather the storm prodding him would induce. Ruthless is a bomb waiting to go off. One wrong touch and he will explode, whether he realizes it or not. I can barely handle the chaos of my own pain. I'm in no position to provoke him.

"Back again," I drawl as I approach, dressed in a red corset, feathered skirt, and fishnet stockings. The outfit is finished with tall, black heels that take me from five-foot-six to nearly six feet tall and make my legs look endless.

At the sound of my voice, Ruthless looks up from his phone. Starting at my feet, his eyes slowly lift, pupils dilating with appreciation, as he takes in the thin strip of skin visible between my corset and skirt, hovering on my chest, before finally lifting to my face.

One thing I have come to recognize from working at Lux is when a man is lusting after a woman. And right now, in this moment, Ruthless. Wants. Me.

Of course, he doesn't acknowledge it—our game wouldn't allow it—as he wipes his expression clean with his next blink.

"You know," I begin, "other girls here would happily perform for you."

He smirks, the action cocky and sexy all at once. "None of them are you."

The way he says it, I don't think he means that as a good thing, and I tilt my head as I study him.

"Why me? Is this because I ran into you? Do you not believe that it was an accident—*all three times*?"

"This isn't about that," he states with a conviction I'm inclined to believe.

But if not that, then why?

"Once again," he drawls, expression growing sharp. "I'm here for a dance, not an interrogation."

*Alright, asshole, I get the hint.*

Keeping my mouth shut, I close my eyes to block him out and instead focus on the music as I begin to move.

I do such an effective job that I forget his presence entirely. Until I feel a sharp pinch to my hip.

"Eyes on me," he growls when I flick them open to glare at him.

"Hands to yourself," I bite back.

The asshole smirks, but removes his hand as he rests back in his seat. His eyes remain on mine as I continue dancing. I don't know why I'm even following his orders. Only now that I'm latched on, I can't seem to look away.

I give him my best defiant glare, making it crystal clear that he's not getting to me. Even if he sort of is. This type of situation makes me uncomfortable, made worse by the fact that he is drop-dead gorgeous and has that mysterious bad-boy vibe, and I can't pinpoint why he came back or even tracked me down in the first place.

"Come on, Babydoll. I know you've got better moves than that. You're supposed to be making me want to rip that corset off and come all over those tits of yours."

I gasp at his crude words, seriously glad that the thick fabric of my corset hides the hardening of my nipples as I picture him doing exactly that. I shouldn't be feeling like this... this potent cocktail of trepidation and irresistible attraction that pulls me in like a magnet.

The dark allure of Lux only serves to intensify the moment, adding an air of secrecy. An aura of possibility. An intoxicating liberation that heats my blood as though I'm dancing on the edge of a precipice.

I'm not Riley. This isn't the real world. In this club, we're drawn into a hidden world where real-life rules are disregarded and a passion burns fiercely like a flame on a frozen winter's night.

Still holding his gaze, I steel my spine, and placing my hands on his knees, I slowly glide them up his thighs. Even through the stiff fabric of his jeans, I feel him tense. Bent over, I lean in until the swell of my breasts are right in front of his face, our breaths mingling.

"Like this?" I purr, wondering when I was body snatched because, honestly, I've never heard that husky rasp before.

"Better." His own voice has taken on a rough quality that scrapes along my skin, encouraging me on.

Slowly rising, my chest brushes against his, and I relish his rough swallow and the way his Adam's apple bobs. He stares transfixed at my blushing flesh before slowly lifting his gaze to mine, his ice-blue irises darkening into deep pools of blue. Static charges in the air between us, the moment growing heavy. Too heavy. The intensity is too much, and before I can do something stupid like close the distance and press my lips to his, I spin in my heels.

Sucking in a breath, I fan my flaming skin as I shake my ass in his face. *Remember this is a job,* I mentally chastise as I focus on my body and not the tall, solid, muscular one behind me.

Moving to the beat of the soft, sultry music, I plant my hands on his thighs and lean back until the length of my torso brushes along his.

As though he can't help himself, his hands move to my hips. I stare down at where his long, nimble fingers, ridged with callouses and scored with scars, press into my skin. Instead of the daunting fear I always imagined when being touched while performing at Lux, my skin burns as though branded, and I half expect to see the outline of his hand when he removes it.

Sliding my ass over his crotch, a cocky smirk graces my lips, and I ignore the shot of liquid lust that zaps through me. "Mmm, I'd say I'm doing a pretty good job meeting your expectations." Emphasizing my point, I press more firmly against his straining erection. "Just so you're aware. There are tissues in the bathroom... you know, in case you come in your pants."

His chest vibrates with a silent growl, his fingers digging sharply into my skin. "It would take a lot more than the graze of your ass against my dick to get me off, James."

I suck in a gasp at hearing my surname; it's akin to the shattering of a mirror. The illusion is broken.

It snaps me out of whatever headspace I was in, and I stiffen before pulling away. *What the hell was I thinking? This is not me.*

His hand tightens on my hip, stopping me from putting distance between us, and his breath in my ear elicits a shiver.

Holding me in place with one hand, the fingers of his other skate along my upper thigh.

He moves closer to the junction between my legs, and I snap them together in a moment of self-preservation. At the last second, he wedges his leg between mine, creating enough of a gap to slide his hand through.

"Tut tut. Think you can hide from me that easily? I see everything you don't want me to, James." His hand slides steadily lower. "You think you're getting to me, but I *know* I've gotten to you. So are you going to tell me, or do I have to find out for myself?"

"Find out what?" I ask on an unsteady breath.

"How close *you* are to coming in your panties."

Air sticks to the inside of my lungs as his finger brushes feather-light over the scrap of fabric covering my pussy, and his chest rumbles when he discovers the answer to his question: far closer than I'd ever verbally admit.

Heat engulfs me, sucking all the oxygen from the room, and I launch off his lap as panic constricts my chest.

"Dance over," I state, frantic and unable to hide how affected I am. How completely thrown off-kilter he has me.

Lazily pushing to his feet, he smirks. "Sure thing, James. Same time tomorrow."

He moves to step away but pauses at my question. "Why?"

"Because you don't want me to."

I... what? How does that make any sense?

Does he have some sort of kink where he gets off on seeing me uncomfortable? On pushing my buttons? On dragging my sanity to the edge of a cliff and watching as he casts it over the side?

Confused, wrung out, and frustratingly turned on, I watch as he walks away.

"Girl!" Tara squeals when I step into the dressing room at

the end of the night. "Why has Ruthless been paying you a visit?! Did something happen that night at The Depot? You were in the bathroom for an awfully long time."

I snort, shaking my head. "Definitely not. The universe just hates me," I grumble, tired and weary, as I wipe off my makeup.

"Huh?"

Huffing, I take a seat at my dresser and fill Tara in on how I have now *accidentally* run into the asshole three times, including that night at The Depot, and that he's so obsessed with himself that he believes I'm stalking him.

"I mean, I couldn't blame you if you were," Tara says when I'm finished. "But, ugh, why are the hot ones always so full of hot air?" I snort out a laugh. "What are you going to do?"

"What can I do?" I nibble on my bottom lip as images of Ruthless sitting in that booth, legs spread as his gaze slowly wandered over my bare skin, cause a flush to bloom on my cheeks. There's something about his close proximity, knowing his eyes are on me. The intensity in which he watches me. It's terrifying and electrifying all at once. Makes me almost want to cast aside my insecurities and fall headfirst into whatever danger is lurking in those piercing eyes of his.

Recalling the way it felt to have his hands on my body elicits a shiver, snapping me out of my thoughts. Danger is exactly what I'm trying to avoid and Ruthless has heartbreak written all over him. Clearing my voice, I lift my gaze to meet Tara's in the mirror. "All I can do is continue to dance for him when he comes in and hope he gets bored and moves on to someone new sooner rather than later."

---

"I swear I'm still hungover from Friday's party," I overhear a girl at a nearby table in the library groan.

It's a Sunday, and I like coming to the library on Sundays because it's mostly dead. Admittedly, it's the same today, but these two girls walked in half an hour ago and sat down at the table right beside mine. They haven't shut up since. Nor do they have the common decency to whisper.

It's a library, for Christ's sake.

That's like taking the Lord's name in vain inside a church. Everyone knows you just don't do it.

Gritting my teeth, I glare at the question sheet in front of me as I re-read the same question for the third time.

"I saw you disappear with Todd," that same grating tone says. The flimsy pen in my hand threatens to snap in two. "Spill. Does this year's captain have skills?"

"I'd give him an eight outta ten," her friend answers, the two of them completely unaware of how degrading their conversation is. "Adequate length and width, and only needed minor help to reach the goal."

They both titter, and I am wholly irritated now, so I lift my head to glare at them. Unsurprisingly, they look like typical Halston girls—stick thin, long, painted nails, primped hair, and glowing skin. They could almost be sisters, except one has waist-length platinum blonde hair while the other has a short, brunette bob.

Unfortunately, neither is looking my way, too busy gossiping with one another for the entire library to hear.

"I went to some of last year's games to cheer on my brother, and the quarterback was *hot*. I was so disappointed to hear he wasn't on the team anymore." The brunette says—the one who didn't fuck Todd, apparently. Her voice dips, taking on a coy quality. "I'd hoped he'd be at the parties so I could give his dick a whirl, but I haven't seen him at a single one all year."

"Are you talking about Royce King?" Blondie asks.

"Ugh, even his name is sexy as hell."

Her friend makes an odd, strangled noise. "Yeah, you might wanna avoid that one."

"Ooh, gossip? Please don't tell me he has a name like that, looks the way he does, and sucks in the sack."

I'm still watching them from the corner of my eye, so I notice Blondie's tight expression before she states, "His problem is more that he only cares about himself."

"Ugh, a selfish asshole."

"Yeah, to the extent he won't take no for an answer."

The other girl gasps. "Are you saying—"

"Yes."

My fist tightens painfully around my pen, my hands shaking at the implication of what they're discussing.

There's an emotional tone to the blonde girl's voice, and her next words come out softer, although still not quiet enough that I can't hear.

"He raped my cousin. That's why he isn't on the team."

Chills run along my skin, the full effect of her admission hitting me like a ton of bricks. The force is enough to nearly have me toppling from my seat, and I hold the edge of the table in a death grip as those deeply buried demons swoop in. The library around me disappears as shadows blot out the light until all I can feel is his rancid breath on my neck. Hear his low grunts.

*Always such a good girl for me.*

Bile burns a vile path up the back of my throat and it's only the feel of the cool, wooden tabletop against my cheek that grounds me in reality. Blinking, I take in the large, stuffed stacks around me, realizing I must have tried to curl in on myself. The side of my face rests on the table, and I've brought my knees up to wrap my arms around.

Still trembling, I push my fingers between my thighs to where I know the white scars lie. I can't feel them through my jeans, but I don't need to. Simply knowing they are there is enough, and I immediately start to feel my heart rate slow.

*You're safe. You're in the library. You're at Halston.*

*Breathe in. Bleed out.*

*He's not here. He can't hurt you. He* won't *hurt you ever again.*

Breathe in; bleed out.

"I survived," I whisper aloud. "I have a heartbeat. Air in my lungs."

It's the same routine I repeat every time. Thankfully, it has become an infrequent occurrence, but when triggered, I can do nothing except allow my mind to be dragged back there and then force myself to remember it's no longer my reality.

Reminding myself of where I am. Acknowledging that he no longer has the power to hurt me. Touching my scars and remembering that he didn't win, that I'm not dead. All of it works to corral those demons and stuff them back into the recesses of my mind.

I can still hear the two girls talking, but my brain refuses to focus on the details. I don't know who this Royce guy is, but I know being suspended from the team isn't sufficient punishment. He should have been expelled. Arrested. Branded a rapist for the whole world to see.

Why do men with money and status always get away with the vilest of crimes?

PASSENGER AIRBAG
RADIO
MEDIA
PHONE
VOICE
Springview Federal Correctional Center
00:57
NAV
TRAFFIC
CAR
MENU

# GRAYSON

## CHAPTER NINETEEN

"How was she today?" the middle-aged receptionist asks as I scrawl my name in the visitor log book.

"I officially know all the lyrics to *My Girl*, which had never been on my bucket list, but it settled her every time."

The woman nods knowingly. "That song is definitely her favorite at the moment. It's so sweet of you to take time out of your Thanksgiving to spend it with her."

My only response is a tight smile. I'm not about to bare my ugly family history to this woman. Everyone here at Sunnyside Nursing Home is great, and I know many of them wonder why I'm the one who's always here. Her emergency contact. The one paying for her place. I'm sure they all have their theories, but none of them will ever know the truth.

"Thanks, Tammy."

"Well, go on and enjoy the rest of your day, sweetie."

No one has ever called me *sweetie*. They know if they did, I'd rip their heads off, but Tammy helps take care of one of the only people in my life who I genuinely give a shit about, so I let her get away with things I wouldn't allow anyone else.

Wishing her a happy Thanksgiving, I stride away from the reception desk as my phone pings. Noticing a text from Royce, I open up our chat and stall halfway out the door as I stare at the photo he sent.

One in which Riley James—the girl responsible for all the shit that has gone wrong in my life—is staring off into the distance with a radiant smile.

In this captured moment, with the sun shining on her face, she looks so innocent. Virtuous. Angelic.

However, I know it's all an act—one big, fat lie.

She couldn't be farther from the wholesome girl she pretends to be.

Beneath that virtuous exterior is a woman who doesn't care who she has to trample over to get what she wants. She paints a pretty picture of innocence, of docility. But she's intelligent and cunning, and when she sets her sights on a target, she sinks in her claws and doesn't let go until her prey is dead and lifeless in her hands.

Which is exactly what she did to my family. She hunted us. Picked us apart until she knew our weaknesses and vulnerabilities. Then she pounced. Caught us in her maw and shook until our necks snapped.

The phone creaks precariously in my hand, my anger bursting at the seams, demanding release. Forcing my grip to slacken, I tear my eyes from her face, instead lowering them over the rest of her body visible in the photo.

She's dressed in lycra leggings that stop at her knees and a loose, floaty top that does nothing to hide her sports bra underneath. Her hair is pulled up in a messy bun, flyaway hairs sticking up everywhere, and her face is red. Based on the way the sun is reflecting off the glass and the grubby wooden floors and dated interior visible in the background, I'm guessing

Royce stalked her to the dance studio she attends near her apartment.

He's been doing a lot of that recently—stalking her.

Which is ideal. Since Logan can't stand to look at her, and for obvious reasons I can't let her see me. Not without kick-starting our plan, and I need the downtime and isolation of winter break for what I'm planning.

My eyes trail over her slim figure, usually hidden behind clothes two sizes too big when she isn't at Lux. Today every curve is on display. Every trim line so familiar and yet so foreign. Sliding my gaze upward, I hover over her face. Her green eyes and freckles always took my breath away. They still do.

When she and her mother lived with me and my father, she spent most of her time squirreled away in her room while I was always out with friends or at some party. We weren't around one another often, but when we all sat down for the odd family dinner, I felt her presence like a beacon calling to me. She'd steal all of my attention without even trying.

However, at that age, two years felt like a huge age gap—not to mention that she was my stepsister—and I had plenty of less complicated girls I could lose my time in. So, besides the occasional admiring of her body over a Sunday roast, she didn't exist in my world.

Until she placed herself front and center.

Dragging my eyes up to her face, my appreciation for a hot body twists into something harsher, harder, tarnished. Her eyes are shimmering with a vibrancy they have no right to contain, and the corners of her lips are pulled up in a slight smile that somehow still shines with radiance.

I want to rip that smile from her face.

She has no right to smile after what she did. No grounds to feel even a single moment of happiness.

*Soon*, I remind myself. Soon, she will face the consequences of her actions. Soon, she will understand that her deeds did not go unpunished. That the Devil always comes to collect.

Soon, my brothers and I will have her all to ourselves, and by the time we're done with her, she'll be nothing but an empty shell incapable of smiling.

That notion has *me* smiling, and I feel lighter than I have all day as I climb into my BMW i8 and start the engine.

I've just pulled out of the parking lot when my phone rings, the sound coming through the car's Bluetooth. I heave out a sigh at the caller ID before accepting the call.

"This is a prepaid call from *Bertram,* an inmate at Springview Federal Correctional Center. All calls are subject to recording and monitoring. Do you accept this call?"

"Yes," I state the second the robotic voice has finished speaking, more than familiar with this song and dance by now.

A moment later, heavy breathing fills the line before my father's voice echoes throughout the car. "*David* just stopped by. Mentioned some new contract you signed with a renewable energy company." His voice is the picture of calm, but I hear the barely contained anger punched into each and every word. I can mentally picture him standing in his gray jumpsuit, the vein in his forehead pulsing as he struggles to keep his cool.

It's one of Dad's weaknesses—his anger. It's always gotten the better of him, especially when he's blindsided, or something doesn't go his way. He rages up a storm, throws a temper tantrum, then storms off to cool down, and when he comes back later, he'll apologize for losing his temper and be more reasonable to talk to.

Except, when you're in prison and only get one phone call a day, it makes it difficult to return later.

If only fucking *David* would keep his goddamn mouth shut and let *me* decide the right time to deliver news like this to my father. Asshole can't wrap his head around the fact that *I'm* the one in charge. The dickhead is always trying to undermine me. Arguing every little suggestion I bring to the table, voting against me at shareholder meetings, and now running to my dad. Fan-fucking-tastic.

For the most part, Dad and I get on well. It's obviously been challenging since his arrest, but I know he loves and supports me. He's always asking about how I'm getting on at Halston, enquiring about my friends and hobbies—not that there's much to tell him on either front—and taking a general interest in my life and wellbeing.

Our only source of contention is Van Doren Holdings. Typically, the changes I've been making recently. It wasn't so bad when I was a clueless eighteen-year-old, suddenly handed the keys to an entire empire I had no clue how to manage. I had to run to him for help with every little thing, but over the years, I've learned to stand on my own two feet.

More than that. I've learned how to thrive.

Over the last few months, I've been making active moves to take the company in a more green direction.

Moves Dad has been vehemently against.

I couldn't understand it at first. Our objectives had always been aligned—mitigating as much damage as possible after the fallout of his arrest. But then I realized it's got nothing to do with the business decisions I'm making and everything to do with the fact *I'm* the one making them. Not him.

"It was the best move business-wise," I state blandly, shoulders bunched in preparation for an impending argument.

I could go into an entire spiel about how renewable energy is where the investments are being made now. Where the money is. But he won't hear any of it. My father doesn't give a shit about my reasoning. Hell, when he cools down, he'll agree with me. His problem is that *he* wasn't consulted. That I'm now capable of making such pivotal decisions without his input.

When he cools off, he'll tell me that he's proud, that I've done a commendable job with the company in his absence—I just have to weather this brief storm for now.

"It's a foolish business move," he counters, talking out his ass. "This environmental nonsense is a fad. In several months, everyone will have moved on to something new, and you'll be signed into a ten-year contract with these people."

Right. The fact the polar ice caps are melting is a *fad*.

I *know* he doesn't believe that shit he's peddling. It's his anger talking.

Not rising to the bait, I state wearily, "It's a done deal, Dad."

"One the lawyers are going to have to get us out of whenever I'm in charge again."

All so he can renegotiate a new contract with his signature? I don't fucking think so!

My hands tighten around the steering wheel, my teeth grinding as I swallow my retort.

I know that's the plan. I'm an interim figurehead. Someone to ensure the smooth running of everything while my dad cannot.

Except, while he's been gone, I've put my blood, sweat, and tears into keeping the company afloat. Stocks crashed after he was arrested. Unsurprisingly, investors didn't trust a CEO who had embezzled money, and for nearly an entire year, I was convinced we would go under.

It took everything I had—every spare second of my time, every contact I had, every favor I could cash and bargain I could strike to get us through.

By no means are we back to where we were, but we're solvent, and with each passing year, our profits grow. Slowly but steadily, I'm getting us back on our feet. In the process, I've made this company mine. Not my father's. Not my family's. *Mine.*

And the thought of handing over all my hard work to my father upon his release grates on me.

A heavy silence sits perched on the phone line in the absence of my response, and eventually, I hear him blow out a long breath. "I know you think you can do all of this alone, son, but you should still run deals like this past me. What if they tried to slip something past you? You've come a long way, though deals like this are my wheelhouse, and a second pair of eyes is just smart."

My gut writhes with guilt, and I wipe a hand down my face, doubting myself as my car eats up the miles back to Halston. "Sorry, Dad. But I'm not an idiot, I got the lawyers to go through the contract with a fine toothcomb before I signed anything. The deal is solid."

A heavy exhale comes down the line. "I'm sure it is, I just don't appreciate being blindsided with these sorts of business moves that will impact us for years to come. I need to know what's going on at the company."

*For when I take over again once I'm released.* That's what he doesn't say, but it hangs in the air, leaving a bad taste in my mouth.

"How's school going?" he asks instead, changing the subject.

"Good. Fine. Same old."

"Not letting that GPA of yours drop, are you? Only one more year to go, it would be disappointing to let it slip now."

My teeth grind, that familiar pressure to be a perfect Van Doren pushing down on me.

"Nope. Still passing all my classes."

"That's my boy." There's genuine pride in my father's voice that alleviates some of that pressure and makes me wish my father was here to talk to in person. It's just not the same with him stuck behind a cell and restricted to one visit and only so many calls a week.

A familiar beep comes over the line. "I gotta go," he says, voice softer now. "Will I see you soon?"

"Yeah," I sigh. "I'll be up to see you next week."

"Good. We can talk about this deal you've signed then. I'll see you soon, son."

He hangs up before I have the chance to respond.

*Sure thing, Dad. Happy Thanksgiving to you, too.*

In the deafening silence of the car, I relax back into my seat, barely aware of my surroundings as drive down the freeway. A whirlwind of guilt, anger, and uncertainty churns in my stomach. That uncertainty has been growing stronger with every month that we grow closer to his release. Uncertainty for what the future will hold once he's released. Uncertainty for my position in the company when he's back in charge.

I shake my head, chastising myself for being so self centred. Whatever happens, I'm sure we will work it out. Everything will be easier once he's released. When he's no longer stuck behind bars and feeling as if he has no control over his own life. My dad is smart. He's got a good business head. He can see the fiscal improvements my decisions have made on our bottom line. When he's no longer trapped in a cell, I'll talk to him—explain that I want to remain a vital part of this company. That I don't want to hand the CEO title back to him and walk away.

He'll understand.

I know he will.

# RILEY

## CHAPTER TWENTY

When I arrive at Lux on Saturday night, I change and head straight for booth number four, not surprised in the least to find Ruthless—or as I have dubbed him: Mr. Moody, Hot, and Arrogant waiting for me. Personally, I think that's a far more suitable name for him. He's not ruthless, he's just a hot, moody, arrogant asshole.

One who has shown up at Lux every night for the last three weekends. He demands a dance or two purely to piss me off, then he goes on his merry way.

It's weird, right?

Yes, it's definitely weird.

And just a little bit hot?

Or maybe that's my inner damage talking.

Now that I've become more comfortable around him, the initial fear has worn off. I'm still wary, mainly because his motives are unclear, but there's no denying a shot of excitement zips through me when I see him waiting for me each night.

Instead of terrifying and tormenting, dancing for him has become sensual. Feeling his heated gaze rake over my skin, the manner in which his eyes eat me up, and his pants grow tight when I perform solely for him... it's a heady sensation. Provocative. It makes me feel powerful. Sexy. Wanted in a way I never have been before. In a way I was somewhat afraid to be.

I've been stuffing myself into a box, pulling away from all forms of human contact to pursue my goals and so focused on becoming the parent I need to be for my daughter. Intent on building a life for us. One in which I can regain custody and provide for her—give her all the love I was denied by my own mother—that I have neglected my own needs.

From the second that stick turned blue and I set down the razor blade, I have been breathing solely for my daughter. Every single thing I have done has been for her. To get back to her.

To the extent that I have avoided confronting my own trauma, and instead allowed it to taunt me from the shadows, to keep me from stepping foot outside of the cage I've locked myself in.

I thought I was content in my pen, living only for Aurora, but it has taken coming to Halston for me to realize it can't be enough. As much as I may want it to be, it simply can't.

In order to be the best mom I can be, I need to live for more than just my daughter.

I need to live for me.

Despite the complex nature of my relationship with Logan, he has been a large factor in helping me understand that. In our short time together, he has breathed new life into me. Shown me a world in which I can be happy for *me*—not solely for Aurora.

And these regular dances my dangerous mystery man has coerced me into have pushed me out of my comfort zone. Forced me to face my fears. To overcome the demons *he* etched into my flesh.

Every time I dance for Mr. Moody, Hot, and Arrogant, I

reclaim a part of myself I thought I'd lost. I steal back some of the power *he* stole.

So it is with a newfound confidence that I step into the booth tonight.

I've stopped asking him questions. He never answers and makes it perfectly clear he's here for a dance, not to talk, so I immediately start my routine.

"No dancing, yet." I pause with my arms half raised above my head. "Let's play a game."

"You want to play a game?" I clarify, confused.

He nods, sultry eyes skating over my skin. "A truth for a truth."

I tilt my head, trying to get a read on him, to understand why he's changing things up. This is... different. Way beyond physical.

"And if I don't give you a truth?"

"Then I get to touch you."

"Where?" I ask hesitantly.

One side of his lips quirks up in a dark, seductive smirk. "Anywhere I want."

Fuck, I should not be contemplating this.

And yet, for reasons I can't explain, I am.

"Alright, but that means I get to touch you, too."

He hesitates, his lips pursing ever so slightly before he gives a curt nod of agreement.

Since we're going off script tonight, I move to sit beside him in the booth, but he waggles his finger at me. "Ah ah." Deliberately spreading his thighs, he points to the spot between them. "No reason why you can't dance *and* talk."

"Seriously?"

"You are a performer, after all."

"Yeah. I can also make balloon animals and shuffle cards

like a pro," I comment, moving into my usual spot between his legs.

"Congratulations," he drawls, unimpressed. "I'll be sure to keep you in mind if I ever need a kids' entertainer."

I roll my eyes at his attitude, but instead of feeding into it, I tune him out as I get into the zone, moving my hips to the sultry rhythm of *River* by Bishop Briggs.

"First question." His rough tone has me snapping my eyes open to look at him, finding his sharp gaze locked on mine.

"You said a truth for a truth. Not a question for a question."

"Same difference."

"They're actually two very different things."

"I don't want to hear some superficial truth about your high school crush or if you got drunk and kissed a girl at a party once."

Okayyy... Good to know I shouldn't expect those sorts of questions.

However, that means he has something specific in mind to ask.

"Fine, questions it is, then. *But,* I get to go first."

His eyes narrow on me, and I smile sweetly back at him, knowing it probably pisses him off.

After a moment, he waves his hand in a *get-on-with-it* gesture.

"What's your name?"

His eyes dart back and forth between mine. "You're supposed to be dancing." I huff out a breath before distractedly swaying my hips, giving a half-assed attempt at a dance.

"*You're* supposed to be answering. It's an easy question."

"Giving someone your name means you are handing part of your power over to them. It gives that person a sense of ownership. They can wield your name like a weapon, using it however they see fit—as a sign of affection, in an outpouring of love. *Or* they can use it to drag you through the mud, spread slander, and ensue defamation of your character. Once given, you can never take it back. So no, it's not an easy question."

Well, it sounds like he's given it a lot of thought.

"Does that mean you aren't going to answer it?"

"No."

Okay, then. My lips quirk up in a cocky smirk. "That means I get to touch you."

The glare he levels me with could topple a building, but I brush it aside like dust as I tap my finger against my lip and look him over, pretending I'm deciding on where I want to touch him. The truth is, I already know. It's something I've been wanting to do since I first walked into this booth and saw him sitting there.

However, I'm enjoying watching how much this irks him. I can feel him growing tenser with each passing second, the air around us turning charged and deadly. Mr. Moody, Hot, and Arrogant doesn't like when the tables are turned on him. *Interesting.*

He grunts at me to hurry up, his steely gaze boring into me. My heart pounds in my chest as I step closer, and my bare legs brush against his jean-clad thighs when I lean in. The sharp smell of leather and damp earth from his aftershave mingles with the natural scent of male skin, igniting a fire beneath my skin.

My eyes drift from the strands of dark hair that constantly fall forward across his forehead to his ice-blue eyes that remind me of the lake near my middle school that froze over every winter. Our eyes lock, sending a bolt of desire straight to my core. I can feel him prying into my soul with his piercing stare. Probing at my deeply-seated scars and picking at my vulnerabilities.

Feeling exposed, I tear my eyes from his, my gaze dipping

further until it catches on the pale pink color of his lips. They're so soft looking, plump, and moist. So in contrast to his hard edges and sharp lines. I long to touch them, to press my fingertips against them to see if they're as soft as they look, and I decide that's what I will do if I get the opportunity to touch him again.

Slowly lifting my hand, I thread my fingers through the wayward strands and push them back from his face. The silky strands are warm beneath my fingers, gliding effortlessly through them, and I find myself lingering, not yet ready to let go. He doesn't rush me, and daringly, I let my hand drift lower, my fingers brushing along the solid line of his jaw and feeling the day-old stubble scrape against my skin, the sensation sending an electric current shooting through my body.

"My turn." His voice rumbles like thunder, low and guttural, as the words escape his throat, making my head whirl and my chest heave. Sensing the fine grip I have on my control slipping, I force myself to step away and remember why I shouldn't act upon my impulsive desires.

Erecting my walls, I resume my dance, ignoring the rapid thudding of my heart as I await his question, dreading the truth he could ask for.

He drags out the moment, penetrating eyes attempting to flay me open so he can root inside me for the answer without asking his question. However, my secrets are carefully guarded. Hidden behind high stone walls and moats, in a castle upon a tall mountain, surrounded by wild terrain no one can venture through. Nevertheless, I ready the cannons and prepare for war while scouring the walls for any signs of a breach.

"Why did you come to Halston?" he eventually asks.

"Why does any scholarship student come to Halston?" I counter.

Lips pursing, his astute gaze remains rooted on me as his

eyes narrow at my deflection. "I didn't ask why every other scholarship student comes here. I want to know why *you* chose to."

Turning in my heels, I shake my hips, my ass dancing in front of him. A pointless distraction as, when I glance back at him over my shoulder, I find him still intently focused on my face. Sighing, I explain, "I wanted an education. Halston is one of the finest institutions in the country, and they offered me a full ride. I'd have had to be insane to turn it down."

I hold his gaze for a moment longer before turning to look at a point out on the club floor, continuing the sensual moving of my body solely for him. I take the time to decide my next question. Considering I know next to nothing about him, choosing what to ask is challenging. What I want to know most. What he might seemingly answer.

"Why do you keep coming back here?" I eventually ask, turning to face him again.

"I want something pretty to look at."

"But why me? If that's the reason, plenty of beautiful women here would happily dance for you."

"Nu huh, one question at a time, James. It's my turn."

Huffing out a breath, I gesture for him to ask his question.

"Why did you come to Halston?" he repeats.

I cock a brow. "I already answered that one."

"You did, but it wasn't the truth. So I'm asking again."

His comeback has me stopping mid-dance to stare wide-eyed at him. *Well, damn. I totally thought he bought that.*

Unwilling to give him the actual truth, or anything even remotely close to it, I slam my mouth shut, lips pressed together in a refusal.

One side of his lips quirk, and I'd hazard a guess he was expecting my non-response. "Better turn around, James."

"Why?" I ask, suddenly feeling anxious.

"Cause where I wanna touch, I can't reach from here."

Yup, that response only ratchets my anxiety up another five notches, and my knees tremble as I hesitantly turn my back on him. My breathing grows heavier with every second that passes, and he makes no move to reach out and touch me.

As the tension in my body reaches a breaking point, I feel an almost imperceptible brush against the back of my calf. It's so soft that I almost believe I imagined it, except it's followed a second later by another feather-light caress on my other leg. My body goes up in flames, as though every nerve has been dipped in caramel and poked with needles, and I know for certain that it wasn't simply my imagination.

Growing bolder, Ruthless slowly trails a scorching path up the back of my calves. The heat from his fingers spreads like wildfire as he reaches my knees, before his palms cup my legs, engulfing them as he slides them up toward my hips. With every inch gained, my breathing grows labored until I'm light-headed and dizzy, the blood pulsing through my veins like molten lava.

When he reaches the hem of my short skirt, I expect him to continue, perhaps grab my ass. However, he surprises me by moving his hands to the outside of the fabric and continuing his ascent until he can grip my hips.

He tugs, and I gasp as I fall back against him. "*This* is where I wanted to touch you," he whispers in a husky voice, his breath tickling my ear as I try my best not to wriggle in his lap.

His hands remain firmly fixed on my hips. Although, since he didn't need me to turn around in order to touch them, I'm guessing that's not what he's referring to.

"Ask your question," he murmurs, his velvety-smooth voice doing inappropriate things to me as his fingers dig into my soft flesh in a clear indication for me to remain where I am.

I'm not entirely sure what the game is at this point, but I do know he's not going to answer whatever I ask. So this time, I don't even bother asking one of my many questions and instead blurt, "What's the most outrageous thing you've ever done?"

His surprised breath whooshes against the sensitive skin of my neck, and I'm already thinking about where I want to touch him next when he murmurs, "Definitely this."

My head whips around to face him, our eyes clashing, but before I can say or do anything, he bites out, "Why are you at Halston?"

This again?

My lips remain sealed, and taking my silence for what it is, he releases one of my hips from his large, calloused palms and slowly slides it lower across the front of my skirt until his fingers curve around the hem. Sliding lower still, his hand cups my entire pussy, and everything in me shivers at the heat that radiates between us.

Curling a finger, he runs it along my thong-covered slit, and I know he can feel the moisture gathered from this little game of ours. It's a dead giveaway to how affected I am by him—just like the hard rod digging into my back gives away his.

"Come on, James," he purrs in my ear. "Be a good girl for me and answer the question."

His words douse me in ice-cold water, obliterating the searing heat from a moment ago as *his* voice infiltrates the room.

*"Such a good girl for me."*

He would always say something to that effect after he was finished, as I was curled up on my side, my back to him so he couldn't see the devastation he wrought. I wanted him to know precisely what he did to me every night, but I also refused to give him the satisfaction of knowing I was splintering piece by piece.

It was the same reason I never allowed him to see how

viscerally his words affected me. They were more potent than his actions. No matter how hard I tried to keep my tears in, they would inevitably spill out when he gently ran his fingers through my hair and whispered *my good girl*. They were my undoing. The final straw that broke me.

With the feel of *his* hand in my hair and his voice in my head, I jump out of Ruthless' lap and race from the booth. The club is a blur as I make a beeline for the staff exit door leading into the back of the building.

Flying through it, my rapid breathing echoes in my head as I hurry blindly down the corridor, not even sure of where I'm going. Away. I just need to get away. To breathe in fresh air. To get somewhere private before someone sees me in the midst of a panic attack.

A hard shove has me stumbling against the wall as a warm heat envelops my back.

"Where do you think you're going, James?"

I hadn't realized he'd followed me. He shouldn't even be back here, but I can't make my lips form the words to tell him as much. As he presses in against me, my panic spikes, and I slam my eyes closed against the onslaught of memories. Some familiar. Some new. Some I had long since buried or forgotten entirely, while others are the ones that like to sneak up on me in the middle of the night.

"Please," I whimper, my throat choked with tears. "Please, don't."

Trapped in my mind, I don't notice him take a step back or cautiously reach out to turn me around, until gentle fingers grasp my chin, forcing my head upward until my eyes clash with baby blue ones. Ones that I'd recognize anywhere.

I latch on to them, using them as a lifeline to reel me in and pull me out of the bottomless ocean of trauma that I'm wading through. Until my breathing once again feels steady and his presence is tucked away.

I'm not sure what comes over me. Except that one moment I'm falling head-first into the cold ocean of his eyes, depending on them for survival; and in the next my arms are around his neck, my lips on his as I use his mouth to empty myself of every ounce of uncertainty, fear, and unease currently eating me alive.

His lips remain hard against mine, and snapping to my senses, I pull back, unable to look him in the eye as I murmur, "Sorry."

*God, what the hell was I thinking?* Not only is kissing a client unprofessional, but I don't even know this man. Not even his name. Yet here I am, throwing myself at him.

He doesn't respond, and after an awkward moment, I gather the courage and glance up at him through my lashes. He's glaring down at me with the muscle in his jaw pulsing and his eyes blazing with a deadly fire.

Fuck, I've really gone and pissed him off now.

Lifting my head, I open my mouth intending to repeat my apology when he surges forward. The air is knocked from my lungs as my back hits the wall, and he swallows the gasp, his lips covering mine.

His kiss is rough, demanding, with a hint of saltiness that lingers on my tongue. His lips are no longer firm and resistant, but soft and pliable, exactly how I expected them to feel. He nips at my bottom lip before sliding his tongue into my mouth and stealing any hope I had of escaping this exchange unscathed.

The darkened hallway fills with the sweet chorus of soft sighs and labored breaths as he presses me more firmly against the wall. His hips grind against mine, the prominent bulge of his erection coaxing my desire higher. Bringing his hand between us, I whimper into his mouth as his fingers skim the wet patch of my panties. He groans, and I rock my hips, needy for more.

Planting one hand on the wall beside my head, he wrenches his lips from mine, staring down at me with wild eyes. His fingers continue to swipe teasingly along the front of my panties, coaxing me into a frenzy.

"Give me one honest truth and I'll make you come so hard you'll truly believe Heaven is a place on earth."

I can't think straight with the way he's infiltrating my senses, leaving me torn as I stare up at him with glazed eyes. As if sensing I need more encouragement, he pushes his fingers beneath the waistband of my thong, sliding them through my wet lips.

"A truth," he whispers in a gravelly voice against my ear.

"Only if you give me one in return," I half moan. He hesitates before nodding in agreement, and I confess, "I like to dance... outside of here."

He continues to stroke me, sending my body into a tailspin, which is the only reason why I continue talking. "It's the only reason I applied for this job. I just wanted to dance. I need it to breathe, you know? It's the one time when I feel whole. When I'm dancing, it doesn't feel like the strings that normally hold me in place are slowly fraying apart. I can let go and not worry about the pieces of myself scattering all around me... because, at the end of the song, I know I'll find a way to piece them back together—even if only for a moment."

At my admission, his thumb circles my clit, sending sparks of electricity shooting along my nerves before he inserts the tip of his finger into my tight channel.

Dropping his head, his mouth rests against my ear as he drives his finger in and out, working me into a wild frenzy. "For weeks, I've thought about what it would be like to feel you pressed against me like this. I've wondered about the noises you'd make. Imagined how fucking good you'd feel strangling the life out of me while I made you come. Every time I wrap my hand around my cock and close my eyes, it's you that I picture. It's *you* that I jerk off to. Your name that I grunt when I come over the shower wall instead of in your hot mouth or tight cunt."

*God, his dirty words are going to be the end of me.*

Death by dirty talk. It might not be a thing, but Mr. Moody, Hot, and Arrogant is about to make it one.

"But that's not the truth I wanted to share with you," he continues in his straining rasp. "My truth for you is... the reality is so much better."

Our breaths mingle as I stare up at him.

"Tell me, James. Have you gotten yourself off to the thought of me?"

"Yes," I answer breathlessly.

It's the truth. I didn't technically have to give him one, yet I wanted him to know. Wanted him to know that in the early Saturday and Sunday hours, I'd laid awake in my bed, picturing his face hovering above mine, his strong, sturdy hands appraising my heated flesh as I slipped my hand beneath the waistband of my sleep shorts and pretended it was him making me feel so good.

After being unable to reach an orgasm before coming to Halston, I've now found two very different men who can make me come—both by their touch and my own. I had written off the orgasm I gave myself in Logan's presence as a one-time thing, but these last few weekends, when I've gotten home and climbed beneath the cool sheets of my bed, it's Ruthless' face I've seen reflected on the back of my eyelids. His voice I've heard as I pictured myself dancing for him in the private booth. Imagined what might happen if we went one step further as my hand slid between my thighs and my fingers stretched me wide.

Perhaps I'm not as broken as I believe. Perhaps there's something in the water at Halston U. Or perhaps their damage speaks to mine in a song without words. One that, instead of breaking us apart, melds us together.

"Good. Now let me hear the noises you'll make when I eventually destroy your pussy with my cock."

*Fuck.*

It was an order, one I'm helpless to defy as my release barrels through me, taking over control of my limbs and consuming me until I'm no longer able to contain it.

By the time I come back into my body, I'm weak-kneed and breathless. Peeling back my eyelids, I look into darkened pools of deep blue lust as Ruthless' face lingers inches above mine.

After what feels like an eternity where we're the only two people left on earth, his features slowly shift back into their usual, haughty expression, before he steps back. Cool air rushes in, causing me to shake as it strokes the hyper-sensitive nerve endings along my skin, and I watch mutely as he grants me one final truth.

Lifting his hand, I watch in awe as he sucks his fingers into his mouth, humming as he keeps his eyes pinned on mine, portraying the dark pits of desire that burn within them. When he's licked them clean, he leaves without a word, and I stare after him as he strides down the hall before disappearing through the door back into the club.

Alone, I sag against the wall and ask myself what I've just gotten myself in for. Because I don't believe for one second that that will be the end of this unusual interplay between us.

# LOGAN

## CHAPTER TWENTY-ONE

The puck slips between my stick and his, and I growl under my breath as my opponent knocks it away, gaining the upper hand. "Fuck," I snarl, taking off after him.

Before I can catch up, he passes it to one of his forwards who has a clear shot. The puck goes sailing through the air, the collective audience holding their breaths as the damn thing shoots past our goalie right as the buzzer rings.

"Fuck." I bang my stick against the boards angrily.

Another fucking loss.

That makes three losses out of the last six games.

The number of games I've played since *her.* Since that night Grayson spotted her at Lux and I discovered the girl I was falling for was a twisted, conniving bitch.

While 50:50 might seem okay to most, the fact I'm in no way responsible for our wins makes it unacceptable in my books. I'm supposed to be fucking carrying this team and instead, I may as well be sitting on the goddamn bench.

Head hanging, I skate toward the edge of the rink, however, I can't help glancing at her empty seat. I shouldn't even be fucking looking. Shouldn't be thinking about her, or the fact she should be here.

She shouldn't be fucking here!

But tell that to my stupid fucking heart who still has a hard-on for the bitch that screwed over my best friend.

A fact I can't wrap my head around. It still feels like two different people—My Riley and the girl Grayson knew. No matter how hard I try, I can't reconcile the two of them in my head. I can't make it make sense. How can the sweet, shy, sensitive girl who has been tutoring me all semester be the same one responsible for destroying an innocent life and ripping apart a family in the process?

More importantly, how could I not have seen it? I believe myself to be a good judge of character. After years of people cozying up to me for their own gain, I've become adept at identifying the snakes, but she slipped right beneath my defenses. She slithered her way into my heart and bit down on the juicy muscle, embedding her poisonous venom into the fibers and fucking decimating me.

Grayson's revelation that night was a shocking blow. It shattered the beautiful illusion I had created in my mind about our relationship. I'd been picturing her at my games, in my jersey. Cuddling up with her in bed afterward. I had images of her five years from now, at my side while we attended Family Day for whatever team I was playing for. On my arm at social events. I pictured coming home to her after away games and it felt so fucking right.

The devastation hits me anew, as it does every time I think of her—which is pretty much every waking moment. Hurt, betrayal, and sadness have become my permanent state of being, and I fucking hate it. I hate feeling this way, but what I despise the most is that, underneath all the heartache and anger, I still fucking miss her. I miss our study dates in the library, watching her face light up when I aced a test. I miss feeling her soft skin beneath my hands and her supple lips on mine. I miss talking to her or seeing her face every day.

I miss *her.*

Which is ridiculous because the person I thought I knew never actually existed.

How fucked up is that?

That's the real reason why I can't look her in the face. Because if I go anywhere near her I can't be sure whether I'll throw her against the wall and scream at her or kiss her.

It would be too fucking easy to fall head-first into those eyes and never come up for air again.

It has nothing to do with the bullshit excuse I fed her about working at Lux. I couldn't give a shit about that.

Although, it *was* nice to hear she didn't do *extras.* The thought of some perv's hands on her. His dick in her mouth... *nope, not going there.*

Regardless, I actually admire her for having the confidence to get on stage and do what she does. That takes guts—to put yourself on display like that.

*You don't know the courage it takes for me to get up there every night.*

No, I don't. But was that all bullshit to try and get me to talk to her? I no longer know what to believe. If I can trust a single word that comes out of her mouth.

Every time we spoke, she seemed so genuine. She made it impossible not to trust her.

She saw me in a way no one else ever has.

How could that have been fake?

Does it matter, even if it wasn't all a lie?

Maybe she never had any ill intention toward me, but she still fucked Grayson over. She might not have lied to *me*, but she has lied to others. About others. Lies that decimated a family and have had severe and lasting consequences.

There's a rain cloud the size of Texas and threatening hailstones hanging over my head as I step off the ice. One that cracks with an impending thunderstorm when Coach calls my name.

"Astor, I want to see you in my office ASAP."

Double fuck.

I can't say I'm surprised, given how completely useless I've been on the ice these last few weeks. Specifically since that night. She was technically only with me for a total of three games, and yet it changed everything for me. She really was my lucky charm—my unlucky lucky charm. A cursed lucky charm, if such a thing even exists.

Now I can't get back into the groove I had before she infiltrated my life.

Is that what she wanted? To fuck with my head? Most women want a ride on my dick or the bump in social status from hanging around me, but this chick has proven before that she's a vindictive cunt. Is this how she planned to screw me over? By messing with my game?

I could tell the first time I talked to her in Statistics that she disliked me. She wasn't impressed by my popularity or ability on the ice. At the time, I thought it was refreshing. Now, I'm not so sure. Perhaps from that very first moment, she was deliberating the best way to fuck with me. I bet she's having a good laugh now, watching me tank my fucking career because I can't get her stupidly beautiful green eyes out of my head.

Vibrating with humiliation, hurt, and anger, I grunt out a response to Coach before stomping in my skates down the hall toward the lockers.

The mood in the changing room is subdued. I don't have any words of encouragement or inspiration for my team. Hell, I don't even have words for myself. I've been fucking up recently, and I know it. Coach does too, if he's calling me in.

So I keep my head down and mouth shut, ignoring the disappointed glances from Gavin.

Once I'm freshly showered and dressed, I grab my bag, but he catches me before I can escape out the door.

"Yo, a bunch of us are going out. You in?"

"We lost," I deadpan.

"Yeah, no shit, Sherlock," he retorts, a tic in his jaw. "Figured it might do us good to get out of our heads for a night. Have a couple of drinks. Let off some steam. Regroup."

*Well, shit. Being the captain and all, I probably should have thought of that.*

Blowing out a breath, I try to let go of some of my tension as I nod. "Yeah. Sounds good."

God knows I could do with regrouping.

Maybe what I need to push her out of my head is to get drunk. I rarely drink during the season. The odd beer at The Depot or post-Saturday-night game. However, if I could just stop thinking about *her*, perhaps I could get my mojo back and stop fucking up on the ice.

"A few drinks and some downtime sounds like a great idea," I tack on more enthusiastically. "Where are you going? I'll meet you there once Coach is done flaying my balls and making a pretty necklace out of them for his wife."

The guys laugh, and for the first time in weeks, I don't feel so alone. So stuck in my head.

"Guys voted for Lux."

His words pop my fragile bubble of contentment and I can hear the air wheezing out of it as I stall on the threshold of the locker room, glancing back at him over my shoulder. *Seriously, can I not escape this girl?*

He's too busy stuffing his gear into his duffel so he doesn't see the look on my face. I contemplate suggesting somewhere else—a bar on campus, a frat party. I really don't give a shit, just anywhere but there. However, that seems selfish. If that's where the team voted to go, then that's where we should go.

Maybe I could back out...

*No. You're the team captain. You need to start acting like it.*

Besides, it will only raise questions if I back out now.

Fuck.

I have no choice but to go.

Gritting my teeth, I let the locker room door slam shut behind me as I head toward Coach's office.

"Are you trying to fuck up your career before it even begins?" he practically yells the second my ass hits the seat. He's standing behind his desk, hands on his hips as he glares down at me, his anger seeping out to fill the small space.

"No."

He scoffs. "Well, it sure as fuck looks that way. You think that you can stop putting in the effort just because the scouts came to see you play? In case you've forgotten, Astor, there is still no offer on the table. No signed contract."

I haven't. How the fuck could I?

I'm used to Coach's tirades by now, though, so I know he isn't looking for a response from me. A fact that is confirmed when he continues with his rant.

"You're the team captain. That means you're responsible for more than just yourself. If you play like shit, your team does too. *My* team does. I don't give a fuck about you. *I* have worked too damn hard to not make it to the Frozen Four for the fourth consecutive year."

Blowing out a breath, his anger deflates as he collapses into his chair, eyes raking over me. "I'm retiring at the end of this season."

He's what? I'd hazard a guess that Coach is in his mid-fifties. No spring chicken, but I didn't think he'd be retiring for another few years yet... if ever. Honestly, I kinda pictured Coach dying in this office. Hockey—the team—is his life.

"The wife has been nagging at me for years to step back. She wants us to spend more time together. Go on a cruise. I dunno."

"Coach, you can't quit," I splutter. "You *are* this team."

"I've already submitted the paperwork. It's a done deal. I figured with four Championship years under my belt, it was wise to quit while I was ahead."

Well, fuck. Now I'm not only fucking it up for myself but for Coach.

He pierces me with a stern look. "Don't make me regret not filling out the paperwork last year."

"No pressure," I grumble.

"Pressure is exactly what you need," Coach states sternly as he smacks his palm against the desk. "A reminder that it's more than your own career you're fucking up here. However, it is *your* career that I'm concerned with. If you don't pull your head out of your ass and put it in the game, you'll lose everything you've worked toward. You're this close, Logan. Don't fuck it up now in the final period."

---

Coach's words are playing on repeat as I pull into the parking lot of Lux. My phone pings on the seat beside me, another message from the guys wondering where I am. I left Coach's office hours ago. Still I needed time alone to think, so I went to the weight room and worked out, losing myself in the mechanical motion of exercise as I processed everything Coach said.

As tempting as getting drunk sounds, it isn't a permanent solution to my problem. I can't keep letting Riley get to me like this. I need to get my head in the game and focus. This is supposed to be *my* year. Coach's year. He's been there for me since freshman year—pushing, encouraging, yelling.

I don't want to let him down.

Let the team down.

I'm tired of being the weak link.

Especially when I'm the one who should be leading us to victory.

I need to purge myself of her once and for all, except I have no idea how. Obviously, sitting in the parking lot of her place of work isn't going to do me any good. However, I have no desire to go inside.

I should get out and go in. I know I should. The team is expecting me. However, every time I reach for the door handle, I stall. Feeling as though I need another moment to gather myself before I come face-to-face with her.

I've made a point of avoiding Riley. I don't seek her out on campus the way I used to. I avoid anywhere I know she might be. I don't even get coffee from the cart anymore, considering it's located outside the dining hall and I know she eats all her meals there. Plus, the smell of cinnamon and nutmeg makes me think of her.

Rather, I bought myself an insulated cup and I bring my own coffee from home.

The only time I can't avoid her is in Statistics. Although, even then, I make a point of not looking in her direction. Of course, my body intuitively knows whenever she enters the room. I might not catalog her movements with my eyes, but my fucking senses are attuned to her. They know where she is at all times, even where she sits. If she's looking at me. Some days, I can even sense her moods from the opposite side of the room.

The woman is buried so deep in my fucking system that I can't get her out.

"Fuck it," I curse, throwing open the door before I can

continue talking myself out of it. I need to suck it up for my team, so that's exactly what I'm going to do.

Looking more like I'm heading to a funeral than a club, I stalk up to the door, lifting my chin at the bouncer as I walk past. As soon as I step inside, my head swivels toward the stage as I scour it for her. Not seeing her, I breathe out a sigh of relief before focusing on the main reason I'm here: my team.

I spot them huddled around a booth against the far wall, and head in their direction.

"You finally made it!" Gavin holds his beer up as I approach.

"Yeah, yeah. Had to stop and get surgery after Coach ripped me a new one."

The team laughs it up as I slide into the end of the booth and order a beer from a waitress when she passes by.

Thankfully, I don't have a clear view of the stage, and I'm able to lose myself in easy conversation with my teammates. Tension bleeds out of me, and it starts to feel like old times, laughing with them and talking hockey. Gavin and I regale the rookies with stories of the shit we got up to our freshman year, and we all howl with laughter.

It isn't until a wisp of auburn hair catches the light and has my head turning that I remember where I am. Who else is here. My eyes zero in on her like a homing beacon.

*God, she's breathtaking.*

I'd forgotten how entrancing she was to watch on stage. It's mesmerizing. Each movement choreographed and performed to perfection. I can't look away, even after the final notes of the song play out and she walks off the stage. My teammates are entirely forgotten as I watch her pause at the bottom of the steps, her posture tensing as she talks to some man in a suit. The serenity that had been on her face while she danced hardens into a pinched mask as she nods her head, and my eyes narrow, wondering what it is about their exchange that has her on edge.

*Nope. No. It's none of my business.*

Forcing myself to look away, I return to the conversation happening at the table, but don't take part as my mind spins in a hundred different directions.

Before long, we're being told that the club is closing for the night, and we pay our tab before leaving. I walk out with the guys, most of whom are smiling and laughing, tonight's loss apparently forgotten as everyone says their goodnights before heading toward their respective vehicles.

Climbing into my SUV, I watch while car engines rev and tires crunch over gravel as they leave the lot and speed down the street before the noise peters off into the distance, and silence consumes the night.

I should leave. Head home and get some sleep. My muscles are sore, and I'm exhausted after back-to-back games this weekend.

And yet, I don't.

Instead, I sit there as the minutes tick by, suspended in indecision and hating myself for it while I stare out the windshield at the red-brick building, lit up with spotlights and the glow from the backlit sign hanging above the double doors.

"This is stupid," I grumble aloud. "I shouldn't be here."

I move to put the car in gear when I hear voices. A group of women appear from around the side of the building, talking to one another as they walk toward the remaining cars.

Abstractly, I scan their faces for Riley, not seeing her among the group.

The cars peel out of the parking lot, leaving mine and a classy Mercedes sedan as the only two left.

Wearing a frown, I stare at the front door of the club, wondering why Riley is still inside. My gaze slides to the

Mercedes tucked away at the back of the lot as an irrational anger bubbles. What if she stayed behind with a client?

*She said she doesn't give extras.*

Yeah, but that could have been a lie.

Or it could be another worker? That suit-wearing dickhead I saw talking to her? A flashy car like that probably belongs to the manager or owner of the club. Is it just the two of them alone in there?

*Ugh, stop it!*

It's none of my fucking business.

*She* is none of my business.

However, knowing she's most likely alone in there with whoever the asshole is keeps me rooted in my car in the parking lot as the minutes tick by.

Nearly an entire hour passes before two silhouettes emerge from the shadows at the side of the building. My attention snaps to her immediately, eyes scanning her body. The beast that has been banging against its cage for the last hour finally settles, somewhat appeased at seeing her with his own two eyes.

My gaze is so riveted on her that I pick up on how her arms are folded across her chest in a defensive posture, her tight, fake smile in response to whatever the douchecanoe beside her says.

It's enough to have me focusing on him instead, and I snarl quietly when the slimy bastard I saw her talking to earlier gestures toward his car. I don't need to hear what he's saying to know what he's asking. His dirty fucking intentions with *my girl.*

*Not your girl,* the pesky little voice in my head pipes up, and I growl in response, uncaring of that little factoid right now.

Riley shakes her head, but Fuckface doesn't let up, continuing to try and lure her into his car, doling out that smarmy fucking smile of his as though it were candy.

Hell to the motherfucking no.

I don't give a shit who he is; she is not getting in that motherfucking car!

A gust of air passes my lips when she shakes her head, this time pairing it with a step backward that puts more distance between them.

*Good girl.*

Oblivious or uncaring, he continues talking, and Riley glances around her as though seeking an escape. I don't fucking like it.

I don't like that he's not taking no for an answer.

I don't like her standing in a dark parking lot alone with him.

And I sure as fuck don't like the leering way he's looking at what's mine.

My hand tightens around the door handle, and I'm .2 seconds away from tearing it open and storming over there when he finally steps away from her, moving toward his car.

She stands and watches him climb in with a guarded expression, waiting until he leaves the lot before the tension drops from her shoulders. Just as my anger starts to dissipate, she starts walking toward the sidewalk, and in an instant, my rage comes roaring back, full force, this time directed toward *her*.

*Is she for fucking real right now?* I glance down at the clock glowing on my dashboard. It's nearly 2 a.m. and she's going to walk home alone?!

I begin counting in my head, only making it to ten before I throw the car into gear and slowly roll out of the parking lot after her.

# RILEY

## CHAPTER TWENTY-TWO

Shaking off the slimy residue of Ben's ogling eyes, I try to ignore the way his jaw ticked when I refused his offer of a ride home. He has asked me to stay late and lock up with him several times now, and ever since that first night, he has grown bolder with his advances.

He's no longer even trying to be subtle, barely listening whenever I say no or turn him down.

It's starting to make me seriously uncomfortable, and I'm not sure what to do. I can't see a way out of it other than to quit my job, which I can't afford to do.

The street is dead as I briskly walk along the sidewalk, and I push my panicked thoughts aside as I focus on my surroundings. I hate making this journey so late. The streets are eerie in the pre-dawn hours. Especially in this part of town, where the homeless gather and people with nothing better to do drive around aimlessly. My body tenses every time a car passes, and I swear they seem to slow down as they go by.

I always make sure to wear jeans and cover myself up when I'm leaving the club, not wanting to draw any more attention than necessary. The last thing I want is to be mistaken for a prostitute. It's bad enough that men push their luck in the club with the girls working the floor despite the presence of bouncers. I can only imagine how some entitled scumbag would respond to the word *no* from a 'hooker'.

While I walk, my thoughts turn to Ruthless. For the first time in weeks, he didn't show up tonight. It's no coincidence that last week we crossed a line physically and this week he's AWOL. What is a surprise is the fact I was disappointed to discover he wasn't waiting for me. While I enjoyed being back on the stage and performing without any interruptions, I actually missed our strange interactions. The unusual give and take. The heady sexual chemistry.

Perhaps he got what he wanted, and now he's done with me. Now that we've crossed that line, the excitement has worn off. That edge of mystery lost.

Or is it possible he felt what I did, and it sent him running for the hills? He's the type of guy that screams commitment issues, so I wouldn't be surprised if he's currently hiding out somewhere, naively assuming he can ignore his feelings until they go away.

I'm jolted out of my thoughts as xenon headlights paint the sidewalk in an eerie white glow, and the growl of a car engine grows louder as it draws near. The hairs on the back of my neck stand to attention and I keep my head straight, not faltering in my pace as it drives by. I breathe out a sigh of relief, which stalls when the bright red brake lights go on, burning my eyes as the large SUV stops at the curb in front of me.

I slow to a crawl as I contemplate crossing the road. The streetlights are out on the other side, and I'm weighing up my options—walking in the dark versus walking past a potential kidnapper—when the driver-side door is pushed open.

*Fuck.*

Nope.

I turn on my heel, ready to sprint for my life as a dark figure steps out of the car.

"Riley, that you?"

I freeze before slowly turning back around, recognizing that voice.

"Logan?"

He steps forward into the pool of light offered from the streetlamp above. It bounces off his blond hair, illuminating his boyish features.

"I thought it was." His gaze shifts past me in the direction of Lux, lips thinning before he once again meets my stare. Something flashes in his eyes too quickly for me to decipher. "You shouldn't be walking home alone at this time of night."

Seriously? The last words he spoke to me were essentially contempt at how I choose to make a living, and now he's giving me grief for walking home in the dark? Sorry, we can't all afford luxury SUVs to drive around in.

"Noted," I snark, before moving around him and continuing on my way. It's far too late—or early, depending on your perspective—for this shit, and bed is calling my name.

Realizing that he's aggravated me, he blows out a breath. "Sorry. I didn't mean it like that. I just... never mind. Get in. I'll give you a ride."

"I'm good, thanks."

He stares at me for a moment, incredulous.

"Really? You're going to risk walking home alone in the dark instead of getting in the car with me?"

I grit my teeth, knowing he's right. Still, I'm a stubborn bitch and refuse to cave to him.

"Riley," he growls when I make no move toward him. "Get in the damn car."

I hesitate for another second until he takes a threatening step forward. He appears menacing in the darkness. If I didn't know it was Logan and I met him in a dark alley, I'd probably shit my pants. Yet, despite the anger radiating from him, I'm not afraid. I know he won't harm me—not physically, at least.

My heart, though... that's an entirely different matter.

He slowly advances, his eyes filled with a dark promise.

"Logan," I warn, stepping back, even as I continue to glare at him.

"Get in the car, Riley."

When I don't jump at his demand, he reaches out with his long arms, and the world tilts as I'm unceremoniously tossed over his shoulder. One arm wraps tightly around my upper thighs, locking me in place as I struggle against him.

"Put me down, asshole!" I bellow as I bang my fists against his back.

Stomping around to the passenger side of his car, he throws open the door and dumps me inside. I'm instantly drowning in everything *Logan*. The crisp, fresh scent that makes my lungs feel like they haven't inhaled properly in months only grows stronger when he leans in, roughly grabs the seatbelt, and pulls it around me before clicking it into place.

His sudden demonstration of concern for my wellbeing is confusing.

"Why do you even care?" I demand, scowling at him. "You hate me."

He glares right back, the muscle in his jaw clenching, before he shakes his head and steps back to close the door.

Right before it snicks shut, I swear I hear him mutter, "If only it was that easy," and when I look into his face, it's lost that hostile anger. Now he just seems sad. Really fucking sad.

When he climbs in behind the wheel, he pulls onto the street, and I keep my focus cemented out my window, determined not to say a word to him the entire way back to campus.

"Where to?" he asks, ruining that idea.

"The dorms."

I'm still not looking at him, but as the car fills with a fraught tension, I cast him a sideways glance. His hand is wrapped around the steering wheel so tightly that the veins in his arm threaten to pop, and his teeth grind furiously. I can practically hear them all the way over here, but I don't understand what has made him so angry.

"Try again," he practically snarls.

I turn in my seat to glower at him. "Excuse me?"

"I know you don't live on campus," he states, sparing me a scathing glance. "So let's cut the bullshit."

My eyes skim over his face as his acknowledgement settles in.

"Have you been following me?"

He scoffs but keeps his lips firmly sealed.

"I'm not telling you where I live."

"Then I guess we're driving around until sunrise."

"Are you for real?" I seethe. "Just drop me off at the dorms. Or here."

"Kinda defeats the purpose of me giving you a ride home if you still have to walk."

"Why did you pick me up? What are you even doing in this part of town?"

His lips purse and I begin to think he isn't going to answer me when he finally speaks.

"I was out with the team. I needed to clear my head and was just driving around when I saw you risking your fucking life by walking alone in the dark."

"Don't be so dramatic," I snipe, even though I know every night I walk that journey home it's a risk. Maybe not as big of one as if I lived in a large city, but it's still a risk. It only takes one drunken asshole, one entitled shitstain.

"Address, Riley," he growls. "Or so help me, I will make us both miserable by driving around all night."

Good to know that being in my presence makes him *miserable.*

Huffing, I rattle off my address, and he puts it into the GPS, following the directions toward my apartment.

"Why did you need to clear your head?" I venture when we're only a couple of blocks from my apartment.

"What?"

"You said you needed to clear your head... why?"

He's silent for a beat before admitting, "We lost tonight's game."

It's all he gives me, but as I watch him from the corner of my eye, I can see the weight of that loss pressing down on him.

"I'm sorry," I mutter, unsure what else to say.

He doesn't respond as he turns onto my street, and I watch as his gaze bounces over the buildings, lingering on Ava's dance studio before shifting to my apartment building as he pulls to a stop outside. I can't decipher what he's thinking as he takes in where I live.

Tearing my eyes away from him, I glance out the window at the sidewalk. "Uhh, thanks," I mutter, unsure what else to say as I push open the door and slide out of his car.

He lingers there as I unlock the door to my building, waiting until I'm safely inside before driving off.

Alone, I sag against the wall.

Well, that was unexpected.

---

As I step around the side of the building into the parking lot, I immediately spot Logan's car. It's impossible to miss, the expensive-looking SUV appearing entirely out of place alongside the beat-up cars that a few of the other girls own.

However, it could also be the blond-haired hockey god leaning against the bumper that caught my attention more so than the car.

"Ooh, hot date?" Tara asks, eyeing up Logan like he's a juicy gazelle and she's a starved lion.

"Not exactly."

She arches her brow. "Sounds like a story."

"Not a very good one."

"Need me to kick his ass?" Tara asks teasingly, but I sense she's not merely joking. Tara is a bit of an enigma. She's all feminine curves and fluttering lashes, but she's got a tough exterior. Growing up in a poor community not far from here, she hasn't had an easy life. It's made her hard; it taught her how to stand up for herself. However, she's loyal to a fault, and given that her brother owns The Depot, I have no doubt she could get a good shot or two in before Logan would gain the upper hand.

I smile gratefully at her. "Not tonight."

"Well, you just let me know if that changes. I'll dust off my knuckle dusters, especially for you."

I clap my hand over my heart and tease, "Marry me?"

She throws her head back and laughs before something catches her eye and she nudges my shoulder. "Girl." Gesturing to where the other dancers are eyeing Logan with equal interest, she says, "Might wanna claim your man before the vultures descend."

"He's not my man," I point out. My efforts are futile and Tara simply smirks as she backs away.

"Whatever you say, mama. Don't do anything I wouldn't do." She winks before spinning on her heels. She gives Logan a finger wave as she passes him on her way to her car parked at the back of the lot, earning herself an arched brow before he shifts his attention to me.

Swallowing, I steel my spine before moving toward him.

"What are you doing here?"

"Saving a stubborn woman from getting herself into a situation she can't get out of."

"It's not your job to look out for me," I retort, ignoring the unease in my stomach.

He makes a disgruntled noise before gritting, "Get in."

Not wanting him to go all caveman on me like last night, I don't fight him and instead walk around to the passenger side of the car. He nods, seeming appeased by my compliance before he hops in.

"Tara usually gives me a ride home," I tell him when we're nearly at my apartment, feeling the need to show him I'm not as stupid as he seems to think. I only walk home when I absolutely have to, which is only when Ben asks me to stay late. If he asks Tara or if she isn't working that night, I usually grab a lift with one of the other girls.

"The one who waved?" he enquires.

I nod.

"She didn't last night."

"Because I had to stay late."

"Do you do that often?"

I don't know why he's so interested, although I answer him anyway. "Occasionally."

I hear a soft, irritated sigh at my vague answer, and I turn my face toward the window so he doesn't catch my amused smirk.

"Who was that guy you were with last night?" he asks.

"What guy?" I ask, eyes narrowed as I snap my head around to glare at him.

"The pervy-looking dude with the flashy car to compensate for the fact his dick is hamster-sized."

I snort at his surprisingly accurate summation of Ben, even as I pierce him with my suspicion.

"And how do you know I was with *anyone* last night? You said you were driving by and saw me walking."

He gives a casual shrug, except I see right through it. "Okay, so I drove past and saw you two standing outside Lux. You looked uncomfortable so I pulled over and waited until he left. When I saw you walking home, I knew I had to come rescue your ass."

"I did not need rescuing," I fume, choosing to overlook the fact he noticed I was uncomfortable with Ben and stopped. There's too much to unpack from that, and I know it will only raise more questions and leave me even more confused about Logan and what I mean to him. What he means to me.

"Don't change the subject, Riley. Who is he?"

Sighing, I don't see the point in keeping the answer from him. Turning to stare out the window, I explain, "That's Ben. He's the manager."

I can feel his eyes on me, but I don't dare look his way.

"Is he a good manager?"

There's a sharpness behind his question that belies the casual way in which he asks it.

"Yup," I answer with a quality that makes it clear I don't want to discuss Lux or Ben any further.

"Is Tara working next weekend?"

"Yup."

I haven't actually checked, but I do not need *this* to become a regular thing. I don't know his angle, or if his conscience simply won't allow him to let a woman walk home alone in the dark, but my heart is still in tatters. It would take very little for the traitorous organ to forgive him and allow him back into our lives.

His scent alone is weakening my resolve.

I once again feel the probing of his eyes on me, but I continue staring out the window.

"Are you lying to me?"

Okay, now that accusation—even if sort of true—is enough to have me whipping my head around to glower at him. "It's really none of your damn business," I snap. He's the one who is trying to insert himself into my life—after already choosing to remove himself from it. I'm not a fucking door. He can't come and go as he pleases. "Why have you not been playing as well recently?" I fire, deflecting from the ire burning in his eyes.

His body tenses, facial features going rigid as his hand tightens on the steering wheel.

"Who says I haven't?"

I shrug. "People talk." *And* I may have looked it up after he told me they lost last night's game. Turns out that's not the only game they've lost recently. The fire the Huskies had at the beginning of the season seems to have gone out, and they haven't been playing as well recently. *Logan* hasn't been playing as well. The question I want to know is, why?

His teeth grind.

"So... have you?" I ask when he doesn't answer.

"What?" he snaps.

"Been off your game?"

"No." The word is barely more than a snarl as he glares out the front windshield. However I catch the bobbing of his Adam's apple as he swallows, and he stretches his neck from side to side, clearly uncomfortable.

His annoyance leaves us sitting in a tense silence for the remainder of the journey, and as I push open the car door, I sort of feel bad for poking at him.

Standing on the sidewalk, I hesitate before closing the door as I stare at his stiff posture. He refuses to look at me, and after a moment I sigh.

"For what it's worth, I hope you figure out whatever is affecting your game."

His eyes snap to mine, a whirlwind of indecipherable emotions I refuse to delve into as I slam the door closed and head into my building.

# RILEY

## CHAPTER TWENTY-THREE

It has been a grueling week of exams. The pressure has been immense, knowing how much is riding on these grades. My brain hasn't switched off once all week, too busy racing with thoughts about all the materials I need to review and chapters I should revisit. My head is crammed with so many pointless facts, I'm surprised I don't blurt them out every time I open my mouth.

I've never been more aware of the minute hand of the clock, the *tick-tock* a reminder that I'm running out of time and need to make the most of every minute.

The entire week has been nothing but a blur of study sessions, practice tests, and late-night cramming. Sleep is a luxury I can no longer afford. Thankfully, I only have one more exam before I can enjoy some downtime. I'm so ready for my first semester at Halston to be over, even if I have no exciting plans for winter break, unlike most of my classmates, who have talked non-stop since Thanksgiving about their plans to go skiing and vacation with their families.

I'd be jealous, except the thought of vacationing with my mother is equivalent to hell on Earth. Although, I would give anything to spend Christmas with Rora. I was away at school for her first two Christmases and Mom always ensured I remained there during the holidays. After I graduated, I moved in with my mom and Rora, but I had to work a double shift last Christmas and barely got to spend any time with my daughter.

Not once have I been with her on Christmas morning when she discovered her pile of presents from Santa waiting under the tree, and I ache to see her face light up with joy and feel that magical wonder.

I can't think about Aurora without thinking of my mother, and not needing to go into this final exam with a burning rage clouding my thoughts. As I step into the classroom and head for a vacant seat, I focus on the various theories I need to know for my Statistics exam.

The exam is a mixture of multiple choice and short answer questions, so I lift out a pen and pencil, along with a backup of each and an eraser. Only when I have everything set up and I'm waiting for Professor Caldwell to hand out the papers do I look around the room.

That's when I realize the broad, muscular shoulders in front of me. Ones I recognize. Somehow, I've managed to select the seat directly behind Logan's. I hadn't even noticed it was him when I sat down. Wide-eyed, I stare at his back, pain cinching my chest. We haven't spoken since he showed up at my job on Saturday night, although I've seen him around campus with his usual groupies and fucking *Whitney* glued to his side.

Her constant presence irritates me more than it should. Or maybe it's the fact Logan never seems to notice me, his attention devoted to her and his other brainless followers.

The only time I do receive his full and unwavering attention is in the parking lot of Lux.

I'm still not entirely sure what to make of that.

Is it a sign that he still cares?

I mean, why would he go out of his way to ensure my safety if he didn't care?

Whatever his reasoning, I'm not entirely sure that it's a good thing for me, seeing as my reaction to his mere presence is as visceral as ever. Although, it's no longer that excited flutter I used to feel. Instead, it's a sharp ache. A stabbing to the heart.

I feel betrayed. Not only by him but by myself. I thought he was different, but he turned out to be just as narrow-minded and judgmental as everyone else here. I totally misjudged him, and that's on me.

And yet, I still can't look away as I trace the outline of his shoulder blades, visible through the tight fabric of his top, before trailing my eyes down to his trim hips. I'm dying to know if he feels the same aching loss I do. Or has he so easily moved on?

Does he feel the same conflicting emotions? That desire to run away every time I see him, to escape the intensity of this pain, while also being drawn closer, wanting to bathe in his light for a moment longer before being tossed into the cold once more. Despite everything, I still feel that irresistible pull toward him. The lingering connection we once shared. It's a twisted mix of wanting to never see him again and yearning for what we once had.

As though feeling my gaze on him, he turns in his seat, chestnut orbs widening when they connect with mine. His eyes bounce over my face, and I catch a flash of emotions too chaotic for me to distinguish before his features harden and he thrusts out his hand.

Glancing down, I notice the stack of pages, and I realize he didn't turn around because he felt me staring. He's simply sending our Statistics test up the row.

"Take one and pass it on," he states gruffly when I make no move to take the pages.

The second I do, he lets go, spinning around and giving me his back once again. Lifting one of the tests for myself, I pass the rest to the person behind me.

"Alright, everyone, you have one hour. You may commence," Professor Caldwell calls out to the rustle of pages as everyone begins.

Stalling, I lean forward and whisper, "Good luck."

Logan doesn't respond, but his shoulders tense, so I know he heard me, and after another second, I forget all about him as I dive into my own exam paper.

---

"Your admirer is back," Ben snaps, sounding more irritated than normal when I step onto the floor at Lux that night.

Honestly, I'm surprised. Ruthless has been a no-show for the last two weeks since he made me come so hard I thought the universe was being torn apart around me.

A mixture of anxious anticipation thrums through me as I head for his usual booth.

Once there, I hover just outside his line of sight, unsure how to act. How *he* is going to react. Presumably, what happened was too much for him, yet what does it mean that he's returned?

I decide to simply follow his lead, and with my heart beating an irregular rhythm against my chest and my palms damp with nerves, I stride into his booth. He barely looks up from the phone clutched in his hand before dismissing me, and I'm left awkwardly standing there as I gawk awkwardly around the booth.

"I believe I paid for a dance," he bites out in his raspy voice.

My teeth grind. *So we're back to this, then.*

Fine, asshole. You wanna act like nothing happened, I can play that game, too.

Refusing to give him anything, I merely block him out as I begin moving to the rhythm. Three songs have played before he deigns to lift his gaze from his phone and actually look at me. Unable to help myself, my eyes flick to his, and I immediately regret it. His stare is sharp enough to cut glass, his piercing eyes like two icicles, ready to inflict permanent damage.

Sliced to my core, I wrench my eyes away and focus on a point on the wall behind him as the song's final notes play out. Before another one can begin, he stands. "That's enough for tonight."

Seriously? That's all he has to say? Why did he even bother coming back?

He moves to step past me, and in a last-ditch effort, I reach out and wrap my fingers around his arm.

"Don't," he snarls, removing himself from my grip. His eyes don't meet mine as he bites, "Don't touch me."

I flinch at his harsh tone, momentarily stunned before waves of anger crash through me. Eyes narrowing, I bite, "Oh, but it's okay for you to touch me?"

I watch warily as his teeth grind against one another, his fists repeatedly clenching and releasing at his sides. Anger rolls off him—directed at me? What the hell did I do?

"I didn't ask you to chase after me. I didn't ask you to touch me. To-to..."

"To what, Babydoll?" His tone is half purr-half sneer. "Make you come harder than you ever have before."

*Smack.*

Ruthless's eyes go wide, his jaw dropping, and it's the sharp sting of my palm that has me registering that I just slapped him. A response that is becoming a habit in his presence.

"Get out," I hiss.

He stares me down, his eye twitching with unrestrained anger. Lifting my chin, I stand my ground, even as my heart slams painfully against my chest and a voice in the back of my head begs me to run.

Without saying another word, he turns on his heel and storms away. I don't breathe until the door closes behind him.

The rest of my shift passes in a blur. I'm in a foul mood the entire night, one that is only compounded when Ben asks me to stay late *again.*

"You seem stressed," he purrs, his gross-ass fingers reaching out to wrap around my shoulder as I wipe one of the tables down. "I could help you with that."

Revulsion tastes like battery acid in my mouth as I fight my body's natural instinct to recoil and instead slowly ease away from him. "I'm good," I state as politely as I can, throwing him a tight smile over my shoulder, even as the remnant of his brief touch lingers on my skin.

"You sure?" he pushes, my temper spiking as I strangle the cleaning cloth in my hand.

*Dude, take a fucking hint!*

"Yup. Just that time of the month. Feel like I'm running to the bathroom every five minutes to change my tampon, and all I wanna do is put on my favorite spaghetti-stained pajamas and drown myself in ice cream."

Looking truly disgusted, his hand jerks back as if burned.

*Mission accomplished.*

"Uhh, right. Guess we should hurry up and finish, then."

"Sounds good."

Shockingly, we're done for the night sooner than ever before. *Note to self: telling the sleazy perv you're on your period is a total turn-off.*

"Raincheck on that, uh, de-stressing," Ben says as he locks the door half an hour later.

I keep my lips tightly sealed, refusing to agree to anything as we step into the parking lot, and I heave out a silent breath when I spot Logan's SUV idling. I admit, I'm not entirely surprised to see him, even If I am confused as to why he cares.

I'm actually relieved. Although, I'm aware that means he's been sitting here for an entire hour after everyone else left.

Just so he can ensure I get home safely.

Now that I am aware of his presence, I swear I feel his eyes on me through the tinted windshield as Ben babbles about some new exercise regime he's been doing. Apparently, he's put on all this muscle. It must be somewhere inauspicious because I don't see any difference.

"Let me give you a ride home," Ben offers. "I won't take no for an answer."

*Seriously? What just happened to a raincheck?*

I give him a tight smile. Every single fucking time he offers, I decline. Learn the definition of no, you single-brain-celled idiot.

I open my mouth to decline yet again when he cuts me off. "I can't have an employee of mine walking home in the dark after work. It's not safe. It would eat away at my conscience if something were to happen."

He's really pulling out the guilt card tonight, and it makes me even more reassured knowing Logan is here.

Even if I am also pissed at him. The second our Statistics exam ended, he bolted from the room like the hounds of hell were on his ass. Yet, here he is. It doesn't make any sense. He can't stand to be near me on campus, but he shows up every Friday and Saturday to ensure I make it home okay. He's giving me emotional whiplash.

"That's so sweet," I say in a tone so sugary it would give an Olympic athlete diabetes. "But I actually have a ride."

I point toward Logan's SUV, noting Ben's surprise. There's a flash of something darker in his expression, even if he masks it well. "Oh, that's good."

After that, he doesn't hang around, muttering goodbye as he makes a hasty retreat.

I wait until he's in his car before making a beeline for Logan's.

Expression pinched, I yank open the passenger door but make no move to get into his car. "Why are you here?"

I might be secretly relieved that he is, but that doesn't mean I forgive him.

He arches a patient eyebrow. "Are we doing this again? I thought we'd already established this."

"And I thought I told you I had it covered."

He makes a dramatic point of looking around the otherwise empty parking lot. "Is your car invisible? Because unless it is, I don't fucking see it. That girl, Tara, left with the others ages ago."

"I didn't know I'd be asked to stay late," I mutter.

"Then it's a good thing I'm here, isn't it?" His tone is snarky, but he does have a point, so I keep my mouth shut as I get into the car.

However, Logan makes no move to leave, and when I look over, he's scowling out the windshield.

"Why is he always trying to get you into his car?"

The hostile bite in his voice takes me by surprise. Is Logan jealous?

"He was just offering me a lift home," I state with a fake nonchalance.

When Logan turns to look at me, there's an arrogance to his expression. "Why did you turn him down?"

"Because you were here, and I wanted to yell at you for being an asshole to me earlier."

"Then why did you turn him down last week and all the times before that?"

*Cocky asshole.*

I'm sure as hell not about to admit to Logan, of all people, that no matter how angry I may be with him or how pissed he might be at me, I will always choose to get in his car over Ben's. Logan might have the potential to obliterate my heart if I was to ever hand all of it over to him, but I know all the way to the deepest recesses of my soul that he'd never physically harm me. That he'd never cross the lines Ben constantly steps over without any care or concern.

He'd never do anything I didn't want him to. Never put me in a situation where I was uncomfortable.

"It's called maintaining professional boundaries," I snap defensively, refusing to admit to Logan, of all people, how uneasy I feel in Ben's presence. "How come you were a total dick today?"

Flinching, his cocksure expression falls away, and he finally starts the car and puts it in drive. "I don't know what you're talking about."

"Sure you don't," I mutter with a roll of my eyes. Resting my elbow on the armrest, I pretend the dickhead doesn't exist as I stare out the window at the passing buildings.

The journey to my apartment passes in tense silence. It's not exactly pleasant, although it isn't altogether uncomfortable either.

When he stops, I don't immediately move to get out. Taking a moment to gather my thoughts, I then shift in my seat to face him. "Look," I begin. "I'm not sure what exactly is going on here,"—I wave my finger between us—"But I don't want you picking me up after work if you're going to be an ass and ignore me, or worse, treat me like shit when we're at school."

His eyes bounce around the inside of the car, never landing

on me for more than a second before moving on, and his nostrils flare with some annoyance I can't pinpoint. Regardless, I continue with my speech.

"You can't be both guys, Logan. You can't be the one who picks me up after work because you don't want me walking home *and* the guy who thinks it's okay to treat me like dirt when we're at Halston. You need to figure out what you want, 'cause this Jekyll and Hyde act, is not okay. I have more self-respect than that."

Finally, I open the car door and step out, but before I close it, I turn and state, "Until you've figured it out, don't pick me up."

# RILEY

## CHAPTER TWENTY-FOUR

"Might want to change at home," one of the dancers whispers as I walk past her, me entering the dressing rooms and her exiting. "Ben is hovering in there being a creep."

*Ugh, great. Of course, he chooses tonight to hang out in the dressing rooms and make small talk when all of us are covered in glitter from tonight's performance and need to shower. Coincidence? I don't think so.*

Thanking her for the heads up, I push open the door to the dressing room and immediately hear Ben's stupid guffaw. Each of the girls don tight smiles plastered to their faces and share uneasy glances as they hurry to get dressed without giving Ben a front-row seat to their tits or ass.

"Riley! There you are. I'm just getting to know you all a little better before I get back to work," Ben says, smiling at me in what he probably thinks is an enticing way, but comes across as phony.

I give him the same fake smile all the other girls do before hurrying to my dressing table. "Any of you girls got exciting plans tonight?" Ben asks, a hopeful twinge to his voice that I'm sure none of us miss.

Seriously? It's 1 a.m. I bet the most exciting plans any of us have is to eat food in bed while we watch late-night TV reruns.

Murmured no's are exchanged, and I tune them out as I grab my jeans and t-shirt and, feeling gross with the glitter still smeared across my chest, arms, and legs, I pull my clothes on. I'd rather wash it off at home. Finishing up, I stuff my feet into my sneakers, grab my coat, and head for the door.

"Leaving already?" Ben asks, pouting at me like a stupid man-child.

"Yeah. I've got assignments due." I rush out the door before he can point out that it's officially winter break, so technically I shouldn't have any assignments due for weeks.

Hitting the fresh air, I finally exhale a deep breath. What a weird night. Ruthless was once again MIA. Although, after last night's encounter, I'm thinking that's for the best. Not that my idiotic heart agrees. It's stupid. I should be happy to be back on the stage all night, every night, but I miss our intimate interactions, and throughout every performance, I found myself scouring the room for him.

After the way he behaved last night, I shouldn't want to be anywhere near him. I should be staying far away from him and his mood swings. If he can't handle getting a girl off, that's on him. He shouldn't take it out on me.

Besides, no distractions, remember?

Rounding the side of the building, I step into the parking lot and falter. After my speech last night, I wasn't expecting to find Logan waiting.

Yet that's exactly who is sitting in the black Range Rover parked in front of me.

"Two weekends in a row," Tara points out, walking up beside me and wagging her eyebrows.

Before I can tell her it's not what she thinks, she talks over me. "Girl, don't give me that. No guy sits outside a club on a Saturday night waiting for a girl if he doesn't have every intention of pursuing her."

She points at Logan's awaiting car. "Whether or not you realize it, that right there is boyfriend shit."

Her parting words leave me stumped as I watch her walk to her car before shifting my attention to Logan's now familiar SUV.

As I slowly approach, his door opens and he steps out. Running my gaze over his face, I try to get a read on him. His emotions seem all over the place. His face is contorted into tight lines making him appear pained, and his mouth is pressed into a thin, angry line, yet his eyes are dilated with lust.

Not sure what to expect, I stop several feet away. "Thought I told you not to come tonight."

"I believe your exact words were not to pick you up until I figured shit out."

Crossing my arms in front of my chest, I cock a hip. "And have you?"

If anything, his expression only seems to darken. Torment flashes across his features, and I have to wonder what has him so conflicted. Is whatever he feels for me that complicated? Is the fact I work here really such an issue?

"It was never a choice." His voice cuts like gravel, and in the next instant he's in front of me, hands in my hair and lips on mine as he upends my world with a searing kiss.

His body is pressed flush against mine, and my fingers dig into his arms, clinging to him as his tongue sweeps in and claims my mouth. There's something darker about this kiss. It lacks Logan's usual sunlight. Instead of a fulfilling warmth, there is a cold intensity. It's harsher, more desperate, and with every hard press of his lips, it becomes crystal clear.

This isn't an *I choose you* kiss.

It isn't an *I'm sorry, I was an idiot.*

It's a goodbye.

That knowledge has me wrenching away, staring up at him with questions brimming in my eyes. My lips tingle, swollen already from the sheer intensity of our kiss. I press them together, and Logan's eyes dip, observing, until he pulls away.

Letting go of me, he curses under his breath, looking even more conflicted than he previously did, before snarling out in a furious tone, "Get in the car, Riley."

It's on the tip of my tongue to refuse, but he seems nearly unhinged in his anger. Besides, I'm not sure what is going on, but I have questions, and after that kiss, I deserve answers.

So instead, I hurry around the front of the car and climb in.

Whatever is going on with him is palpable as he pulls out of the parking lot and onto the road. Deciding it's best to wait until he's ready to talk, I choose to watch him subtly from the corner of my eye while he drives.

His forearms repeatedly flex, his face contorted. What I'd pay to gain even a fraction of insight into his mindset. Slowly, my gaze travels lower, noticing for the first time his workout gear. It's a bit late for a training session. Did he come straight from the gym? If that was the case, you'd think he'd have burned off some of that aggression eating at him.

The large armholes of his beater offer me a glimpse of his toned chest and chiseled torso. There's not an ounce of fat anywhere on him. His arm shifts, and I catch sight of a tattoo across his ribs—an EKG heart rhythm ending in the silhouette of an ice hockey player.

Before he can catch me ogling him like a slab of meat, I tear my gaze away to stare out the windshield.

"Uhh, Logan," I hedge when I realize we're not taking the usual route to my apartment. "Where are we going?"

When he doesn't answer, I turn to look at him. "Logan."

No response.

I know he hasn't suddenly gone deaf.

"Logan!" His name is barked with a hint of panic. I trust him, I do, but *fuck*, what if I was wrong?

My palms sweat as I dart my frantic gaze between him and the windshield.

"Can I ask you something?" he suddenly asks in a gruff voice before slowing the car to a stop at the side of the road. My eyes dart around the street, unable to pinpoint where we are, until the sudden loud click of the car's locking system grabs my attention, and I whirl to face him.

I find him staring at me with an expression I have never seen him wear before. His face has been wiped clean. A blank slate. It's unnerving. Terrifying.

This isn't the easy-going Logan I've gotten to know over the last several months.

This isn't even the asshole Logan who couldn't bear to be around me when he discovered what I did for a living.

I'm not even entirely sure if this is ice hockey Logan.

He tilts his head to the side, and I get the distinct impression he's trying to figure me out. I can practically feel him probing underneath my skin and pushing against the outskirts of my mind.

"Why do you put on this whole innocent act?"

His question catches me off-guard, and I blink at him, confused.

"I don't—what do you mean?"

He leans toward me, and I press back, heart thumping erratically as I try to maintain some distance between us, but I very much feel like a cornered animal right now.

"Why do you act like this goody-two-shoes when we both know you're anything but?"

My fight or flight instincts are on full alert, telling me to get out of the car, but when he reaches out and winds a lock of my hair around his finger, the tormented, damaged part of myself that I've spent the last four years pretending doesn't exist finally raises her head. Using my eyes as windows, she peers out at him, taking a visceral interest in the threat in front of her, while at the same time in my head I hear *mine.*

My rational brain is shouting for me to run, but the mutilated, tortured fragments of my soul are screaming for *him.*

I instinctively lean into his touch, my lips parting as my tongue flicks out. His eyes widen in surprise as he zeros in on my mouth, and I watch his throat bob as he swallows. Time stands still, and my heart hammers against my chest as I wait to see what will happen next.

His gaze catches on something over my shoulder, and I turn in my seat to see what it is, but with his finger still holding my hair hostage, he tugs on the strand, snapping my attention back to him as a cloth is pressed firmly over my nose and mouth.

My eyes bug out of my head and my fingers claw at Logan's hand, a sweet smell filling my nostrils. My efforts are futile though, and I stare helplessly into his conflicted eyes as I silently implore him not to do this.

Tears leak out of the corner of my eyes as my vision blurs, and with every passing second, my body grows weaker. I blink furiously, trying to focus on Logan's face. A face I once found so handsome, is now twisted and haunting as he watches me with a cold ambivalence.

The brief thought flitters through my mind, *who is this guy?* Because evidently, the Logan I thought I knew never existed.

My mouth is dry, and there's a dull thudding at the back of my head as I groggily open my eyes. Feeling the hard ground beneath me, memories rush back, and I jolt upright, immediately regretting that decision when my stomach churns precariously.

Fear consumes me and I shiver. It only gets worse when I register the cool metal around my wrists and, squinting in the dark room, I can just make out my hands cuffed to some sort of pole. *What the...*

I can taste vomit at the back of my throat and the chain of the cuffs rattles against the metal pole as my hands tremble. Shifting on my ass, I squint around the dark room, making out the outline of sofas—some sort of living room, I'd guess.

With a stripper pole in it.

No normal person has a stripper pole in their living room. I mean, bedroom, *maybe*, if that's their kink, but not their fucking living room.

I stand on unsteady legs, thankful that I'm at least still wearing the jeans and t-shirt I left the club in earlier, although my coat and shoes have disappeared, and the glitter I should have washed off hours ago is beginning to itch. Turning my attention to the pole, I give it a good shake, desperately hoping it will come loose. I need to get the fuck out of here before Logan, or whoever lives here, comes back.

It rattles loudly against the bolts, but that's all.

"It's not going to give."

At the sound of the low, menacing tone, I squeal, half jumping out of my skin as I quickly move to place the useless metal strip between us and squint in the direction of the voice.

This time, I see what I missed before—the faint outline of three bodies sitting on a couch at the back of the room.

I lick my lips nervously. "Wh-Who are you? What do you want?"

The three shadows rise in unison, faces hidden by the darkness. Without answering my question or saying anything at all, they cross the room toward me. My unease builds as their heavy footsteps echo around the room, intensifying until my heart threatens to leap from my chest, screaming at me to move. To run.

Except there's nowhere to go. Nowhere for me to hide.

Their dark silhouettes come into focus as they draw near, my mouth drying as my palms sweat. Terrified, I step back as far as my shackles will allow, until my arms are outstretched in front of me, the metal digging sharply into my wrists.

My gaze swivels between the three shadows, each more prominent and more ominous looking than the last, as they move to surround me. One on my left, one on my right, and most petrifying, one at my back.

I hardly dare to breathe.

Silence consumes the darkness as the three of them press in around me, and I let out a whimper when the warm air of one of their breaths hits my cheek.

My breaths are ragged pants, my head dizzy from the lack of oxygen as I squeeze my eyes shut.

*I have survived worse.*

*I can survive this.*

I repeat my mantra twice more, gathering strength from it before opening my eyes and straightening my spine. The small move has my shoulders brushing against the person behind me, and I sense him freeze before ever so slightly stepping back.

I stare into the darkness, waiting.

"You mean you don't recognize me?" that same low menace growls in my ear.

My brain whirs, trying to put a face to the voice, but I come up empty. *Maybe* it sounds familiar, but I can't place it.

"No?"

No. I'd remember a voice that sounded like that. While his deep husk terrifies me, I would remember the low timbre and commanding tone. I couldn't possibly forget the primal response that stirs low in my belly. Even laced with danger, the allure is irresistible. There's a seductive edge to his menace that draws me in even as my brain pleads for me to escape.

His stubble scrapes along my skin, the coarseness sending a tremor of exhilaration and fear skittering along my spine as the tip of his nose runs up the side of my face. Lips at my ear, he whispers darkly, "You don't recognize your own brother?"

His words are like a bucket of ice water being poured over me, dousing any scandalous thoughts the baser part of me was considering.

"G-Grayson?"

His low chuckle has shivers zinging down my spine.

"That's right, little sis. You didn't think you were rid of me for good, did you?"

My whole body begins to tremble, and I feel lightheaded as I struggle to remain on my feet.

"I don't—what are you...Why am I here?" My voice is a helpless whimper.

He keeps me waiting, his silence terrifying me more than his words ever could.

"Why, you have sinned, little sis. Committed such heinous crimes, for which you must be punished." His breath is a gentle caress against my skin, but the sinister threat of his words turns my stomach to stone.

"And we are your judge, jury, and executioner."

# RILEY

## CHAPTER TWENTY-FIVE

Forcing a confidence I don't feel, I ask, "What is your plan, Grayson? You can't keep me here indefinitely. People will be looking for me if I disappear."

Grayson's low chuckle is cold and heartless as it sweeps over my skin. "Surely, you don't think I'm that stupid, Riley. I've made it my mission to learn everything I need to know about your life."

I stiffen at his confession. There's no way he could know about Aurora. Things would not be unfolding the way they are if he had. He'd have confronted me in a rage, demanding to know her parentage. There wouldn't be any of these mind games.

"Other than rehearsals and your shifts at Lux, you have no other plans for winter break. You haven't made any friends on campus, and even your own mother doesn't want to see you for Christmas."

I internally groan as I recall a late-night phone call with Logan before everything blew up between us, where we discussed our plans for winter break. Well, mostly, he told me about the huge family dinner his parents host every year and how excited he was to go home and see them, albeit he could only spend Christmas Day with them because of his hockey schedule.

When I told him I had no plans other than to work and get ahead of my schoolwork, he invited me to go home with him. Somehow, I doubt that invitation still stands.

Regarding the mother barb, if Grayson intended for that to sting, he missed the mark. I'd far rather not see my mother over Christmas. Aurora is the sole link between us. She is the only reason why I would ever want to see that vile woman. However, he is wrong. Assuming my mom doesn't cancel—and there's still plenty of time for her to do just that—then I *will* be seeing my mother on Christmas day. Which gives me two weeks to figure a way out of this situation.

Unfortunately, Ava and Isabella left today to stay with their mother for Christmas, so they won't notice my disappearance, and the only other person who would is Tara.

"One of us will escort you to each of your shifts," Grayson continues, answering that predicament before hope can grow roots and germinate in my chest. "But before you go getting any grand ideas of tattling or trying to slip away, we will always have eyes on you. And in case you need further incentive to toe the line, we have enough clout between the three of us to ensure your scholarship is revoked and you lose your place at Halston."

My teeth grind as I swallow my scoff. Of course, they're playing the *we're rich so we own you* card.

However, I can't afford to call their bluff. I've already missed out on so much of Rora's life, and knowing it will be another four years before I'm graduated and in a situation to provide for her eats at me every day. I can't allow any wrenches to be thrown in the works that may delay that any further.

"So, what? You're planning to keep me here as your own

personal hooker for the entirety of winter break?" I snap, irritated and concerned purely at the thought of spending the next three weeks being degraded and demeaned, being punished for a crime I didn't commit and made to feel less than all because Grayson is unable to open his eyes and see his dad for the piece of shit he truly is.

Not to mention the fact he's somehow dragged Logan—and whoever else—into this.

Logan's sudden change in behavior is now making a lot more sense, and I have the nagging suspicion that it wasn't seeing me at Lux that changed his mind about us but rather Grayson whispering in his ear.

*You have survived worse*, I remind myself, repeating my usual comforting statement. However, the words don't have their usual bolstering impact.

Grayson's disparaging chuckle only rattles me further. "A hooker? You wish, Riley. Hookers get paid for what they do. You can think of yourself as more of a... sex slave."

"Ooh, kinky," Logan mutters from where he's standing on my left.

The third shadow remains ominously silent, and I flick my gaze his way, struggling to get a read on him in the darkness. It concerns me that I don't know who he is. Especially with all this talk of hookers and sex slaves.

Through the dark, I can feel his eyes boring into mine with a familiar intensity, but I struggle to place it. It's on the tip of my tongue to ask who he is when Grayson speaks. "You better rest up tonight. You've got one hell of a show to put on tomorrow—and every day for the next three weeks."

With a sinking weight growing heavier in my stomach, Grayson, Logan, and the third mysterious shadow silently stalk out of the room, leaving me alone to ponder my predicament as my legs give out and I collapse to the hard floor, lost to the swarming of my own thoughts.

I can't comprehend how this happened. I made sure this *couldn't* happen. I checked that no Van Doren attended this school before I applied. Yet, somehow, we've ended up at the same college together. What are the chances?

Resting my weary head against the cold metal of the pole, I release a long exhale as I allow my thoughts to drift to the last time I saw him.

It was the day the cops showed up.

*"What is this about?" Bertram barks at the uniformed officers standing in the doorway.*

*I'd only come downstairs to force some food into me. Normally, I wouldn't bother, but I'd only just found out I was pregnant, and while most days I still wanted to curl into a ball and die, I knew that was no longer an option. Not for another nine months, anyway.*

*However, when I heard the house manager inform Bertram that there were two police officers at the door, my feet became rooted to the floor. I knew I should run and hide, but I couldn't bring myself to look away.*

*"Mr. Bertram Van Doren?" one of them questions.*

*"Yes. What is the meaning of this?"*

*"Sir, your presence has been requested at the station."*

*"What? Is this a joke? Do you have any idea who I am? My time is valuable. I demand to know what this is regarding."*

*The two officers exchange uneasy glances. "Uh, Sir," the older one begins. "Allegations have been made against you. Ones which we would prefer to discuss down at the station."*

*"Dad?"*

*At the sound of Grayson's voice, my body unlocks, and I go to scurry away when a hand reaches out and snatches my wrist.*

*He's only two years older than I am, but he towers over me at six-*

*foot-two. Seventeen and going into his senior year of high school in the fall, he is rarely home, usually out with his friends or at parties.*

*When me and my mom moved in with him and his dad six months ago, I developed the biggest crush on him. I had these wild, inappropriate fantasies that he felt the same way—imagined what would happen if the two of us fell in love.*

*It's laughable how naive and childish it all was.*

*A match was taken to those ridiculous, youthful fantasies that first night my door squeaked on its hinges, and I realized it wasn't him sneaking in to see me but his dad. Since then, I've gone out of my way to avoid Grayson. The way he looks at me when we're in the same room... I swear he can see through the front I put on for everyone else. It's almost as though he's reacting to the cracks his father inflicts each night. I know I'm no longer the happy, bubbly girl I was when I first moved in, but I can't let him see just how broken I've become.*

*"What is going on?" Grayson asks me in a quieter voice when his father fails to respond.*

*Looking up at him, his face is lined with creases, and my heart clenches. I had to do what I did, but I hate that it's going to hurt him.*

*His eyes search mine before turning to look at his father as Bertram demands, "Allegations? What allegations?"*

*The officers share another uneasy glance, and I stiffen in Grayson's hold as the older one leans in and says in a quieter tone, "Sir, someone has come forward with claims of sexual abuse."*

*"What?" Bertram barks. "That is absurd."*

*"Nonetheless, Sir, we need you to come with us so we can get to the bottom of this."*

*"Dad?" Grayson tries again, taking a step toward his father.*

*"It's nothing, son. A misunderstanding. Call the lawyers."*

*Grayson drops my arm, nodding along with his dad's instructions. However, all I can do is watch on as Bertram's incensed glare shifts to me, and the promise of retribution shakes me to my core.*

*Grabbing his coat and looking like he is heading to the office rather than the police station, Bertram's dress shoes clip against the hard floor as he strides out of the house without a backward glance.*

*The door snicks shut behind him, enveloping Grayson and me in a weighted silence. One that extends until infinity before his shoulders drop on a haggard exhale. Running his fingers through his overgrown, dark hair, he turns to look at me with a pained expression.*

*His eyes scour my face in that penetrating way of his, and I'm convinced he already knows it's me.*

*"I'm sorry," I whisper brokenly before racing up the stairs and hiding behind my locked door.*

His father was arrested a few days later, although not for the initial charges against him. Grayson kicked my mother and me out of the house that same night, and I never saw him again... until tonight.

It's obvious Grayson is harboring a lot of resentment toward me for the part I played in his father's arrest. He wants me to pay, and based on the lengths he's gone to and the fact I'm chained to a stripper pole, I can guess his payment method.

I feel my insides rearranging themselves, hardening into a concrete mass. There's no way out of this other than to bide my time and wait. In the meantime, I'll have to play by their rules. Grayson may think I have something to repent for, but the fact remains I've done nothing wrong.

And he might believe this little stunt of his will break me, but I'm stronger than he could possibly know. Moreso, I have someone worth fighting to get back to. So I will suffer and endure, and when they're done playing their games, I'll emerge from the ashes and show them all that fire doesn't burn me; it only makes me stronger.

# RILEY

## CHAPTER TWENTY-SIX

I get a fitful night's rest on the cold, hard ground. It doesn't help that the glitter I didn't get to shower off yesterday has irritated my skin, causing me to scratch incessantly at it all night. I give up on sleep entirely when the dull gray of morning begins to creep around the edges of the heavy curtains. It offers a dim view of what appears to be a living room. A sofa and chairs have been rearranged to fit around the stripper pole I'm currently attached to, which stands proudly in the center of the room and is brand-spanking new from the looks of it.

*How sweet of them to go out of their way to accommodate me.*

I roll my eyes at the idiocy of it all.

In the harsh light of day, I should probably be feeling more fearful of my situation. And don't get me wrong, anxiety is absolutely one of the emotions pounding through my veins, but it's not as potent as it was when I first came to last night.

Something about knowing Grayson is the one behind this, and not some creepy psycho stalker, has eased the worst of my fear. Grayson wouldn't go so far as to irreparably break me, right? We were siblings once, even if only for a short time.

Perhaps he can even be reasoned with. I never had the opportunity to explain to him properly, and I have no idea what lies his father will have spread. Perhaps I can make him see my point of view. Somehow, prove to him that I'm the one telling the truth.

I hear a shower running somewhere in the house, and a short while later, the floorboards outside my room creak as someone walks past. The sound of life in the house is shortly followed by the smell of bacon permeating the air, making my stomach growl as it reminds me it's been too long since I last ate. I refuse to call out or ask for anything from these assholes though, even if my stomach protests at the idea of not getting any of the delicious-smelling bacon.

More footsteps pass the closed door, followed by muffled voices coming from the room beneath mine. At the clattering of plates and cutlery, I assume the kitchen is directly below me, and the guys are currently tucking into their nice warm breakfast, not giving a shit about the hungry girl chained up in their living room.

I'm not sure how much later it is when the door creaks open, and I lift my head, finding Logan standing in the doorway, watching me with a curious yet indifferent expression. He looks exactly like he always does, casual in his jeans and white t-shirt, feet bare, and blond hair mussed up. In comparison, I probably look like a haggard mess.

"I need to use the bathroom," I blurt out flatly, meeting his gaze with an unflinching one of my own.

He doesn't react, acting as if I never spoke. Looking at me like he's never seen me before. It's more cutting than I'll ever admit.

"Logan." His name is snapped off the end of my tongue, and my sharp tone breaks him out of his trance. In the time it takes to blink, his features harden, and a wall slams over his face until I'm faced with ice-rink Logan.

"What?" That one word is a harsh bark, reminding me the Logan standing before me is not the one I'd come to know over the last few months.

"I need to use the bathroom."

He huffs like I'm being a huge inconvenience. Well, my bad. Maybe if they didn't fucking kidnap and chain me to a pole, I wouldn't have to *ask* him to let me use the toilet.

He closes the distance between us, digging a small key out of his pocket. He pauses before inserting it into the handcuffs. "Don't try anything stupid." I roll my eyes. Does he seriously think the second he takes the cuffs off me, I'm going to make a mad run for it? Grayson already delivered his threats of what would happen if I pulled anything. I don't need a repeat from Logan.

When he unlocks the cuffs, I rub at the skin before he grabs a hold of my arm and roughly pulls me to my feet.

"I can walk," I snap, attempting to pull my arm out of his tight grip.

He only tightens his hold, glaring at me as he escorts me out the door and into the hall. My eyes bounce around the place, taking in the two sets of stairs—one leading up and one leading down—the three closed doors, and the faint sound of life coming from outside. The walls are bare, covered in dark navy wallpaper, and the wooden floor beneath my feet is warm and clean.

*Underfloor heating. Fancy.*

Straining my ears, I can't hear anyone else in the house. "Who all lives here?" I ask.

"Just the three of us," Logan responds gruffly, not paying me any attention.

"You, Grayson, and..."

He glances at me as he pushes open one of the closed doors, revealing a large, modern bathroom with a whitewash sink, toilet, a gorgeous, deep, freestanding tub in the middle of the room, and a large shower in the corner, complete with a bench and more jets than any shower should need.

I'm left waiting as he closes the bathroom door behind us and leans against it, crossing his arms over his chest. When I remain standing and staring at him, he lifts his chin toward the toilet. "Hurry up."

Eyes widening, I glance between him and the toilet. "I am not peeing with you watching me."

He quirks a brow, not moving a muscle as he silently observes me.

Frowning, I continue, "I also need to shower off this glitter." I hold my arm out so he can see the raised bumps and red abrasions from where I've been scratching at it all night.

His lips flatten as he takes in the irritated skin before he huffs out a breath. Not meeting my eye, he snaps, "Fine. Towels are in the cupboard. You have fifteen minutes," before stepping out of the bathroom and leaving me alone.

The second the door clicks shut behind him, I rush toward it, flicking the lock. I hear him chuckle through the door. *Fucking shithead.*

"A flimsy lock won't keep me out. You have thirteen minutes left."

I scowl at the piece of wood separating us but quickly turn my back on it and scope out the rest of the bathroom. There's a frosted window above the toilet, and I lower the lid to climb on top of it. Unlocking the latch, I push up the window, giving me a view out the back of the house. I'm on the second story, overlooking a pretty garden complete with a decking area and hot tub at the end of a row of terrace brownstones. Beyond the house, fields stretch as far as the eye can see, and I can only assume we're on the outskirts of Halston.

Pulling my head back in, I do another scan of the bathroom, but there isn't anything else I can do right now except shower.

Hurrying into the cubicle before Logan barges in here and tells me my time is up, I quickly scrub the glitter from my skin and lather it in vanilla-scented shower gel. I've just wrapped a towel around me when there's a loud rap on the door.

"Time's up, Cinderella," Logan barks.

"Hold on!"

The words are barely out of my mouth when the door flies open and Logan stomps in.

"Hey! I locked that!"

"And I told you a locked door wouldn't keep me out," he retorts with a conniving smirk before he takes in the fact I'm wearing nothing except a towel, my damp hair hanging limply around my face. His eyes flash with heat, which should maybe make me uncomfortable, but all I feel is relief. He can't wholly hate me if he still finds me attractive, right?

"Logan," I hedge, taking a step toward him.

Ripping his eyes away, he glowers at a point on the wall as he throws out his arm. "Put these on."

Swallowing back the words lodged in my throat, I take the garments from his outstretched hand. "Seriously?" I growl, holding the piece of string masquerading as a bra with the tip of my finger. The two tiny triangles have barely enough fabric to cover my nipples. It and the thong are more revealing than anything I've worn at Lux.

"If you prefer, I can take back the T-shirt."

"No," I blurt, clutching the T-shirt like it's a lifeline. Holding the articles of clothing to my chest, I stare at Logan, and when he notices I'm not getting changed, he drags out a weary sigh and finally turns his head to face me. "You need to turn around," I explain to him.

"Really, Riley? You put your body on display for a living, yet you can't change in front of me?"

"I'm not naked when I'm on the stage," I snap irritably. "And you lost any right to see my body."

Shaking his head, he thankfully does as I say and turns his back to me as he stares at the bathroom wall.

"I'm not the repugnant human who lied about being raped and got an innocent man sent to prison."

*Oh, so we're going there.*

My laugh is insolent and caustic, and it's with sharp, angry movements that I loosen the towel and allow it to drop to the floor before yanking on the undergarments. "I'm guessing that's what changed your mind about us? Why you switched from Doctor Jekyll to Mr. Hyde? Because Grayson found out who I was?"

The muscles in his back flex and bulge as his hands clench at his sides. "He was with me that night, at Lux."

*Just fucking perfect.* Seeing me on campus would have been bad enough, but to see me at the club. No wonder he thinks a sex slave is appropriate.

"And it's just as well he was," Logan continues in a harsh tone, unaware of the grave he's digging for himself. "Saved me from what would probably have been the biggest mistake of my life."

*Ouch.*

He shakes his head but doesn't turn around, even though I'm now dressed in the bra, thong, and oversized T-shirt that falls to nearly my knees and smells of Logan.

Pushing past the hurt, I focus instead on the issue at hand. "Grayson's father was proven guilty. He embezzled money. That is hardly on me."

"The police wouldn't have even been looking if you hadn't

directed their attention his way," he half yells, spinning to glower at me.

"Are you fucking kidding me?" I'm now absolutely furious as I glare at him from across the room. "He committed the crime he was accused of. And got away with a far more serious one." I sigh as my anger gives way to a desperate sort of plea. "We spent weeks getting to know one another while in the library. Do you truly believe I'm capable of falsely accusing someone of something so heinous?"

Logan comes at me so fast that I stumble back. "I don't even know if that Riley exists," he snaps. His eyes are glowing with a fire, raging flames of anger, but as I stare harder, I can see the hurt, the confusion that they're hiding. "It could all have been a ruse."

"A ruse?" I parrot, confused. "A ruse for what?"

Throwing up his hands, he growls, "I don't know, Riley. For all I know, you planned on doing the same thing to me that you did to him."

It would have hurt less if he'd slapped me. I physically cringe at his harsh words, gaping at him for a full minute before my rage rises like a tidal wave. Locking away the hurt, I advance toward him. "You're the one who approached me, you dipshit. The one who asked for *my* help. The one who *kissed* me. Who asked that I go on a date and to your game. And you have the fucking gall to say that to me."

I shake my head, thoroughly disappointed and disgusted with him.

"I'm on my way to the pros," Logan continues to argue, but he doesn't sound as incensed as before. "If everything goes well, I'd be a prime target. It wouldn't be the first time I've known a girl to pull such a stunt."

"And I'm not arguing that, but you were never a target to me, Logan." I sigh in exasperation. "I don't know how many times I have to tell you, I liked you for *you.* Not the number on your jersey, the money in your bank account, or your potential future in hockey."

"Liked?" Logan queries. Creases form deep crevices across his forehead. *Seriously, did he hear anything I said after that point?* "As in, past tense?"

"Yeah, Logan. Past tense, 'cause I won't let myself fall for a man who thinks I'm capable of what you've accused me of and who believes I'm out to destroy him when I've only ever wanted the best for you."

Uncaring that I'm supposed to be *his* captive, I shove past him and out of the bathroom door. I'd rather be chained to that stupid pole than forced to spend another moment in there with Logan.

Storming down the hall, I re-enter the room they're keeping me in and drop onto the couch. I bring my legs up, stretching the t-shirt over my knees and wrapping my arms around them before resting my cheek on top.

It hurts to be thought so little of. It's one thing for Grayson to side with his father. It's his dad. Of course, he's going to believe him over me. But Logan? We'd spent weeks getting to know one another before he flipped the switch. Shouldn't that have accounted for some doubt? Warranted me at least the opportunity to defend myself?

I tense as I hear him approach, only relaxing when he walks on by, moving down the stairs.

I'm not sure how long I'm lost in my thoughts, but I don't even hear him returning until he shoves a plate of food under my nose. "Here."

My stomach growls at the smell of bacon and scrambled eggs, and I'm not stubborn enough to refuse food when offered, so I take the plate from him.

He hovers in front of me, but I stare steadfastly down at the plate in my lap as I wait for him to leave. After a moment, he sighs and turns to leave. Unable to help myself, I lift my gaze, watching him through my lashes as he strides out of the room and disappears. I stare at the empty doorway for another minute, contemplating how different things could be between us if Grayson hadn't been at Lux that night before my growling stomach reminds me of its presence.

---

I must drift off on the sofa at some point, my lack of sleep from the night before catching up with me. Wriggling on the couch, I huff out a breath when I can't find a comfortable position, not yet ready to open my eyes and face the reality of my shitty situation.

At the sound of a throat clearing, I go still, ears straining. That's when I hear the soft sound of someone breathing, and I jackknife upward as my eyes fly open.

I have to blink several times, my sleep-addled brain conjuring tattooed muscles and piercing blue eyes that are startlingly similar to Ruthless'. I lift my hands to rub at my eyes, but the image doesn't change, and that's when it registers that it's not a dream.

Mr. Moody, Hot, and Arrogant *is* standing before me.

"Ruthless? What—what are you doing here?" I ask, eyes darting around the otherwise empty room before resting on him. He's dressed in his typical outfit of all black, tattoos peeking from the collar of his top and cascading down both his arms before disappearing where his hands are stuffed into the front pockets of his jeans as he stares down at me with cold indifference.

His veiled gaze rolls over my body, lingering on my exposed legs, and glancing down, I realize the hem of my t-shirt rode up while I was asleep, giving him a clear view of, well, everything.

Yanking it down, I tuck my legs beneath me.

"Royce?" Logan calls before he appears in the open doorway. His gaze bounces between us before he directs it at Royce, "Everything alright in here?"

"Yeah," Royce responds, not once taking his eyes off me.

"R-Royce? Your name is Royce?"

A sick sort of niggle, like a spider weaving a web in the back of my brain, pricks at my consciousness.

*Royce King. He raped my cousin.*

What are the chances that more than one Royce currently attends Halston University?

His lips twitch in what could possibly become a smile. "Guess that answers one of your questions, James."

"Royce, come on. Leave her be. I need your help."

Not seeming in any rush to leave, Royce's eyes continue to bore into mine, his expression as unreadable as ever. It's unnerving, especially given the niggling panic gathering momentum and slowly sliding into my veins, freezing like ice in my blood.

Eventually, he turns and strides toward the door.

"Your last name. W-what's your last name?"

He halts mid-stride, turning his head to look at me over his shoulder. His eyes dart between mine before he answers, "King."

Something vital inside me shatters. It takes everything I have to keep my expression neutral beneath his piercing stare, and I count every one of the seconds until he turns his head and strides out of the room.

As soon as I'm alone, and their footsteps and lowered murmurs have faded into the distance, the veil covering my actual expression drops.

He's Royce King.

The same Royce King who that girl said raped her cousin.

The same Royce King who has been coming to the club and demanding I dance for him every weekend for over a month now.

The same Royce King who pushed me against the wall and made me come all over his fingers.

The same Royce King that I am now trapped in a house with.

*Oh, God. I think I'm going to be sick.*

All of my thoughts swirl around in my head.

*He raped someone. He's been watching me dance. He's been pulling me out of my self-made shell. He made me come.*

Except, only one sentence is the outlier.

I know next to nothing about Royce—clearly. However, I know he pushes my boundaries. I also know he has stopped any time I've said no or when he can physically see he has pushed me too far. Hell, he managed to bring me back from the brink of a meltdown.

He has respected my fiercest of boundaries.

The Royce I've come to know, he challenges, he pushes, he thrives off driving you to the brink. But he doesn't ever cross that line.

At least, he never has with me.

That somewhat settles me. Enough that I no longer feel as though I'm going to vomit. However, it does leave a plethora of unanswered questions. I'm curious to know what truly happened. Is that why he thought I was initially crashing into him on purpose?

At least now, I understand why he's been coming to Lux. He's probably Grayson's little spy. He couldn't send himself or Logan, which left Royce to suss out what I did within the club's walls.

Although, he could have sat in the corner of the room and simply observed. He didn't have to engage with me. Didn't have to get so close. He certainly didn't have to kiss me back.

And yet, he did.

I just don't understand what that means.

On the other hand, it now makes sense why he kept persistently asking why I was at Halston. Did he think I was here for Grayson? Ha, that's rich. I didn't even know Grayson was here. I wish he *wasn't* here. After he kicked me and my mom out of the house, I lost track of what happened to him. My mom wasted no time shipping me off to St. Maria Maternity Home, where I was sequestered away from the rest of the world until Aurora was born. I wouldn't have had a hope of discovering where Grayson ended up even if I'd wanted to.

I idle away the time, thinking about each of the three men living in the rooms surrounding me until the room is pitched in darkness and I hear the ominous creak of floorboards as one of the shadows stalks toward my room.

# GRAYSON

## CHAPTER TWENTY-SEVEN

"Inmate's name," the prison guard orders, fingers poised over his keyboard and gaze fixed to his screen. One thing I've learned over the years visiting my dad is that customer service isn't a priority in a prison.

"Bertram Van Doren."

I tap my foot impatiently while he types the name into his computer. I nearly didn't come today. The thought of staying home and playing with our new toy sounded much more appealing. But it's wise not to let myself get drawn into Riley's orbit. Coming here—seeing Dad—will help me keep my priorities in line. Remind me of the purpose for all of this.

Then I can go home reinvigorated and make her pay.

I haven't told Dad about Riley attending Halston. I'm not entirely sure how he will react, and I don't want to be responsible for him losing his shit and ending up with a black mark on his record this close to his parole hearing.

"Go on through," the guard states, not once looking my way. "Next!"

Dismissed, I move over to the security scanner, emptying my pockets of my wallet, phone, and car keys into the tray before stepping through. Another guard waves me on, and I retrieve my belongings once they've been scanned before moving down the corridor to the visitors' area.

The room is a bustling hive of activity. Nearly every table is occupied as prisoners meet with their families and friends. I scan the busy room until I find my father sitting at a table in the far corner. Even in his bland gray prison uniform, he still dominates a room. His back is ramrod straight, dark hair cut short with flecks of gray that become more prominent every time I visit him, and he cuts his eyes around the room like he owns it.

Gaze catching mine as I make my way toward him, his face splits into a smile. "Son," he greets, getting up from the metal table and giving me a quick, regimented, one-armed embrace. A slap on the back. "How have you been?"

I slide into the hard plastic bench on the opposite side of the table. "Good."

"Classes going well? Grades solid?"

I give a curt nod. "Yup. Top of my year."

"That's my boy," he states with a proud smile. "Living up to the Van Doren name."

*Yup, that's me. The living embodiment that the Van Dorens are not self-righteous criminals only out for their own gain.*

It's who I've *had* to be since the day of his incarceration. The day the judge declared him guilty and sentenced him to five years behind bars. The day our family name took a hit, everyone started looking at us with disdain and whispering how we were just like the other wealthy, white, generational families who think only of themselves. I can't say or do anything without first thinking it through from a hundred different angles, questioning how it might be perceived—by the media, investors, shareholders, clients, and the general public.

"How are you holding up?" I ask instead, directing the conversation back to him.

"Same old," he says with a resigned sigh. "Bored. Ready to get out of here."

"I'm sure. It hopefully won't be much longer," I try to appease, knowing there's nothing else I can say or do to make it any easier for him. He's already endured four years in here, what's another couple of months?

He nods, glaring at the table as he blows out a tense breath.

"We need to start making preparations for after I'm released. The parole hearing is only a few weeks away." His face has hardened when he lifts his gaze to mine; father mode switched out for 'Business Bertram'.

"Okay..."

"I'll need somewhere to live."

"I can organize something for you when the time comes," I assure.

"Not some shitty little apartment, Grayson. A proper house. Everyone will be watching and I need to show them that the Van Doren name hasn't completely crumbled. They need to see that this is nothing but a bump in the road. One we will easily bounce back from."

What does he think I've been doing these last four years? Sitting on my ass, twiddling my thumbs? Buying him a fancy, expensive house isn't going to prove shit to anyone. No one is even watching. The newspapers moved on from his arrest years ago and I highly doubt they will give a shit when he gets released.

Not that highlighting any of that will do either of us any good. "Of course," I agree instead. What the fuck does it matter to me where he lives? He's spent four years inside a six-by-eight cell. He can live in a motherfucking castle after he gets released for all I care.

The only thing I care about is not losing my place in the company. Of course, I understand we can't both be CEOs. He can have the title; I don't care about that. While I believe I've earned it over the last four years, I understand that it's rightfully his until such a time as he retires and hands it to me. What I don't want is to be cast aside, given a bottom rung role that I would have been handed upon graduation under normal circumstances.

What I want is to be his second-in-command.

To be making the decisions along with him.

To have a say in the vital workings and decisions made.

Which is precisely what I have been doing. So basically, I want to continue doing what I've been doing, but he can have the CEO title if it makes him feel better.

"Dad," I hedge, since we're talking about life post-release.

"I know, Grayson." With a waned smile, he reaches across the table, placing his hand over mine and giving it a quick squeeze. "You've done a commendable job these last four years. You've truly stepped up, and I could not be prouder. I'm a firm believer in repaying hard work. We can discuss your place in the company once I'm out of here, okay?"

I sigh, some of the tension loosening in my chest as I take in the proud gleam in his eyes. Our relationship has been tumultuous recently, and I know part of that is because I've been so anxious about how things will change once he's back at the helm, but I know he wants what's best for the company and for me.

Equally, I understand that his upcoming parole hearing has been eating at him. The possibility of the freedom that awaits. It's made him more irritable than usual. Caused us to be at one another's throats more often.

But it's a temporary glitch. Once he's out, everything will go back to normal. Better than normal. It will go back to the way it *was*.

"Sure thing, Dad," I say with a tight smile, ignoring the

unease twisting my guts. "We'll have plenty of time to discuss it when you're on the outside."

I've basically been accountable to no one but myself since his arrest. I've been in charge of my own life, my own future. I've been the sole person responsible for the success and failures of Van Doren Holdings. The ultimate figurehead making all of the decisions. I'm the one who weathered the storm created by his arrest. Who reassured our employees and investors that this wasn't the end of VDH. Who had to watch our stocks plummet and come up with ways to salvage it, without any experience or even really a full understanding of the significance of it all.

And I did it. I did all of it. Not only did I keep the company afloat, but thanks to the latest deal I negotiated, our share price is officially higher than it was before my dad's arrest.

I did that. Me. All on my own, without him.

And yet, sitting here, despite his assurances and knowing he wants the best for the company, I am also aware that *he* wants to be the one to obtain it. That he'll tear apart the company upon his release. He'll destroy everything I've worked so hard to achieve just so he can put it back together with his name on the dotted line. He has no appreciation for everything I've sacrificed to keep us equitable. The friends I lost because I no longer had time to hang out with them. The classes I missed because I needed to put out some new fire at the office. The press I had to dodge as a scared, overwhelmed eighteen-year-old kid.

For the entirety of that first year after he was arrested, my life was a literal shitshow. I was thrown into shark-infested waters with no clue how to swim and left to sink or build myself a life raft.

Know what I did? I built myself a motherfucking raft.

One that I improved upon year after year until that flimsy strip of wood that was barely keeping my head above water became a top-of-the-line cruise liner. A warship built for battle. An unsinkable barge large enough to carry all the baggage I lug around on a daily basis.

And I never told him any of it. Never confided in him. Because I didn't want him to feel any more guilty than he already did. Didn't want to put that weight on his shoulders when there was damn all he could do about it.

So while I understand; while I want to see my dad released and have him back in my life, to have a purpose and to help with the company, I also know I can't let him destroy everything I've worked so hard to achieve.

---

"Yo, how was your dad?" Logan asks when I step into the kitchen later that day. He and Royce are sitting at the table, mid-conversation, which is set aside when they both look my way.

"Same old. His parole hearing is set for January."

I move to the fridge, grab a bottle of water and twist off the lid before downing half of it.

"He'll get out, man," Royce encourages while Logan nods.

I'm hopeful, but one can never truly know how these things will go, and the closer we get to that day, the more unsettled I become. Our relationship, while complicated, works the way it is, and I can't fathom how that dynamic will change when he no longer needs to rely on me. I swipe a hand over my face, suppressing the ball of dread in my stomach at the thought of how bad things will get if he is denied parole.

"How's our hostage?" I ask instead, desperately needing the distraction.

Logan shrugs. "Angry," he mutters bitterly.

"Huh, she didn't seem angry when I went in to check on her," Royce muses, only causing Logan's scowl to deepen.

I watch him closely, his forehead creased as he mulls something over before lifting his gaze to meet mine. "Gray, can I ask you something without you biting my head off?" My eyes narrow as I wait him out, and he eventually spits out, "Are you sure she's the girl?"

"Why the fuck are you asking me that, Logan?" I growl, my heart pounding with a mix of anger and frustration. "Am I certain she's the one who falsely accused my dad of raping her? Yes, I'm fucking certain."

"Why?" he argues, unfazed by my outburst.

"Why? Because as they pulled my dad out the door and placed him in the back of the cop car after stating the allegations against him, she turned to me and told me she was fucking sorry." My voice cracks with emotion, body trembling with the weight of my hatred for that bitch. "Why are *you* suddenly doubting me?"

"I'm not," he says, holding his palms up in defense. "I'm just trying to understand. Was there ever any proof? Did she testify or anything?"

I search his face, struggling to control my emotions as rage crashes like a tidal wave over my head. "What. The. Fuck. Did she say to you?"

"Nothing." When I simply continue to stare, he confesses, "She went off on me earlier, saying how your dad committed the crime he was accused of and got away with a far more serious one."

"If that isn't proof enough that it was her who accused him," I counter, voice rising with frustration.

"True. It's just the Riley I got to know... I didn't think she'd be capable of doing that."

"Because she's a manipulative liar!" I half yell, unable to

contain the lid on my anger. Staring him right in the eyes, I bluntly state, “I’m sorry to break it to you, man, but the girl you thought you knew doesn’t exist. Trust me. Once upon a time, I thought I knew her, too.”

He nods but doesn’t meet my eyes, clearly struggling with the conflicting information he’s received. It lessens some of that rage inside me, and I continue in a softer tone, “She’s trapped and searching for a way out of her predicament, and she sees *you* as the weak link. She has a connection to you and thinks she can manipulate and use it for her own gain.”

Logan’s lips press into a scowl, his eyes drilling into the tabletop. “You’re right, man. I’m sorry. I let her get in my head and I shouldn’t have.”

Blowing out a breath, I place my hand on his shoulder; my anger snuffed out at seeing his turmoil. “It’s okay, dude. I know you’re having a rough time with this. It’ll get easier, I promise. We’ll break her until she finally confesses to what she did, and then you’ll see her for who she truly is.”

Deep down, though, I’m worried. I can’t help but wonder if Logan will be able to resist her manipulation and see through her lies. Concern that she will sink her claws in and destroy him the same way she has my dad, has my hatred toward her sharpening into a finely tuned weapon, and with fresh determination, I lift my head and meet Royce’s ice-cold stare. “You still on board?”

The same cold, hard determination is reflected back at me. “You know it, man.”

Confident that between us, we’ll be able to keep Logan out of her clutches, I smirk. “Good, ‘cause I stopped on the way home and got a *welcome to hell* gift for her for tonight.” I hold up the paper bag in my hand, and both Logan and Royce eye it critically.

“That’s tonight’s fun sorted, then, but what do we do with

her tomorrow when we're at Logan's game? Just chain her up and leave her?" Royce asks.

"Actually," Logan begins hesitantly, eyes shifting between Royce and me. Even before he opens his mouth, I know I'm not going to like whatever he's going to say. "I was thinking she could come to the game with you guys."

*Yup. Knew I'd fucking hate it.*

"Why?"

"Fucking hell, is this that superstitious bullshit, man?" Royce gripes, rolling his eyes. Logan has always been into that shit. He's got a puck from his first Championship win that he kisses before every game because he believes it brings him good luck. And now he's set Riley on the same pedestal. "You do realize it's all hocus pocus. Only you can determine if you have a good game or not."

"Yeah, maybe," Logan says, clearly not truly believing that. I've heard enough times about the weird rituals some of his teammates have to know there's no point in trying to tell him—or apparently any hockey player—otherwise. They will continue to do whatever they believe is necessary to win their game. Whether it be wearing the same pair of boxers for each one, listening to the same song on repeat in the locker room, or sleeping in their opponent's uniform—yes, the captain his sophomore year did actually do that.

Royce should understand it better than I do. Some of the guys he played football with were just as superstitious. However, Royce is a firm believer in devising your own luck. He had his own pre-game ritual, but it had nothing to do with superstition and everything to do with getting his head in the right mindset before he went out onto the field.

"I need all the help I can get, though," Logan continues. "We all know I've been off my game since... you know. Even Coach called me on it, and if I don't improve soon, I will end up benched for the rest of the season. Which will be the least of my concerns if we don't make it to the Frozen Four and I don't get a pro contract."

Well, fuck, when he puts it like that...

Royce clearly feels the same as we share a pained, *what the fuck can we do?* glance.

Warring internally with myself, I eventually grit my teeth and sigh. "Fine," I reluctantly agree. "She can come with us." Fuck me. This is *so* not what I had in mind when I was installing that stripper pole. "But win or lose, the three of us meet back here tomorrow night afterward."

"Yeah, man, whatever you want," Logan says, looking lighter than he has since I got home as he pushes to his feet and grins at me before walking away. "I gotta get my workout in before tonight's festivities begin."

Royce holds my gaze, patiently waiting until Logan's footsteps have faded before asking, "You sure you can handle that?"

"Do I have a fucking choice?" I grumble, dropping into Logan's vacant barstool. "It's not like I could have said no to him."

He nods, agreeing.

"Still. Not exactly the sex slave ideal you were spouting last night."

"Tell me about it. She's supposed to be our prisoner, not a fucking ride-along." Sighing, I confess, "I'm worried about him."

"Are you worried she'll be at his game and he'll play like shit, or that she'll be there and he'll play as well as he did last time?"

Well, fuck. The asshole knows me too well.

I glare at his astute insight. Of course, I want Logan to win his game. To take his team to the Frozen Four and get a pro contract. I want all of that for him. But does *she* seriously have to be the magical fucking charm that helps him obtain all of that? What was wrong with relying on his lucky puck? It's gotten him this far in his career!

Chuckling when I don't deign to answer him, Royce changes the topic. "So... Which one of us is breaking the news to Babydoll?"

Arching my eyebrow at his nickname for her, I deadpan, "Unless we're humiliating her, I'm not going anywhere fucking near her." Before he can argue, I'm out of my chair and storming from the room, my head a chaotic mess of pent-up aggression and frustration.

"Guess that leaves me to break the news to her then," the asshole calls after me. "Awesome. Excellent chat, dude. Let's do this again." Giving him the bird over my shoulder, I stomp up the stairs, intending to go straight to my room on the third floor and remain there until Logan's done with his workout and we can finally start messing with Riley.

However, my steps involuntarily slow as I pass her closed door until they stop altogether and I'm left contemplating what she's doing right now. What she's thinking.

An exhilaration like nothing I've felt thrums through my veins at the possibility of storming in there and seeing her, eyes wild with fright at my presence. I used to get a similar feeling when I'd walk into the kitchen and see her there, or when we'd sit down for the occasional family dinner. Only now, sharp thorns have wrapped their way around that feeling, tightening and stabbing at it until it turned into something darker. Something twisted.

I once wanted to know what it would be like to kiss her. To worship her skin with my lips and feel her quivering between my thighs.

Now...

Now, I want to destroy her. To force her to feel this ugliness that has consumed me since the day she turned my world upside down.

Before I know it, my hand is wrapped around the handle, and I throw the door open with enough force that it ricochets off the wall. She jumps off the couch, eyes wide, just like I pictured.

I take a second to roam my eyes over her. Noting that she's no longer restrained to the stripper pole. No doubt that is Logan's doing. Sentimental idiot. However, she has changed out of her jeans and top from the night before. One of Logan's T-shirts drowns her, hiding her curvy figure and falling to just above her knees.

After a second, when I make no move toward her, she deflates slightly, that wild-eyed expression dimming as she collapses back onto the couch. She brings her legs up, wrapping her arms around them as she continues to watch me warily.

"Ready to confess?"

Unflinching, she stares right back. "I can't confess to a crime I haven't committed."

I scoff. "We both know that's not the truth. Why don't you just own up to what you did and this can all end."

She perks up, and I know I've got her.

"You're saying, if I come clean, you'll let me go? You'll leave me in peace to finish out the rest of the year? No stalking me on campus, no sending Royce to watch me at the club, no Logan picking me up after work."

*Huh. Apparently, my boys have been keeping secrets. Think the three of us need to sit down and have a family meeting.*

Not giving away my surprise, I merely nod. "Yup. You won't see any of us again. Pinky promise."

Lies, obviously. But she doesn't need to know that.

Her eyes narrow to slits, assessing me for any hint of deception. Unable to see past my poker face, she eventually nods.

"Alright then." Standing on long, slim legs, she takes a step toward me. "Grayson Van Doren, I confess..."

Blood rushes in my ears. This is it. Fucking finally, she's going to admit what she did to me.

"... that I am truly sorry for the pain I have caused you. For being the trigger that changed your life."

Wait, what?

"But I am *not* sorry for what I did. Between ensuring you continued living in your perfect little bubble and my survival, I chose me. I chose to live. To have a future. And I'm sorry if that ruined yours, but honestly, it looks like you're doing pretty fine anyway."

One second I'm blinking dumbly at her, and in the next my hand is around her throat as I throw her against the wall.

"You lying little cunt," I snarl, spittle flying from my mouth and hitting her face. "*Confess*."

Her whole body trembles against my rage, even as her eyes burn with wildfire. "Your dad raped me, Grayson. Repeatedly. He'd sneak into my room after Mom was asleep or while you were out with your friends. He'd stroke my hair and tell me I was his good little—

"STOP!" My hand slams against the wall beside her head, and I can feel the vein pulsing in my forehead. "Stop lying!"

"Stop being daddy's little bitch!" she screams back.

My hand shakes with the force of my anger, my fingers pressing into her skin until her eyes go wide. Genuine fear douses the flames as her fingers wrap around my wrist and begin to tug on it.

"Grayson," she croaks.

But all I hear is her lies. Repeating over and over, fanning the flames as I tighten my hold around her throat.

I can feel her pulse hammering beneath my thumb, quick-ening with each passing beat. Her nails dig into my skin, splitting flesh, but I'm numb to the pain.

"What's going on—Grayson!"

I'm knocked off my feet, my grip loosening as I stumble to the side. "What the fuck, dude?" Royce snarls, glaring at me in shock and horror before turning his attention to Riley.

I stare too, as she slides down the wall to the floor, bringing her legs up and pressing her forehead against her knees. Her shoulders shake as a confusing jumble of emotions war within me. That ever-present anger still bubbles, volatile and toxic, but it's covered in a layer of guilt and regret.

"Fuck," I curse, unable to deal with this shit or how it feels as though it's eating me alive. Without sparing her a second look, I storm out the door and up to my room. Unless I'm with Royce or Logan, I need to stay the fuck away from her.

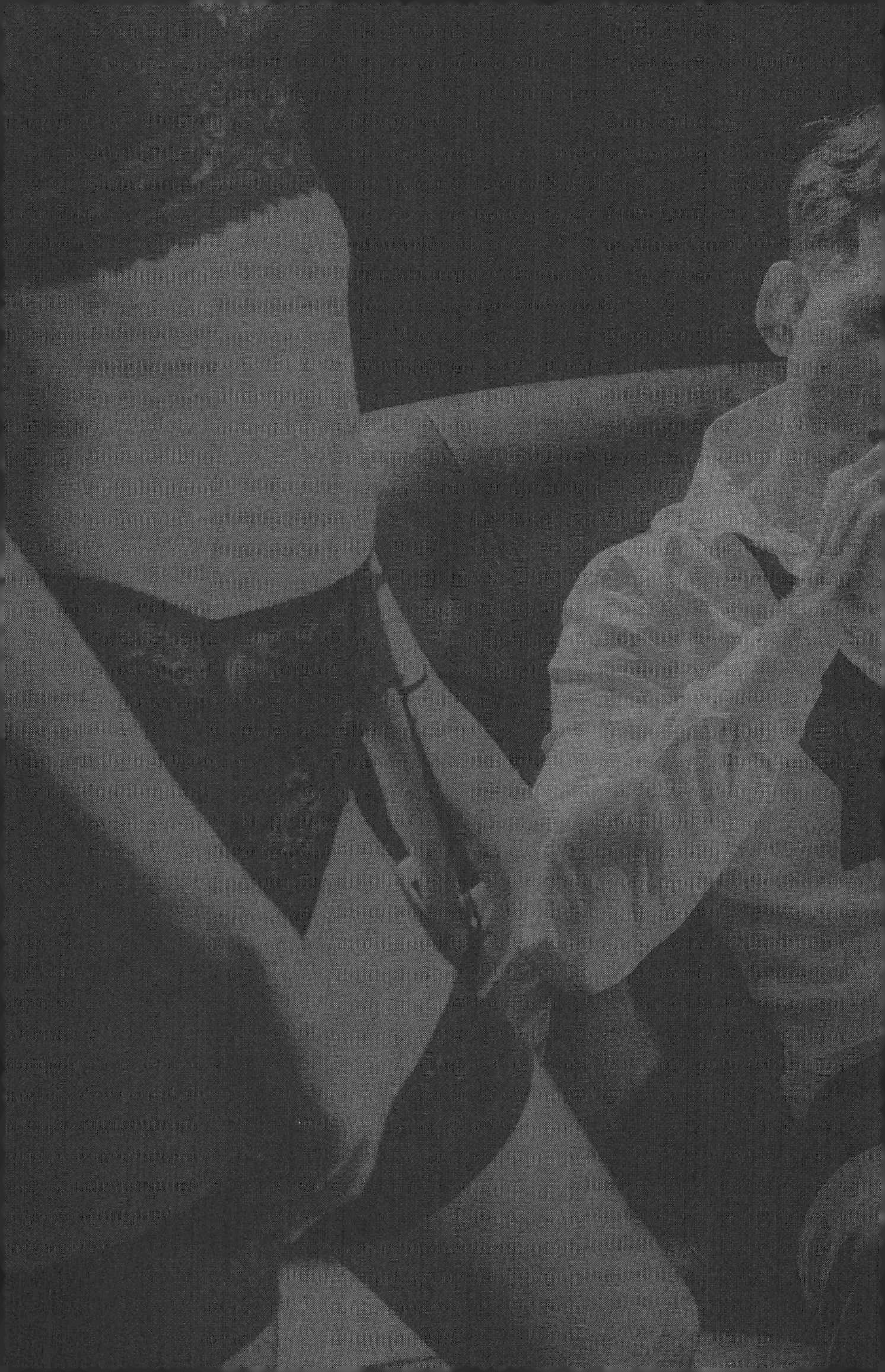

# RILEY

## CHAPTER TWENTY-EIGHT

My heart threatens to launch itself from my chest and my body shakes so severely that the floor vibrates beneath my ass. My throat is on fire and my lips tingle as I curl into myself.

"Hey, are you alright?" Royce murmurs gently. He presses a hand against my shoulder, and instinctively, I jolt away.

Glaring at him with hate in my eyes, I growl, "Don't touch me!"

To my surprise, his face shows no signs of being affronted at my outburst, and he remains crouched in front of me, patiently watching.

I stare right back, my inner turmoil on display for him to gawk at. There's an empathy in his eyes that I've never seen before. I hate seeing it. Loathe how it makes me shrink further. I don't want his sympathy. Don't want him to see me as weak and helpless. That's not who I am anymore.

Undeterred by my hostility, he repeats, "Are you okay?"

"Do I look fucking okay to you, Royce?" I snap, anger burning a path through my veins. I know I'm taking my anger out on the wrong person, but sue me. Grayson just pushed me off the goddamn ledge.

"No."

"Then there's your answer."

He nods, seeming satisfied, before shifting onto his ass and crossing his legs in front of him. I watch, confused. "What are you doing?"

"Figured I'd sit with you until you do feel okay."

"Why would you do that? Why do you even care?"

Royce is a complete enigma. He keeps himself locked behind so many layers, never giving anything real away. Every time I think I have him sussed, he surprises me and I am once again thrown off kilter.

The only answer I receive is a shrug. I know better by now than to push him. If he doesn't want to give an answer, he won't.

Instead, I rest my chin on my knees and silently watch him. He watches me right back. The two of us are strangers attempting to gain an honest read of one another. Words have never been our language. It's our bodies that do all the talking.

Like, right now, his posture is open, offering me surprising reassurance. Yet, at the same time, he's still so shut down. He's telling me without words that he's here but unwilling to share any of himself.

I'm not entirely sure why I decide to cross that divide, but my lips part on their own accord, the words spilling from my tongue. "He never used to be so angry." My tone is hushed as I stare at the faded band logo on Royce's T-shirt. "He had the best smile. There were days when I lived just to see it. The way it reached his eyes and made them sparkle. And his laugh, *ugh*." I can't help but smile as I dig up the sound from the depths of my memory. It was the kind of laugh that wrapped around you like a thick blanket on a freezing winter's night, keeping the cold at bay and ensuring you were warm and cozy.

"You liked him," Royce keenly observes. It's not a question so I don't answer, and eventually, he tacks on, "I've never seen him smile like that. Or, at all, really."

That's sad. I know I'm partially to blame, but equally, I don't believe that it's my fault. Why should I carry the guilt of that? Grayson losing that light magnetic energy surrounding him is not what I wanted. None of this is what I wanted.

"How long have you known each other?" I ask Royce, needing to veer the topic off my memories of Grayson.

"Since freshman year. The three of us met one night in a bar. Well, more like they saved me from getting my drunk ass handed to me."

"You got into a fight?"

He nods, not elaborating further.

"And you became instant BFFs."

His lips quirk at my teasing tone. "Something like that."

"Have you always fought like you do at The Depot?"

"Nah. I started doing it in the off-season when I started at Halston. It only became a more regular thing this year."

"You used to be a football player, right? Quarterback?"

He stiffens, his gaze hardening. "Yeah."

"Do you miss it?"

He instantly relaxes when I don't start peppering him with questions about what happened. Again, I know better than to ask questions he won't answer.

Dropping his gaze to the floor, he sighs. "Like you wouldn't believe."

"I'm sorry," I say softly, thinking how lost I'd feel if I could no longer dance. "It must be incredibly difficult to adapt to a life without it. I know, not being able to dance would feel like a death sentence for me. And having to see your teammates on campus all the time..." I shake my head. I can only imagine how torturous that would be. "It must be agony," I empathize. "All that rage needs to be channeled somewhere. No one could blame you for taking it out on the world around you." He merely blinks at me, his expression unreadable, although something passes between us—an understanding, and I dare to ask, "Does drawing help?"

"That's enough questions for today, Babydoll," he says, bringing our conversation to an abrupt halt as he gets to his feet. "I believe Grayson has a special evening planned for all of us."

"How delightful," I deadpan, wishing we could stay in this moment. I like talking to Royce, even if he doesn't really do much in the way of actual talking. It still feels as though he's contributing to the conversation through his body language alone.

He smirks down at me. "On the plus side, you get to come out with us tomorrow night."

"Where?" I ask with a frown. As far as I was aware, this is the only place other than Lux that I need to be for the next three weeks, and I'm not on the schedule to work tomorrow night.

"It's Logan's final game before the break, and he wants you there."

"Me? Why?"

Royce arches an eyebrow. "Because he is under the deluded belief that your presence is required for him to play well."

"And what if I don't want to go?"

Chuckling darkly, he holds out a hand to pull me up. "If whatever is going on between you two is real, then you'll come because you want what's best for him."

With a sigh of defeat, I slip my hand into his and allow him to help me to my feet.

"Fine, I'll go, but there is nothing going on between me and Logan. Not anymore."

"Sure, you tell yourself that, James." He eyes me a moment longer. "You know, the two of you might just make the perfect couple. You're both as deluded as each other."

I elbow him in the ribs, smiling when he grunts in pain.

"Well, I can't go dressed like this, so I'll need my clothes returned before tomorrow night."

Royce's eyes drop down to my bare legs, lingering as a coy smirk plays along his lips. "What's wrong with what you're wearing?"

"You asshole. You know damn well I can't go like this. Just like I can't do whatever Grayson has planned for me on an empty stomach, so since you're keeping me captive, I demand that you feed me."

He snorts. "Why do I feel like I'm the one being turned into the minion?"

I smirk back at him until he leaves to get me some sustenance. However, by the time I've finished eating, I'm left with nothing to distract me as I wait for tonight's *festivities* to commence, and the food twists in my stomach precariously until I regret eating anything at all.

Soon enough, I hear their footsteps approaching. I'm a ball of stress, and my heart threatens to explode out of my chest as the door opens and the three of them stand like ominous silhouettes in the doorway.

Grayson tosses a bag at my feet. "Put that on."

With shaking hands that I hope he can't see, I open the bag and pull out the clothing within.

My stomach hollows out as I stare at the slutty cheerleader outfit. "Really?" I sigh.

"I know how much you always wanted to be one," Grayson drawls, seeming far too fucking smug.

Yeah, I contemplated it for all of .2 seconds because Grayson played on our high school football team, and I thought it would be a good way to get him to notice me. Nevertheless, once his father started stealing pieces of my soul for himself, I stopped thinking of Grayson altogether.

Tossing it on top of the bag, I snark, "Thanks, but no thanks. I've moved on from high school dreams."

"Tough shit. None of this is about what you want," Grayson retorts, marching toward me.

I swear the skin around my throat throbs with every step he takes closer, and my body vibrates with the urge to retreat. Every muscle is pulled taut as I force myself to remain in place, air sealed in my lungs as I track his every move.

"Grayson," Royce warns, his tone sharp enough to stop Grayson in his tracks, several feet from where I stand.

His gaze drops briefly to the visible bruising on my still tender skin and his features tighten almost imperceptibly, eyes flashing with what looks like... regret? Except it's gone in the next second and I'm left wondering if I imagined it.

"Get dressed," he barks in the next second, confirming that any guilt I saw was concocted by my own imagination.

I shake my head in disappointment as he storms across the room, before shifting my attention to Royce and Logan. I arch a brow, and the two assholes smirk at me with zero intention of stepping in and putting a stop to this madness.

Mentally cursing all three, I turn my back on the room and snatch up the cheerleader outfit as heavy, sultry music starts playing.

"Happy?" I snipe once I'm dressed, spinning to face the room in my bright yellow and blue skirt that should be remade as a belt because it's so short and a matching crop top that pushes my breasts together and is one deep inhale away from splitting at the seams.

"Fuck," Logan rasps, drawing my attention in time to watch his throat bob as he swallows, his eyes slowly raking up my legs and over my torso. I suddenly recall our conversation where we teased about me being his own personal cheerleader.

*"I'm totally picturing you in a short little skirt, a tight crop top, and your hair tied up in one of those high ponytails. Do you own pom poms? 'Cause you might make me come in my pants for a second time today if you do."*

I'm literally dressed up as his wet dream right now.

Fuck Grayson and his stupid shitty ideas!

Logan's eyes lift to mine, and I can tell he's also recalling that moment in the library. Our frayed and bruised connection flares with newfound life, that ever-present chemistry sizzling between us before Grayson interrupts.

"Well, what are you waiting for?"

Ripping my gaze from Logan's, I huff out a breath and move to the pole. Forcing thoughts of all of them from my mind, I close my eyes and turn my focus inward, concentrating on my body and the song as I begin to move.

Grayson may think that this is degrading or humiliating for me, but what he doesn't realize is that dancing is my happy place. It's the one time when I can tune out the rest of the world and simply be. Me, my body, and the music in tandem.

I fall into such a deep trance that I fail to notice when the music abruptly cuts off. A sharp tug on my arm causes me to stumble and I snap my eyes open, finding Grayson glowering down at me. "Why the fuck are you smiling?"

I was? I hadn't even realized.

"I didn't know I wasn't allowed to do that. Any other rules I'm not aware of that you'd like to point out?"

His jaw tics with his irritation, and I find it extremely satisfying.

"Just fucking dance," he growls, remaining in place in front of me.

"Without smiling?" I ask, making it sound as though I'm clarifying when really I just want to poke at him some more.

"Yes." The word comes out in a low, barely contained hiss as the threads of his control sever.

"Got it." I throw him a cheeky wink, knowing I'm playing with fire before I go back to my dance. However, he doesn't return to his seat, instead remaining directly in front of me. I can feel his presence like a breeze against my skin, making it impossible for me to get lost in the music.

I end up staring into his face as I put on a performance. One that feels far more intimate than it did a minute ago. The irony isn't lost on me that all these years later, I have Grayson's undivided attention. And it's just as potent as I knew it would be. Terrifying and intoxicating.

There's no denying, I might know how to get under his skin, but he's also capable of getting under mine.

The air grows cloying until Grayson's presence presses against my skin like a physical force, compressing my lungs until it becomes a struggle to breathe.

Just when I think I'm about to break beneath the pressure, Grayson growls before turning on his heel and storming from the room.

"Wow," Logan murmurs. "That was intense."

Royce grunts out an agreement, and tearing my eyes from the now empty doorway, I turn to find him frowning as he stares at a point on the wall. After a second, he shakes his head, muttering something too low for me to hear, before following Grayson. "I'm out," he calls over his shoulder when he reaches the threshold, before disappearing altogether.

Left alone in the room with Logan, the air thickens with tension.

"I'm not dancing for you," I snap, crossing my arms across the front of my chest.

Seeming to accept that, Logan nods, still looking at me with far too much intimacy for someone who supposedly hates me. Pushing to his feet, he makes a point of walking right by me as he heads for the door, and it's possible that I'm mistaken, but I'd swear I hear him murmur, "So beautiful," as he passes.

# RILEY

## CHAPTER TWENTY-NINE

I wasn't left on my own for long last night before Royce came in to lock me back in my cell—AKA tie me up to the stripper pole. When I protested, he said they couldn't trust me not to run off while they slept, which, I get. However, I was still wearing the stupid cheerleader outfit which I wasn't about to run outside in, especially without any shoes, and in the middle of winter.

I want to escape, but not badly enough to risk frostbite or hypothermia. I wouldn't jeopardize my chance to spend time with my daughter on Christmas Day, nor my ability to dance, by getting sick or losing a couple of toes.

Regardless, I was left with no choice while he tied me up, and I'm blaming the hard floor and cold draft for my sour mood today.

"Here you go." Royce tosses my clothes at me, and I give them a sniff.

"You could at least have washed them."

"We're not a hotel, Babydoll."

"Yeah, no kidding. You'd only have a one-star rating on Yelp if you were. Zero outta ten. Do not recommend. Lacks any sort of bed or blankets. Into some kinky shit. And forgets to feed its guests."

"Cranky today, aren't we?"

"If you would like an un-cranky captive you should feed and clothe her properly and ensure she gets her eight hours of *comfortable* beauty sleep."

He snorts, seeming to find me amusing when that's not what I was going for. "Get dressed. It's game time."

Sighing, I pull on the clothes I was wearing when Logan so thoughtfully kidnapped me. I'm both excited for and not exactly looking forward to this game tonight. I haven't been to one since Logan asked me to attend, and while I know he wants me there tonight, I'm not entirely sure what to expect. What if he loses? Will he blame it on me?

More concerningly, what if he wins? Will he expect me to be at his games? He'd mentioned as much before, but by the time his next match rolls around, this little hostage situation will be done and dusted. Once the new semester starts up, they can't keep me here, and I refuse to have anything to do with any of them. Including going to Logan's games.

Once I'm dressed, Royce ushers me down the stairs. I'm halfway down them when I stop, spotting Grayson standing by the front door, waiting for us. My abrupt halt causes Royce to bump into my back, and his hand flattens across my abdomen as I pitch forward.

"Always crashing into me, Babydoll," he murmurs against my ear, his sultry voice raising goosebumps along the flesh of my arms.

"I believe you're the one who just crashed into me," I mutter, eyes still focused on Grayson.

As if sensing my presence, his head snaps up, gaze roaming over my face before dropping to linger on my throat. Small, circular, fingerprint bruises decorate the sides of my neck, and it's a little tender to touch, but I refuse to let him see any of that as I stare boldly back.

"About time," he barks, ripping his gaze away and yanking open the front door before storming out.

"I won't leave you alone with him," Royce murmurs in my ear. "He won't hurt you."

Scoffing, I turn my head to look at him. "You mean you won't let him kill me. But everything else is on the table, right?"

His only response is the pursing of his lips.

"Yeah, that's what I thought." I snap scathingly. "I appreciate your assistance yesterday, but I've got it from here. Believe it or not, I've survived worse than whatever Grayson Van Doren throws at me."

The journey to the stadium is filled with awkward silence, and I'm glad to breathe fresh air when we finally get out of the car.

"Let's grab some food," Royce says once we've made it past the ticket kiosks. The two of them are practically glued to my sides as we make our way through the crowd and get in line for food.

"Two beers and nachos with cheese," Royce tells the girl once we reach the counter.

"Certainly," she says in a peppy tone all while batting her eyelashes at him. "Will that be everything?"

"Ye—"

"No," I interrupt. "Make that three beers, and I'll take a hotdog with all the toppings, a second nacho with cheese, and a tub of popcorn."

The girl blinks at me for a full minute before inputting the order into the computer.

"Seriously?" Royce questions when she moves away to grab our food.

"Yes, *seriously,*" I state, turning to glare at him. "None of you bothered to feed me since breakfast so I'm fucking starving."

"Leave her be," Grayson drawls, staring at a poster advertising the stadium's new vegan options. "She'll need her energy for later anyway."

My hand on the counter tightens into a fist, and the three of us fall silent as the girl comes back with our food and beers.

"You sit in the middle," Grayson demands once we reach our seats.

I roll my eyes but follow behind Royce as we squeeze between the row of seats until we reach ours. Grayson drops into the chair on my other side and it takes everything in me not to recoil. I'm still so angry at him.

I keep my focus firmly on the ice rink in front of us. I'm once again sitting rink side, and memories of the last time I was here have my heart clenching in my chest. How did everything go to fucking shit within such a short period of time? It doesn't seem fair.

I munch on my food while the teams warm up on the ice and the seats around us fill with spectators. Several times, my eyes clash with Logan's as he sits in the center of the ice, stretching out his muscles before the game, but just as quickly, one of us always looks away, and eventually all of the players head back into the locker room to get ready for the game.

Shortly before the game is due to begin, I spot the older man who sat beside me at the last game ambling down the aisle. I wave at him, and he returns it with a nod before moving to sit on the opposite side of the aisle.

"Who is that?" Grayson snaps, glaring daggers at the man.

"My sugar daddy."

His head whirls around to face mine so quickly that I'm shocked he doesn't pull a muscle.

"Oh my God, you should see your face right now!"

"Dude, she's right," Royce agrees with a rare laugh. "You look like you're about to lose your shit."

He does. Interesting. I wonder why that would be.

"Asshole," he grumbles, glaring daggers at Royce before dismissing us as the stadium lights dim and the music builds in crescendo. The same adrenaline-fueled thrill I felt last time starts up inside me as names are called over the speaker system, and one by one the Halston Huskies pour onto the ice.

The stadium erupts when Logan's number, seventeen, is called, and I clap and hoot alongside everyone else when he shoots onto the ice, stick raised above his head as he does a loop of the rink. He slows as he passes, tilting his chin to Grayson and Royce. However, his eyes remain glued to mine, an intensity I haven't seen since the last time I was here shining back at me.

The force is enough to suck the air from my lungs as I stare unblinkingly back, a tidal wave of emotions threatening to drag me under and pull me out to sea. It's almost a relief when he lets me go, tossing me back into the ocean as he continues on his loop for his adoring fans.

Looking away, I find Royce watching me, and when I catch his gaze he quirks an eyebrow. "Still fooling yourself?"

"Shut up," I grumble, stuffing a handful of popcorn into my mouth as the game gets underway.

---

"Yes! Go, Logan! Go! GO!"

I'm on my feet, screaming alongside everyone else as Logan shoots toward the goalie with the puck. If he gets this, it will be his fifth goal of the night. Something that is practically unheard of—according to Royce and Grayson, who have been talking over my head like I don't exist every time there's a break in the play.

I can feel both of them watching me quizzically every time I jump to my feet and scream for Logan. They're probably as surprised as I am, but it's impossible not to get caught up in the atmosphere. The entire stadium is rooting for the Huskies. At least, that's how it feels, and I tell myself it's the team I'm screaming for, even if it's Logan's name on my tongue. *That's only because he's the one scoring all the goals.*

*Yeah, right.* I don't even believe myself.

He sets up the shot, swinging his stick, and the puck goes sailing past the goalie and into the back of the net right as the final buzzer blares.

"YES!" I scream, bouncing up and down on my feet.

"Holy shit!" Royce's grin is the brightest I've ever seen as he cups his hands around his mouth and whistles. Glancing down at me, his eyes skate over my face as if seeing me in a new light. "Maybe you are his lucky charm."

Blushing, I turn my attention back to the rink as Logan untangles himself from his teammates, and pulling off his helmet, he skates toward us, grinning like a damn golden retriever as he pushes his sweat-slicked strands out of his face.

"Did you see that?" he yells through the plexiglass as he slams his gloved hand against it.

"See, what?" Grayson teases. "Did you do something?"

Logan sticks out his tongue at Grayson, and their antics make me laugh despite the odd situation I've found myself in.

Hearing me, Logan's gaze snaps to mine as though we're two opposing magnets. My teeth sink into my bottom lip at the heat I find reflected back at me. I know it's probably just his residual adrenaline, but still, it goes straight to my core and sets it on fire.

"Well done, man," Royce yells. "You played amazing. Now, go change so we can go home and celebrate."

Every muscle in my body pulls taut, images of how they

plan to *celebrate* filtering through my mind as Logan's gaze turns practically feral. *Oh, fuck.* When I pictured myself dancing for them around that pole, I imagined myself hating it. Hating them. But with the way Logan is looking at me and how my body is responding, I'm not so sure I'm going to despise it as much as Grayson hopes I will. As much as I thought I would.

Licking his lips in the sexiest way possible, he pushes off the plexiglass and skates away.

"Let's go, Babydoll. Now it's your turn to put on a show," Royce whispers in my ear before nudging me down the aisle after Grayson.

# RILEY

## CHAPTER THIRTY

"Clothes off," Grayson barks as soon as we're through the door into my new living quarters. Like the king he is, he drops onto the couch with one of the beers they brought up while Royce pumps music through the speakers.

Logan was still in the locker rooms when we left, but no doubt he'll be along shortly to join in this debauchery.

Turning my back to them, I pull my T-shirt over my head before kicking off my shoes, and refusing to feel any embarrassment over this situation, I hurriedly unbuckle my jeans and shove them down my legs.

"Dance," Grayson barks as soon as I'm stripped down to my bra and panties. Biting my tongue, my gaze flicks to Royce, who merely smirks at me.

Assholes. The pair of them are complete fucking assholes.

Blocking them out, I turn my thoughts inward and sway my hips seductively. As my body puts on a show for them, I don't let my mind get caught up in the present. Instead, I do what I've repeatedly done over the last few years—I look to the future. To the daughter I'll be able to take care of, thanks to the steady job

I'll get when I graduate. The cute little house I'll be able to afford. The bills I'll be able to pay.

All of this—every painful second—is merely a means to an end.

Okay, so I didn't plan for Grayson or his brainless followers to kidnap and hold me hostage until he's got his revenge, but even this is only a minor blip in my plan.

See, Grayson might think that he's gaining something by punishing me, but degrading me won't make *him* feel any better. Even after he's had his fun with me, he's still going to be pissed about his dad and angry over our past. He will still hate himself, and no amount of blaming me will ever fix that.

Fingers tighten in my hair, a squeak slipping past my lips as the hand fists the strands. My eyes fly open and I startle, blinking at Grayson in confusion.

"Our boy deserves a lap dance after his win tonight, don't you think?"

He twists my head toward where Logan is sprawled out on the couch with a beer dangling between his fingers as his eyes devour me with a carnal hunger.

*Damn.* I was so lost in my head that I didn't hear him coming in.

With his hand still in my hair, Grayson shoves me roughly toward him, and I stumble over my feet before righting myself, glaring at Grayson before dismissing him altogether.

Pushing past the butterflies that have taken flight in my stomach, I slip effortlessly into Aurora Noir and sway my hips as I stride confidently toward Logan. His grin grows wider with every step, eyes slowly drinking me in as his gaze drops down my scantily clad body. The desire I felt watching him on the ice earlier returns, and this no longer feels like a punishment. It resembles the way I felt when I danced for Royce at Lux. Sexy. Seductive. Empowering.

Rather than beating me down and making me feel like shit, every moment beneath Logan's hungry gaze fills me with strength.

He spreads his legs wide in invitation for me to step between them, which I do, and he licks his lips as I place my hands on his shoulders. A move that has my tits bouncing in front of his face as I start to move my hips.

His gaze drops, and he groans as though in pain. His eyes never once leave my body, his beer forgotten in his hand as I put on a show for him, and I don't miss the noticeable bulge that forms in his jeans.

I try to remind myself that he isn't the Logan I once thought he was. That, despite the fact I still care for the asshat on some level, and we clearly have undeniable chemistry, that we can never be the couple I once hoped we'd inevitably become.

However, it doesn't have the desired effect of helping me distance myself from him. Instead, my gaze roams over his face while I dance, trying to piece the Logan before me with the carefree one I met that first day in class, but it doesn't quite fit. There's a hardness in his eyes that I never remember seeing before and a cruel curl to his mouth that makes me uneasy.

He bites his lower lip, and his hand moves to touch my outer thigh, slowly climbing until it rests on my hip. I can see the desire in his eyes, the thoughts racing across his mind—to push me further or accept what he's getting.

His hand tightens around my hip bone, and I'm fairly certain he's about to pull me into his lap and take this to second base, if not third, when he glances up at my face. He seems taken by surprise to find me watching him. For a second, that hardness in his eyes melts away, the lines around his mouth smooth out, and he looks like the Logan I remember from before. *My* Logan.

However, before I can work out what any of it means, someone latches onto my wrist, and I'm tugged away.

"That's enough for him, Babydoll. My turn now."

---

"Riley," Logan hisses.

"Go away, Logan," I groan, refusing to open my eyes. They kept me awake until the early morning hours, dancing for them while they guzzled beer after beer.

Based on how groggy I feel, I can't have been asleep for more than a few hours. Grayson insisted on cuffing me to the damn pole before they all went to bed, so the simple fact that I was even able to fall asleep on the hard floor says everything about how exhausted I was.

"Riley." He puts more of a demand behind his tone, and sighing, I reluctantly peel open my eyes.

"Logan," I groan when I realize the room is bathed in weak light, indicating it's barely dawn. "It's not even morning yet. Why are you awake?"

"Trust me, Shortcake. I'm not happy about the early wake-up call either, but your mom won't stop calling you."

That immediately sweeps the cobwebs from my brain and I sit up, instantly alert.

"What? When? Did you answer?"

"No, I didn't answer, but I figured you should."

He holds the phone up to my face as it begins to ring again, and I blow out a breath before taking it from him.

"Ehh, privacy," I snap, arching a brow when he remains crouched in front of me.

He shakes his head. "Not happening, Shortcake. I need to make sure you don't tell your mom anything about our... situation."

*Yeah, like she'd come bounding to my rescue.*

"Whatever," I grumble, before gathering myself and pressing *answer.*

"Mom," I hedge.

"Speaker," Logan mouths.

I roll my eyes as I hit the speaker button just in time for him to hear my mom snap, "Where the hell have you been, Riley?"

"Sleeping, Mom. It's.." I glance at the time at the top of my screen, frustration giving way to concern when I realize just how early it is. "Is something wrong, Mom? Did something happen?"

"Yes, something has happened," she snaps. "And if you'd answered my earlier calls, you'd know that."

God, if I could reach through the phone and strangle her, I would.

"I've answered now," I hiss through gritted teeth, silently praying that nothing is wrong with Aurora but unable to actually ask aloud with Logan listening in on every word.

I don't know what Logan and I are. There are feelings there, on both ends, but Grayson's anger is a toxic fuel dousing any potential we may have, and so long as that remains the case, I can't trust him enough to tell him about my daughter. Protecting her is my primary goal. I'd sooner endure this bullshit a hundred times over than have them find out about her.

"Our heating went out last night," she snipes, as though that's somehow my fault.

"Okay... did you pay the heating bill?"

"Do you take me for an idiot, Riley? Yes, I paid the heating bill," she mimics in a high-pitched voice that has me curling in on myself in shame at the mere fact Logan is listening to all of this. I can't even bear to look at him to see what he's thinking.

"You better fix this," she demands.

"What do you expect me to do, Mom?" I sigh wearily.

"I don't care, Riley, but unless you want me and—"

"I'll sort it, Mom," I exclaim, cutting her off before she can say something she shouldn't. "I'll see if I can get a heating repairman out to you today."

"It better be today, Riley. We're going to freeze if we have to sit in this cold house for much longer."

"It'll be today," I promise her, even though it's not one I can technically make. I'll have to call around and see if anyone is available to have a look at it today. And God only knows how much an emergency call is going to cost.

"I need money to pay for it."

"Of course," I grit out.

"And a little extra to cover the stress."

"Fine."

At this point, I just want her off the goddamn phone.

My shoulders sag in relief when she hangs up, and still refusing to look at Logan, I begin Googling heating repair men.

"Your mom is a bit of a bitch," Logan interrupts several minutes later.

"Yeah, no shit."

I can feel his gaze drilling into the top of my head, but I remain pointedly fixed on my phone as I dial the number for the first guy I come across.

"Hi. The heating has gone out at my mom's place and I need someone to go out right away and take a look. Would you be available?"

"Sorry, love. I'm not working this week. Holidays and all that."

"Right, thanks anyway."

Sighing, I hang up and go back to scrolling for the next number I can try. However, my search comes to a halt when a large palm lands on top of my phone, blocking the screen.

"Riley," Logan coaxes with surprising gentleness. He waits until I muster the strength to gaze up at him. "Talk to me."

"I don't have time to talk to you, Logan," I bite back. "I have to sort this shit out before Grayson wakes up and decides to make me his dancing monkey for the day. Then I've got to go to work tonight and see if any of the girls would be willing to give me any of their shifts. And even if I didn't have to do all of that, I still wouldn't talk to you about my mom because you and I aren't friends, Logan. Forget you heard that entire conversation." Dropping my eyes back to the phone, I desperately tack on, "Please."

A heavy silence follows my outburst as I compile a list of various handymen to contact. Until Logan snatches the phone from my grip.

"Hey!" I bark as he gets to his feet. "That's mine! I need it."

"No, you don't. I'll sort out your mom's heating."

"No, Logan. You won't."

He doesn't appear to be listening as he strides toward the door with my phone in hand.

I move to chase after him, but the jiggling of the cuffs and sharp press of metal against my wrist reminds me that I can't.

"What if my mom calls back?" I shout at his back, frustrated and panicking.

"Then I'll deal with her too."

# RILEY

## CHAPTER THIRTY-ONE

"You didn't need to come in," I grumble as Royce follows me into Lux later that night.

"Babydoll, I'm not just escorting you inside. I'm staying for your entire shift."

"Seriously?" I groan. "That is *so* not necessary."

"Hmm," is the only response I'm warranted before he points toward a table in the back corner of the club. "I'll be right over there."

"You mean, you don't want your usual booth?" I partially tease.

His lips form a smug grin and he wraps his arm around my shoulders before leaning in to whisper, "Now, why would I need a booth when I've got my own personal lap dancer at home?"

Rolling my eyes, I shove at his arm before striding toward the dressing room. I'm in a surprisingly good mood tonight, and I keep telling myself it has nothing to do with the fact Logan totally came through for me. He sorted out a heating guy to go to my mom's today, and I got word from my mom that it had been fixed and everything was working as it should.

Moreover, when I asked him how much I owed him, he told me not to worry about it. Of course, I have no intention of owing Logan Astor—or any of them—anything, so I fully intend to pay back whatever amount it cost.

Still, the fact he actually sorted out the problem and didn't hang me out to dry is a huge weight off my shoulders.

"Well?" Tara asks as I step into the dressing room. "Please tell me something finally happened with that cutie?"

"Which one?" I ask distractedly as I move to my usual dresser and begin getting ready.

"Which one, she says." Tara cackles. "I was referencing the cutie who has been picking you up every night, but if something happened with Mysterious and Dangerous, then I'm all for that too."

"Nothing has happened with either of them. Turns out they're both giant dickheads." Because despite Logan's sweet gesture today, it doesn't make up for everything he has done.

I can feel her eyes on me before her arms wrap around me from behind. "I'm sorry. Are you okay?"

I smile at her through the mirror. "I'm fine. Just tired."

She nods knowingly. "Well, if you need a break from the humdrum, hit me up. We can go out for a girls' night."

"Sounds good," I respond, knowing I won't take her up on the offer. I can't, even if I wanted to. I can't imagine Grayson being okay if I ask him for a night off from being tortured.

We chatter—well, Tara mostly chatters—while we change into sparkly gold dresses and heels for tonight's performance before heading onto the floor. The lights are off above the stage as we hurry up the steps and into position, forming a circle with all of our toes in the center and hands perched on one knee.

Usually, I focus solely on the other dancers, but tonight I can't help looking out into the room. I glance over the numerous patrons staring expectantly at the stage until I find

Royce tucked away in the back corner. He's nearly invisible, shrouded in darkness. However, his focus is zeroed in on me, and I suck in a gasp as our gazes collide. I have no idea how he even sees me. We can't be more than black shadows to the rest of the club, and yet, he's looking directly at me.

It's exhilarating and electrifying, igniting a subtle tingle, a spark of recognition in my core that slowly penetrates outward, taking over my body one inch at a time.

I'm still staring at him when the bright lights burst to life, dazzling me as the opening notes of *Video Phone* by Beyoncé and Lady Gaga play out around the club and each of us begin clicking our fingers in time to the music.

The opening beat builds to a crescendo before we spin out and our performance really gets underway. The entire time, my focus remains on Royce. On the way his riveted gaze is glued to mine. Dancing is when I feel most empowered, but beneath the weight of his penetrating stare, I feel liberated of my inhibitions. Emboldened as I embrace the potency of my own allure. A newfound confidence blooms, fueled by the knowledge that Royce craves my presence as much as I'm beginning to relish his.

It's as though he possesses the ability to see beyond the surface as he strips away my layers of doubt and insecurity until he has a first-row seat to the deepest parts of my soul.

I'm exposed. Vulnerable. A live wire with the plastic casing pulled back.

And yet, I'm not afraid. His icy-blue eyes don't hurt as they caress my skin. Instead, it's like a warm embrace, awakening my dormant desire and passion.

Every cell in my body responds to his gaze. I dance on autopilot, not hearing a single word of the song. The club, the stage, the other dancers... all of it fades away until there is only me and him.

Every single one of my senses is held captive by him. *Owned* by him.

I'm not dancing for those watching. I'm not even dancing for myself.

I'm dancing for *him*.

By the time our performance comes to an end, I feel seen in a way I never have. I'm transformed as I step off the stage on shaky legs. Stripped bare and raw but also invigorated and unshackled.

That feeling only intensifies as the night wears on. With each performance, Royce's probing gaze only grows more ardent until it sizzles along my skin. Desire becomes a palpable force between us, the chemistry crackling in the air. I don't know how everyone in the room isn't aware of it. We're opposing magnets, drawing closer with every dance, as though our two souls are reaching out across the room to touch, to merge, to intertwine.

Our song is a dance of desire, a symphony of passion.

One that is sure to set me on fire and leave my ashes blowing in the wind after all is said and done.

The second my foot hits the bottom step after my last performance of the night, I'm pulled back into the shadows behind the stage as a hand clamps over my mouth. There's a moment of panic, which quickly ebbs when Royce growls in my ear, "You drive me insane."

He punctuates his point by grinding his crotch against my ass, and I feel the prominent outline of his hard dick. It's like a spark to a flame, dousing me in desire and I melt against him, arching my back as I grind along his length.

He hisses in my ear, wrapping his lips around my earlobe and sucking it into his mouth until I whimper.

"Do you feel how fucking hard I am, James? I've been like this since the moment you stepped foot on that stage. You had me goddamn hypnotized. I wanted to drag you off that stage and into my lap, bend you over my knee and smack your ass until it's raw for making me want you the way I do."

My entire body has gone up in flames. My *soul* is on fire as our hips grind and my mind screams for more. "Please," I plead, not even entirely sure what I'm begging for. Just that I need *something*.

"You'd like that, wouldn't you?" He chuckles darkly. "Is that what you're trying to do? Get me to fuck you in the hopes I'll turn my back on my friends and convince Grayson to let you go?" Even though his words are scathing, his low, seductive tone melts like dark chocolate over my skin. "I'm not Logan, and your pussy isn't magical."

Turning in his hold, I reach up and grab his face in my hands. My fingers dig into his cheeks as I glare up at him. "Lie to yourself all you want, Royce. But you know as well as I do that whatever this is between us has nothing to do with Grayson." Leaning in, I trail my nose along the column of his neck, breathing in his scent of leather and something earthy; masculine. Reaching the underside of his jaw, I press onto my toes, dragging my lips along the sharp edge. "Sooner or later, you'll have to face the fact that you want me as badly as I want you."

Our gazes collide for a single second before he surges forward, pressing his lips to mine in a hard, demanding, scalding kiss. His hand slides into my hair, wrenching my head to the side as he deepens it. He controls every one of my movements as his tongue glides over mine, the hard planes of his body pressing into me and igniting a fire everywhere we touch.

My hips rock against his, and I shiver as his erection twitches in his pants. Before either of us can get carried away, he uses his hold on the back of my head to tug me away.

"Not here," he half growls. "You want me, Babydoll, then

you can have me back at the house where the others can watch."

*God.* There's something exhilarating and intimidating about that, although I don't altogether dislike it. The thought of Logan watching is hot and kind of a turn-on. Grayson, however, is less so.

Not giving me the chance to overthink it or change my mind, Royce spins me around and gives my ass a hard slap. "Now go get changed so I can find out just how talented that mouth of yours really is."

Thank God he can't see the deep red blush on my cheeks as I totter away. However, as we step out from behind the stage, we come face-to-face with Ben.

His narrowed gaze darts between us before landing on me, and his jaw tics with irritation. "Riley. I've been looking for you. I need you to stay late tonight."

My shoulders drop as I release a silent sigh before nodding. "Sorry," I mutter to Royce before scurrying off to the dressing rooms to change.

By the time I re-emerge on the main club floor, Royce is standing there waiting for me and Ben is nowhere in sight.

"Ready to go?" Royce asks casually.

"Uh, I have to help Ben tidy up?" My inflection rises at the shadows dancing in his eyes until it comes out as a question.

"Nope. Not anymore." My gaze narrows on Royce, searching for the hidden meaning behind his words, but he's an impenetrable fort keeping his secrets locked down tight.

Before I can argue, he moves beside me, pressing a hand to the base of my spine and leading me out of the club. Right before we step outside, I turn to look behind me. My eyes clash with Ben's, where he stands hidden behind the bar, glaring at us through one eye as he holds an ice pack to his other.

"Did you hit him?" I mutter as Royce pulls me through the door and it slides shut behind us.

He doesn't answer as he directs me over to his truck, and I wait until we're inside before repeating more firmly, "Royce, did you hit Ben?"

"Forget about it, James," he growls, navigating out of the car park with more speed than necessary.

My eyes dart down to his hands perched on the steering wheel, spotting the tell-tale red knuckles that confirm my suspicions.

"I can't just *forget about it,*" I snap. "He's my *boss.* You can't go hitting my boss, Royce." When he remains silent, the only sign that he's listening at all the whitening of his fingers around the steering wheel, I press harder. "I mean it. If you go causing issues, I'll be fired. The three of you can play your stupid little games with me, I don't give a shit, but you *cannot* interfere in my life. I still need to have my job once Grayson is done torturing me and the three of you have kicked me to the curb."

He's silent for a minute longer, his grip on the steering wheel growing so tight that it groans beneath the pressure. "Fine," he finally hisses. "I won't do anything that will result in you losing your job."

Blowing out a breath, I finally relax against the seat and mutter, "Thank you." He nods, and we fall into silence as I lean my elbow on the armrest, rest my head in my palm and stare out the window.

We're nearly home when I glance his way out of the corner of my eye and hedge, "So, why did you hit him?"

His forearms flex, jaw tightening. "Doesn't matter," he grunts.

Turning back to the window, I roll my eyes. "Given that it happened at the club and that I have the sneaking suspicion it had something to do with me, I'd say that it does, in fact, matter."

His only response is the creaking of the steering wheel, and I glance his way out of the corner of my eye, finding him strangling the leather.

We drive the rest of the way home in silence. However, as I open my door and move to climb out, he reaches across the car and, wrapping his large hand around my wrist, stops me. When I turn to look at him, he's frowning down at the center console before he lifts his gaze to mine. "Just... be careful when you're around him."

Brows furrowed, I stare at him in confusion. What the hell transpired between them to warrant this warning? Of course, I know to watch my back around Ben. All us girls do. He's pushy and a sleaze, but what could he have said to Royce to have him suddenly concerned for my safety? His grip tightens, and I realize he's waiting for me to agree. Slowly, I nod. "Okay. I will."

He holds me hostage for a moment longer, gaze searching mine before he relents. "One of us will be with you at all times when you're at the club."

Grayson already delivered this warning, and yet... the way Royce says it. It doesn't sound like it's a warning. It sounds more like a promise.

---

"On your knees."

As soon as Royce and I stepped into the house, Grayson barked at me to get upstairs and undress while the three of them lazily followed behind, beers in hand and hungry eyes devouring every inch of skin as I exposed it.

Heavy rock music pumps through the speakers, entirely at

odds with the sultry songs from Lux, adding a rough and dirty edge to the atmosphere.

I'm not sure if it's because I'm still keyed up from the club, but the second we entered the room, I knew tonight would be different. No more dancing around a pole and lap dances. The games were being amped up, and I'm not entirely sure if I'm turned on or terrified.

Blinking, I stare into Grayson's cold, dark eyes, and the defiance I've been giving him since I walked through the door flickers. He only smirks like the arrogant asshole he is and quirks a brow when I hesitate to obey his orders.

I grit my teeth, glaring to let him know I'm imagining his death in a thousand painful ways as I, reluctantly, lower myself to my knees in front of Royce. It was one thing to stare at one another across an emotionally charged room. Another for him to mention the others watching while I suck him off when his erection was pressed against my stomach and my brain wasn't capable of thinking straight.

But this... this is so out of my wheelhouse.

I've never done anything like this. Never even given a guy head before.

I'm not sure I recognize the woman I've become.

The girl who enrolled at Halston for the sole reason of winning custody of her daughter is long gone. While that still remains the ultimate goal, somewhere along the way, each of these men has pried open different layers of the shell I was encased in, and with each crack in my armor, I've discovered a part of myself I never knew existed.

It's intoxicating and terrifying, too much and not enough all rolled into one. I no longer know who I am, but I think I like who I'm becoming. Grayson brought me here to tear me down, to break me, to destroy what his father didn't, but the opposite is happening.

Instead of growing weaker, I can feel myself becoming stronger.

Every time Logan looks at me with those soft, impassioned eyes.

Every time Royce challenges me.

Every time Grayson tries to break me.

So despite the nerves wracking my body as Royce steps in front of me, his large body towering over mine and blocking my view of Grayson, I acknowledge and accept the simmering coil of desire that unfurls deep in my core and meet his haughty gaze with a steadfast one of my own.

He takes his sweet time unbuttoning his pants and lowering the zip. Reaching into his boxers, he pulls out his dick, and any confidence I was feeling shrivels up and dies.

*Holy fuck, that thing is humongous.* There is no way it is fitting inside my mouth. I'll suffocate. I absolutely refuse to have 'asphyxiation by giant cock' written as my cause of death.

To make matters worse, there's a metal ball poking out the top and bottom of his shaft, right below the head, making it look even more intimidating.

He chuckles darkly as I stare bug-eyed at the giant, pierced snake bobbing inches from my face. "Open up, Babydoll."

It takes a massive amount of effort for me to relax my jaw and drop it open. It's only the flash of pure desire that darkens his blue irises that reassures me as he trails the tip of his cock along my lips, leaving a smear of precum before he threads his soft head past my lips.

"That's it, take my cock like a good little slut."

I close my eyes as my cheeks flush with heat. I definitely shouldn't find that erotic. Perhaps it's because *he* always called me a good girl, but hearing the opposite has pleasure pooling in my panties as his hand comes to rest on the back of my head, pushing me down further until he hits the back of my throat and I gag.

His fingers press into the back of my skull and he groans as I work my jaw, trying to accommodate him. “Oh yeah, just like that.”

He pulls back, and I suck in a deep lungful of air before he slams back into me, blocking my airway once more.

“Swirl your tongue around me.”

I blink, and the gathered tears overflow, blurring my vision before they roll down my cheek. I try to do as he wants, but when my teeth accidentally graze along the delicate skin of his shaft, causing him to hiss, I freeze, expecting some sort of blowback.

Instead, his cock jerks and his hand cups my cheek before he brushes away the tears. I blink furiously, clearing my vision to find him staring down at me with an odd expression on his face that I can't quite place, as he continues to use my mouth like it's his own personal cock warmer.

I return his stare with an unfaltering one of my own, and this time, I deliberately let my teeth graze along his length as he thrusts into me. His hold on my cheek tightens, keeping me still, and he emits a throaty groan that goes straight to my core and has me clenching my thighs.

Watching me, he growls in a strained voice, “You’re going to swallow every drop of my cum like the dirty little whore you are.” It’s not a question but an order. One I am helpless to obey as he buries his dick in the back of my throat and comes.

Rope after rope of cum hits the back of my tongue before sliding down my throat. I can feel the excess leaking past my lips, and when he pulls out, he tucks his soft dick in his pants before lowering to a crouch in front of me.

Eyes raking over my face, he swipes his thumb across my chin before pressing it against my lips. “Open.”

I do as he says, and he pushes it into my mouth. My tongue swirls around the calloused pad, gathering the last of him before I swallow it too.

He lingers there, thumb in my mouth, as something more profound, electrically charged, and transcendent passes between us. He might have used crude words. This may have been done in a strange way with his friends watching, but it wasn't a dirty act. It wasn't shameful or embarrassing.

It was fucking hot.

And I'm not the only one who thinks so.

"Wow. Never thought I'd get off on watching you get your dick sucked, man, but that shit was fucking fire." Logan whistles, his interruption breaking the moment as Royce slides his thumb out of my mouth and gets to his feet.

I blink up at him as he continues to stare down at me, his expression unreadable, except for the darkened hue of his irises, giving away the hint of desire he refuses to acknowledge.

Grayson scoffs, reminding me of his presence as my body stiffens. "Speak for yourself. Looked sloppy as hell to me. You'd think she would be well used to sucking dick by now."

My cheeks redden in both anger and embarrassment, that shame I hadn't felt before creeping in as I duck my head and wish for the ground to swallow me whole.

"That's enough for tonight." Royce's tone cuts like a blade through the tension. "It's late."

"Yeah, I never got to sleep in this morning so I'm beat," Logan agrees. I watch from the corner of my eye as he gets to his feet, squeezing his hard-on through his jeans.

"Fine," Grayson reluctantly agrees, and I silently let out my relief. "One of you lock her back up."

"Can't we just leave her on the couch?" Logan whines. I don't see what transpires between the three of them, but he tacks on, "She'll be no fun if she's complaining of a sore neck."

"No!" Grayson barks. "If a sore neck is the worst of her worries, then we clearly need to up our game."

That is the absolute last thing I want. I'll happily accept sleeping on the floor over more torture from Grayson.

"It's fine," I intervene. "I don't mind sleeping on the floor."

"See. She's fine." With that, Grayson strides out the door. I remain steadfast on the floor as the room descends into silence.

"I'll sort her out," Logan says after several long minutes, where I can only assume some sort of silent communication was happening between him and Royce.

I can feel Royce's probing gaze drilling into the top of my skull, yet I don't lift my head. I can't. I'm terrified of what I'll read in his eyes if I do. Grayson successfully took what felt seductive and intoxicating and turned it into something disgusting and shameful. I'm officially fucking done with this night, and I just want them all to leave me alone to wallow in self-pity.

"Fine," he eventually grunts out, turning on his heels, and his heavy boots stomp across the floor before the squeaking of hinges signals the shutting of the door.

And then there were two.

Silently, I get to my feet and move over to the pole. I'm so numb, I don't even stop to redress or at least grab a t-shirt as I lower back onto my knees. The entire time, I can feel Logan watching me, but my gaze never once leaves the wooden floorboards.

Eventually, he sighs and moves toward me.

Instead of crouching in front of me like I expected, he lowers himself to the ground behind me.

"W-what are you doing?"

"Shh," he soothes in my ear as his large palm moves to rest on my hip before slowly sliding low across my abdomen. His fingers brush the waistband of my panties and I suck in a startled breath.

"I saw you earlier," he whispers, his warm breath dancing along my ear and sending shivers racing down my spine. "You acted like you didn't want it, but I saw the way you clenched your thighs, the blush on your chest."

His heat sears into my back, and I can feel his erection pressing into my ass as his fingers trace patterns on my flesh right above my panties.

My breath hitches with every flex of his fingers, and I *know* I shouldn't be allowing this to happen, but he's right. I *did* enjoy it, at least until Grayson opened his big, fat mouth and ruined it.

Flattening his palm against my skin, he drags his hand upward, over my abdomen, and along my ribs until he cups a heavy tit in his hand. My head falls back as he pushes his hand beneath my bra and kneads my heated skin, a soft sigh passing my parted lips.

"That's it, baby. Give yourself over to me."

His other hand strokes along my inner thigh, slowly climbing higher. Too distracted by the desire his talented fingers are stoking, I don't notice until his fingers brush along the raised scars just below my apex. My legs clamp together as panic sweeps through me.

Chuckling darkly, he pries them apart, and I sag against him as his hand moves past the scars to brush over my wet panties, sending me spiraling headfirst into a whirlwind of need.

"Call this your reward for a job well done."

He pushes aside the fabric of my panties, his fingers circling my sensitive nub and only emphasizing how much I've been needing someone to touch me. The tension at the club all night between me and Royce, the dirty words he whispered in my ear, and the way he fucked my face... all of it was the best sort of foreplay, only it's left me weak and desperate for release.

Pathetic whimpers fall from my lips as he drives me higher, fingers expertly playing with my clit. "I love the sounds you make," he murmurs huskily in my ear as I grind my ass against his cock and tilt my hips in a silent plea for him to slide them lower.

"Logan," I moan as his fingers slip through my wetness before he pushes them inside, stretching my walls in the most delicious of ways.

He scissors his fingers inside me and I groan as I rock my hips, driving him deeper. His nose is buried in my hair, and he licks my ear in a surprisingly seductive move that only intensifies the sensations wracking my body. His fingers pump into me, pushing me higher, and I can feel myself slowly unraveling beneath his touch.

"I knew there was more to you than meets the eye." He nips along my neck, making me clench around his fingers as they pick up their pace. "You act all innocent, but you're just as wild and lost as the rest of us, aren't you?" His spare hand moves to my other tit, sliding beneath the fabric until he can roll my nipple between his thumb and forefinger. I'm moments away from falling apart, both loving and hating every second his talented fingers drive me closer to oblivion.

"You'd be perfect for us, you know. Your demons match ours. If only you'd let them out to play."

He presses down on my clit and simultaneously pinches my nipple, sending me over the edge as I cry out.

"Fucking beautiful," he praises as I sag against him, panting and breathless.

17
Personal Care
Feminine Hygiene
Family Planning

# LOGAN

## CHAPTER THIRTY-TWO

Lying in my bed, I stare up at the ceiling above me, but all I see is her. All I feel is her velvety smooth skin against mine. All I hear are her soft, sweet moans as she came apart beneath my touch.

Like a disease, she has infiltrated all of my senses, reprogrammed my cells, and taken hostage of my brain. She's a cancer, but instead of slowly killing me, she's bringing me back to life.

Still, it's not her husky moans or the feel of her coming on my hand that has kept me awake all night, pondering into the darkness. It's the raised marks I felt along her inner thigh. The way she clamped her legs shut and stiffened in my arms.

It's played on repeat in my head all night as my mind contemplates the numerous possibilities. The various scenarios as to why she might have them. Why she'd want to hide them. Although there's one, in particular, I keep circling back to. The darkest yet most likely reason. One I refuse to contemplate too deeply because I'm unsure what it means—and admittedly a little horrified at the notion.

Unable to ruminate in my thoughts a moment longer, I

throw back my covers and pull on a pair of sweatpants before padding barefoot from my room. I pause briefly at Riley's door next to mine, listening for any sounds coming from within. I felt like a total shit leaving her on the hard floor to sleep last night, and I very nearly told Grayson to go fuck himself—in my head, of course—and took her to my bed, but I needed the time alone to think.

Not hearing anything from behind her closed door, I saunter down the stairs, following the smell of bacon and eggs. I'm not surprised when I walk into the kitchen and find Royce in front of the stove and Grayson sitting at the island, nursing a steaming cup of coffee while he scrolls through his iPad. Unless I have an early morning practice, I'm usually the last one up.

Royce raises a surprised eyebrow. "What are you doing up so early?"

"Couldn't sleep," I grunt as I drop into a bar stool beside Grayson.

"Too excited for Santa coming," the jackass teases, earning himself my middle finger.

Ignoring Royce's barking laugh, I turn to Grayson. "I wanted to talk to you, actually... about Riley."

Sighing, he doesn't lift his gaze from his iPad until he sets his coffee down on the marble countertop. "I thought you were done letting her get into your head?"

"I am. It's not her. It's just..." Already frustrated with this conversation, I rake my fingers through my sleep-tangled hair. "What do you know about her mom?"

His eyebrows pinch before he shrugs. "Not much. She was always nice enough. Pleasant. Adoring to my father. Polite with me."

"What about with Riley?"

He gives another blasé shrug. "I dunno, Logan. Like any

mother with a teenage daughter. I never looked too closely at the dynamic."

"What's this all about?" Royce asks, pulling the pans off the stove before turning to face us. "Why are you asking about her mom?"

"She was blowin' her phone up the other morning, so I gave it to Riley and got her to put it on speaker. The way she talked to her..."

"The way Riley talked to her mom?" Royce questions.

"No. The way her mom spoke to *her.* Her mom's heating had gone out and she was demanding Riley to fix it. Threatened her. Made it clear Riley would have to cover the cost."

"What the fuck? What a bitch!" Royce comments.

I nod in agreement while focusing entirely on Grayson, who gives nothing away. "She *was* being a total bitch."

"Wouldn't you, if your daughter blew up your perfect little life with lies and false accusations?"

"She's still her daughter," Royce retorts.

"Her daughter, who resulted in both of them being left homeless and destitute. My father's accounts were frozen, and even if they hadn't been, I doubt he'd have given a penny to either of them—Even if her mom did refute her daughter's claims."

"She did?" I ask, not having heard any of this before. Grayson has told us about the accusations Riley levied against his dad and how they were dismissed, but that in the process, his father was convicted of embezzlement and sentenced to prison, but he's never mentioned the logistics around Riley and her mom. Honestly, until now, I never cared to ask.

Gray scoffs. "Yeah. She told the police her daughter was struggling to adjust after she and my dad got married and that she was acting out to get attention. Evidently, her grades had fallen at school and her mom found alcohol in her room. Typical teenage shit but out of character for Riley."

"Bit of a fucked up way to get attention," Royce points out, face scrunched.

"Yeah, tell me about it. I guess nothing else had worked, so she pulled out the big guns."

I chew on the inside of my lip as I mull over everything Gray has said. It makes sense. If Riley was struggling with her mom's new marriage, and perhaps the loss of her mom's attention, then it would be logical that she'd act out. Escalate her behavior if she didn't receive the reward she wanted from earlier attempts.

*On paper*, it makes sense, but when I think about the quiet, shy, yet fierce girl I got to know the first couple of months of this semester, it just doesn't match up. She's not attention-seeking. Not someone who needs to be in the limelight. The opposite, in fact. And perhaps in her teenage years, she was different, but do people really change that much?

Tapping my finger anxiously against the countertop, I blurt, "Do you know about her scars?"

"What scars?" Grayson asks casually, sipping on his coffee.

"She's got scars on her inner thighs."

His eyebrows dip, a flash of actual emotion shifting across his face before he brushes it aside.

"I felt them too," Royce inputs, and I turn to raise a questioning eyebrow at him. *When the hell was he close enough to be touching her there?*

His expression is as guarded as Gray's as he stares at me, unblinking. *Fucking assholes and their poker faces.*

"They're self-harm scars, right?" I ask him anxiously. "I mean, what else could they be?"

"I dunno, man." Despite his apathetic tone, there's a tightness around his eyes that belies his concern.

Tilting my head, I stare at him. A silent standoff ensues until I find that crack I was searching for, and the realization hits me like a hockey stick to the face.

*Holy fucking shit. Royce gives a damn about Riley.*

I thought he was firmly on Gray's side in all of this. Didn't think he *knew* Riley, never mind gave any sort of shit about her. Sure, he followed her around a bit over the last few weeks, but I hadn't realized it was enough to form any sort of attachment.

However, that tiny bit of emotion he's demonstrating says a lot.

It says fucking everything.

It's equivalent to Royce standing at the top of the Empire State Building and screaming his feelings for all of New York to hear.

"So?" Grayson drawls, regaining my attention as I tear my gaze from Royce to level him with an unamused glare. His attitude is seriously beginning to piss me off.

Unperturbed, he holds my gaze. "Probably just another way for her to get attention when accusing my dad didn't work."

I blink at my best friend in shock for a minute before anger wells up and consumes me. "Fucking seriously, Grayson? You think she cut herself for attention? Why wouldn't she slice open her wrists if that were the case? Why would she hide them away?" Smacking my hand against the table, I shove to my feet. I'm the tallest out of the three of us, so I have a good few inches on him perched on his stool. "Have you ever considered you might be *wrong*?"

His chair legs screech against the floor as he pushes to his feet, appearing far more calm than I am. However, I can feel the tension radiating from him. See it in the tense set of his shoulders as he turns so we're chest to chest.

"No," he snarls, jabbing a finger in my chest. "But the fact you're questioning me means your loyalty is shot to hell. You let her get to you."

I swat his hand away. "No, it's not, but can't you see shit isn't adding up? Nothing makes any fucking sense anymore!" His eyes narrow, but I continue. "You're so hellbent on revenge that you can't see past it to actually look at the girl living beneath our roof. Maybe if you took a second to talk with her instead of making demands or choking her out, you'd have the same reservations I do."

"Oh, so you have reservations now?" Gray sneers. "Good to know." Lips pressed into a tight line, he shakes his head, looking thoroughly disappointed in me. "I thought you were a better friend than that, Logan."

"Fuck you," I seethe, enraged. "Being a good friend doesn't mean I'm going to take your side if you're fucking wrong."

"You don't know that I am wrong!"

"I don't know that you're right."

"Maybe we should table this conversation until everyone's calmed down," Royce suggests, and I turn my ire on him.

"Fuck you too, Royce! You felt those scars too, yet you're still letting Gray call all the shots."

He cocks an unimpressed brow. And, pissed off at the pair of them, I shove past Grayson and out of the kitchen. At the front door, I stuff my feet into sneakers and grab a coat to put on over my bare chest before storming out the door. I'll eat breakfast elsewhere. Fuck knows, I don't want to sit in there with those two assholes.

With anger rattling my bones, I stalk down the street to my favorite breakfast spot, a small hole-in-the-wall cafe that does the best avocado on toast. While waiting for my order, I review everything from this morning. Royce, Grayson, and I have been tight since the first night we met. We instantly clicked, and nothing has come between us, until now.

My head's a fucking mess. I'm at constant war with myself, a clash of blades between my head and heart as an ongoing battle ensues. I don't know who to trust or what to believe. Grayson is my best friend. If he believes Riley is at fault, then I don't doubt him.

But what if what he believes is wrong?

The evidence is starting to stack up against him.

When he initially told me and Royce about the shit that went down with his dad, I took him at his word. Especially once Royce opened up about his past. Who was I to refute the truth? So when he pointed Riley out at Lux that night, I was a loyal friend and shoved my feelings for her aside. I got on board with the plan to make her life miserable. I was all fucking in because he's my best friend, and I knew he would have done the same for me.

But shit is no longer black and white, and I can't stop remembering the disappointment in Riley's eyes when she went off on me in the bathroom. Despite putting my feelings for her on lockdown, I felt awful that I'd let her down. Seeing her disappointment slayed me.

Still, I couldn't be sure it wasn't a ploy to manipulate me. Regardless of the niggles of doubt already taking hold in my stomach.

But then there was the phone call with her mother.

The scars on her inner thighs.

The fact that she still talks to me like the girl I was falling in love with and not the narcissistic bitch Grayson has painted her as.

None of it makes any fucking sense!

So caught up in my thoughts, I barely taste my food as I swallow it down.

"Will that be all?" the server asks when I'm finished.

"Yes." I remove some dollar bills from my wallet to pay for

the food, but I pause, glancing up at the woman. "Actually, can I get a pumpkin spice latte to go, please?"

"Certainly," she states with a professional smile, and I hand over enough money for my breakfast and Riley's coffee.

I no longer have any fucking idea what I'm doing, but I think it's past time I find out what Riley's side of the story is.

---

"Good morning, Shortcake," I greet when I enter her room. My earlier anger has given way to curiosity, and I'm suddenly bursting with the need to hear her side of things. The questions press against the inside of my lips, demanding freedom. Still, if I stand any chance of Riley confiding in me, I have some making up to do. I can only hope that coffee and the willingness to hear her out is enough.

My lips tug down in a frown when I find her huddled against the stripper pole, her head resting against it. She's only wearing one of my T-shirts, leaving her bare legs exposed, and I can see the goosebumps pebbling along her skin.

My displeasure only intensifies when she lifts her head and I see the dark circles forming beneath her eyes. *Well, fuck. If that doesn't make me feel like shit.*

"Speak for yourself," she sasses. "A good morning would be one where I woke up in my own bed, with my lumpy mattress and the window that isn't properly insulated so there's a constant draft." *Sounds... awful.* Mumbling to herself, she tacks on, "Ugh, never thought I'd miss my crappy apartment."

In an attempt to salvage the morning, I hold out my hand carrying her coffee. "Maybe this will cheer you up."

She stares at it, her nostrils flaring as she inhales the delicious scent of coffee, nutmeg, and cinnamon before her eyes flash to mine, filling with suspicion. "What's the catch?"

"No catch," I assure her.

"Is it laced with laxatives?"

"What?" I ask, laughing. "No. Why would I do that?"

She shrugs, saying in an equally hurt and angry tone, "Could be Grayson's new way to fuck with me."

"It's not. He's not even here, so he has no idea I got this for you. I cross-my-heart-and-hope-to-die promise this is a laxative-free—and every other kind of drug-free – pumpkin spice latte."

Her gaze switches to the coffee, remaining glued there as she licks her lips. "But it has caffeine, right?"

"Yes. The only drug this coffee contains is caffeine. And a fuckton of sugar."

"Okay, I'm sold." She makes a grabby-hands motion that has me chuckling as I pass the coffee cup over to her and watch as she lowers her nose and inhales deeply. "Ugh. So good. Truthfully, I probably still would have drunk it, even if it did contain laxatives."

Crouching in front of her, I watch perplexed as she rests her forehead against the lid of the takeaway cup. I can't figure out what she's doing—praying to the coffee gods?—until she sniffles.

"Are you... crying?" I ask, starting to panic.

"No," she bites, the word coming out muffled because she still hasn't lifted her head.

"Riley." Her name is laced with concern. "You are. Why? Did something happen? Are you hurt?"

She sniffles again, and I'm ten seconds away from uncuffing her and pulling her into my lap when she finally lifts her head. The cuffs jangle against the pole as she wipes a hand and swipes the telltale signs of her tears away.

"It's nothing. I'm just tired. Maybe hormonal. My period is probably coming."

I scan her face, hating the redness around her eyes and the fact she won't meet my gaze.

"Okayyyy," I say, because what the fuck else does one say in this situation? Feeling awkward as shit, I grab the key for her cuffs from my pocket and undo them before carefully helping her over to the sofa. She practically collapses onto the seat, tucking her feet beneath her as she slowly sips on her drink.

I sit and silently watch her, which thankfully, she doesn't object to. Pressing her shoulder into the back of the sofa, she closes her eyes and rests her head against the leather fabric as she nurses her coffee. While she enjoys her morning fix, I try to reconcile the girl in front of me with the one Grayson talks about, but honestly, I can't.

To me, they are two different people.

And unless Riley has a personality disorder, I'm beginning to think that's the truth.

Perhaps Grayson has it wrong, and it wasn't Riley who made the false allegations against his dad? Is it possible that she apologized because she knew who did? However, that doesn't explain her telling me that Grayson's dad got away with a far more severe crime. Unless she truly believes whoever made the false allegations?

There are countless possibilities as to what could have happened. Grayson is only focusing on one side of the story, and I'd be a fool not to at least hear Riley out.

"Riley," I hedge, waiting patiently until she opens her eyes and looks at me. "What happened back then?"

I don't need to be any more specific. She knows exactly what I'm referring to. I can tell by the way her shoulders bunch and her serene expression falls.

"Why do you want to know, Logan?"

She sounds tired more than anything, like she doesn't expect discussing this will make any difference.

"I'm just trying to understand."

"I thought you already had all the information you needed."

Pursing my lips, I glance away. "Maybe I'm beginning to realize I don't."

"You mean you no longer believe Grayson?"

"No, I'm not saying that. I just... what if Grayson is wrong?"

She chuckles, but it lacks any warmth. "You couldn't have come to this little realization before you upended my life?"

"I'm trying now, Riley." I sigh in frustration before taking a calming breath. "So, will you tell me what happened?"

Her eyes search my face, her coffee forgotten.

"How about you tell me what Grayson told you and what you think, and I'll tell you if you're right or wrong."

It's not quite what I was after, but I guess it's better than nothing.

Blowing out a breath, I begin, "He said a girl—you—went to the police, falsely accusing his father of, uh, sexual assault."

"Rape."

"Erm, right. Yes. That."

*Fuck, this is awkward.*

"Grayson believes you did it for attention. Being that you were having difficulties adjusting to your mom's new marriage. Seemingly, that's what your mom told the cops back then, anyway."

She snorts at that but remains silent and gestures for me to continue.

"Ugh, well, that's it, really."

"Why does Grayson believe it's me?" she asks.

"Because apparently, you said you were sorry the day the police came to arrest his dad?" It comes out as more of a question, and I watch as a heavy sadness fills her eyes. "And I think his dad confirmed it."

"What do *you* think?"

I run my hand through my hair, feeling all sorts of uncomfortable. "Well, uhh, I thought maybe it wasn't you. Maybe his dad just *thought* it was you, considering it made the most sense. Maybe it was a friend of yours? Someone you believed—still believe?"

Tilting her head, she studies my face. "You don't think I'm capable of making false allegations against Grayson's dad?"

"He was your dad at the time, too," I point out.

"Hmm," she says through tight lips, waiting for my answer.

"Honestly," I begin, swiping my palm down my face. I can feel myself starting to sweat. "When Gray pointed you out at the club, I couldn't believe that you and the girl he'd talked about were the same person. It just didn't make sense to me. It was like trying to fit two jigsaw pieces together only to discover they were from different boxes. It didn't add up, but Grayson's my friend. I owed him my loyalty."

"You don't any longer?"

"No, I do. I feel fucking awful simply having this conversation, but I equally can't stand by him if he's wrong."

She sucks her lower lip into her mouth, gnawing on it as she considers everything I've said.

"It wasn't a friend of mine."

"Huh?" Her statement momentarily takes me aback. "Then, was it someone else?"

She shakes her head, her eyes wide, as the hand clasped around her coffee cup trembles.

"It was me. Grayson is right about that part. I was the one who went to the police."

"*You* made the false allegations?"

*What the fuck?* I expected her to provide a different theory to Grayson's, not to fucking back up what he's been saying about her. Does this mean he's been right this entire time, and I've allowed Riley to take me for a fool?

Her hand wraps around my wrist, and I realize how cold her fingers are as they squeeze tightly. It pulls me out of my head, and I blink into her beseeching eyes. Eyes pleading with me to listen, to believe.

"*I* went to the police, Logan. But the allegations weren't false."

"What?" My head is spinning. I've jumped off a diving board into the ocean and now can't tell which way is up. "But that would mean..."

"His dad raped me."

"I don't... that can't be right."

"It is. Nearly every night for six months, his dad snuck into my room and assaulted me."

"No," I argue, shaking my head. "Grayson would have known."

"Grayson was never home! He was always out with his friends or off partying. On the odd night he stayed in, those were the only nights his dad left me alone."

Rather than balking at her accusation, I force myself to sit still and appropriately take her in. To take in her ashen skin. Her shimmering eyes wet with unshed tears.

Seeming to realize that I'm listening, the words start to spill out of her. It's as if she's kept them bottled up for so long that, now, she's loosened the cork. The momentum slowly gaining until it pops off like on a champagne bottle sending the contents spraying everywhere.

"I went to the police, but they couldn't do anything without physical proof. The sheriff took pity on me—Apparently, his teenage daughter had been assaulted at a party and the culprit was never convicted. He looked into Bertram and levied the only charge that would stick against him. And honestly, I didn't care. He was out of my life, and that was all that mattered."

Feeling like I might throw up, my eyes inadvertently travel to the juncture between her thighs. "Your scars..."

She quickly closes her thighs, redirecting my attention to her face. Gone is the pain and anguish, replaced with a sharp mask. "Do you believe me?"

Do I believe her? Fuck. How could I not?

"Why have you never told Grayson this?"

She scoffs. "Because he's never allowed me the opportunity. He's never been willing to listen. He kicked me and my mom out of his house without any questions asked, and I never saw him again until I woke up in this god-forsaken fucking house." Frowning, she waves a hand toward the closed door. "He hasn't exactly been in the frame of mind to listen to anything I have to say. Not that I think for one second that he would believe me, anyway. He's so convinced that what he believes is the truth. It would take a lot more than me telling him otherwise to change his mind."

I chew on my bottom lip. "And you don't have any proof?"

It's subtle, but I catch the slight change in her posture. The straightening of her spine, the squaring of her shoulders.

"You do, don't you."

"No," she snaps quickly. Too quickly.

My eyes narrow on her. "It's nothing," she counters, not meeting my eyes. "Nothing irrefutable. Not enough to prove to Grayson."

Before I can push to know more, her eyes snap to mine, narrowing as she tilts her head in thought. "You said Bertram told Grayson it was me who made the claim?"

"Yeah."

"How did he know?"

I shrug. "I assume the cops told him."

She shakes her head. "They wouldn't have. My statement was confidential. They'd have told him about the allegation but not who made it. The only way Bertram could have known for certain that it was me is if it couldn't have been anyone *but* me."

Well, fuck. I don't know what other proof she thinks she has, but that sounds pretty fucking damning to me.

We talk for a bit longer before I move to leave.

"Are you going to tell him?" she asks, sounding small and unsure.

"I don't know," I admit, feeling wrung out. Ninety minutes on the ice is less draining than this conversation has been. "I need to think."

She nods. "But you believe me?"

I meet her wide, green eyes, holding them before saying, "Yeah, Riley. I believe you."

---

*With wings. Without wings.*

*Long. Normal.*

*Oh, look. That one has super wings—whatever the hell that means.*

"Can I help you, Sir?"

I lift my head from the box I'm holding in each hand to gape at the saleswoman. "Erm, I don't know what to buy."

She takes one glance at the boxes of sanitary pads before giving me an empathetic smile. "Well, for starters, is she a pad or tampon girl?"

"Umm. I'm not sure."

Nodding, she claps her hands together. "Okay, then I think we should be safe and get some of each. I'm guessing you don't know anything about her flow?"

"No." *Jesus Mother Mary, what did I do in a past life that resulted in me ever having to have this conversation?* I just wanted to do something nice for Riley. I didn't realize there were twenty different types of sanitary pads. Or that a woman could be *a pad or tampon girl.* I should have known it wouldn't be so simple.

*Nothing* with women ever is.

Nodding again, she grabs several boxes off the shelf before moving down the aisle to the tampons. Furthermore, there are a hundred different types. Different strengths, applicator vs. non-applicator, large ones, mini ones... I swear to fuck, women make life ten times more complicated than it needs to be.

The saleswoman lifts another couple of boxes and adds them to the basket I'd lifted. "Do you need anything else?"

"Erm." I look into the basket, confidently admitting that I am officially out of my depth. "Maybe you should tell me?"

"Well, does she get bad cramps?"

"I don't know," I admit, realizing I know nothing about Riley James. The woman currently living in my house. Occupying every single one of my thoughts.

"A heating pad and some painkillers never go amiss, so I think we should add that and some chocolate. Every girl likes chocolate when the Devil is banging on her uterus."

I nod in agreement, and she fills my basket with the final few items before taking me to the register.

"It's sweet, what you're doing," she says as she scans the items and fills a paper bag. "I've never had a boyfriend do this for me."

Boyfriend.

Is that how I'm behaving?

I've never done this for a girl I've dated before.

And the irony isn't lost on me that Riley is not my girlfriend. Yet here I am, making a fool of myself in the *female products* aisle of the pharmacy.

"Thank you. I appreciate your help," I tell the woman as I hand over my card and take the bag from her, making a mental note to never return here again. I'd probably die of embarrassment the second I walked through the door.

"Oh, were you at the store? Did you get protein powder?" Royce asks, jumping on me the second I get through the door, my earlier outburst forgotten for now.

He snatches the paper bag from my grip before I can shove him away.

"Dude, what the fuck is this?" he asks, lifting out one of the boxes of tampons. "Eww, what is this for?"

"In case you hadn't noticed, there is a *woman* living in this house," I snap, stealing the box back from him and dropping it in the bag.

"She made you go out and get her *monthlies* for her?" he teases, laughing his head off.

I refuse to answer him, knowing he'll find the reality even more pathetic. However, the asshole can read me like an open book.

"Oh, shit, man. She didn't even have to ask, did she? Fuck, you are so whipped."

"Shut up, asshole." I shove at his shoulder.

"Grayson is going to murder you."

"I'd like to see him fucking try."

"Dude," he says, his voice taking on a more serious tone. "You gotta get over this girl. You can't go falling for her."

Yeah, he's about four months too late with that advice.

"What if Grayson's got it wrong and she's not the girl he thinks she is?" I hedge, unwilling to outrightly spill Riley's secret.

Royce's lips pinch, his eyes lowering to the breakfast bar situated between us. "You can't think like that, man. Grayson is our brother."

"Yeah, but we are all capable of making mistakes. What if this is his?"

Shaking his head, he refuses to answer me. "Don't go falling for her, Logan. It won't end well."

"So you haven't developed any feelings for her?"

His head rears back, and he stares at me, looking stunned. "Fuck no!"

I quirk a brow. "How long have you been visiting her at the club?"

"I was only doing that to keep an eye on her. Mess with her a little."

"Right. You still didn't answer my question, though." Leaning across the breakfast bar, I tilt my head, "But maybe you'll answer this one. How did you know about the scars on her legs?"

"I told you. I was messing with her. Trying to get in her head."

I scoff, not believing a word out of his mouth. "Sure you were, Royce. Keep telling yourself that bullshit. You know what I think?"

He waves his arm at me. "No doubt you're going to fill me in any way."

"I think you're starting to see what I see. You're starting to have your doubts and question things. But more than that, you're starting to feel something for her, which scares you. So, instead of tackling it head-on, you're hiding behind Grayson. Behind his truth. Like a little fucking bitch."

"What the fuck did you just call me?" Royce snarls, surging forward to grab my T-shirt in his fist and haul me further over the breakfast bar.

"You heard me. Stop being a goddamn pussy."

He snarls in my face, looking more animal than human, before he shoves me away. "Fuck off, Logan. We're not all so happy to be led around by our dicks like you are. You know better than anyone why I might be having some fucking reservations about this entire situation. Just because you've decided you're Team Riley and are willing to throw four years of friendship with Grayson under the bus doesn't mean I'm in the same boat."

He storms out of the room, and I hear the front door slam a minute later. Sighing, I sink onto the bar stool, dropping my head in my hand. *Fuck.* I didn't mean for that to get so heated. I wanted to get him to acknowledge what he's feeling, not push him all the way over the fucking edge.

Feeling bad, I decide I'll apologize to him when he gets home. In the meantime, I should check on Riley to see how she's doing after our talk earlier.

Bringing the bag with me, I leave it in the bathroom before going to her door and pushing it open. I stop in the doorway when I find her curled up asleep on the sofa. She looks so small and fragile, and the black rings around her eyes are fucking with my head.

Before I've properly thought it through, I'm across the room, an arm hitched under her legs and another around her shoulders as I reel her into my chest.

"What are you doing?" she mumbles groggily.

"Shh, go back to sleep," I whisper, satisfied when she buries her face in my T-shirt and her breaths even out once more. Holding her closer, I carry her out of the room and across the hall to my bedroom, where I gently set her down on the bed. Her auburn hair fans out against my navy sheets, and I can't help thinking how right it feels to have her there.

"I don't know what you're doing to me," I murmur as I pull the covers up around her. "But I'm not entirely sure I hate it."

# RILEY

## CHAPTER THIRTY-THREE

Burying my face in the softest pillow known to man, I try to go back to sleep. I'm nearly there, too, when I realize something is off. It's the soft sheets against the bare skin of my thighs. The crisp, winter scent in my nostrils. The lack of a hard floor beneath my shoulder or pinch of cuffs against my wrists.

But what really confirms it for me is the low, masculine chuckle that comes from my left. My body goes tense. Not out of fear, but because I can't remember how the hell I ended up in Logan Astor's bed.

Turning my head to face him, I pry open an eyelid, finding him on his side, leaning on his elbow with his head resting in his hand as he watches me with a knowing smirk. His chestnut eyes gleam in the morning light, and I groan as I bury my face back in his pillow.

Eventually, I roll to face him, my nose scrunching when I have to look at his face again. "Ugh. Your face."

He barks out a surprised laugh, lifting this hand to rub at his morning stubble.

"You're delightful in the morning."

I wave my hand at his face. "No one has the right to look that good first thing in the morning. Have you even brushed your teeth yet?"

"Nope. I just wake up looking this amazing." He flips his non-existent long hair.

I snort, cuddling deeper into my pillow as I stare up at him. "You brought me to your bed."

What I don't say aloud is, *"You believe me."* I know he said he did, but the fact he went against Grayson and brought me to his room says more than his words ever could.

I have to physically swallow back the tsunami of emotions threatening to spill over.

*He believes me.*

He believes me when my own mother doesn't.

When the entire police department wrote me off as attention-seeking because *Bertram Van Doren, upstanding citizen and millionaire, couldn't possibly do something so heinous.* The only one who took pity on me was the sheriff.

Still, this is different because I care what Logan thinks of me. What all of them think of me. And knowing they thought I was an attention-seeking bitch who would happily let an innocent man sit in prison for a crime he didn't commit made me feel like utter shit.

"I did," Logan says, seeming to see into my soul as he gazes into my eyes.

"Will you get in trouble with Grayson?"

He shrugs a shoulder. "He'll get over it."

My lips flatten. Grayson is not one to simply *get over* anything, but I'm choosing to stay out of it for now.

"So, what is the plan for today?" I ask instead, rolling onto my back.

"First, breakfast. I'm starving." Logan throws back the

covers, and for the first time since we woke up, I realize he's only wearing a pair of boxer shorts.

*Holy shit! My vagina is officially pitching a tent in this bed and calling it home, since I most definitely want to wake up to that sight every morning.*

All that hockey training has *definitely* paid off because he is cut from fucking stone. There isn't an ounce of fat on him. His entire body is lean muscle that has me wanting to trace each individual one with my tongue.

I'm so absorbed in my fantasy that I don't notice that he has turned to look at me until he's waving his hand in front of my face. "Earth to Riley."

"Huh?" I blink and find him smirking cockily.

"I asked what you wanted for breakfast, except now I think I know."

Wholly embarrassed, I grab the pillow from under my head and chuck it at him. "Shut up, asshole!"

He effortlessly grabs it, and before he can throw it back at me, I dart out of bed.

"Can I borrow a T-shirt and some sweats?"

"You mean you aren't enjoying walking around with just a T-shirt on?" he teases.

I snort. "Maybe in my own apartment, but not here."

He nods knowingly and points to the dresser. "Help yourself."

"Thanks." I root around in his drawers until I find a fresh shirt and a pair of sweats that look like they won't drown me. I still have to roll the waistband five times to stop them from dragging on the floor. I also grab a pair of thick socks, which I imagine are meant to go inside his skates, and at the last minute, I lift a hoodie and pull it on to complete my ridiculous ensemble.

"What the hell are you wearing?" Logan asks, failing to hide his laugh behind his hand when he takes me in. "You've gone from wearing practically nothing to half my wardrobe."

"You are aware that it's December, aren't you? My toes get cold on the hard floors." I hold out a sock-covered foot and wiggle my toes to emphasize my point. "Admittedly, the hoodie is just because it's cozy. Besides, you told me to help myself, so I did."

He holds up his hands, palms forward. "You don't need to justify your clothing choices to me. My clothes are your clothes."

"*Or...* you could let me go home and I could wear *my* clothes."

"Nice try, Shortcake. Grayson would actually have my balls if I let you do that. Besides, aren't you having fun staying with us?"

I arch a brow at him, wondering if he's taken a puck too many to the head. "You and I clearly have very different definitions of fun."

He shrugs, unbothered before ushering me out of the room for breakfast.

---

"You're going to behave yourself, right?" Logan asks for the hundredth time that afternoon.

"Yes." I sigh in exasperation. "Do I need to point out again that I'm not the one who did the strangling?"

He throws me a blatant *don't be dramatic* look while stuffing the last of his gear in his bag. Grayson and Royce have been MIA all day. However, Grayson came back an hour ago and holed himself up in his room. The problem is, Logan agreed to a friendly game with some of his teammates, so he has to leave the two of us alone... and we all know how that went last time.

Lips pursed, he grumbles, "I wish Royce was here, at least."

"Where is he anyway?" A guilty look flashes across his face that has me asking, "What did you do?"

"Nothing," he responds too quickly before confessing, "I said a few things to him yesterday. Pissed him off."

"About me."

His warm eyes meet mine. "Yes."

I sigh, my shoulder's dropping. "I don't want any of you to fight over me."

"It wasn't... He was being an ass."

"That's Royce's default setting."

That statement has Logan arching a brow. "I didn't realize you knew Royce well enough to *know* his default setting."

Shrugging a shoulder, I pick at an invisible thread on his bedsheet. "We've been hanging out."

"At the club."

"Yeah. So?"

My tone is defensive, and I can't meet Logan's eye. He lowers himself onto the bed beside me, his hand reaching out to squeeze my thigh just above my knee. "I think it's good that he's been hanging out with you."

"You do?" I question, peering up at him.

He nods. "Yeah. He's been... lost recently." His eyes bounce back and forth between mine. "You'd be good for him. Royce doesn't let anyone in. If he's willing to open up to you then I'm glad."

I nibble on my bottom lip. "I dunno if I'd say he's opening up to me..."

"No, but he's not pushing you away either," Logan counters.

Well, I mean, he definitely has. However, Royce keeps coming back, and that's got to mean something, doesn't it?

"I'm sure wherever he is, he'll be back soon," I say, changing the subject and attempting to reassure Logan. And myself.

He grunts, mumbling, "Not until his knuckles are too bruised to fight."

My lips flatten, brows lowering as a niggle of worry settles in my gut.

"In the meantime, just don't antagonize Grayson."

*Oh great, we're back to talking about Grayson. Yay!*

I pout when he looks my way. "Me? I would never."

"Riley," he growls in warning. "I mean it."

"Fine." I sigh. 'I'll do my best, but you know he just has to look at me and it sets him off."

"Then stay out of his way. Just keep to your room until Royce or I get back. *Please.*"

"Well, because you asked so nicely."

He brightens my day with that boyish grin I haven't seen in so long, and I swear it nearly sends my heart into an arrhythmia. *Fuck, I've missed that.* I don't know what the dynamic between me and Logan is now. Do I forgive him? I'm honestly not entirely sure. But he believes me, and ultimately, that's all that matters. Where we go from here... well, I guess we'll see.

There are too many unknown factors to know anything for certain, and honestly, I'm not sure if I'm ready to jump back into what we had before. I'm not even sure if it's possible to get back to what we had.

"Thank you." He quickly kisses my temple before hitching his bag on his shoulder, and I follow him out of his room.

Standing outside my door, I watch him continue down the stairs. "Enjoy your game," I call, and he glances up at me with a smile before disappearing.

Alone, I look up the stairs to the third floor where Grayson sleeps and silently send up a prayer that he remains there until Logan or Royce come home before I slip into my room carrying some science fiction book I found beneath Logan's bed.

Since I don't have my phone or any way to tell what time it

is, I don't know how long Logan has been gone when my stomach rumbles for the third time. I've been doing my best to distract myself, but the pangs are getting difficult to ignore.

Slamming the book shut—science fiction really isn't my thing, so it's doing fuck all to distract me from my hunger. Desperate times call for desperate measures and all that, so I drop it onto the couch and quietly creep toward the door. I press my ear to it, listening for any sounds of life within the house. I haven't heard anyone walking around, but that doesn't mean Grayson isn't sneaking about like a creeper.

When I don't hear anything, I slowly open the door and peek my head onto the landing. I hear the faint sound of music playing from Grayson's room upstairs, thankful he's still up there. I sneak down the stairs to the kitchen and grab myself some food.

Standing in front of the fridge, I laden my arms with stuff to make a sandwich and turn to kick the door closed with my foot when a dark shadow in the doorway has me jumping out of my skin.

"Holy shit!" Half the food in my arms goes tumbling to the ground as my heart slams like a jackhammer against my ribs.

Grayson slowly stalks into the light of the kitchen, not the slightest bit perturbed by the heart attack he nearly gave me.

"Jesus. Warn a girl next time before you sneak up on her."

"Maybe if you weren't in *my* kitchen, I wouldn't have had to sneak up on you."

"Maybe if *you* weren't holding me hostage, I wouldn't be in your kitchen," I snipe back.

What did Logan say about antagonizing Grayson? Oh, yeah. *Not* to do it.

Pursing my lips, I take a deep breath through my nose before slowly letting it out as I set the things in my arm on the counter and bend to retrieve whatever dropped.

"I'm making a sandwich for dinner. Would you like one?"

See! Look at me being all polite to the douchecanoe who is holding me captive.

My question doesn't seem to warrant an answer since he doesn't respond. *Whatever.* I go about making one for myself, choosing instead to leave the bread and condiments out so he can help himself before I sit down at the breakfast bar with my plate.

I have the sandwich poised halfway to my mouth when he makes his move.

"Hey!" I yell when he steals it right out of my hand, stuffing the entire thing into his fat mouth.

His face scrunches. "Butter instead of mayo? Seriously?"

"I like butter!" I snap. Refusing to point out that it's cheaper so it's what I'm accustomed to. Besides, it can't be that bad since he chews the entire thing instead of spitting it out.

"Of course you do. It's all sweet tasting, luring you in. Meanwhile, behind the scenes, it's clogging your arteries and lining your cells with fat."

I'm sorry, does he think mayo is a healthy alternative? Dude needs some nutritional education if that's the case.

"Grayson," I sigh, shaking my head. "You can't blame me just because you've put on a few pounds since the last time I saw you."

He slams his hand down on the table beside my empty plate, causing it to rattle as I jump. "*You* are a cancer, destroying everything you touch. First my family, and now my friends. What will you take next, eh?"

"I didn't *take* your family, Grayson. And I'm not trying to steal your friends either. *You're* the one that brought *me* here. That chucked *me* into your life again and is *forcing* me to remain in it. If you have such a fucking problem with me being here, then why don't you let me leave?!"

His hand comes up quicker than I can process, grabbing me by the back of my neck and forcing me to my feet. “You want to leave?” he snarls as he drags me out of the stool and across the kitchen.

“Grayson!” I try to grab at his hand, but it’s futile. “Let go! You’re hurting me!”

He doesn’t listen to my pleas as he throws open the back door and shoves me through it. Crisp, cold air circles around my wrists and ankles, and my breath fogs in front of my face.

“Then leave!” Using his grip on the back of my head, he thrusts me forward and I stumble before righting myself. “Go!”

I blink at him, only faintly aware of the frigid night air brushing against my skin and eliciting goosebumps in its wake. “What the fuck are you waiting for?” he yells. “GO!”

I blink at him for another second before taking off.

Fuck that shit, and fuck him. I needed out of that house anyway. I’m not about to look a gift horse in the mouth. Except I’m in their enclosed backyard. Brick walls line the boundary between their neighbors, with a privet hedge backing onto a field at the end of the garden. That’s what I aim for, figuring I can probably find a spot to climb through and circle around to the street out front.

I don’t make it more than a handful of steps before Grayson’s cutting tone slices through the crisp winter night. “Tick-tock, Riley. You’ve got ten seconds to find a way out before I drag you back inside. This time, I’ll gag you so you can’t use that smart mouth of yours.”

What the fuck? This isn’t him showing mercy. He isn’t letting me go. He’s playing with my fucking head. This is a mind game.

Realizing I’m not being set free, but rather hunted, adrenaline floods my body and I pick up my pace as I jog toward the hedge and begin to run along it, searching for a gap.

Halfway along, I notice one large enough for me to squeeze through, and grateful for the sweats and hoodie I'm wearing, I wiggle through the hole. The hoodie catches on a sharp thorn, tearing the fabric, but thankfully, it misses my skin, and I drop down onto the field on the other side.

"Five seconds," I hear Grayson call from what sounds like the other side of the hedge. *Fuck.*

Mouth dry and hands shaking, I take off into the darkness. I rush past stalks of corn, barely feeling the hard soil beneath my socked feet as I try to keep as quiet as possible.

After several minutes, I slowly stop, breathing heavily as I spin in a circle. I've lost all sense of my bearings, and I can't see over the crops to see the lights from the houses to tell where I came from.

Panic sets in as I spin in a circle, keeping one ear out for Grayson while I figure out which direction to move in.

Before I can make a decision, a large body crashes into mine, arms banding around me. "I caught myself a pesky little rabbit," Grayson growls in my ear as I writhe and wriggle in his arms.

"Let me go!" I scream, trying to kick at his legs.

"Not before I teach you a lesson," he snarls.

Tightening his arms, he lifts me off the ground, and I scream louder as I fight against him. I arch my back, trying to break his hold. The move presses my ass against his front, and I go still when I feel a stiff rod pressing into me.

*Is he fucking hard right now? I should have known this sort of twisted game would be his kink.*

Bending forward, he slams me into the ground, knocking the air from my lungs, and I hurry to turn onto my back, fighting back the fear and memories that begin to creep in from the shadows as he looms over me.

With every blink, his facial features shift. One minute it's Grayson hovering over me, and the next it's his father.

The past clashes with the present until I'm not sure what's real and what isn't.

"Please," I beg.

Or maybe it's my former self pleading.

With another blink, Grayson comes back into focus, and in a split second of panic, I lurch forward and press my lips to his. Desperate for something solid to ground me in the present.

Grayson remains unmoving, his lips hard as stone against mine. Regardless, it's enough to quell the rising panic. To push the shadowy figures back into the darkness where they belong. However, as I go to pull away, his hand slides to the back of my head, holding me in place as his lips move over mine.

Now I'm the one paralyzed as his lips skate along mine, nipping in a demand for me to open, to surrender. On autopilot, I do, granting him entry as his tongue delves in, exploring in a rough, hasty manner, as though this is the one opportunity he will get, so he's going to take everything he can.

As the shock slowly ebbs, my lips unlock until I'm returning his kiss with equal fervor. Each stroke of our tongues is like the clash of a sword. Neither of us willing to relent as we battle for dominance. He strikes, and I weave. I return, and he ducks. A war ensues. One in which neither of us will come out victorious because there can be no victor when the scars of our past remain a gaping wound festering between us.

My sweats are shoved down my legs, my panties hastily pushed aside and I feel him line up at my entrance a split second before he drives past the boundary. My entire body goes rigid, but I'm so wet that the resistance is minimal as he shoves his way inside.

"Fuck," he grunts against my mouth, going still as I clench around him. Needing him to move more desperately than I need my next breath, I bite down hard on his lip, drawing blood that trickles into my mouth. Snarling, he fists my hair, yanking my head back as he begins to pump into me with long, hard thrusts that I can feel throughout my entire body.

I feel alive in a way I never have before.

My body goes taut, a feeling more intense than what I felt when I got myself off in front of Logan and darker than what I experienced beneath Royce's touch is growing speed and building in momentum until it erupts through my nerves, chasing everything else into oblivion as I throw back my head and scream to the stars above.

I feel Grayson tense above me, his thrusts growing harsh and brutal. His eyes close, the muscles in his neck straining until I can see the pulsing of his artery before he goes still.

In the aftermath, our breaths fog up the air between us. Crickets chirp in the distance as the world seeps back into existence. And still, I continue to gaze into his face, committing every eyelash, every laugh line, every short hair of stubble to memory.

I suck in a gasp when his eyes snap open with a cold intensity, the heavy weight of his stare boring into mine before he pushes off me. Getting to his feet, he reaches down to grab a hold of my arm, yanking me off the ground. I scramble to pull up my sweats, conscious of our shared release dripping down my thighs.

Without saying a word, he frog-marches me back toward the house, standing guard as I wriggle through the hole in the hedge before hauling me up the back garden.

As we approach the house, Logan appears in the doorway, eyes wide. "What the hell happened?" he asks, eyes roaming over our dusty, disheveled clothing.

Instead of answering, Grayson shoves me into Logan's arms. "Deal with her," he snaps before storming off. And the second I hear his bedroom door slam shut upstairs, I fall apart.

# RILEY

## CHAPTER THIRTY-FOUR

Logan lifts me into his arms and carries me up the stairs. All the while, I cling to his T-shirt, unable to stop the flow of tears. I'm not even entirely sure *why* I'm crying. It's all just been too much. The secrets and lies. The hatred. The mind games and constant pushing and prodding at my partially closed wounds. I'm coming apart at the seams, and I don't know how to stop the unraveling.

With every curled lip and haughty remark, Grayson tugs on another thread. Picking and picking until loose strands poke out everywhere, the frayed ends like exposed nerves threatening to undo me with every raw touch.

"I'm going to run you a bath, okay?" Logan murmurs gently as he carries me into the bathroom and sets me on the counter. "Girls like that sort of thing, right?"

I nod, wiping under my eyes as he moves to run the water and fill the tub.

"Then we can get into bed and watch a movie or just go to sleep. Whatever you want."

"You want me to sleep in your bed again?" I ask. I hadn't given it much thought since this morning. Sure, sleeping in a proper bed for a change was nice, but I didn't want to get my hopes up that it was anything more than a one-off.

Leaving the water to run, he stalks back toward me, cupping my chin with his hand. "You're welcome in my bed for as long as you want, Shortcake."

"What about Grayson?"

He scoffs. "After what he just did, he can eat a dick." I chuckle weakly. "I don't care what he says, you're not sleeping on that floor any longer."

I smile wearily at him, and he softly strokes my cheek before moving back to check the temperature of the water.

"Uhh, I don't have any bubble bath. Shower gel will suffice, won't it?"

"Shower gel is fine," I assure him, watching with a strange sort of detachment as he pours half the bottle into the tub until a thin layer of bubbles forms.

Once he's done that, he turns awkwardly in the small space, clearly having no idea what to do. It's sweet and endearing, even in my numb state. "Erm, should I leave you alone?"

I shake my head. "You don't have to. The company would be nice if you don't mind staying."

"If you want me here, I want to be here, Shortcake."

Giving him a small smile, I twirl my finger in a signal for him to turn around, and when his back is to me, I slide off the bathroom counter and shimmy out of my clothes before getting into the tub.

"You can turn around now," I tell him when I'm submerged up to my shoulders.

Leaning my head against the edge, I sigh as I stare up at the ceiling while Logan gets himself comfortable on the floor facing me.

"Wanna talk about it?" he asks after several drawn-out moments of silence.

My head falls to the side as I shift my focus to him. “I had the biggest crush on Grayson when we first moved in with him and his dad,” I tell him. “He was older, popular, and he always acknowledged me if we crossed paths at school, and talked to me when we were at home.”

There was a soft smile on my face as I recall how Grayson looked and behaved back then, but it instantly falls as my memories start to shift.

“That first night, my stupid, naive heart thought it was him coming into my room. I remember being so nervous as I lay in bed, pretending to be asleep. I was certain he’d hear my heart smashing against my ribs. It took everything in me to stay still when the bed dipped. And when he brushed my hair back from my face, I thought I’d died and gone to heaven. But then it was *his* voice I heard and the fantasy shattered like broken glass.”

If Logan is uneasy by my topic choice, he doesn’t show it while holding my gaze as I flay myself open for him to see every withered, scarred, rotten piece of my soul.

I chuckle, the sound arctic and foreign. “If you’d told fifteen-year-old me that when she finally got to be with her crush, it would be a hate-fuck in a field, she’d be mortified.”

“You fucked him?” Logan blurts, and I don’t miss the flare of hurt in his eyes.

“Yup,” I say, popping the ‘p’. “You can go back to hating me now.”

Unable to look at him, I turn my head away to stare at the wall instead.

“I don’t hate you, Riley,” Logan whispers after a long moment. I keep my focus firmly fixed on the wall. “You and Grayson... it’s complicated between you.”

Complicated... that’s a nice way of putting it.

Fucked up. Ill-fated.

“Just like I know it’s complicated between you and Royce.”

His voice is carefully neutral, making me curious enough that I turn to face him again, studying his face to see what he makes of that.

"I haven't slept with Royce," I tell him, needing him to know that.

His eyes search mine. "But you want to."

"There's chemistry there," I admit warily. "Whatever it is, though, it's purely physical."

He arches an eyebrow. "Is it?"

"I'm certain it is on his end."

"And on yours?"

I shrug. "I don't think it matters, given the predicament we're all in."

He sighs, shifting so we're sitting side by side instead of staring at one another. "Things will improve, Riley. They won't always be like this."

Moving so I can rest my head on his arm perched on the edge of the tub, I murmur, "All you can do is keep moving forward."

---

"There's got to be something else we can do around here other than watch TV," I complain.

It's been several days since Grayson chased me into the fields, and he's been AWOL ever since, leaving me alone with either Logan or Royce for company when I haven't been at work. It's actually been nice. I'm not sure what is going on in Royce's head because trying to interpret anything he doesn't want you to know is like trying to read Sanskrit. Still, he hasn't been opposed, or even frowned, whenever he's come in and seen me and Logan sprawled out on the couch watching TV, and I know he's seen me going into and emerging from Logan's room each morning and night, yet he hasn't said a word. Which leads me to believe he's not on my side like Logan is, but he's not entirely on Grayson's either. He's floating in no man's land, trying to stay clear of the shit that is currently flying everywhere.

I've been working the last couple of nights, so today is my first full day off in a few days, and honestly, I'm bored. If I was at home, I'd be getting ahead in my schoolwork or cleaning the apartment and doing laundry, but there isn't any of that for me to do here.

It's just me and Royce in the house while Grayson is doing who knows what, and Logan had a final training session before everyone goes home for Christmas; apparently, all Royce wants to do is watch Supernatural reruns.

"There isn't," Royce drawls, not once looking away from the TV as I pace the floor in front of him. I'm getting antsy being cooped up inside, and the closer we get to Christmas Day, the more anxious I become.

"Can I see your drawings?" I ask, spinning to face him.

"No."

I push my lower lip out in a pout. "Why not?"

Removing his gaze from the television, he stares up at me. "Then I want to see you dance. *Properly* dance. Not the shit you do upstairs or at the club."

I bristle. "No." I do that for me. Sometimes people watch or can't help but see if they're walking past on the street or if Ava is around, but mostly, I dance for me. I don't want Royce to see that. To see me so exposed. When I dance, it's akin to stripping myself bare, and honestly, I'd feel more comfortable walking around naked in front of him.

He arches an eyebrow in a *see, we don't like to have our secrets laid bare* way.

Crossing my arms over my chest, I counter, "What if we play for it?"

He chuckles. "Play what, Babydoll?"

I quirk my lips. "Do you know how to play Gin Rummy?"

"Sure. Do *you?*"

I give him an innocent shrug of my shoulder. "Guess you'll find out. Are you in?"

He snorts under his breath, and I can already tell by the sly tilt of his lips that he thinks he's won. "Sure, James. Let me find a pack of cards."

We move to the kitchen, settling at the table while he shuffles the playing cards. "So, if I win, I get to see one of your drawings," I state.

"And if I win, I get to see you dance."

"Deal."

"Deal," he confirms with a smirk before dealing the cards.

Lifting mine from the table, I lean back in my chair while I look over my hand. It's admittedly been a while since I played, but Gin Rummy was a form of currency at Breakthrough Academy, a school for troubled teens that my mom sent me to after I had Rora. It was a strict, military-style institution that worked to 'correct' our behavior via stringent routines, manual labor, and harsh punishments. However, no matter how rigid they were, we were still teenagers. We always found a way to work around the rules. Gin Rummy was used to barter for sugary snacks, which were strictly prohibited, or for cell phone usage.

After two years of playing the game in order to get whatever I needed that made Breakthrough Academy bearable, I'd call myself a little bit of a pro.

Not that Royce needs to know that... yet.

We take turns lifting cards from the stock deck or discard pile and discarding whichever card from our hand that we don't want. The room is so quiet you could hear a pin drop. The only sound is the shifting of cards and when one of us either knocks the tabletop or calls Gin.

I study Royce closely, noting the tells that give away his growing frustration as the gap between our scores widens and I pull ahead.

When he sets a five of diamonds in the discard pile, I know I've won. Lifting his discarded card, I slot it in amongst the two other fives and smother my smirk. "Gin."

His brows, which have been scrunched in concentration as he frowns at his hand, jump to his hairline. "What? There's no way."

Smirking, I place my hand on the table so he can see the three cards of fives, alongside the three cards of sevens, plus the ten, Jack, Queen, and King of Spades that I was holding.

"Fuck," Royce growls, setting his hand down. It doesn't even matter how many unmatched cards he has. I was only twenty points off winning, and my Gin just pushed me over the finish line.

His eyes narrow on me, before he barks, "Go again."

"Fine." I shrug. "But new stakes. I won fair and square. I'm not about to let you weasel your way out of showing me your sketches."

His face contorts, teeth clenching until it looks like his head might explode. I can't help but chuckle at his pain as I grab the cards and reshuffle before dealing another hand.

"I win," I sing-song twenty minutes later.

"What the... how did you get so good at this game?"

I distract myself by gathering the cards and putting them back in their packet as I say, "Not a whole lot else to do at a school for problematic teenagers." I can feel his probing gaze on my face and hold my breath for the inquisition that is undoubtedly to follow.

However, I'm pleasantly surprised when he says, "Okay, what do you want?"

I tap my finger against my lip, thinking it over before deciding. "An IOU. A favor to be cashed in at a time of my choosing. Whether it be a foot massage, a lap dance, or for you to buy me one of those big foam fingers the next time we go to one of Logan's games."

He snorts. "Hell will freeze over before I give you a lap dance, but the rest of it... fine."

I grin triumphantly. "So, those drawings?"

His blue eyes instantly shadow over, his features growing taut before he nods. "Yeah, fine. A deal's a deal." He gestures for me to move, and I follow him out of the kitchen and up the stairs to his room.

He pushes open the door, and I linger on the threshold, taking in the dark navy walls and bedspread that give the room a warm, cozy feel. I've never been in Royce's room. Unlike Logan, who always leaves his door open and doesn't appear to care who comes and goes, Royce's door is constantly shut, and knowing him as I do, I imagine he values his privacy. His room is his safe space. His sanctuary. I don't want to invade that.

Once he's across the room, standing in front of his desk, he turns to look at me over his shoulder, finding me still hovering in the doorway. My eyes catch his, noticing the raw vulnerability there. I suddenly realize that this is a huge deal for him, and it makes me feel bad for pushing if he doesn't want to show me his art.

"You know what, it's fine. We can just go watch a movie or something instead."

His gaze continues to bore into mine, the air between us fraught with tension. "No. We made a deal. It's not a problem." Searching his face for any signs he's putting on a brave front, I nod when I don't see any. When I remain frozen in the doorway, he lets out a soft laugh. "You can come in."

Taking a step over the threshold feels akin to walking on holy ground. This is Royce's sacred space, and it feels like a massive deal that he's granting me entry. I pad across the carpet to stand beside him, noticing balled-up pieces of paper piling up in his wastepaper basket and lying on the floor around it.

A drawing pad lies open on his desk, a pencil placed on top of it, and the sketch illuminated in the harsh light of his desk lamp.

My eyes skim over the page with the reverence of a sweet caress, memorizing every stroke of the pencil as I picture the moody, muscular, hostile man beside me bent over this desk, pencil in hand as he memorialized this moment in time. It's a mundane moment—students dining at the food court on campus—but the way Royce paints each of them makes me feel as though I'm standing in the food court with them. I can practically hear the clattering of plates, the raucous laughter, and loud voices.

My hand reaches out, my fingers brushing along the edges of the page. "You have such a talent, Royce," I murmur in awe as I drink in every part of the drawing. Thumbing the edge of the page, I go to turn it when a large hand clamps around my wrist.

"The deal was one drawing."

My lips part in protest until I recall that that is the deal we made. *Damn, my stupid wording.*

He leans in, his lips hovering above my ear, and his voice dips as he says, "However, I'd be willing to make another deal with you."

"You really want to lose at another game of Rummy?" I tease.

He shakes his head. "Not Rummy."

"What then?" I ask in a breathless voice.

"Sit for me."

"Sit for you..." my eyes dart down to the sketch lying open on the table. "While you draw me?"

He nods. "And in exchange, I'll show you another drawing."

Looking back up at him, I ask, "Why would you want to draw me?"

His fingers brush along my hairline, down the side of my face and along my jaw. "I've been trying to for weeks but I can't get it quite right."

He's been drawing me for weeks?

I think about the scrunched-up balls of paper filling his wastebasket and wonder how many of them contain my face.

"Okay," I agree, unnerved. "But that's the sketch I want to see... when you're finished."

He hesitates before agreeing. "Go sit over there." He points toward his bed and I walk over and perch on the edge, watching as he sinks into the chair at his desk and turns the notepad to a fresh, clean page.

Looking up, his gaze rakes over me in an astute, critical fashion. "You're going to be sitting there for a while, so you may as well get comfy."

"Can I lie down?"

"Sure."

Climbing onto the bed, I lie on my stomach, head in my hands and feet crossed at the ankles. "Okay," I say with a smile, a thrill of excitement washing through me. "I'm ready."

I've never had someone draw me before. Never even posed for a photograph, so this is kind of exciting... and a little ruffling, knowing the two of us will be alone in here for the next few hours.

He shifts in his chair as his eyes roam over me in a slow perusal that sparks a heat in my core and has me clenching my thighs. Clearing his throat, I watch as his Adam's apple bobs before he tears his gaze from my body and focuses on the page in front of him.

The next few hours are the most beautiful kind of torture as I silently watch him work. Even though I'm just lying there, I never once find myself bored or zoning out. I'm too entranced by the sharp line of his brows as he concentrates, and the way he presses his lips when whatever he's drawing doesn't come out how he wants. The flexing of his biceps and forearms as he makes quick strokes across the page or fills in areas with soft shading. I can honestly say I have never found arms to be as sexy as they are on him, and while he traces my curves and edges, I trace the outline of his tattoos running from his wrist to disappear beneath the sleeve of his T-shirt, before reappearing around the collar.

Some of the designs I recognize, like the football helmet on his forearm and the bloody fist on his bicep that I imagine represent the fighting he does in the ring. While other designs resemble patterns, and woven in amongst them, I catch sight of lines of text, too small for me to decipher from this distance.

Eventually, he straightens in his chair, stretching out his neck as he rolls his shoulders. "That's probably enough for now."

"Can I see it?"

"It's not finished yet," he states, closing the notebook.

*Ah, he's one of those artists. A perfectionist. I should have guessed.*

"Okay," I say, sitting upright on the bed. "Do you need me to sit for you again?"

He shakes his head. "I should be able to do the rest from memory."

"And you'll show me when you're finished?"

"We made a deal, didn't we?"

I nod. A surprisingly comfortable silence falls over us, and I notice how relaxed he is in his own space. He doesn't wear the armor he dons outside this room. The black leather jacket and resting moody asshole face.

"You're quite the enigma Royce King," I state, almost laughing aloud at the fact his facial expression doesn't so much as twitch.

"How's that?"

"Football player. Fighter. Artist... It's quite the eclectic mix."

"Ex-football player," he corrects with an edge to his voice. One that blatantly tells me not to push against that door. So I don't.

"Do you have any other secret talents?"

He smirks, and it's dark and mysterious and oh-so sexy. Pushing out of his chair, he closes the distance between us until he's standing over me where I'm sitting on the end of his bed.

Lifting a hand, he tucks a finger beneath my chin and tilts my face up until I'm staring into the dark depths of his eyes. "You mean the kind that would have you creaming my cock over and over until you're too sore to move?"

My breaths come in short pants as my nipples pebble against my bra. He smirks down at me. "You'd like that, wouldn't you? All doe-eyed and innocent looking, but you know exactly what to do with that tight body of yours. How to entice men. You enjoy being at our bidding. Knowing you're getting under Grayson's skin. Basking in Logan's glow. Kneeling at my feet." His hand lowers until it wraps loosely around my throat, fingers caressing the skin. "Don't you?"

"Yes," I confess, admitting aloud what I have refused to accept for myself.

Because while sometimes Grayson pushes me too close to the edge, I have found a sick sense of pleasure in watching them bend to me little by little. It's seductive. Empowering. Heady in a way I've never experienced before.

"I bet you're soaking wet right now," he continues in his low, gravelly voice.

The heat burning in his eyes sparks a challenge within me and I daringly part my legs, taunting, "Why don't you find out for yourself?"

His fingers tighten around my throat as he releases a pained groan, stepping into the gap I've made for him between my thighs. Releasing me, he drags his hand down to the base of my throat, and lower still between my breasts and down over my abdomen. Reaching the top of Logan's sweats, he begins gathering the excess fabric of the T-shirt in his hand until he can push his fingers beneath the waistband.

I suck in a breath as his fingers glide over my skin, sliding lower to dip under my panties. Our mingled breaths heat the air between us, anticipation crackling like static electricity.

When his fingers graze over my mound, I suck my lower lip into my mouth, swallowing back my whimper as I tilt my hips, needing more.

"Such a needy girl," Royce teases, voice thick with desire. "Tell me what you want, James."

"I—" I trail off, having never actually said such things aloud. I love how dirty he talks, but I'm not sure if I can pull it off the same way. I worry I'll just sound stupid.

"Go on, Babydoll. Tell me..." Leaning down, he trails his lips over my ear. "...and maybe I'll do it."

"I want—"

"Yo, fuckers!" Logan bellows from downstairs, his voice piercing through the charged atmosphere and unintentionally ruining the moment as I jolt away from Royce's touch. "Where you at?"

Ignoring him, Royce and I stare at one another as that

fragile bubble of anticipation shatters. It feels like a cruel twist of fate, or perhaps it's a blessing in disguise. How far would I have let this go? How far would he?

The moment, once brimming with heat and possibility, dissolves into frustration for what could have been, and I force an awkward smile to my lips as I get to my feet, dislodging his hand from my sweats.

He doesn't step back, forcing me to press against his front as I shift to maneuver past him. Except as I step away, he reaches out and grabs my wrist. I turn to look at him over my shoulder, finding his heated, intense gaze boring into mine. "To be continued."

# GRAYSON

## CHAPTER THIRTY-FIVE

"Three days in a row? Cecilia is a lucky woman," the receptionist teases as I sign the visitor log book. Giving her a polite smile, I navigate through the building toward room 173.

I tap my knuckles lightly against the door, listening for any sounds from within before easing it open. "Gran?"

"Grayson, is that you, dear?"

"Yeah, Gran. It's me," I respond as I step into her room and softly close the door behind me.

"It's late, I was growing worried," she chastises.

It's 11 a.m. and she didn't know I was stopping by today. "Sorry, Gran. I didn't mean to worry you."

"Come sit with me." She pats the arm of her worn armchair, and I lean in to press a kiss to her temple before taking the spare seat beside her.

"How are you today?" I ask, casting my eyes over her. She looks the same as she always does these days. Frail. I remember thinking she was elderly and *past it* when I first moved into her house after Dad went to prison, but now her skin is wafer-thin.

I can see the blue veins through it, and when I touch it, it feels as though it will slough off in my hand.

"Old," she answers.

A rare smile graces my lips, albeit it's fleeting; a brief moment where the turmoil that eats away at me is suspended in time. Gran is one of the few people who make me feel genuine serenity. One of the few I can stand to be around these days. Her presence has always been a comfort to me. I barely have any memories of my mom, so Gran is the only maternal figure I've ever really known.

Usually, coming to see her grants me a peace I rarely get these days, but today that sense of calm is absent, the storm brewing within me too chaotic to be tamed.

I thought dragging Riley under my roof would grant me closure, but it's only opened a floodgate of emotions I can't seem to contain. All the unresolved anger that has been festering like magma inside me for years has bubbled to the surface, exploding in a devastating eruption of lava and destroying everything in its path, including my friendship with Logan if I don't sort shit out soon.

Shouldn't time have mended the wounds and smoothed over the scars left by her betrayal? Instead, the pain is as fresh as it was the day the judge delivered Dad's sentence. In my mind, I replay the moments from the past when my feelings for Riley were simpler, back when she was the object of my teenage infatuation and not the lying temptress chained up at home, tormenting me without even having to be in the same room.

And yet, despite it all, she still drives me as wild as she used to. I didn't expect her presence to affect me as strongly as it is, but *fuck*, every time I lay eyes on her, I want to strangle or fuck her. Or both. I never anticipated I'd feel so conflicted when I saw her again. So torn. It should be simple. It *is* simple. I hate her. The rest of it is... my body's physiological reaction to her. Nothing more.

That old infatuation is long gone. Smoke in the wind. Scorched embers torched in the flames of her spitefulness.

"How was school?" Gran asks, distracting me from thoughts of Riley. "Are those kids still being bullies?"

I sigh, not wholly surprised by her question. More often than not these days, her brain is stuck in the past.

"No. You were right, they moved on to other things."

She reaches over to pat my leg. "I knew they would. People like that... if you don't give them any response, they get bored and move on to the next scandal."

Yeah, or the school year ends and we all go our separate ways, and I enroll in college under Gran's maiden name.

Fuck. It's been a long time since I thought about my final year of high school. What a shitshow that turned out to be. I went from Mr. Popular to the new kid whose dad embezzled thousands of dollars. Even after I moved schools, kids still knew who I was; what my dad had done. And unsurprisingly, no one wanted to hang out with me. I was teased relentlessly. Treated by the other kids as though I was the one who had committed the crime. The moment news of my father's arrest went public, I'd been ostracized at my old school, and it was no different at this new one.

Hence why I changed my last name when applying to colleges.

Gran's wrinkled hand moves to cup my cheek. "You look tired, my dear. You're taking on too much. Helping me with the company, school, and all that while still dealing with your father's absence."

"It's not too much, Gran."

She shakes her head, not believing me. "You think I don't see that hatred eating you up inside? You've been through a lot these last six months, Grayson. Your life has changed irreparably, and no one can blame you for being angry, dear, but don't let it fester and spoil. It will rot you at your core if you don't find a way to let it go. Life hasn't been easy on you, losing your mom at such a young age, and now your father, but holding on to the pain of it all won't do you any good." She taps my chest, a wizened glint in her eye. "How can there be any room for love in that heart of yours if it's so full of anger?"

"You're the only woman I need room to love," I appease.

Guffawing, she shakes her head. "Don't be daft, boy. You're eighteen. You should be falling in love multiple times over." She reaches over to squeeze my hand, a surprising urgency behind the gesture. "Promise me, Grayson, that you won't close your heart off to love."

My eyes search her beseeching ones, and I know it's a lie when I say, "I promise."

"Good." She pats my cheek like she didn't just try to impart some deep wisdom. "Now help an old lady to the bathroom. Tea goes through me like water through a fire hydrant these days."

"TMI, Gran," I mutter, too low for her to hear with her poor hearing. I help her to her feet, remaining close as she ambles over to the bathroom with her walker.

"Do you need help?" I ask. "Or I can call someone."

"I'm not an invalid, Grayson. I'm perfectly capable of using the latrine on my own."

I suppress my small smile as I reluctantly leave her alone in the bathroom. However, I remain right on the other side of the door in case she needs me.

Gran was diagnosed with Alzheimer's disease not long after I went to live with her. The doctors think the stress of everything—my father's arrest, taking me in, and being left to run the company was too much for her to handle.

The gaps in her memory became glaringly obvious quite quickly when I was always around her. Before then, she was able to keep the issues she was having hidden. However, I quickly realized she couldn't run Van Doren Holdings by herself. At first, I helped her with whatever I could, but as her condition progressed and her memory worsened, more and more responsibility fell on my shoulders.

Despite the stress of it all, I didn't mind. VDH is as much her company as it was my grandfather's. After his death, she took over the running of the company. Poured everything she had into not only maintaining what he had built, but also fulfilling every ambition he'd ever had. My chest tightens and I lift a hand to rub over the skin as my thoughts drift to my mother, who sought to continue my grandfather's legacy until her death. That was when my father took control... until it fell into my hands.

The company means *everything* to Gran; thus, it has always meant everything to me. What was initially my grand-father's legacy became hers, and ultimately now mine. It was devastating for both of us to watch our stocks plummet in within those first few weeks after Dad's arrest. So for Gran, and even myself, I have been determined to ensure we don't go under.

Unfortunately, Gran is rarely lucid long enough to appre-ciate how far I've managed to bring VDH. Still, knowing that she'd be proud of the changes I've been making gives me courage in my moments of self-doubt.

Concerned that she is taking too long, I listen intently at the bathroom door, and I'm about to call out when I hear the toilet flush, and several minutes later, she re-emerges. She startles when she sees me. "Bertram, what are you doing here?"

I blink, taken aback. Despite the similarities in appearance, she has never mistaken me for my father. In fact, she's always telling me how *unlike* him I am, which I never really understood.

"You shouldn't be here." Her eyes dart anxiously around the room, her sudden uneasiness giving me pause as I stare at her in confusion, unable to comprehend what she's talking about. "You need to go," she states authoritatively, voice shaking as she backs away from me.

My father and maternal grandmother have never gotten along. They're both incredibly stubborn and used to getting their own way. It makes for a tense environment when they're both in the same room, but I've never actually seen her *afraid* of him. I always believed their issues were due to their differing visions for VDH. They'd butt heads over the conference table at every shareholder's meeting and rarely deigned to see one another outside the office, but this is different.

Personal.

"Do you think I don't know what you're doing to my daughter?" She barks in a moment of defiance. "You've already taken her from me, what more can you possibly want? Haven't you hurt my family enough?"

A sickening pit forms in my stomach, questions piled precariously on the tip of my tongue that I know I won't get answers for tonight.

"Gran," I hedge, keeping my voice low and gentle.

"No!" She becomes visibly distressed. "Get out! I don't want you here. Get out!"

"Okay," I assure her, keeping my voice low and soothing as I hold my hands up in front of me and back across the room. "I'll go."

Turning, I move to her record player and put on *My Girl* by The Temptations.

"Oh, Freddy. Dance with me, won't you?" Gran asks, moon-eyed as she now mistakes me for my grandfather. "I do love this song."

It's a relief to see that anger and fear gone from her eyes as she stares at me in adoration. Smiling broadly at her, I hold out my hand as I cross the room toward her before reeling her into my arms, happy to play the part of my grandfather if it settles her.

"I know," I murmur in her ear. "That's why I put it on."

As I lead my grandmother around the room in a dance, pretending to be her dead husband, her words play on repeat in my head, leading me to question everything I thought I knew about my father.

# RILEY

## CHAPTER THIRTY-SIX

I wait until the front door closes, counting to sixty before sliding off the sofa and creeping into the hall. Royce and Logan have gone to the store to grab snacks for our Christmas movie marathon, and Grayson is still avoiding me like the plague. I haven't set eyes on him since that night four days ago. Although I've heard the floorboards creaking beneath his feet early in the morning and late at night, so I know he's been sleeping here. I have no idea what he's been doing with himself all day or where he goes, and I haven't dared ask Logan.

Pausing in the hall, I stare at the front door. It would be so easy to sneak out and walk home. Logan even stopped at a clothing store while he was out yesterday and bought me some clothes of my own so I didn't have to wear his all the time.

Only I know that one of them would come after me, regardless. Whether it was Grayson or Logan. At this point, it's a safer bet for me to stay, especially with Grayson not around to torment me. Tomorrow is Christmas Day, and I'm supposed to be meeting my mom and Aurora. I've already decided I'm going to sneak out early in the morning and make my way home. By the time Logan wakes, I'll be at the park with my baby girl, and the rest I can deal with after that.

However, that brings me to my other problem—the fact I haven't heard from my mom since her phone call about the heating. She's not a regular caller per se, but she does have an uncanny habit of phoning to cancel the day or two before our scheduled meetings. Yet, there hasn't been a word from her, and when I've asked Logan if she's called, he deftly dodges answering.

Which has left me to find out for myself, because there is no way in hell that I am letting her get out of meeting with me tomorrow. Especially not because I didn't answer my goddamn phone.

So, turning my back on the front door, I march up the stairs to Logan's room. Since he's the one who had my phone when my mom called, I'm guessing he's the one in charge of it, so it's most likely hidden somewhere in here.

I stand on the threshold and look around his bedroom. I wouldn't describe Logan as the neatest person. His clothes are strewn over the floor, and his laundry basket is overflowing, but he is a minimalist.

Moving to stand in front of his desk, I stare down at it. The only things on his desk are his laptop and a stack of textbooks. Not spotting my phone, I start pulling open drawers and searching through them, coming up empty.

Next, I move to his bedside table.

"Ah ha." My phone is sitting in the top drawer alongside my purse, which I had on me when Logan drugged me. Lifting both out, I bend down to sit on the edge of the bed as I tap on the screen. Nothing happens, and hoping that it isn't dead, I press the power button, breathing out a sigh of relief when it comes to life.

"Shit." My phone starts beeping rapidly, notification after

notification popping up on the screen. Missed calls. Text messages. Most of them are from my mother. Not bothering to go through them all, I instead dial her number and bring the phone to my ear, tapping my foot as it rings.

"About time," my mother snaps as soon as it connects.

"Is everything okay?" I ask, ignoring her sniping tone. "How is Rora?"

"She's fine. *I'm* fine, too. Thanks for asking."

"You're still coming up tomorrow?"

"About that..." she begins, instantly raising my hackles. "It's just not fair on Aurora."

"Keeping her from her mother *is* unfair to her?" I argue, vibrating with restrained anger.

"It's Christmas Day. She shouldn't be spending it in a car, outside in the cold."

Like my mother gives a fuck about my daughter's wellbeing.

"Mom," I growl in warning. "You agreed to this. You have yet to follow through with one of your agreements so far. I haven't seen *my daughter* in four months. You bring her tomorrow, or I won't transfer you any money for next month."

"You can't do that. You *wouldn't* do that."

"I can and I will. I'll pay your bills and arrange for food for you and Aurora to be delivered, but I won't send *you* any money. You think I don't know my daughter hardly sees a penny of that extra money?"

My threat is met with silence.

"Can I assume your silence means that you'll be there?" I ask in the fakest of sweet tones.

"We'll be there," my mother grits out.

"Perfect. I'll see you then. Don't be late."

I hang up before she can protest. Feeling good that, for once, I had the upper hand in our conversations. It feels good to stand up for myself. To fight back. If only I had the power to do it more often.

The sound of a key being inserted into the front door has me hurriedly powering down my phone and placing it and my purse back in Logan's bedside table before scurrying from his room.

Descending the stairs, I don't hear any sounds of Logan and Royce in the kitchen. "Logan?" I call, reaching the bottom step. I could have sworn I heard the front door. However, the kitchen is empty when I walk into it, and doing a quick check of the other rooms, they are the same.

*Huh. Guess I imagined it.*

I decide to lift bowls out of the cupboards for the snacks that Logan and Royce went to buy because you can't have a Christmas movie marathon without enough snacks to send you into a sugar coma.

As I'm stretching up to the cupboard, I hear a floorboard creak behind me and with a spike of adrenaline, I spin in place. "Fuck." I jump back against the countertop in fright before I recover. "Still sneaking up on people I see," I bite angrily at Grayson, who lingers in the doorway.

I turn to dismiss him, but something seems off, and I slowly turn back around, eyes roaming over him as I take in his flushed skin, white eyes brimming with contempt. The shaking of his hands, as though he's struggling to restrain himself. Even so, it is the palpable tension radiating from him, the negative energy pressing against my skin like a physical force. The temperature feels as though it drops as we stare at one another, and my stomach twists into a knot, making it difficult to breathe.

I swear I can see the physical cracks forming in Grayson's armor. He's on the verge of coming undone, and with his name on my tongue, I push him over the edge.

He lurches forward, eating up the distance between us in

the blink of an eye. Before I can suck in a lungful of air, his hand is around my throat as he shoves me against the breakfast bar. He pushes me down until my back is pressed against the cold surface, a hostile glare piercing my skin as he hovers above me.

I should be shoving him away, fighting back, *something*, but all I can do is lie there as his fingers flex around my throat and his spitting glare burns me. I must be broken, because fear is not the predominant emotion I'm feeling, even though I'm pretty sure it's fifty-fifty whether Grayson chooses to strangle me to death or fuck out the hate.

The situation is precarious at best, but I can see the unraveling. The turmoil that consumes him from within. He desperately wants to cling to what he knows. What he believes. But I see the doubts, the insecurities. They swirl in his dark eyes like a turbulent storm. If Grayson hopes to break out of his self-contained prison, then this is it. I may hate him, but I still remember the man he used to be, and I firmly believe that goodness is buried deep inside him, smothered beneath years of hardship, hate, and teenage angst.

"It meant nothing," he snarls venomously. "*You* mean nothing."

The cracks in his voice betray his strain, and his hand trembles with the weight of his feelings, all of it becoming too much for him to bear.

The problem is, I have no idea how to reach Grayson. *If* I'm even the person who should. I'm partially responsible for breaking him, and I want to be the one to offer solace, to fix what I broke, but I'm as adrift as he is, and I haven't the first clue how to bridge the expansive divide between us. I'm no more capable of offering him a lifeline than I am of saving myself.

Perhaps we're destined to drown together. Suffocate in one

another. Asphyxiate in the tangled web of the hurt we've inflicted.

He rips my sweats and panties down my legs, and they hit the floor as he wedges himself between my thighs. He uses his spare hand to push my legs wider, baring me to him as he stares down at my most intimate part.

"*This* means nothing," he hisses, shoving his sweats down before fisting himself in his hand. He glowers at my pussy like it personally offended him. "A hole to be filled. A warm body to come in."

He slams all the way into me with a harsh, brutal thrust that has me crying out. I'm momentarily blinded by the pain of his intrusion as he fucks me relentlessly. With each hard stroke, he imbues me with his hostility until I swear I can feel everything he does.

It's crushing, the weight of it all.

"You seem to have forgotten that's what you're here for," he grunts between thrusts, his fingers flexing on my neck to remind me who's in charge. "Our sex slave. Our doll. To use and fill and discard however we please."

His strokes become savage, pain clashing with pleasure.

"Confess," he demands in a strained growl.

Unable to find my voice, I shake my head instead.

My refusal causes the dark shadows in his eyes to expand as his grip on my throat turns bruising. My pulse hammers against his hand as the precariousness of the situation causes the fine hairs along my arms to rise.

Pulling back, he slams in, his hips smashing against mine. I whimper at the bite of pain, wincing as he continues his relentlessly ferocious pace.

"I'm not going to stop until you submit to me," he snarls. Removing his hand from my throat, he yanks on my hair, pulling my head back and exposing my neck.

His other hand wraps around the neckline of my T-shirt, tugging on it until the fabric gives and a *rip* reverberates through the air before the material slides down my arm, exposing my shoulder and breast.

Lowering his face, he wraps his lips around my nipple, sucking it into his mouth before biting down—hard. "Ouch!" I cry, lifting a hand to push him away. Instead, he captures it in his, ensnaring my other one before yanking both above my head.

Chuckling darkly, he trails his lips over the swell of my breast. "Aww, did the dirty little sex slave not like that?"

"Grayson," I snap, reaching my limit. It's not about me not liking it. I've come to learn that I *do* enjoy this rough, primal side to him. I like watching him unravel; I like being the cause, but this feels like... *more.* There's a tension building between us, and it's not the good kind. It's the type that speaks of destruction. Of ultimate ruination. "Stop this."

His gaze snaps to mine. "Only when you admit what you did."

"I can't!" I yell, exasperated.

Running his tongue up to my collarbone, he tilts his head as he buries his face in the crook of my neck before a sharp sting triggers my pain receptors, and I scream. "What the fuck, Grayson?"

I fight against his hold, the juncture between my neck and shoulder throbbing as he laps at the bite before lifting his head and grinning at me like a predator about to go in for the kill.

His lips are smeared red.

Blood.

His lips are smeared with *my* fucking blood.

It hits me then: there's no potential breakthrough for him here. Grayson isn't cracking open and on the verge of a *come-to-Jesus* moment. He's devolving. Spiraling out of control.

Descending deeper into the fucking madness in his head, and I refuse to be a part of that. "Grayson," I growl in warning. "Get off me."

His chest vibrates against mine as he chuckles. "But the fun is only getting started."

I arch against him in an attempt to buck him off, but he's far heavier than I am and has the advantage of gravity and the fact his feet are on solid ground while mine can barely get leverage on the edge of the counter.

The move only seems to seat him deeper inside me, and I may as well be a fly banging its head against the wall for all the good it does as he continues to stare menacingly down at me.

Returning this focus to the obliteration of my pussy, he snarls, "Aren't you having fun, whore?"

"No, I'm not. And when you finally pull your head out of your ass, you're going to regret this."

He full-on laughs. "I regret many things, but this won't be one of them."

My neck throbs, my pussy aches, and I'm going to be bald from the bruising hold he has on the back of my head if I don't put an end to this soon.

"Grayson," I beg, softening my tone as I stare into his face with pleading eyes. "Please don't do this."

His harsh expression softens for the briefest of seconds, long enough for hope to swell, for me to believe this situation is somewhat salvageable. That *he* is somehow saveable.

However, I realize how foolish and naive that ideal was when a sharp blade presses against my skin, and my eyes go wide as cold, hard panic floods my system. "W-what are you doing?"

"I told you. This won't stop until you finally submit." He presses the blade harder against my throat, and I flinch as it nicks the skin. "How many cuts will it take before you finally do, huh?"

"You mean until I finally tell you what you want to hear?" I snap, mad more than anything else.

"Until you *repent*."

I breathe out a sigh, sagging in relief when I feel the weight lift from my throat, only to tense a moment later when he slashes the tip of the knife across my chest. It's a shallow cut but stings, nonetheless.

Blade pressed to my skin, his hips slam against mine as he ruts into me, his furious face inches from mine as he snarls, "Repent."

"No."

I hiss between my teeth at another slash of skin, and the cycle repeats. I wonder how many cuts it will take for him to realize I'm not lying. That I have nothing to feel remorse over. I've already admitted to him that the only thing I'm sorry for is hurting him. But I can't take sole responsibility for this level of rage. For this plunge into depravity.

My chest is littered with little nicks and red lines, and we appear to be in some sort of standoff when the front door opens, and I hear Logan's laughter before it cuts off. Something drops to the floor before he appears in the doorway, eyes wide as they bounce between us. "What. The actual. Fuck?!"

Royce appears beside him, the two of them gaping at the sight of Grayson bent over, dick embedded inside me and blood knife poised at my flesh. "What the hell are you doing, man?"

Grayson doesn't once look up. His eyes are leveled on mine as he thrusts once more, groaning as he empties himself inside me. "Next time, I'm going to stay buried in your poisonous little cunt until you finally face the truth of what you did," he snarls in my face before he's hauled backward. His cocks slips out from between my legs as he is slammed into the fridge.

An infuriated Logan steps in front of him, and I watch in shock as he pulls his arm back before driving his fist into Grayson's face. "There won't be a fucking *next time*, asshole!" Shaking his head, disgust is written over his face as he stares at his best friend as though seeing him for the first time. "I can't believe what you just did. We're fucking done, man. Unless you come to your senses, we're fucking done. I want you out of this house, right now!"

Grayson snorts, rubbing at his jaw as he glowers at Logan. "So much for loyalty, huh? Her gold-plated pussy won you over so completely. I really don't get the big deal. It's not that spectacular, especially given all the experience she's gotten."

As Logan winds his arm back for another punch, Royce intervenes, grabbing a hold of his wrist and shoving Logan aside. "Stop it!" He glares at each of them. "Shit is getting out of control. It can't go on like this any longer. You"—he directs his glare at Grayson—"need to get your shit together. Go stay somewhere else tonight. Both of you are having dinner with your families tomorrow. Then after that, we need to sit down and talk all of this out before we throw away years of friendship." His sharp glare shifts between the two men. "Agreed?"

Grayson and Logan both mumble their agreements.

"Good." Royce nods, seeming satisfied before he turns to level his intense stare on me. "That goes for you too, Babydoll. All of us are sitting down and talking. One way or another, the truth is being laid out, then we're all going to move the fuck on."

I nod, too numb to do anything else.

"Good, then get the fuck out of here," Logan snarls at Grayson. "Don't come back 'til tomorrow night."

He glares until Grayson leaves the room, casting me one final *you'll fucking pay for this* glower before he turns on his heel and storms off, taking all the toxic energy with him. A minute later, the front door slams shut. The loud noise acts like the bursting of a bubble, and my extremities begin to shake profusely.

"Shit," Logan gasps when he turns toward me. "Royce! Fuck. Call an ambulance. She needs to go to the hospital!"

I blink at him in a daze, trying to understand why he looks so freaked out. I know I'm a mess right now, but I wouldn't say I'm anywhere near needing to go to the hospital.

"Fucking hell," Logan continues. "What the hell did he do to you?!"

Following his gaze, I look down between my legs, noticing the bright red smears on my thighs and the blood pooling beneath me.

"It's fine," I groan, wincing as I push myself upright.

"Fine," Logan screeches, his voice hitting an octave I didn't know men could reach. "That is not fucking *fine*, Riley. You're bleeding! Did his dick, like, pierce your uterus or something?"

Fuck me, I'm wrung out, wrecked, and on the verge of crashing, but somehow I find the energy to laugh, and once I start, I can't seem to stop.

"Why is she laughing?" I hear Logan asking. "Fuck, did he break her brain too?"

"I'm fine," I wheeze, perfectly aware that I'm the picture of insanity right now.

"Riley," Logan snaps, his tone laden with concern and panic. "You're bleeding out of your, erm, uhh... kitty cat."

"Kitty cat?" Royce queries, speaking for the first time. "Seriously, man? That's what you're choosing to go with at this moment."

The entire ordeal sends me into another fit of laughter, and I double over, nearly falling off the counter as I giggle manically.

"Kitty cat," I wheeze. "It's okay, Logan. My *kitty cat* is just fine."

"But... the blood."

"It's my period." *Damn, venomous bitch chose the worst possible time to show up.* "I really am okay. Well, my kitty cat is. Jury is still out on the rest of me."

As the laughter passes, all I feel is hollow as I blink at Logan and Royce. Logan's face is pale, and it's clear that he's freaking out. Royce looks the same as always. I'd almost think he was entirely unaffected, except his eyes haven't once left my face, and there is a slight tightness of the skin around his lips belying his worry.

"Fuck. Jesus. Fuck." Logan curses before stomping across the kitchen and enveloping me in his arms. I collapse against him, damn near unconscious. "Let's get you cleaned up, yeah?"

I nod against his shoulder. "Then a nap, please."

"Whatever you want, Shortcake. You can have any fucking thing you want."

---

It's dark out when I finally wake from the sleep of the dead. It was so deep that I didn't even dream. I passed out the second Logan tucked the sheets around me, and I don't even think I've moved since then.

Stretching, I pull back the covers, noticing that I'm dressed in fresh sweats and a hoodie. I smile as I burrow my nose in the neckline and inhale Logan's fresh scent. *That man is pretty damn good at taking care of me.*

I refuse to acknowledge what happened earlier with Grayson. A numbness has taken root, but I don't want to look at any of it too closely. Not yet. Not now. I just want to have the nice relaxing night with Logan and Royce that we had planned. Then tomorrow, I'm going to see my daughter for the first time in months, and after that... *then* I can deal with Grayson.

Slipping into the hall, I pause when I come face-to-face with Logan. "Ugh, hi," he begins awkwardly.

"Hi."

"How are you feeling?"

"Better. Refreshed."

He runs his hand along the back of his neck, a sure sign that he's out of his comfort zone. "Good."

"Thank you for taking care of me."

He nods, a long pause following before he rambles, "I, uhh, cleaned your wounds. They're shallow. Didn't require anything more than a Band-Aid."

"Thank you." Another awkward pause, which I break this time. "Are we still doing a Christmas movie marathon?"

"We can if you want."

"I do. With alcohol."

He smiles, his shoulders finally losing some of that tension. "We got eggnog."

I smile back. "It's not Christmas without eggnog."

"That's what I said! Royce wanted scotch, can you believe that? Who drinks scotch on Christmas Eve?"

Shaking my head, my grin feels more real as I respond, "Royce. And probably Grayson."

*Ugh, no. Not thinking about him!*

I follow Logan down the stairs to the kitchen, where Royce is filling a punch bowl with eggnog. The kitchen has been cleaned, and when he spots me, Royce lifts his head, eyes meeting mine as he silently enquires, *are you good?*

I give him a firm nod, which he returns, and that's it. That's all we need for me to know he was concerned, and for him to be content that I'm okay for now and if and when I'm not, I'll let him know.

Glad to have that over with, I grab the pile of junk food off the counter while Logan gets glasses, and the three of us move over to the sofa.

"Which Christmas movie should we watch first?" Logan asks, snatching the remote and starting to flick through the movie choices. It's a relief to see him back to his normal, boyish self. Even if it's a front he's putting on for me, it at least brings a sense of normality back to the day. "I vote for *Elf*."

"No. God, no. Anything but that," Royce gripes. "Can't we watch *Die Hard*?"

"That's not a Christmas movie," Logan protests, frowning at Royce as though he's an idiot.

"I don't give a shit. It's better than *Elf* or *Love Actually*, or whatever other crappy movie you're going to suggest."

Logan gasps. "You don't like *Love Actually*?" When Royce simply gives Logan a deadpan stare, he shifts the focus to me. "Tiebreaker... what will it be, Riley?"

"Ehh." Looking at Royce, I wince. "Sorry, but I vote for *Elf*."

Rolling his eyes, he collapses against the couch cushions. "Of course you do."

"But we can watch *Die Hard* afterward?" I offer, trying to appease them both.

"Don't sweat it, James. After a couple of eggnogs, it won't be so bad."

By the time we're halfway through the movie, Royce is smiling as Will Ferrell discovers all the best things New York City has to offer.

Movie bleeds into movie. My glass of eggnog never seems to diminish, and I find myself laughing and smiling more than I have in an incredibly long time.

I feel comfortable, relaxed even, huddled between Logan and Royce on the sofa as we binge Christmas movies. Not once is it awkward. I'm not sure when exactly things shifted between us—particularly between Royce and me—but we've gone from sex-driven dances to being comfortable in one another's presence. It's nice. I like it.

"This is nice," I mutter aloud, my head resting on someone's shoulder. My eyes are too heavy and my head spinning too much to find out whose, but I figure it doesn't matter.

Warmth presses in on my other side before Royce murmurs, "Yeah, James. It is." Someone kisses the top of my head before sleep rises up and claims me.

# RILEY

## CHAPTER THIRTY-SEVEN

"Mmm," I groan, rolling onto my back as I blink my eyes open. "Ugh." A drum starts up in my head as the daylight assaults my eyes, and I'm totally regretting my life choice to drink yesterday. Even if it was warranted at the time.

Turning my head to face Logan, I pause when I find his side of the bed vacant. Lifting my head, I look around the empty room before returning it to his pillow, where a folded piece of paper sits.

Reaching out, I open it and begin to read.

> *You looked so cute, I didn't want to wake you. I'm at my parents' for the day, but I'll be back later tonight. Have fun with Royce. Don't do anything I wouldn't do ;)*
>
> *Merry Christmas,*
>
> *Logan x*

Realizing that Logan has already left for his parents', I jump out of bed, panicking as I scour the room for a clock. Spotting his laptop sitting on his desk, I hurry over and open the lid. It asks for a password to be inserted, but thankfully I don't need one in order to see the time.

A panicked squeak escapes my mouth. I have ten minutes to get ready and get to the park. Knowing my mom, if I'm not there when she arrives, she will turn around and leave, even with my warning to withhold her money.

I dress faster than I ever have in my life, not giving a single damn about what I'm throwing on, before grabbing my phone and purse from Logan's bedside table and racing out of his room and across the hall to Royce's.

"Royce," I call as I bang on his door. "Royce!"

The door flies open, a half-asleep, half-naked Royce standing in front of me with every one of his tattoos on display for me to gawk at. My brain momentarily glitches as I blink stupidly at his chest.

"Jesus, woman. Where's the fire?"

"Huh?" I blink again before managing to redirect my dazed stare to his face.

*Daughter. Park. Urgent.*

"I have to be somewhere. You need to take me. We need to go."

"What? Where?"

"I just... *Please,* Royce. I need to be somewhere, and I need you to drive me."

Crossing his large, muscular, tattooed arms across his chest, he stands in the doorway, stubborn as a mule. "I'm not going anywhere until you tell me what this is all about."

"You owe me," I blurt out in a panic, only making his frown deepen. "From Rummy. You owe me. I'm cashing it in, right now."

He glares me down for a minute longer, but I remain determined. Nothing, and I mean absolutely *nothing,* will stand in the way of me getting to my daughter. I will bulldoze over Royce to get to his car keys if necessary. He thinks he could take me because he fights men as big as him in the ring? Well, he has never seen a mother hellbent on getting to her child.

His teeth grind before he finally grits out, "Fine."

"Good. Thank you." When he doesn't move, I shimmy him with my hands. "Go get your car keys."

"Slow your roll there, Babydoll. I need to get dressed."

"Hurry up, *please.* I need to be there, like, right now."

His eyes search my face for another second before he relents, and sighing, he moves to get dressed.

Breathing out a sigh of relief and trying not to panic, I turn my phone on while I wait for Royce, marginally relaxing when I don't have a last-minute missed call or text from my mom.

"Are you ready yet?" I call through his bedroom door when he hasn't emerged after thirty seconds.

"Jeez. Yes, I'm ready." He appears in the doorway, and I don't even spare him a second glance as I turn and race down the stairs and out the front door.

"You need to tell me where we're going," he points out as we get into his truck.

"Do you know the park on the side of the road on the way to Springview?"

"Sure." Starting the engine, he pulls onto the road and heads in that direction.

My foot taps the entire way there, and I check the time on my phone every few seconds. "Can you go any faster?" I grumble. "You're driving like a granny."

"I'm doing forty in a thirty," he points out.

Huffing, I turn to stare out the window.

"Are you going to tell me what this is about?"

I remain silent, nausea preventing me from opening up to him even if I wanted to. There isn't time to explain. He'll no doubt figure it out as soon as we arrive, and this definitely isn't how I saw any of this unfolding, but it is what it is. There's nothing I can do about it now.

We drive the rest of the way in silence, and the second we pull into the parking lot, I scan the cars for my mom's. The second I spot it, I unbuckle my seat belt and throw open the door.

"Jesus Christ," he snarls, as I half fall out of the still-moving vehicle.

"Stay here," I call over my shoulder before taking off toward the children's play park.

I immediately spot my mom sitting on a bench at the edge of the play area and scanning the faces of the handful of other children running around, I quickly identify Aurora.

"Aurora," I call out as I reach the gate.

"Mommy!" she comes running toward me, and tears overflow as I crouch down and bundle her into my arms. Standing, I spin her around as I hug her close.

"Mommy, you're squishing me."

"I'm sorry, baby girl. I'm just so happy to see you."

She smiles up at me, and it makes my entire year. All the shit I've endured since moving to Halston, all the crap Grayson has put me through, the bullshit I put up with with Ben... none of it matters. It doesn't mean a damn thing.

"Merry Christmas," I tell her, kissing the top of her head.

"Merry Christmas, Mommy."

"Let me get a good look at you," I say, setting her on her feet. She twirls in front of me, and I laugh as I take her in, noting that her coat is a size too small and her hair *still* hasn't been cut. Forcing back my frown, I smile at her. "Beautiful as ever."

For the next hour, I let her lead me around the playground. I push her on the swings, hold her up while she attempts to cross the monkey bars and catch her when she reaches the bottom of the slide. My grin is permanently glued to my face, and I memorize every smile, every giggle, every time she says my name.

"It's time for us to leave," Mom interrupts, coming to stand beside me. I haven't spoken a word to her since I arrived. These visits aren't about her. They're for Aurora and me.

"She needs a new coat," I bite out.

"Yes, well, money has been tight recently."

"And you said you'd trim her hair."

She sighs, exasperated. "I haven't had the time."

It's on the tip of my tongue to ask her what the hell she does all day that she can't find half an hour to trim her granddaughter's hair. The woman doesn't work. She should have nothing but time. Instead of causing a scene in the middle of the play park, I rip open my purse and, grabbing the handful of bills inside, I stuff them into her hand. "Get her a new coat and cut her damn hair," I snarl.

My mother glowers back at me. Her makeup is done to the nines, and her outfit is pristine and clearly designer. My daughter can't afford a winter coat that fits her, but my mom can afford designer clothing.

*Yeah, someone call bullshit on that one.*

What I've never been able to figure out is *how* she affords it. There have been a handful of wealthy boyfriends over the years, but they don't usually stick around for long, and in the interim, where does she get the money from?

"Come on, Aurora," my mother calls in that falsetto tone of hers, jarring me from my thoughts. "Time to go."

"Okay." Aurora comes running over and I bundle her into my arms for the last time, fighting back my tears. "Love you, Mommy."

"To the moon and back."

She grins, planting her small hands on my cheeks. “To the moon and back.”

*God damn, don’t cry yet.*

“I’ll see you real soon, okay?”

She nods her head fervently. “Okay.”

When I set her down, she reaches for my mom’s outstretched hand. “My money?” my mother hedges, like I didn’t just give her fifty bucks.

“Yeah, I’ll send it to you.”

Transaction completed, she turns and strides away with my little girl bouncing beside her, completely oblivious to the fact my heart is fracturing in two.

I watch as she bundles my daughter into the car seat before the car reverses out of the space and drives out of the parking lot. Even then, I continue to stand there, numb and oh so broken as the tears flow down my cheeks.

Eventually, I pull myself together enough to turn toward Royce’s truck. It’s parked directly in front of the playground, but as I look through the windshield, I don’t see him inside the cab.

Turning my head, I scan the rest of the park until I spot a lone figure sitting on a picnic table overlooking the lake. Inhaling a deep breath, I walk over and climb up beside him.

Neither of us says anything for a long time.

“She’s yours, right?” he eventually asks.

“Yeah.”

“What age is she?”

“She’s three.”

He nods knowingly.

“Grayson’s dad lied.”

“Yeah,” I sigh. “He did.”

# ROYCE

## EPILOGUE

My mind is a mess as, hours later, I trudge numbly through the front door of the townhouse I've shared with Logan and Grayson since Freshman year.

The townhouse we locked Riley up in. Where we took away her rights. Stole her voice. Forced her to bend. To compromise. To hand over one of the few parts of herself she had left.

Where *I* forced her to do all those things.

In the hall, I sag against the wall, shoulders slumped as I stare unseeingly at the floor. Every time I close my eyes, I see her diving out of my truck. Watch as she races toward the play park. Toward the little girl that looks so. Like. Her.

That dark red hair. Those cheekbones...

However, that straight nose, the sharp eyebrows...

... features disturbingly similar to a tall, dark-haired, surly bastard I've shared these walls with for the last three years.

One of my closest friends.

My brother, for all intents and purposes.

I can still feel the bone-deep chill that settled over me as the realization dawned.

The realization that Grayson had been wrong. That *I* had been wrong.

Feeling like I might puke, I stumble into the living room, collapsing into the nearest chair. My head falls back, eyes closing.

I'm instantly assaulted with images of today. Riley pushing the little girl—*her daughter*—on the swings. The first truly genuine smile, bright and radiant, filled with hope and for once not fractured or riddled with anguish on Riley's face.

The light that entered her eyes. I'd never seen that before. Never seen her so... at peace. So content. So lost in the moment. Her mind is always on something else, always trying to figure out how to stay ahead, ascertaining how much of herself she is willing to compromise for the bigger goal. It's always fascinated me, watching her ingenious mind at work, but seeing her press pause today, seeing how truly happy she was for that brief moment... I caught a rare and precious glimpse of the *real* Riley. At the best version of herself. Not the person she needs to be when she's on campus. Not the dancer she portrays at Lux. Not the woman unleashing every ounce of pent-up emotion in the dance studio. And certainly not the cornered cat fighting for survival, for the safety of her daughter that she had to become to navigate the predators in this house while we tried to tear her limb from limb.

Round and around I go. Thoughts swirling. Emotions raging.

Shock.

Outrage—at myself, at Grayson, at his father.

Understanding.

Newly acquired insight as I turn over every interaction I've had with Riley and assess it with new eyes, with this new information at my fingertips.

Seconds turn to minutes. To hours.

The sun traverses the sky, day passing. And still, I sit there, lost in thought, my limbs too laden to move.

The rug feels as though it's been pulled out from beneath my feet, and I'm left questioning everything Grayson has told me. Recalling every fucked up thing we've done in the name of revenge.

Riley didn't give me any details, nor did I ask. We sat on that bench until the cold sneaked in under our clothing, leaving a chill behind and Riley started to shiver. Then, I walked her to my truck, helped her in, and drove her to her apartment.

Done with the games. Done with the secrets. With the lies.

I hadn't intentionally planned to take her home. I drove in a fog, but when I blinked and realized I was parked outside her building, I knew it was the right thing to do.

What I should have done weeks ago.

Had I only known.

Had I only listened to the feeling in my gut that something was off.

I suspected. I... I wasn't convinced that all was as Grayson believed.

Nor was I as adamant as Logan that Riley's version of events was the truth.

I had spied her subterfuge. Sensed there was more than what she was saying.

And I'd been right... just not in any way that I could have possibly imagined.

Riley wasn't telling the whole truth, but it was Grayson who got it all wrong.

*So fucking wrong.*

There were no false accusations.

No heinous lies or petty allegations to regain her mother's attention.

Whatever report Riley filed contained only the stone-cold truth.

One which Grayson's dad spun into a web of lies to cover his own vile crimes.

And he convinced everyone around him, Grayson included, that his version was the truth. After all, who would people believe: him or a confused, insecure teenage girl?

The thought of it all leaves me sickened, and it takes hours more before I allow the cold, hard facts to fully penetrate my reality.

Bertram Van Doren raped his fifteen-year-old stepdaughter. Got her pregnant. And when she found the courage to come forward, he turned the entire world, her family included, against her.

This whole time, Riley has been telling the truth.

And we're the idiots who didn't believe her.

But not any longer.

This stops now.

Today.

I no longer give a shit about what Grayson says or believes. That beautiful, fiery, sparkling woman I saw in the play park today... I want to see her again. To *know* her. To protect her from the cruelty of this world so that her light may shine even on the bleakest of days.

I will be her protector. Her silent shadow in the night. Her invisible weapon to wield. The soldier at her side. The shield at her back and the breastplate over her heart. I will be whatever and whoever she needs to feel safe in this world.

And in return, I can only hope that one day I will be worthy of basking in the beauty of that sweet, glowing smile I bore witness to today.

By the time Grayson strolls through the door, the inky

blackness of the sky matches the oily darkness of my mind and soul.

I watch from my perch in the shadows as he wipes his feet on the mat, closing the door behind him with a heavy, resigned sigh. I remember that the four of us were meant to sit down tonight. That, one way or another, the truth would be heard.

Irony. Such a fickle bitch.

The truth was heard all right. Like whistles blasted in my ear loud enough to burst the drum. Permanently enough that I will forever bear the scars. The lesson learned. The consequences doled out.

He does a double take when he notices me sitting there in the dark, not having bothered to turn on a light when the sun slipped behind the earth and out of sight.

Lifting a hand to the wall, he flicks on the light, casting shadows across my face. Across the room. Across everything we ever knew. "What—"

Eyes on mine, he goes no further, as if sensing the weight of the truth dangling in the room, a devastating blow waiting to fall and crush us all.

Or perhaps he can taste the bitterness of my emotions. The guilt. The anguish. The unfairness of it all.

Pinning him in my harsh stare, my voice a guttural rasp, I lay bare the only words I can find in me to say. "We fucked up. You. Me... Logan. We really fucked up."

# ACKNOWLEDGMENTS

Every now and again, a character pops into your head, and you just resonate with them. This book was that for me. I connected with not just Riley but Logan, Royce, and Grayson. Their pain and heartache. Their hope and how they strived for a better future for themselves. These characters sucked me in and wouldn't let me go until their story was out in the world for you all to read. I hope these characters have ingrained themselves in your DNA as deeply as they are in mine.

Certainly, this book would be nowhere near as good as it is without the help of my amazing team. Nikki who is always ready to listen to my rants and suggest ideas when I get stuck (which is a lot). Thank you so much for being on this crazy journey with me.

Another thanks to my alpha readers, Melissa, Cheria, and Katie for trudging through the mess that was my first draft and still loving it. And to my beta readers for fine tuning everything.

A massive thank you to my editor and friend, Angie for dealing with every single "I know I told you I was done, but I just added this little bit" comment I dropped her after telling her it was all hers.

I also have to thank my tiktok and street teams, and those who signed up for the blog tour with Peachy Keen to help promote and spread the word about this series. I appreciate all your hard work promoting every week.

I need to thank my husband who is always my rock and support. He dealt with a lot during this book. Mostly me being a hermit for 2 months because these characters barely let me sleep until I'd told their story.

Lastly, thank you to all of you, the readers, for picking up this book and reading it. Without you none of this would be possible!! If you loved this book, please help me spread the word by leaving a quick review.

# ALSO BY R.A. SMYTH

**Crescentwood Series**

A dark, high school bully reverse harem with a stalker and gang element.

**Pacific Prep Series**

A dark, academy bully reverse harem with a taboo relationship.

**Black Creek Series**

A rival gang-mafia reverse harem with a vigilante FMC. Contains MM.

**The Ruthless Boys of Ridgeway**

A college, friends-enemies-lovers, second chance reverse harem with a stalker and secret society elements.

**Halston U**

A college, hockey, stepbrother, enemies-to-lovers reverse harem with a revenge plot.

# ABOUT THE AUTHOR

R.A. Smyth is best known for writing contemporary dark romance filled with unexpected twists, mystery, and plenty of steam. Rachel lives in the UK with her husband and two golden retrievers, and when she's not busy thinking up crazy cliffhangers to drive her readers insane, she enjoys inflicting the same torture on herself by reading incomplete series.

She has always been an avid reader, starting from the Harry Potter books as a kid. It's an interest that has grown into an obsession over the years and becoming an author has been a secret lifelong dream of hers.